LINDSAY McKENNA

presents the powerful, passionate story of Inca and the rugged warrior who wins her heart. It's the MORGAN'S MERCENARIES book you've been waiting for!

* * *

"What is it about you that makes me feel as I do?" Inca demanded.

Roan smiled at the spark of challenge in her eyes. "What do you mean? Do I make you feel bad? Uncomfortable?"

"No...I *like* being close to you."

He saw her eyes fill with confusion for a moment over her admission. He knew Inca was a virgin and, more than ever, he realized just how innocent she was.

"You make me feel safe in my world," she continued. "And in my world there is no safety. How can that be?"

Roan's heart soared. She trusted him. He needed—*wanted*—that trust. Just as much as he wanted her...

* * *

"Lindsay McKenna continues to leave her distinctive mark on the romance genre with... timeless tales about the healing powers of love."

—*Affaire de Coeur*

Also available from

LINDSAY McKENNA

and
Silhouette Special Edition

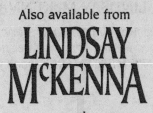

*Morgan's men are born for battle—
but are they ready for love?*

Available July 2000:
MAN OF PASSION
(Silhouette Special Edition #1334)

Available November 2000:
A MAN ALONE
(Silhouette Special Edition #1357)

Available February 2001:
MAN WITH A MISSION
(Silhouette Special Edition #1376)

Available March 2001:
MORGAN'S MERCENARIES: HEART OF STONE
(Silhouette Books)

LINDSAY McKENNA

Morgan's Mercenaries:
Heart of the Warrior

Silhouette Books

Published by Silhouette Books
America's Publisher of Contemporary Romance

SILHOUETTE BOOKS

ISBN 0-373-48416-X

MORGAN'S MERCENARIES: HEART OF THE WARRIOR

Copyright © 2000 by Lindsay McKenna

This edition published by arrangement with Harlequin Books S.A.

Visit Silhouette at www.eHarlequin.com

Printed in U.S.A.

To Karen David, a real, live warrioress and healer.
And a good role model for the rest of us!

Chapter 1

"No...!"

Roan Storm Walker's cry reverberated around the small, dark log cabin. Outside, the rain dripped monotonously off the steep, rusty tin roof. Breathing harshly, Roan pressed his hands to his face, dug his fingers frantically into his skull as he felt his heart pounding relentlessly in his chest. His flesh was beaded with sweat. Lips tightly compressed to halt another scream, another cry of grief and loss, he groaned instead, like a wounded cougar.

Lifting his head, Roan turned the dampened pillow over and dropped back down onto the small, creaking bed. He had to sleep. *Great Spirit, let me sleep.* Shutting his eyes tightly, his black lashes thick and spiky against his copper-colored skin, he released a ragged sigh.

Sarah...how he missed her. Brave, confident, foolhardy Sarah. It had been two years and he still missed her. How badly he wanted to touch her firm, warm shoulder or to smell that jasmine scent that always lingered tantalizingly in the strands of her short red hair. Gone...everything was gone.

Swept from his life like litter before some invisible broom. Sarah, his wife, was dead, and his heart had died, too, on that fateful day. Even now, as he lay listening to the rain splattering against the roof of his cabin high in the Montana Rockies, he felt the force of his aching grief. The waves of agony moved through him like waves crashing in from the ocean and spilling their foamy, bubbling essence on the hard, golden sand.

Unconsciously, he rubbed his fingers across the blue stone hanging around his neck—his medicine piece. He'd worn the amulet continually since his mother, a Lakota medicine woman, gave it to him—before her death many years ago. Composed of two cougar claws representing the cougar spirit that was his protector, and two small golden eagle feathers, it hung from a thick, black, sweat-stained leather thong around his neck. The center of the medicine piece was an opalescent blue stone, roughly fashioned in a trapezoid shape. The bezel around the stone was of beaten brass that had long ago turned dark with age. No one knew what the stone was, or where it came from. He'd never seen another one like it in all his travels. His mother had told him it came from their ancestors, passed on to the medicine person in each succeeding generation of the family. He always touched this piece when he was feeling bad. In a way, it was like sending a prayer to his mother and her line of ancestors for help with the heavy emotions he wrestled with. Roan never took off his medicine piece; it was as much a part of him as his heart beating in his chest.

He closed his eyes once more. He was good at forcing himself to go back to sleep. His mother, a Lakota Yuwipi medicine woman, had taught him how to lucid dream. He could walk out of one harsh reality into the more amorphous world beyond the veil of normal human reach. More than likely he was able to do this because he had the genes of that long line of medicine people coursing richly through his bloodstream. His father was an Anglo, a white man—a physics teacher. Between both parents, Roan found it easy to surrender over to a power higher than himself, give himself back to the night owl's wings of sleep, which almost instantly embraced him again.

As he moved from the pain of the past, which continued to dog his heels like a relentless hound on the scent of the cougar spirit that protected him, his grief began to recede. In lucid dream and sleep, he could escape the sadness that was etched in his heart. This time, as he slipped into sleep, Walker heard the distant growl of thunder. Yes, a Wakan Wakinyan, a mighty thunder being who created the storms that roved across the Rockies, was now stalking his humble cabin hidden deep in the thick Douglas firs on a Montana slope.

A slight, one-cornered smile curved Roan's mouth as he felt his mood lightening, like a feather caught in a breeze and being wafted gently into the invisible realm of the Great Spirit. Yes, in dreaming there was safety. In dreaming there was relief from the pain of living in human form. Roan expected to see Sarah again, as he always did whenever this shift in his consciousness occurred. The Lakota called the state dreaming "beneath the wings of the owl," referring to the bird they considered the eagle of the night. Within the wings of this night protector, the world of dreams unfolded to those who knew how to access this realm. Reaching this altered state had been taught to Roan at a very young age and he had found it an incredible gift, a means of healing himself, really, over the last twenty-eight years of his life.

Sarah? He looked for his red-haired Sarah, those flashing Celtic blue eyes of hers, and that twisted Irish grin across her full, soft lips. Where was she? Always, she would meet him while in the embrace of the owl. Full of anticipation, he spied a glowing light coming out of the darkness toward him. Yes, it had to be Sarah. As he waited impatiently within the darkness, the golden, sunny light grew ever closer, larger, pulsating with brilliant life of its own.

His cougar spirit's senses told him this wasn't Sarah. Then who? Even as he felt his disappointment, something strange happened. His cougar, a female spirit guardian with huge, sun-gold eyes, appeared out of the darkness to stand in front of him. He could see that her attention was focused fully on the throbbing, vital orb of light drawing closer. Walker felt no fear, simply curiosity, despite the fact that it was unlike Anna, his cougar spirit guide, to appear like this unless there was danger to him. Yet he felt no danger.

The mists surrounding the oblong light reminded him of thickly moving mist on a foggy morning at the lake below his cabin, where he often fished for a breakfast trout. Anna gave a low growl. Roan's heart rate picked up. The golden oval of light halted no more than six feet away from him. Slowly, it began to congeal into a body, two very long legs, slender arms, a head and...

Walker felt his heart thundering in his chest. His cougar guardian was on full alert now, her tail stiff, the hackles on her neck ruffled and the fur raised all the way down her lean, supple spine. Roan was mesmerized as he watched the person—a woman?—appear. What the hell? He wasn't sure what or who he was looking at.

Huge, willow-green eyes with large black pupils stared fiercely back at him.

Swallowing hard, Walker felt every cell in his body respond to this unknown woman who now stood before him. Although the golden light had faded to a degree, so he could see her clearly, it still shone around her form like rays of brilliant sunlight. She warily watched him as the tension built and silence strung tautly between them.

This was no ordinary human being. Walker sensed her incredible power. Few humans he'd ever known had an aura of energy like hers. It was so brilliant that he felt like squinting or raising his hand to shield his eyes from the glow. Her eyes drew him. They were magnetic, commanding, fierce, vulnerable and magical all at the same time.

He tried to shift his consciousness; it was impossible. She held him fully within her powerful presence. She was tall, at least six feet. Her skin was a golden color. What she wore confounded him. She was dressed in army camouflage fatigues and black, shiny military jump boots. On her proud torso she wore an olive-green, sleeveless T-shirt crisscrossed with two bandoliers containing bullets. Slung across her left shoulder was a rifle. Around her slender waist was a web belt with a black leather holster and pistol, several grenades and a wicked looking K-bar knife. Down her back, resting between her shoulder blades, hung a huge leather sheath, knicked and scarred, that held a machete with a pearl handle. She was obviously a warrior. An Amazon. A soldier used to fighting.

Roan could see and sense all these things about her. Despite her dynamic presence, the threat she presented in the armament she wore, the way her hand curled around the thick leather strap that bit into her shoulder as it held the rifle in place, she was beautiful. Roan could not tear his gaze from her full, square face, those high, proud cheekbones. From her narrowing, willow-green eyes, that fine thin nose that flared like the nostrils of a wary wild horse, or those compressed, full lips.

Her hair was thick and black and hung in one long braid over her right shoulder and down between her breasts, which were hidden by the bandoliers of ammunition. There was such pride and absolute confidence in her stance, in the way her shoulders were thrown back. As she lifted her chin imperiously, Roan wanted to simply absorb the sight of her and the feeling of that incredible energy swirling around her. He wondered if she was a figment of his imagination, a hybrid between Sarah and some kind of superhuman woman.

The instant he thought that, her eyes snapped with rage and utter indignation.

"Do not waste precious energy and time on such speculations!" she growled at him. "You were born into a medicine family. You know better!'' She jabbed a finger at the amulet he wore around his neck. ''You carry the stone of the Jaguar Clan. You are one of us! I am Inca. I am asking for your help, Roan Storm Walker. Well, will you give it? I do not beg. This will be the only time I stand before you. Answer me quickly, for many will die without you here by my side to fight the fight of your life and mine. I am in a death spiral dance. I invite you into it.''

Walker felt her outrage at the very thought that he might say no to her request. *Inca.* A mysterious name. The name of a woman from…where? Perhaps from the Inca empire in Peru? Her accent was thick, reminding him of Spanish. He touched the blue stone that lay at the base of his throat. It felt hot, and throbbing sensations moved through his fingertips. The amulet he wore was powerful; his mother had told him so, and Roan had often experienced strange phenomena regarding it. But he'd never before felt the level of energy that was emanating from it now. He glanced down and saw a strange turquoise-white-and-gold light pulsating around it, like a beacon.

''Where do you come from, Inca?'' he demanded in an equally fierce voice. He was not afraid of her, but he respected her power. Where he came from, women were equal to any man.

''I come from the south, Storm Walker. The stone you wear around your neck tells me of your heritage. The spirits of your ancestors led me to you. You are needed in my country. Time is short. Many lives are at stake. My guardian says you are the one.'' The woman's green gaze grew demanding. ''Are you? the *one?*''

''I don't know. How can I help you?''

''You will know that when you see me the second time.''

He searched her shadowed features. She had the face of an Indian, all right—most probably of Incan heritage if she was from the south. Her stance was uncompromising. This woman feared nothing and no one. So why was she approaching him? He looked around, feeling another, invisible presence near her.

"Your guardian?" he asked.

A sour smile twisted her mouth and she gazed down at his gold cougar, which stood guard. "Watch," she commanded. "I run out of patience with you."

In moments the golden light enveloped Inca once more. Roan watched with fascination as the woman disappeared within spiraling bands that moved like a slow-motion tornado around her. But what walked out of the light moments later made him gasp. It was a huge stocky, black-and-gold male jaguar.

Roan vaguely heard Anna growl. In response the male jaguar hissed and showed his long, curved fangs. His golden eyes were huge, with large, shining black pupils. As the animal stalked around them, his tail whipping impatiently from side to side, his thick body strong and sensuous as he moved, Walker watched in awe. Anna remained on alert at his side, but did not attack the slowly circling jaguar.

The coat on the cat was a bright gold color, patterned with black crescent moons. To Roan, the massive jaguar seemed formidable, invulnerable. His mind churned with more questions than answers. A woman who turned into a male jaguar? She was a shape-shifter—a medicine person from South America who had the power to change shape from human to animal, and then back into human form at will. That in itself was a feat that few could manage successfully. He recalled that his mother, who worked with the Yaqui Indians of Mexico, had possessed shape-shifting abilities herself. One never knew, seeing a bird, a reptile or a four-footed, if it was in fact human or not. Walker had been taught never to kill anything that approached him in such a bold, fearless manner.

As he watched the male jaguar make one complete circle, Roan was wildly aware of the throbbing power around the animal...around this mysterious woman called Inca. As he stared, he felt an intense, searing telepathic message being impressed upon him, body and soul.

I cannot control the tides of the ocean. I cannot change the course of the winds. I cannot control what is free and yearns to roam. I can only bend and surrender to a higher power through my heart, which rules me. I bend to the will of the Great Goddess, and to the Jaguar Clan. I ask you to willingly, with pure heart and single-minded purpose, to work with me. My people need your help. I ask in their name...

To Walker's surprise, he felt hot, scalding tears stinging his eyes. The impassioned plea made him blink rapidly. Tears! Of all things! He hadn't cried since...since Sarah had died so unexpectedly and tragically. Trying to halt the tumult of feelings radiating through his chest and around his heart, he watched the jaguar through blurred vision. What the hell was going on? This was no lucid dream. This was some kind of phenomenal, otherworldly meeting of the highest, purest kind. He'd heard his mother speak in hushed tones of those times when the gods and goddesses of her people would come to her in her dreams. She had often described rare meetings just like the one he was having now.

Was Inca really a human being? A shape-shifting medicine woman? A shaman who lived in South America? What was the Jaguar Clan? All questions and no answers. The stone at his throat seemed like it was burning a hole in his flesh. He felt it with his fingertips; it was scalding hot. This was the first time it had ever activated to this extent. His mother had said that the stone possessed powers beyond anyone's imagination, and that at the right time, he would be introduced to them. Rubbing his throat region, he understood this was no ordinary meeting. This had something to do with the stone's origin and purpose.

The jaguar stopped. He stared up at Roan with those huge eyes that were now thin crescents of gold on a field of black.

Walker felt the inquiry of the massive jaguar. His heart

was beating hard in his chest, adrenaline pumping violently through him. Fight or flight? Run or stay and face combat? She was a warrior for something. What? Who? *Who does she represent? The light or the dark?* Walker knew she wasn't of the darkness. No. Everything within him shouted that she was of the light, working on the side of goodness. Yet she was a combat soldier. A modern-day Amazon.

Roan felt his cougar rub against his thigh, and he draped his fingers across the female animal's skull. She was purring and watching the jaguar with interest. Looking down, Roan saw Anna was once again relaxed, no longer on guard or in her protective stance. *That* was his answer.

Lifting his head, Walker looked over at the male jaguar. "Yes, I'll come. I'll be there for your people."

Within seconds, the jaguar disappeared into the cloud of brilliant, swirling light. And in the blink of an eye, the light was also gone. *She* was gone. Inca...

The drip, drip, drip of the rain off the tin roof slowly eased Walker out of his altered state. This time, as he opened his eyes, the grayness of dawn through the thick fir trees caught his attention. Twisting his head to one side, he looked groggily at the clock on the bedstand: 0600. It was time to get up, make a quick breakfast, drive down the mountain to Philipsburg, fifty miles away, and meet with his boss, Morgan Trayhern, leader of the super secret government group known as Perseus. A messenger had been sent up the mountain two days ago to tell him to be at the Perseus office in the small mining town at 0900 for a meeting with him and Major Mike Houston.

As Roan swung his naked body upward and tossed off the sheet, his feet hitting the cool pine floor, he sighed. Hands curling around the edges of the mattress, he sat there in the grayish light of dawn and wondered who the hell Inca was. This lucid dream was no dream at all, he was sure. He'd never had an experience like this before. The stone against his upper chest still burned and throbbed. Rubbing the area, he slowly rose to his full six foot six inches of height, then padded effortlessly toward the couch, where a pair of clean jeans, a long-sleeved white Western-style shirt, socks and underwear were draped. *First, make the coffee, then get dressed.* He pivoted to the right and made his way to the small, dimly lit kitchen. Without coffee, no day ever went right for him. He grinned a little at that thought, although his mind, and his heart, were centered on Inca. Who was she? What had he agreed to? First, he had to see what Morgan Trayhern and Major Mike Houston had up their sleeves. Roan knew Houston had worked down in South America for a decade, and he might be the right person to share this experience with. Maybe…

"What the hell are we supposed to do?" Morgan Trayhern growled at Mike Houston from his place behind the huge dark maple desk in his office.

Army Special Forces Major Mike Houston turned slowly away from the window where he stood and faced his boss. "Inca *must* lead that Brazilian contingent into the Amazon basin or Colonel Jaime Marcellino and company will be destroyed by the drug lords. Without her, they're dead," he said flatly. Then his eyes snapped with humor. "They just don't know it yet, that's all."

Rubbing his square jaw, Morgan dropped the opened file labeled Inca on his desk. "Damn…she's a lone wolf."

"More like a lone jaguar."

"What?" Disgruntled, Morgan gave Mike a dark look.

"Jaguars," Mike said in a calm tone, "always hunt alone. The only time they get together is to mate, and after that, they split. The cubs are raised by the mother only."

Glaring down at the colored photo of a woman in a sleeveless, olive-green T-shirt, bandoliers across her shoulders, a rifle across her knees as she sat on a moss-covered log, Morgan shook his head. "You vaguely mention in your report that Inca's a member of the Jaguar Clan."

"Well," Mike hedged, "kind of..."

"What is that? A secret paramilitary organization down in Brazil?"

Mike maintained a dour look on his face. He unwound from his at-ease position and slowly crossed the room. "You could say that, but they don't work with governments, exactly. Not formally..." Mike wasn't about to get into the metaphysical attributes of the clan with Morgan. He tip-toed around it with his boss because Mike felt Morgan would not believe him about the clan's mysterious abilities.

"But you're insisting that Inca work with the Brazilian government on this plan of ours to coordinate the capture of major drug lords in several South American countries."

"Morgan, the Amazon basin is a big place." Mike stabbed his finger at the file on the desk as he halted in front of his boss. "Inca was born near Manaus. She knows the Amazon like the back of her hand. The major drug activity is in the Juma and Yanomami Indian reservation around Manaus. You can't put army troops into something like this without experts who know the terrain intimately. Only one person, someone who's been waging a nonstop war against the drug lords in that area, knows it—Inca."

With a heavy shake of his head, Morgan muttered, "She's barely a child! She's only twenty-five years old!"

Mike smiled a little. "Inca is hardly a child. I've known her since she saved my life when she was eighteen years old."

"She's so young."

Mike nodded, the smile on his mouth dissolving. "Listen to me. In a few minutes you've got to go into that war room with emissaries from those South American countries that are capable of raising coca to produce cocaine, and sell them on this idea. Inca has a reputation—not a good one, I'll grant you—but she gets the job done. It ain't pretty, Morgan. She's a Green Warrior. That's slang for a tree hugger or environmentalist. Down there in Brazil, that carries a lot of weight with the Indian people. She's their protector. They worship her. They would go to hell and back for her if she asked it of them. If that Brazilian army is going to make this mission a success they need the support of the locals. And if Inca is there, leading the troops, the Indians will fight and die at her side on behalf of the Brazilian government. Without her, they'll turn a deaf ear to the government's needs.''

"I read in your report that they call her the jaguar goddess."

Raising one eyebrow, Houston said, "Those that love her call her that."

"And her enemies?"

"A Green Warrior—" Houston grimaced "—or worse. I think you ought to prepare yourself for Colonel Marcellino's reaction to her. He won't have anything good to say when he hears we're going to pair him up with Inca."

Studying Houston, Morgan slowly closed the file and stood up. "Mike, I'm counting on you to help carry the day in there. You're my South American expert. You've been fighting drug lords in all those countries, especially in Peru and Brazil. No one knows that turf better than you."

"That's why Inca is so important to this operation," he said as he walked with Morgan toward an inner door that led to an elevator to the top secret, underground war room. "She knows the turf even better than I do."

Morgan halted at the door. He rearranged the red silk tie at the throat of his white shirt. Buttoning up his pinstripe suit, he sighed. "Did you ever find anyone in our merc database who could work—or would want to work—with the infamous Inca?"

Grinning a little, Houston said, "Yeah, I think I did. Roan Storm Walker. He's got Native American blood in him. Inca will respect him for that, at least."

Morgan raised his brows. "Translated, that means she

won't just outright flatten him like she does every other male who gets into her line of fire?''

Chuckling, Mike put his hand on Morgan's broad shoulder. The silver at the temples of his boss's black hair was getting more and more pronounced, making Mike realize that running Perseus, a worldwide mercenary operation, would put gray hairs on just about anyone. ''She'll respect him.''

''What does that mean? She'll ask questions first and shoot later?''

''You could say that, yes.''

''Great,'' Morgan muttered. ''And Walker's in the war room already?''

''Yes. I told him to stay in the shadows and keep a low profile. I don't want him agreeing to this mission you've laid out for him without him realizing he has to work directly with Colonel Marcellino. And—'' Mike scowled, looking even more worried ''—he needs to understand that the ongoing war between Marcellino and Inca will put him between a rock and a hard place.''

Snorting, Morgan opened the door, heading for the elevator that would take them three stories down into the earth. ''Sounds like I need a damned diplomat between the colonel and Inca, not a merc. Roan's always taken oddball assignments, though. Things I could never talk anyone else into taking—and he's always pulled them off.''

''Good,'' Mike murmured, hope in his voice as he followed Morgan into the elevator, ''because Walker is gonna need that kind of attitude to survive.''

''Survive who?'' Morgan demanded, ''Marcellino or Inca?''

The doors whooshed closed. Mike wrapped his arms around his chest as his stomach tightened with tension. The elevator plummeted rapidly toward their destination.

"Both," he said grimly. "There won't be any love lost between Marcellino and Inca, believe me. They're like a dog and cat embroiled in a fight to the death. Only this time it's a dog and a jaguar...."

Chapter 2

*W*hat in the hell am I doing here with all this fruit salad?
Roan wondered as he slowly eased his bulk down into a
chair in the shadows of the huge, rectangular room. Fruit
salad was military slang for the ribbons personnel wore on
their uniforms. Ribbons that spoke of various campaigns and
wars that they served in, and medals they'd earned when
they'd survived them. His own time in the Marine Corps as
a Recon came back to him as he scanned the assembled
group of ten men. Roan recognized two of them: Morgan
Trayhern, who sat at the head of the large, oval table in a
dapper gray pinstripe suit, and Major Mike Houston, who
was a U.S. Army advisor to the Peruvian military. Roan
amended his observation. Mike was retired. Now he was
working for Perseus and for Morgan.

Roan was the only other person besides Morgan and Mike
wearing civilian attire. In his white cotton Western shirt, the
sleeves rolled up haphazardly to just below his elbows, his
well-worn jean's and a pair of dusty, scarred cowboy boots,
he knew he stuck out like a sore thumb in this assemblage,

members of which were now scrutinizing him closely. Let them. Roan really couldn't care less. At twenty-eight he was already a widower, and the dark looks of some colonels and generals were nothing in comparison to what he'd already endured.

"Gentlemen, this is Roan Storm Walker," Morgan began. "He's an ex-Recon Marine. I've asked him to sit in on this important briefing because he will be working directly with the Brazilian detachment."

Roan noticed a tall, thin man in a dark green Brazilian Army uniform snap a cold, measuring look in his direction. The name card in front of him read Marcellino, Jaime, Colonel, Brazil. The man had hard, black, unforgiving eyes that reminded Roan of obsidian, an ebony rock, similar to glass in its chemical makeup, which was created out of the belching fire of a violent volcano. Instinctively Roan felt the controlled and contained violence around the Brazilian colonel. It showed in his thinned mouth and his long, angular features that hinted of an aristocratic heritage. Everything about the good colonel spoke of his formal training; he had that military rigidity and look of expectation that said his orders would be carried out to the letter once he gave them.

Maybe it was the intelligence Roan saw in Marcellino's restless, probing eyes that made him feel a tad better about the man. Roan knew he would have to work with him, and his instincts warned him that Marcellino was a soldier with a helluva lotta baggage that he was dragging around with him like an old friend. People like that made Roan antsy because they tended to take their misery and unconscious rage out on others without ever realizing it. And Roan wouldn't join in that kind of dance with anyone. It was one of the reasons why he'd quit the Marine Corps; the games, the politics choked him, and he withered within the world of the military. His gut told him Marcellino was a man who excelled at those bonds of politics.

Clearing his throat, Morgan buttonholed everyone seated

around the oval table. One by one he introduced each man present. Roan noted there was either a colonel or a general from each of the South American countries represented at the table. In front of him was a file folder marked Top Secret. Roan resisted opening it up before being asked to. When Morgan got to his corner, Roan lowered his eyes and looked down at the well-polished table.

"I've already introduced Roan Storm Walker, but let me give you some of his background. As I mentioned, he was a Recon Marine for six years. A trained paramedic on his team, he saw action in Desert Storm. His team was responsible for doing a lot of damage over in Iraq. His specialty is jungle and desert warfare situations. He holds a degree in psychology. He speaks five languages fluently—Spanish, German, French and Portuguese, plus his own Native American language, of the Lakota Sioux nation. He will be working with Colonel Jaime Marcellino, from Brazil. But more on that later."

Roan was glad once the spotlight moved away from him. He didn't like being out front. People out front got shot at and hit. He had learned to be a shadow, because shadows could quietly steal away to live and fight another day. As he sat there, vaguely listening to the other introductions, Roan admitted to himself that the fight had gone out of him. When Sarah died two years ago, his life had been shattered. He had no more desire to take on the world. With her his reason for living had died. If it hadn't been for Morgan nudging him to get back into the stream of life, he'd probably have drunk himself to death in his cabin up in the mountains.

Morgan would visit him about once a month, toss a small mercenary job with little danger to it his way, to keep Roan from hitting the bottle in his despair. Trayhern was astute about people, about their grief and how it affected them. Roan knew a lot about grief now. He knew what loss was. The worst kind. He tried to imagine a loss that would be greater than losing a wife or husband, and figured that would probably be losing a child. It was lucky, he supposed morbidly, that he and Sarah never had children. But in truth he wished that they had. Sarah would live on through that child, and Roan wouldn't feel as devastated or alone as he did now. But that was a selfish thought, he knew.

Still, he felt that losing a loved one, whether spouse or child, was the hardest thing in the world to endure. How could one do it and survive? As a psychologist, he knew the profound scarring that took place on the psyche. He knew firsthand the terrible, wrenching grief of losing a woman he loved as well as life itself. And Roan swore he'd never, ever fall in love again, because he could not afford to go through that again. Not ever. His spirit would not survive it.

"Gentlemen, I'm turning this briefing over to Major Mike Houston. You all know him well. He was a U.S. Army advisor up until very recently." Morgan allowed a hint of a smile on his face. "Mike is now working for Perseus, my organization. He is our South American specialist. One of the reasons you have been handpicked to represent your country is because you have all worked with him in some capacity or another. Major Houston is a known quantity to you. You know he's good at his word, that he knows the terrain and the problems with the drug trade in South America. You know he can be trusted." Morgan turned to Mike. "Major Houston?"

Mike nodded and stood up. He, too, was in civilian attire—a pair of tan trousers, a white cotton shirt and a dark brown blazer. When he turned on the overhead, a map of Brazil flashed on the screen in front of the group.

"The government of Brazil has asked this administration for help in ridding the Amazon basin of two very powerful drug lords—the Valentino Brothers." Mike moved to the front and flicked on his laser pen. A small red dot appeared on the map. "We know from intelligence sources in the basin that the brothers have at least six areas of operation.

Their business consists of growing and manufacturing cocaine. They have factories, huge ones, that are positioned in narrow, steep and well-guarded valleys deep in the interior of the rain forest.

"The Valentino Brothers capture Indians from the surrounding areas and basically enslave them, turn them into forced laborers. If the Indians don't work, they are shot in the head. If they try to escape, they are killed. What few have escaped and lived to tell us about their captivity, relate being fed very little food while working sixteen hours a day, seven days a week. If they don't work fast enough, the overseer whips them. There is no medical help for them. No help at all."

Mike looked out at the shadowy faces turned raptly toward him. "All of you know I'm part Quechua Indian, from Peru. I have a personal stake in this large, ongoing mission. We have drug lords enslaving Indians in every country in South America in order to produce large quantities of cocaine for world distribution. If the Indians do not do the work, they are murdered. The captured women are raped. After working all day they become unwilling pawns to the drug dealers at night. Children who are captured are forced to work the same hours as an adult. They suffer the same fate as an adult." His mouth became set. "Clearly, we need to make a statement to these drug lords. The head honchos aren't stupid. They use the rain forests and jungles to hide in. Even our satellite tracking cannot find them under the dense canopy. What we need, in each country, is someone who knows the territory where these factories are located, to act as a guide, to bring the army forces in to destroy them."

Mike grimaced. "This is no easy task. The Amazon basin is huge and the military must march in on foot. The only way units can be resupplied is by helicopter. When they get farther in, helicopters are out of range—they can't reach them without refueling—so we must rely on cargo plane airdrops. The troops' medical needs aren't going to be met. If there is an emergency, a sick or wounded soldier will have to be carried out to a place where a helicopter can pick him up and transport him back to the nearest hospital. As you all are aware, I'm sure, there are a lot of deadly things out in the Amazon. Piranhas in the rivers, channels and pools. Bushmaster snakes that will literally chase you until they sink their fangs into you. Mosquitoes carrying malaria, yellow fever and dengue. There's always the threat of unknown hemorrhagic viruses, victims of which can bleed out before we can get them proper medical help. There are insects that with one bite can kill you in as little as forty-eight hours if you are without medical intervention."

Mike paused, then moved on. "Colonel Jaime Marcellino has been chosen to lead the Brazilian Army contingent, a company of their best soldiers—roughly one hundred and eighty men. He is their rain forest specialist. He has knowledge of the problems inherit in that environment."

Jaime bowed slightly to Houston.

Mike went on. "We all agree that Colonel Marcellino's experiment with a company of men in Brazil will teach us a lot about how to organize military attacks against drug strongholds in other countries. What we learn from his mission will help all of you in preparation for yours. He will be our guinea pig, so to speak. Mistakes made there we will learn from. What works will be passed on in an after-action report to all of you."

Moving toward the front of the room, Mike tapped the map projected on the huge screen. "We have it on good authority where six factories, in six different valleys, are located. We have a guide who will lead the colonel's company to the nearest one, which is about ten hours southeast of Manaus, up in a mountainous region known as Sector 5. The colonel's company will disembark at Manaus, motor down the Amazon and, at a predestined spot, off-load and meet their guide. The guide will then take them through a lot of grueling hilly and swampy terrain to reach the valley where the factory is located. Once there, Colonel Marcellino will deploy his troops for a strategic attack on the facility." Mike shrugged. "It is our hope that the Indians who are captive will be freed. We don't want them killed in the cross fire. The Valentino Brothers have heavily fortified operations. Their drug soldiers are men who live in the rain forest and know it intimately. They will be a constant threat."

Jaime held up a long, narrow hand with closely clipped carefully manicured nails. "Major Houston, I am sure my men will be able to take this factory. Do not look so worried." He smiled slightly.

"Colonel, I wish I could share your optimism," Mike said heavily. "I don't question your willingness and passion for this mission. But it's going to be hard. No army in South America has tried such a thing before. There's bound to be a steep learning curve on this."

"We are prepared," Marcellino answered in his soothing well-modulated tone. He looked at Morgan. "My men are trained for rain forest warfare."

Morgan nodded. "We realize that, Colonel. That's why you're being asked to lead this mission. Even though your men have trained for it, that doesn't mean they've actually undertaken missions in the basin, however. There's a big difference between training and real-time experience."

Jaime nodded. "Of course, Mr. Trayhern. I'm confident we can do this."

Mike Houston cleared his throat. "For this mission, we are sending Roan Storm Walker with you, Colonel. He'll be your advisor, your translator, and will work directly between you and the guide. He will answer only to you and to Morgan Trayhern at Perseus, which has the backing of this administration to undertake this plan of attack. Even though Storm Walker has no military designation, his judgment will be equal to your own." Houston drilled Marcellino with an incisive look. "Do you understand that?"

Jaime shrugged thin, sharp shoulders beneath a uniform resplendent with shining brass buttons and thick, gold braid and epaulets. On his chest were at least twenty ribbons. "Yes, yes, of course. I will order my officers to acknowledge that he has full authority to override their decisions in the field." Frowning, he turned and looked down the table at Storm Walker. "However, he must check with me first before any action is taken."

"Of course," Mike assured him. "Roan knows chain of command. He recognizes you as the ultimate authority over your men."

Nodding, Jaime raised his thin, graying brows. "And what of this guide? What is his status with me?"

Mike sent a brief, flickering glance in Morgan's direction and kept his voice low and deep as he answered. "The guide knows the terrain, Colonel. You should listen to the advice given to you. This is a person who has lived in the basin all her life. Storm Walker will be her liaison with you, and she'll be your point man—woman—on this mission. You'd best heed whatever advice she gives you because she knows the territory. She's had a number of skirmishes with the Valentino Brothers and has every reason for wanting them out of the basin."

Curious, Jaime straightened, his hand resting lightly on the table. "Excuse me, Major. Am I hearing you correctly? You said 'she'? I thought our guide would be a man. What woman has knowledge of the basin?" He laughed briefly and waved his hand. "Women stay at home and have our children. They are wives and mothers—that is all. No, you must have meant 'he'. *Sim?*"

Mike girded himself internally. He flashed a look of warning in Roan's direction. Now the muck was going to hit the fan. "No," he began slowly, "I meant *she*. This is a woman who was born and raised in the basin. She knows at least fifteen Indian languages, knows the territory like the back of her hand. No one is better suited for this assignment than she is. Roan Storm Walker will interface directly with her, Colonel. You will not have to if you don't want to.''

Though he frowned, Jaime said laughingly, ''And why would I not want to meet this woman and hear her words directly? If she is Indian and knows Portuguese, there should not be a language problem, eh?''

Biting down on his lower lip for a moment, Mike said quietly, ''She is known as the jaguar goddess, Colonel. Her real name is Inca.'' He saw the colonel's eyes widen enormously, as if he'd just been hit in the chest with an artillery shell. Before the Brazilian could protest, Mike added quickly, ''We know the past history between Inca and yourself. That is why Roan Storm Walker is going along. He'll relay any information or opinions from Inca to you. We know you won't want to interface with her directly due to…circumstances….''

Marcellino uttered a sharp cry of surprise. He shot up so quickly that his chair tipped over. His voice was ragged with utter disbelief. ''No! No! A thousand times no!'' He swung toward Morgan, who sat tensely.

''You cannot do this! I will not allow it! She's a ruthless killer! She murdered my eldest son, Rafael, in cold blood!'' He slammed his fist down on the table, causing the wood to vibrate. ''I will not permit this godless woman anywhere near me or my troops!'' His voice cracked. Tears came to his eyes, though he instantly forced them back. ''I lost my eldest son to that murdering, thieving traitor! She's a sorceress! She kills without rhyme or reason.''

Choking, he suddenly realized how much of his military bearing he'd lost in front of his fellow officers. His face turned a dull red. He opened his hands and held them up. ''I apologize,'' he whispered unsteadily. ''Many of you do not know me, know of my background. My eldest son, the light of my life…the son who was to carry on my name, who was to marry and someday give me grandchildren…was senselessly and brutally murdered by this woman named Inca. She is wanted in Brazil for thirteen murders. Thirteen,'' he growled. Straightening up, his heart pounding, he again apologized. "I had no idea you would suggest her," he told Morgan in a hoarse tone.

Morgan slowly rose and offered a hand in peace to him. "Please, Colonel, come and sit down."

An aide scrambled from near the door to pick up the colonel's fallen chair and place it upright so that he could sit down. Hands shaking, Jaime pulled the chair, which was on rollers, beneath him. "I am sorry for my outburst. I am not sorry what I said about this sorceress." Sitting down, he glared across the table at Morgan and Mike Houston. "You know of her. You know she's a murderer. How can you ask me to tolerate the sight of her, much less work with her, when she has the blood of my son on her hands?" His voice cracked. "How?"

Houston looked to his boss. This was Morgan's battle to win, not his. Sitting down, he watched Morgan's face carefully as he rose to his full height to address the emotionally distraught colonel.

"Jaime…" Morgan began softly, opening his hand in a pleading gesture, "I have four children. I almost lost my oldest son, Jason, in a kidnapping and I know of your grief. I'm deeply sorry for your loss. I truly am." Morgan cleared his throat and glanced down at Mike who sat looking grim. "I have it on good authority that Inca did *not* kill your son Rafael. She said she was on the other side of the basin when he and his squad surprised a drug-running operation in a village. Inca denies killing your son. The person in this room who knows her well is Mike Houston. Mike, do you have anything to add to this, to help the colonel realize that Rafael was not murdered by Inca?"

Mike leaned forward, his gaze fixed on Jaime's grief-filled face. The colonel had lost his hard military expression, and his dark eyes were wild with suffering and barely checked rage. Mike knew that in most Latin American countries, the firstborn male child was the darling of the family. In the patriarchal cultures in South America, to lose the eldest son was, to the father of that family, to lose everything. The eldest was doted upon, raised from infancy to take over the family business, the family responsibilities, and carry on their long heritage. Mike knew the people in Jaime's social strata were highly educated. Jaime himself, descended from Portuguese aristocracy of the 1700s, had a proud lineage that few others in Brazil possessed. Rafael had been trained, coaxed, nurtured and lovingly molded according to this prominent family's expectations. Mike knew even as he spoke just how devastating the loss was for the colonel.

"Colonel Marcellino. Inca is my blood sister." He held up his hand and pointed to a small scar on the palm of his hand. "I met her when she was eighteen years old. She saved my life, quite literally. She almost died in the process. The Inca I know is not a murderer. She is a member of the Jaguar Clan of Peru, a group that teaches their people to defend, never attack. If someone fires on Inca, or someone attacks her, she will defend herself. But she will never fire first. She will not ever needlessly take a life."

Marcellino glared across the table at him. "Do not paint a pretty picture of this murdering sorceress. The men in Rafael's squad saw her. They saw her put a rifle to her shoulder and shoot my son cold-bloodedly in the head!"

"Listen to me," Mike rasped. "Inca was two hundred miles away from the place where your son was killed. She was with an old Catholic priest, Father Titus, at an Indian mission on the Amazon River. I can prove it." Mike pulled out a paper from the open file in front of him. "Here, this is an affidavit signed by the priest. Please, look at it. Read it."

Belligerently, Jaime jerked the paper from Mike's hand. He saw the sweat stains on the document and the barely legible signature of the old priest. Throwing it back, he barked, "This proves nothing!"

Mike placed the paper back into the file. Keeping his voice low and quashing his feelings, he said, "No one in your son's squad survived the attack by the drug lord and his men. I saw the report on it, Colonel. All you have is one person's word—a man who was later captured and who is suspected of working with the same local drug lord who indicted Inca. He said Inca was there. You have a drug runner's word. Are you going to believe him? He has every reason to lie to you on this. He wants to save his hide and do only a little bit of prison time and get released. How convenient to lay the blame at Inca's feet. Especially since she wasn't there to defend herself." Houston tapped the file beneath his hand. "I know Father Titus personally. The old priest is almost ninety. He's lived in the basin and has helped the Indians at his mission for nearly seventy of those years. At one time he helped raise Inca, who was orphaned."

"Then all the more reason for the old priest to lie!" Jaime retorted. "No! I do not believe you. The blood of thirteen men lays on Inca's head. There is a huge reward, worth six million cruzeiros, or one million dollars, U.S., for her capture, dead or alive, in Brazil. If I see her, I will kill her myself. Personally. And with pleasure. My son's life will finally be avenged."

Roan shifted slightly in his chair. The atmosphere in the room was cold and hostile. Not one man moved; all eyes were riveted on the colonel and Mike Houston. Roan saw the hatred in the colonel's face, heard the venom that dripped from every stilted English word he spoke. The colonel's black eyes were a quagmire of grief and rage. Part of Roan's heart went out to the man. Jaime had made the worst sacrifice of all; he'd lost a beloved child. Well, Roan had something in common with the colonel—he'd lost someone he'd loved deeply, too. But who was Inca? The woman he'd seen in his dream earlier? She sounded like a hellion of the first order. Warrioress, madwoman—who knew? Roan looked to Mike Houston, who was laboring to get the colonel to see reason.

"Inca's only responsibility is as a Green Warrior for Mother Earth," Mike said quietly. "She has taken a vow to protect the Amazon Basin from encroachment and destruction by anyone. Twelve of these so-called murders were really self-defense situations. Plus, the twelve men who are dead are all drug dealers. Inca does not deny killing them, but she didn't fire first. She shot back only to save herself and other innocent lives." Mike held out a thick folder toward Jaime. "Here is the proof, colonel. I haven't understood yet why the government of Brazil has not absolved Inca of those trumped up charges. I'd think Brazil would be happy to see those men gone." He laid the file down. "But I don't want to get off track here. You can read her sworn statements on each charge when you want."

"It is well known she hates white men!" Marcellino snapped, his anger flaring.

"Not all," Mike countered. "She's my blood sister by ceremony. She respects men and women alike. Now, if someone wants to destroy, rip up, start cutting down timber, hurt the Indians or make them into slaves, then Inca will be there to stop him. She will try many ways to stop the destruction, but murdering a person is not one of them. And as I said, she will fire in defense, she will never fire the first shot."

"And I suppose," Marcellino rattled angrily, "that the thirteen men she killed fired on her *first?*"

"That's exactly what happened in twelve cases," Houston said gravely. "Your son is the thirteenth to her count, he shouldn't have been added. Members of the Jaguar Clan can be kicked out of it by firing first or attacking first. She can only defend herself. So twelve men fired *first* on her, Colonel. And she shot back. And she didn't miss."

"She murdered my son! He's one of the thirteen."

"Inca was not there. She did not shoot your son."

Morgan appealed to Marcellino. "Colonel, would you, as an officer, lead your entire company of men into an unknown area without proper help and guidance?"

"Of course not!"

"Inca knows the basin better than anyone," Morgan said soothingly. He lifted a hand toward Roan at the end of the table. "This man will be standing between you and Inca. You won't have to face her. You won't have to see that much of her. He's your liaison. Your spokesman, if you will. Inca can lead you and your men safely to this valley in the mountains. I know much is being asked of you, and that is why Roan is here—to assist and help you as much as he can. Anything she tells him, Roan will relay on to you or your officers. I realize the pain of your loss, and we tried to come up with a plan that would somehow protect you and her both during this mission."

"I will kill her if I see her."

"No," Morgan said, his voice hard and uncompromising, "you won't. If you really want to take this mission, you will promise to leave her alone."

"And you will not order one of your men to shoot her, either," Houston growled. "Any attempt on Inca's life, and she'll leave you and your company wherever you are. And if you're in the middle of the rain forest, Colonel, without a guide, you'll be in jeopardy."

"Then I will hire an Indian guide to lead us."

Houston shook his head. "There isn't an Indian willing to lead you into the area, Colonel. If the drug lords find out that they did, they'd move into their village and murder everyone in retribution."

Jaime tried to take a breath. It hurt to breathe. His heart was wild with grief. Rafael had been murdered two years ago, but it felt like only yesterday. Rubbing his chest savagely, Jaime snarled, "You cannot ask this of me. You cannot."

Morgan moved around the table and faced him squarely.

"Colonel, if I thought for a heartbeat that Inca had killed your son, I would not have asked you to head this mission. Nor would I have asked Inca to be your guide. I believe Mike Houston. I've never met her, I only know of her reputation in Brazil. I know that if a person becomes a legend, many times the truth gets tattered and distorted. I believe the old priest's affidavit. He has no reason to lie to protect her. Priests don't lie about something like this. I've also read her sworn statements on each charge. I believe she's innocent in such charges." Morgan eased his bulk down on the table next to Marcellino's chair.

"Colonel, you are a man of consummate honor. Your family's heritage stretches back to the kings and queens of Portugal. You were the only person we wanted for this mission. You are a brave and resourceful man. You are someone who is good at his word. Your love of your country has been obvious in the twenty years you've served in her military. You are one of the most decorated men in your country." Morgan held the officer's dark gaze. "I believe, Colonel, that if you will give me your word that you will not harm Inca for the duration of the mission, that you can be trusted. Look beyond her. Look at what you will accomplish for all the people of Brazil. You will be a hero."

Morgan raised his hand and swept it toward the rest of the men sitting around the table. "And think of the glory you will receive, the recognition, for going in first to strike a blow for freedom from these drug runners. Your name will be on the lips of people around the globe. Is that not a credit to your son? Could this mission be undertaken in his name? In his memory?"

Morgan saw Marcellino sink back into the chair. He knew the officer's ego and pride were tremendous. And typical of South American aristocracy, fame and power would appeal strongly to the colonel. Morgan was hoping it would break the logjam on this mission. He tried to sit there appearing

at ease, even though his gut was knotted while he waited
for the man's answer.

Roan watched the proceedings with rapt attention. So, he
was to be a bridge, a liaison between this wild woman from
Amazonia and the colonel who wanted to kill her in the
name of his lost son. Roan realized the immensity of his
mission. Was this woman, Inca, sane? Was she manageable?
Would she respect him enough to stay out of Marcellino's
way so they could successfully complete the assigned task?
Roan wasn't sure, and he had a helluva lot of questions to
ask Houston when the time was right.

All eyes were on Marcellino as he sat back, deep in
thought over Morgan's softly spoken words. No one moved.
The Brazilian finally looked at Houston. "What makes you
think she will work with Storm Walker?"

"He's Indian like she is. Inca respects Indians."

"He's a man." Marcellino's voice dripped with sarcasm.

"Inca doesn't hate men. She respects men who have
honor, who have morals and who aren't destroying Mother
Earth. Roan, here, comes from a similar background. He'll
be able to understand her, and vice versa. I believe it is a
good match, and I believe Inca will get along well with
him."

"And what if she doesn't?"

"Then," Mike said, "the mission is off. Morgan and I
realize your loss, Colonel. We've worked hard to put the
right people in key positions to help you get through this
mission successfully. If Roan can't forge the bond of trust
we need with Inca, in order to work with you, then this
mission is scrubbed."

Nodding, Marcellino glared up at Morgan. "If it had been
anyone but you asking this of me, I would tell him to burn
in hell."

Relief shuddered through Morgan, though he kept his face
expressionless. Reaching out, he placed his hand on the
colonel's proud shoulder. "Jaime, I share your grief and

your loss. But I'm convinced Inca is innocent of your son's death. She is the only person we know who can give you success on your mission. I know I'm asking a lot from you in begging you to rise above personal hurt, grief and rage, and look at the larger picture. You can be the deliverer of hundreds of people. The name Marcellino will be revered in many Indian villages because you had the courage to come and eradicate the drug lords from the basin. I know you can do this. And I don't deny it will be difficult…''

The colonel slumped slightly. He felt Morgan's grip on his shoulder, heard the sincerity in his rumbling voice. "Very well," he whispered raggedly, "you have my word, Morgan. I will reluctantly work with Inca. But only through this man." He pointed at Roan. "I don't know what I'll do if I see her. I want to kill her—I won't deny it. He had best make sure that she never meets me face-to-face.…''

Morgan nodded and swallowed hard. "I know Roan will do everything in his power to convey that message to Inca. She will be your scout, your point person, so the chances of seeing her are pretty slim. But I'll make sure he tells her that. I have no wish to hurt you any more than you've already been hurt by your son's loss."

Eyes misting, Jaime forced back tears. He looked up at Morgan. "And do you know the terrible twist in all of this?"

"No, what?"

"My youngest son, Julian, who is a lieutenant, will be leading one of the squads under my command on this mission."

Morgan closed his eyes for a moment. When he opened them, he rasped, "Colonel, your son is safe. Inca is not going after him—or any of your men. She is on *your* side of this fight."

"This time," Marcellino said bitterly. "And for how long? She is infamous for turning on people when it suits her whims and wiles."

"Roan will see that things go smoothly," Morgan promised heavily, shooting him a glance down the table.

Roan waited patiently until the room cleared of all but him, Morgan and Mike. When the door shut, he slowly unwound from his chair.

"I didn't realize what I'd be doing."

Mike nodded. "I'm sorry I couldn't brief you beforehand, Roan."

Morgan moved toward the end of the table, where Roan stood. "More importantly, do you *want* to take this assignment?"

With a shrug, Roan said, "I wasn't doing much of anything else."

Morgan nodded and wiped his perspiring brow with a white linen handkerchief, then returned it to his back pocket. "I've never met Inca. Mike has. I think you should direct your questions to him. In the meantime, I'm going to join the officers at a banquet we've set up in their honor in the dining room. See me there when you're done here?"

Roan nodded, then waited expectantly as the door closed behind Morgan. Silence settled over them, and Roan discovered Mike Houston's expression became more readable once they were alone. Roan opened his hand.

"Well? Is she a killer or a saint in disguise?

Grinning, Mike said, "Not a killer and not a saint."

"What then?"

"A twenty-five-year-old woman who was orphaned at birth, and who is responsible for protecting the Indian people of the Amazon."

"Why her?"

"She's a member of the Jaguar Clan," Mike said, sitting down and relaxing. "You're Native American. You have your societies up here in the north. Down in South America, they're known as clans. One and the same."

"Okay," Roan said, "like a hunters' society? Or a warriors' society?"

"Yes, specialists. Which is why the societies were created—to honor those who had skills in a specific area of need for their community. The welfare and continuing survival of their families and way of life depends on it."

"So, the Jaguar Clan is...what?"

"What kind of society?" Mike sighed. "A highly complex one. It's not easy to define. Your mother, I understand, was a Yuwipi medicine woman of the Lakota people. She was also known as a shape-shifter?"

Roan nodded. "That's right."

"The Jaguar Clan is a group of people from around the world who possess jaguar medicine. They come from all walks of life. Their calling is to learn about their jaguar medicine—what it is and what it is capable of doing. It is basically a healers' clan. That is why Inca would never fire first. That is why she defends well, but never attacks. Her calling is one of healing—in her case, to help heal Mother Earth. She does this by being a Green Warrior in Brazil, where she was born."

"The colonel called her a sorceress."

"Inca has many different powers. She is not your normal young woman," Mike warned him. "Combine that with her passion for protecting the people of the Amazon, the mission she is charged with, and her confidence and high intelligence, and you have a powerful woman on your hands. She doesn't suffer fools lightly or gladly. She speaks her mind." Mike grinned. "I love her like a sister, Roan. I don't have a problem with her strength, her moxie or her vow of healing Mother Earth and protecting the weak from drug runners. Most men do. I figured you wouldn't because, originally, Native American nations were all matriarchal, and most still have a healthy respect for what women have brought to the table."

"Right, I do."

"Good. Hold that perspective. Inca can be hardheaded, she's a visionary, and she can scare the living hell out of you with some of her skills. They call her the jaguar goddess in the basin because people have seen her heal those who were dying."

"And do you trust Marcellino not to try and kill her?"

"No," Mike said slowly, "and that is why you'll have to be there like a rock wall between them. You'll need to watch out for Inca getting shot in the back by him or one of his men. You're going to be in a helluva fix between two warring parties. Inca has a real dislike for the military. According to her, they're soft. They don't train hard. They don't listen to the locals who know the land because they are so damned arrogant and think they know everything, when in reality they know nothing."

"So I'm a diplomat and a bodyguard on this trip."

"Yes. You're at the fulcrum point, Roan. It's a messy place to be. I don't envy you." He smiled a little. "If my wife and child didn't need me, and vice versa, I'd be taking on this mission myself. Morgan wanted someone without family to take it, because the level of risk, the chance of dying, is high. And I know you understand that."

Nodding, Roan ran his long index finger across the highly polished surface of the conference table enjoying the feel of the warm wood. "Is Inca capable of killing me?"

Chuckling, Mike said, "Oh, she can have some thunderstorm-and-lightning temper tantrums when you don't agree with her, or things don't go the way she wants them to, but hurt you? No. She wouldn't do that. If anything, she'll probably see you as one more person under her umbrella of protection."

"Will she listen to me, though? When it counts?"

Shrugging, Mike said, "If you gain her respect and trust, the answer is yes. But you don't have much time to do either."

"Where am I to meet her? Hopefully, it will be without Marcellino and his company."

"On the riverfront, near Manaus, where the two great rivers combine to create the Amazon."

"How will you get in touch with her?"

Houston gave him a lazy smile. "I'll touch base with her in my dream state."

Roan stood there for a second absorbing Houston's statement. "You're a member of the Jaguar Clan, too?"

"Yes, I am."

Roan nodded. He vividly recalled the experience he'd had earlier—the dream of the woman with willow-green eyes. "What color are Inca's eyes?" he asked.

Mike gave him a probing look. He opened his mouth to inquire why Roan was asking such a question, and then decided against it. "Green."

"What shade?"

"Ever seen a willow tree in the spring just after the leaves have popped out?"

"Many times."

"That color of green. A very beautiful, unique color. That's the color of Inca's eyes."

"I thought so...." Roan said, his own eyes narrowing thoughtfully as he realized he and Inca might have already met....

Chapter 3

Inca was lonely. Frowning, she shifted on the large stack of wooden crates where she sat, her booted feet dangling and barely touching the dry red soil of the Amazon's bank. Her fine, delicately arched brows knitted as she studied the ground. In Peru, they called the earth *Pachamama,* or Mother Earth. Stretching slightly, she gently patted the surface with the sole of her military boot. The dirt was Mother Earth's skin, and in her own way, Inca was giving her real and only mother a gentle pat of love.

Sighing, she looked around at the humid mid-afternoon haze that hung above the wide, muddy river. The sun was behind the ever-present hazy clouds that hugged the land like a lover. Making a strangled sound, Inca admitted sourly to herself she didn't know what it was to feel like a lover. The only thing she knew of romantic love was what she'd read about it from the great poets while growing up under Father Titus's tutelage.

Did she want a lover? Was that why she was feeling lonely? Ordinarily, Inca didn't have to deal with such an odd assortment of unusual emotions. She was so busy that she could block out the tender feelers that wound through the heart like a vine, and ignore them completely. Not today. No, she had to rendezvous with this man that her blood brother, Michael Houston, had asked her to meet. Not only that, but she had to work with him! Michael had visited her in the dream state several nights earlier and had carefully gone over everything with her. In the end, he'd left it up to Inca as to whether or not she would work as a guide for Colonel Marcellino—the man who wanted to kill her.

Her lips, full and soft, moved into a grimace. Always alert, with her invisible jaguar spirit guide always on guard, she felt no danger nearby. Her rifle was leaning against the crates, which were stacked and ready to take down the Amazon, part of the supplies Colonel Marcellino would utilize once they met up with him and his company downriver.

She was about to take on a mission, so why was she feeling so alone? So lonely? Rubbing her chest, the olive-green, sleeveless tank top soaked with her perspiration from the high humidity and temperature, Inca lifted her stubborn chin.

She had a mild curiosity about this man called Roan Storm Walker. For one thing, he possessed an interesting name. The fact that he was part Indian made her feel better about this upcoming mission. Indians shared a common blood, a common heritage here in South America. Inca wondered if the blood that pumped through Walker's veins was similar to hers, to the Indians who called the Amazon basin home. She hoped so.

Her hair, wrapped in one thick, long braid, hung limply across her right shoulder with tendrils curling about her face. Inca looked up expectantly toward the asphalt road to Manaus. From the wooden wharves around her, tugs and scows ceaselessly took cargo up and down the Amazon. Right now, at midday, it was siesta time, and no one was in the wharf area, which was lined with rickety wooden docks that stuck

fifty or so feet off the red soil bank into the turbid, muddy
Amazon. Everyone was asleep now, and that was good. For
Inca, it meant less chance of being attacked. She was always
mindful of the bounty on her head. Wanted dead or alive by
the Brazilian government, she rarely came this close to any
city. Only because she was to meet this man, at Michael's
request, had she left her rain forest home, where she was
relatively safe.

Bored by sitting so long, Inca lifted her right arm and
unsnapped one of the small pouches from the dark green
nylon web belt she always wore around her slender waist.
On the other side hung a large canteen filled with water and
a knife in a black leather sheath. On the right, next to the
pouch, was a black leather holster with a pistol in it. In her
business, in her life, she was at war all the time. And even
though she possessed the skills of the Jaguar Clan, good old
guns, pistols and knives were part and parcel of her trade as
well.

Easing a plastic bag out of the pouch, Inca gently opened
it. Inside was a color photo of Michael and Ann Houston.
In Ann's arms was six-month-old Catherine. Inca hungrily
studied the photo, its edges frayed and well worn from being
lovingly looked at so many times, in moments of quiet. She
was godmother to Catherine Inca Houston. She finally had
a family. Pain throbbed briefly through her heart. Abandoned
at birth, unwanted, Inca had bits and pieces of memories of
being passed from village to village, from one jaguar priestess to another. In the first sixteen years of her life, she'd had
many mothers and fathers. Why had her real parents abandoned her? Had she cried a lot? Been a bad baby? What had
she done to be discarded? Looking at the photo of Catherine,
who was a chubby-cheeked, wide-eyed, happy little tyke,
Inca wondered if she'd been ugly at birth, and if that was
why her parents had left her out in the rain forest to die of
starvation.

The pain of abandonment was always with her. Wiping

her damp fingers on the material of the brown-green-and-tan military fatigues she wore, she skimmed the photo lightly with her index finger. She must have been ugly and noisy for her mother and father to throw her away. Eyes blurring with the tears of old pain, Inca absorbed the smiling faces of Michael and Ann. Oh, how happy they were! When Inca saw Mike and Ann together she got some idea of what real love was. She'd been privileged to be around these two courageous people. She'd seen them hold hands, give each other soft, tender looks, and had even seen them kissing heatedly once, when she'd unexpectedly showed up at their camp.

He's coming.

Instantly, Inca placed the photo back into the protective plastic covering and into the pouch at her side, snapping it shut. Her guardian, a normally invisible male jaguar called Topazio, had sent her a mental warning that the man known as Storm Walker was arriving shortly. Standing, Inca felt her heart pound a little in anticipation. Michael had assured her that she would get along with Roan. Inca rarely got along with anyone, so when her blood brother had said that she had eyed him skeptically. Her role in the world was acting as a catalyst, and few people liked a catalyst throwing chaos into their lives. Inca could count on one hand the people who genuinely liked her.

The slight rise of the hill above her blocked her view, so she couldn't see the approach of the taxi that would drop this stranger off in her care. Michael had given her a physical description of him, saying that Roan was tall with black hair, blue eyes and a build like a swimmer. Mike had described his face as square with some lines in it, as if he'd been carved out of the rocks of the Andes. Inca had smiled at that. To say that Roan's face was rough-hewn like the craggy, towering mountains that formed the backbone of South America was an interesting metaphor. She was curious to see if this man indeed had a rugged face.

Inca felt the brush of Topazio against her left thigh. It was a reassuring touch, much like a housecat that brushed lovingly against its owner. He sat down and waited patiently. As Inca stared into the distance, the midday heat made curtains where heat waves undulated in a mirage at the top of the hill.

Anticipation arced through her when she saw the yellow-and-black taxi roar over the crest of the hill on the two-lane, poorly marked road. She worried about the driver recognizing her. Although there were only a few rough sketches of her posted, artists for the government of Brazil had rendered her likeness closely enough for someone to identify her. Once Storm Walker got out of the cab, it would mean a fast exit on the tug. Inca would have to wake the captain, Ernesto, who was asleep in the shade of the boat, haphazardly docked at the nearby wharf, and get him to load the crates on board pronto.

The taxi was blowing blue smoke from its exhaust pipe as it rolled down the long hill toward Inca. Eyes narrowing, she saw the shape of a large man in the back seat. She wrapped her arms against her chest and tensely waited. Her rifle was nearby in case things went sour. Inca trusted no one except Mike Houston and his wife, Rafe Antonio, a backwoodsman who worked with her to protect the Indians, Grandmother Alaria and Father Titus. That was all. Otherwise, she suspected everyone of wanting her head on a platter. Inca's distrust of people had proved itself out consistently. She had no reason to trust the cab driver or this stranger entering her life.

The cab screeched to a halt, the brakes old and worn. Inca watched as a man, a very tall, well-built man, emerged from the back of the vehicle. As he straightened up, Inca's heartbeat soared. He looked directly at her across the distance that separated them. Her lips parted. She felt the intense heat of his cursory inspection of her. The meeting of their eyes was brief, and yet it branded her. Because she was clairvoyant, her senses were honed to an excruciatingly high degree.

She could read someone else's thoughts if she put her mind to it. But rather than making the effort to mind read, she kept her sensitivity to others wide open, like an all-terrain radar system, in order to pick up feelings, sensations and nuances from anyone approaching. Her intuition, which was keenly honed, worked to protect her and keep her safe.

As the man leaned over to pay the driver, Inca felt a warm sheet of energy wrapping around her. Startled, she shook off the feeling. What was that? Guardedly, she realized it had come from *him*. The stranger. Storm Walker. A frisson of panic moved through her gut. What was this? Inca afraid? Oh, yes, fear lived in her, alive and thriving. Fear was always with her. But Inca didn't let fear stop her from doing what had to be done. After all, being a member of the Jaguar Clan, she had to walk through whatever fears she had and move on to accomplish her purpose. Fear was not a reason to quit.

The cab turned around and roared back up the hill. Inca watched as the man leaned down and captured two canvas bags—his luggage—and then straightened up to face her. Five hundred feet separated them. Her guard was up. She felt Topazio get to his feet, his nose to the air, as if checking out the stranger.

The man was tall, much taller than Inca had expected. He was probably around six foot five or six. To her, he was like a giant. She was six foot in height, and few men in the Amazon stood as tall as she did. Automatically, Inca lifted her strong chin, met his assessing cobalt-colored eyes and stood her ground. His face was broad, with the hooked nose of an eagle, and his mouth generous, with many lines around it as well as the corners of his eyes. His hair was black with blue highlights, close-cropped to his head—typical of the military style, she supposed. He wasn't wearing military clothing, however, just a threadbare pair of jean's, waterproof hiking boots and a dark maroon polo shirt that showed off his barrel chest to distinct advantage. This was not the

lazy, *norte americano* that Inca was used to seeing. No, this
man was hard-bodied from strenuous work. The muscles in
his upper arms were thick, the cords of his forearms distinct.
His hands were large, the fingers long and large knuckled.
There was a tight, coiled energy around him as he moved
slowly toward her, their gazes locked together. Inca dug
mercilessly into his eyes, studied the huge, black pupils to
find his weaknesses, for that was what she had to do in order
to survive—find an enemy's weakness and use it against
him.

She reminded herself that this man was not her enemy,
but her radarlike assessment of him was something she just
did naturally. She liked how he moved with a boneless kind
of grace. Clairvoyantly, Inca saw a female cougar walking
near his left side, looking at her to size *her* up! Smiling to
herself, Inca wondered if this man was a medicine person.
Michael had said he was Lakota, and that his mother was a
medicine woman of great power and fame. His face was
rough-hewn, just as her blood brother had described. Storm
Walker was not a handsome man. No, he looked as if his
large, square face had been carved from the granite of the
Andes. She spotted a scar on his left cheek, and another on
the right side of his forehead. His brows were thick and
slightly arched and emphasized his large, intelligent eyes as
they held hers. Few men could hold Inca's stare. But he
did—with ease.

Her pulse elevated as he stopped, dropped the luggage
and straightened. When his hardened mouth softened tem-
porarily and the corners hooked upward, her heart pounded.
Her response to him unnerved Inca, for she'd never re-
sponded to a man this way before. The sensations were new
to her, confounding her and making her feel slightly breathless as a result. When he extended his large, callused hand
toward her, and Inca saw a wand of white sage in it, she
relaxed slightly. Among her people, when one clan or nation
visited another, sacred sage, ceremonially wrapped, was al-

ways given as a token of respect before any words of greeting were spoken.

Just this simple acknowledgment by him, the sacred sage extended in his hand, made Inca feel a deep sense of relief. Only Indians knew this protocol. Something wonderful flittered through Inca's heart as she reached out and took the gift. If the sage was accepted, it was a sign of mutual respect between the two parties, and talk could begin. She waited. The dried sage's fragrance drifted to her flaring nostrils. It was a strong, medicinelike scent, one that made her want to inhale deeply.

"I'm Roan Storm Walker," he said in a quiet tone. "I've been sent here by Mike Houston."

"I am called Inca," she said, her voice husky. He was powerful, and Inca wanted to back away from him to assess the situation more closely. Ordinarily, men she encountered were not this powerful. "I was not expecting a medicine person. I do not have a gift of our sacred sage to give you in return."

Roan nodded. "It's not a problem. Don't worry about it." His pulse was racing. He wondered if she could hear his heart beating like a thundering drum in his chest. Roan had realized for certain as he got out of the cab that Inca was the same woman who had entered his vision state that morning at his cabin. It was definitely her. Did she remember talking to him? Asking him to come down here to help her? If she did, she gave no hint to him. He decided not to ask, for it would be considered disrespectful.

She was incredibly beautiful in his eyes. There was a wildness to her—a raw, primal power as she stood confidently before him dressed in her military attire. Even though she wore jungle fatigues, black GI boots, a web belt around her waist and an olive drab T-shirt, she could not hide her femininity from him in the least. She wore no bra, and her small breasts were upturned and proud against the damp shirt that provocatively outlined them, despite the bandoliers of ammunition criss-crossing her chest. Her face was oval, with a strong chin, high cheekbones and slightly tilted eyes. The color of her eyes made him hold his breath for a moment. Just as Mike Houston had said, they were a delicious willow-green color, with huge, black pupils. Her black lashes were thick and full, and emphasized her incredible eyes like a dark frame. Her hair was black with a slightly reddish tint when the sun peeked out between the sluggishly moving clouds and shined on it. The tendrils curling around her face gave Inca an air of vulnerability in spite of her formidable presence. He rocked internally from the power that surrounded her.

Roan had spotted the rifle leaning up against the crates, and he sensed her distrust of him. He saw it in the guarded look of her eyes. Her mouth was full and soft, yet, as she turned her attention to him, he watched it thin and compress. Mike was right: he'd have to earn her trust, inch by inch. Did he have the necessary time to do it? To protect her? To work as a liaison between her and Marcellino's troops?

"Why do you worry about me?" Inca growled. She turned and put the sage into a small, coarsely woven sack that sat on top of the crates. "I would worry more for you."

Frowning, Roan wondered if she'd read his mind. Mike had warned him that she had many clairvoyant talents. He watched as she shouldered the rifle, butt up, the muzzle pointed toward the ground. Any good soldier out in a rain forest or jungle situation would do that. Water down the barrel of one's weapon would create rust. Clearly Inca was a professional soldier.

"Come," she ordered as she strode quickly to the dock.

"*Olá!* Hello. Ernesto! Get up!" Inca called in Portuguese to the tug captain. The middle-aged, balding man roused himself from his siesta on the deck of his tug.

"Eh?"

Inca waved toward the crates. "Come, load our things. We must go, pronto."

Scrambling to his feet, the captain nodded and quickly rubbed his eyes. His face was round, and he hadn't shaved in days. Dressed only in a pair of khaki cutoffs that had seen better days, he leaped to the wharf.

Inca turned to Storm Walker, who stood waiting and watching. "We need to get these crates on board. Why don't you stow your gear on the tug and help him?"

"Of course." Roan moved past her and made his way from wharf to tug. The boat was old, unpainted, and the deck splintered from lack of sanding and paint to protect it from the relentless heat and humidity of Amazonia. Dropping his luggage at the bow, he watched as Inca moved to the stern of the tug. Her face was guarded and she was looking around, as if sensing something. He briefly saw the crescent-shaped moon on her left shoulder though it was mostly hidden beneath the tank top she wore. Mike Houston had warned him ahead of time that the thin crescent of gold and black fur was a sign her membership in the Jaguar Clan.

Inca barely gave notice to the two men placing the supplies on board. Topazio was restless, an indication that there was a disturbance in the energy of the immediate area. A warning that there was trouble coming.

"Hurry!" she snapped in Portuguese. And then Inca switched to her English, which was not that good. "Hurry."

"I speak Portuguese," Roan stated as he hefted a crate on board.

Grunting, Inca kept her gaze on the hill. Nothing moved in the humid, hot heat of the afternoon. Everything was still. Too still for her liking. She moved restlessly and shifted her position from the end of the wharf to where the asphalt crumbled and stopped. Someone was coming. And it wasn't a good feeling.

Roan looked up. He saw Inca standing almost rigidly, facing the hill and watching. What was up? He almost mouthed the query, but instead hurried from the tug to the shore to retrieve the last wooden crate. The tug captain

started up the rusty old engine. Black-and-blue smoke
belched from behind the vessel, the engine sputtered,
coughed like a hacking person with advanced emphysema,
and then caught and roared noisily to life.

"Inca?" Roan called as he placed the crate on the deck.

His voice carried sluggishly through the silence of the
damp afternoon air. The hair on his neck stood on end.
Damn! Leaping off the tug and running along the dock,
Roan ordered the captain to cast off. He had just gotten to
the end when he saw two cars, a white one and a black one,
careening down off the hill toward them. His breath jammed
in his throat. He could see rifles hanging out the open windows of both vehicles.

"Inca!"

Inca heard Storm Walker's warning, but she was already
on top of the situation. In one smooth movement, she released her rifle and flipped it up, her hand gripping the trigger housing area and moving the barrel upward. She saw
the guns stuck out of the windows. She felt the hatred of
the men behind them. Turning on her heel, she sprinted toward the tug. It was going to be close!

To her surprise, she saw Storm Walker running toward
her, his hand outstretched as if to grab her. Shaken by his
protective gesture, she waved him away.

"You have no weapons!" she cried as she ran up to him.
"Get back to the tug!"

Roan turned on his heel. He heard the screech of brakes.
The first shots shattered the humid stillness. Bits of red dirt
spurted into the air very near his feet. *Damn!* More shouts
in Portuguese erupted behind them. Inca was following
swiftly behind him. He didn't want her to get shot. Slowing,
he reached out and shoved her in front of him. He would be
the wall between her and the attackers. Who the hell were
they, anyway? Digging the toes of his boots into the red dirt,
Roan sprinted for the wharf. Already the tug was easing

away from the dock. The captain's eyes were huge. He wanted out of here. Pronto!

More gunfire erupted. Inca cursed softly beneath her breath. She halted at the end of the wharf and shouldered her rifle. With cool precision, with wood exploding all around her, she squeezed off five shots in succession. She saw Storm Walker leap to the tug, which was sliding past her. Turning, she jumped from the wharf onto the deck of the vessel herself. It was a long jump, almost five feet. Landing on her hands and knees, she felt Roan's large hands on her arm drawing her upward. He was pushing her behind the cockpit of the tug in order to protect her.

Growling at him, she jerked her arm free. "Release me!" she snarled, and then ran to the side of the cockpit closest to the riverbank. The men were tumbling out of the cars— six of them. They were heavily armed. Inca dropped to one knee, drew the leather sling around her arm and steadied the butt of the rifle against her shoulder and cheek. She got the first man in the crosshairs and squeezed off a shot. She watched as the bullet struck him in the knee. He screamed, threw up his weapon and fell to the earth, writhing in pain.

Rifle fire rained heavily around them. The captain was swearing in Portuguese as he labored hard to get the tug turned around and heading out to the middle of the mile-wide river. Pieces of wood exploded and flew like splinters of shrapnel everywhere. He ducked behind the housing of the cockpit, one shaking hand on the old, dilapidated wooden wheel.

Crouching, Roan moved up alongside Inca. He reached out. "Let me borrow your pistol," he rasped, and leaned over her to unsnap the holster at her side.

Inca nodded and kept her concentration on the enemy. Ordinarily, she'd never let anyone use her weapons, but Roan was different. There was no time for talk. He took her black Beretta, eased away from her and steadied his gun arm on top of the cockpit. She heard the slow pop at each squeeze of the trigger. Two more men fell. He was a good shot.

Those left on the shore fell on their bellies, thrust their weapons out in front of them and continued to send a hail of fire into the tug. They made poor targets, and Inca worked to wound, not kill them. It wasn't in her nature to kill. It never had been. To wound them was to put them out of commission, and that was all she strove to do. Wood erupted next to her. She felt the red-hot pain of a thick splinter entering her upper arm. Instantly, the area went numb. Disregarding her slight injury, Inca continued to squeeze off careful shots.

Finally the tug was out of range. Inca was the first to stop firing. She sat down, her back against the cockpit, the rifle across her lap as she pulled another clip from her web belt and jammed it into the rifle. Looking up, she saw Storm Walker's glistening features as he stopped firing. This man was a cool-headed warrior. Michael had been right about him being a benefit to her, and not a chain around her neck. That was good. His face was immobile, his eyes thundercloud dark as he glanced down to see how she was doing.

"You're hurt...."

Roan's words feathered across Inca. She glanced down at her left arm. There was a bright red trail of blood down her left biceps dripping slowly off her elbow onto the deck.

Without thinking, Roan stepped across her, knelt down and placed his hand near the wound. A large splinter of wood, almost two inches long and a quarter inch in diameter, was sticking out of her upper arm. Her flesh was smooth and damp as he ran his fingers upward to probe the extent and seriousness of her wound.

"Do not touch me!" Inca jerked away from him. Her nostrils flared. "No man touches me without my permission."

Shocked by her violent response, Roan instantly released

her. He sat back on his heels. The anger in her eyes was very real. "I'm a paramedic.... I'm trained—"

"You do not presume anything with me, *norteamericano*," she spat. Scrambling to her knees, Inca made sure there was at least six feet between them. He was too close to her and she felt panic. Why? His touch had been gentle, almost tender. Why had she behaved so snottily toward him? She saw the worry in his eyes, the way his mouth was drawn in with anxiousness.

Holding up his hands in a sign of peace, Roan rasped, "You're right. I presumed. And I apologize." He saw the mixture of outrage, defiance and something else in her narrowed eyes in that moment. When he'd first touched her, he'd seen her eyes go wide with astonishment. And then, seconds later, he saw something else—something so heart-wrenchingly sad that it had blown his heart wide open. And within a fraction of a second, the windows to her soul had closed and he saw righteous fury replace that mysterious emotion in her eyes.

Shaken by his concern and care for her, Inca got to her feet, despite the fact that she felt some pain in the region of the wound. They were a mile away from the dock now, the little tug chugging valiantly along on the currents. For now, they were safe. Placing the rifle on top of the cockpit, she turned her attention to the captain.

"Captain, I need a clean cloth and some good water."

The grizzled old man nodded from the cockpit. "In there, *senhorinha*." He pointed down the ladder that led below.

"Do you want some help removing that splinter?" Roan was behind her, but a respectful distance away. As Inca turned she was forced to look up at him. He was sweating profusely now, the underarms and center of his polo shirt dampened. His eyes were not guarded, but alive with genuine concern—for her. Inca was so unused to anyone caring about her—her pain, her needs—that she felt confused by his offer.

"No, I will take care of it in my own way." She spun around and headed down the stairs.

Great, Roan, you just screwed up with her. He stood there on the deck, the humid air riffling around him, cooling him as he placed his hands on his narrow hips. Looking back toward shore, he saw the men leaving. Who were they? Who had sent them? Was Marcellino behind this? No one knew Roan's itinerary except the good colonel. Worried about Inca, Roan stood there and compressed his lips. He'd forgotten Native American protocol with her. In his experience and training, Indians did not like to be touched by strangers. It was considered invasive. A sign of disrespect. Only after a long time, when respect and trust were developed, would touching be permitted.

Running his fingers through his short hair, Roan realized that he had to think in those terms with her. He was too used to being in the Anglo world, and in order to gain her trust, he must go back to the customs he'd grown up with in his own nation—the Native American way of doing things.

Still, he couldn't get the feel of her skin beneath his fingers out of his mind or heart. Inca was firm and tightly muscled. She was in superb athletic condition. There wasn't an ounce of spare flesh on her tall, slender frame. Not many women were in such great shape, except, perhaps, some in the military. Rubbing his chin, he moved back to the cockpit.

Ernesto was mopping his forehead, a worried look in his eyes. He obviously hadn't expected such an attack, and his hands still shook in the aftermath. He offered Roan a bottle of water. Roan took it and thanked him. Tipping his head back, he drank deeply.

Inca reemerged at that moment. She saw Roan, his head tipped back, his Adam's apple bobbing with each gulp he took. Again, fear rippled through her as she made her way up the stairs. A soft breeze cooled her sweaty flesh as she moved topside. Wanting to keep distance between them, she took another bottle of water that Ernesto proffered to her. She thanked him and drank deeply of it.

Roan finished off the water. He'd felt Inca's return. The sense of her power, of her being nearby, was clear to him. As he put the plastic bottle back into the box near the wheel, he glanced up at her. His mouth dropped open. And then he snapped it shut. Roan straightened. He stared at her—not a polite thing to do, but he couldn't help himself.

The injury on her upper left arm was now completely healed. No trace of swelling, no trace of blood marred her beautiful skin. As she capped the bottle of water and gave him a glaring look, he shifted his gaze. What had happened to her wound? It looked as if she hadn't even been injured. But she *had* been and Roan knew it. The captain, too, was staring with a look of disbelief on his face. He was afraid of Inca, so he quickly averted his eyes and stuck to the task of guiding the tug.

Roan had a *lot* of questions. But asking questions was a sign of disrespect, too. If Inca wanted to tell him what she'd done to heal herself, she would in her own good time. Mike Houston had told him that she was a healer. Well, Roan had just gotten a firsthand glimpse of her powerful talents.

"How far do we go downriver?" Inca demanded of him. Despite the tone she used, she was enjoying his company. Normally, men managed to irritate her with their arrogant male attitude, but he did not. Most men could not think like a woman; they were out to lunch instinctually and jammed their feelings so far down inside themselves that they were out of touch completely. Inca found the company of women far preferable. But Roan was different. She could see the remnants of his worry and concern over her wounding. He didn't try to hide or fix a mask on his feelings, she was discovering. The only other man she knew who was similar was her blood brother, Michael. Inca liked to know where a person stood with her, and when that person showed his feelings, whether they were for or against her, Inca appreciated it.

Roan smiled a one-cornered smile. At least she was still talking to him. He saw the frosty look in her eyes, the way she held herself, as if afraid he was going to touch her again. Remaining where he was, he said, "Let me get the map out of my luggage." He brightened a little. "And there's a gift in there for you from Mike and Ann, too. I think things have calmed down enough that we can sit and talk over the mission while you open it."

Inca nodded. "Very well. We will sit on the shady side of the boat, here." She pointed to the starboard side of the tug. Suddenly, she found herself wanting to talk to Roan. Why did he have the name he did? How had he earned it? She watched as he moved to the bow of the tug to retrieve his luggage.

Settling her back against the splintery wall of the cockpit, Inca waited for him. Roan placed the canvas bag, which was tubular in shape, between them and slowly sat down, his legs crossed beneath him. As he unzipped the bag, she watched his deft, sure movements and recalled his touch.

Men did not realize their touch was stronger and therefore potentially hurtful to a woman or a child. Mentally, she corrected herself. Not all men hurt women, but she'd seen too much of it in South America, and it angered her to her soul. No one had the right to hurt someone frailer or weaker.

"Here," Roan said, digging out a foil-wrapped gift tied with red ribbon. "Mike said this was special for you." And he grinned.

Inca scowled as she took the gift. She made sure their fingers did not touch this time. Oh, she wanted to touch Roan again, but a large part of her was afraid of it, afraid of what other wild, unbidden reactions would be released in her body because of it.

"Thank you."

Well, at least Inca could be civil when she wanted to be,

Roan thought, laughing to himself. He was discovering it was all about respecting boundaries with her. He watched covertly, pretending to search for the map, as she tore enthusiastically into the foil wrapping. She was like a child, her face alight with eagerness, her eyes wide with expectation. The wrapping and ribbon fluttered around her.

"Oh!"

Roan grinned as she held up smoked salmon encased in protective foil. "Mike said you had a love of salmon."

For the first time, Inca smiled. She held up the precious gift and studied it intently. "My blood brother knows my weaknesses."

"I doubt you have many," Roan said dryly, and caught her surprised look. Just as quickly, she jerked her gaze away from him.

"Do not be blinded by the legend that follows me. I have many weaknesses," she corrected him throatily. Laying the package in her lap, she took out her knife and quickly slit it open. The orange smoked fish lay before her like a feast. Her fingers hovered over it. She glanced at him. "Do you want some?"

"No, thank you. You go ahead, though, and enjoy it." Roan was pleased with her willingness to share. Among his people, it was always protocol to offer food first to those around you, and lastly, help yourself.

She stared at him through hooded eyes. "Are you sure?" How could he resist smoked salmon?

She was reading his mind. He could feel her there in his head, like a gentle wind on a summer day. For whatever reason, Roan felt no sense of intrusion, no need to protect his thoughts from her. He grinned belatedly as he pulled the map from the plastic case. "I'm sure. The salmon is your gift. Mike and Ann said you love it. I don't want to take a single bite of it away from you. Salmon's a little tough to come by down here," he joked, "and where I come from, there's plenty of it. So, no, you go ahead and enjoy."

Inca studied him. He was a generous and unselfish person. Not only that, he was sensitive and thoughtful to others' needs. Her heart warmed to him strongly. Few men had such honorable traits. "Very well." She got to her feet and went over to the tug captain. Roan watched with interest. Ernesto, his chest sunken, his flesh burned almost tobacco brown by the equatorial sun, reached eagerly for part of the salmon. He took only a little, and thanked Inca profusely for her generosity. She nodded, smiled, and then came and sat back down. Lifting a flake of the meat to her lips, she closed her eyes, rested her head against the cockpit wall and slid it into her mouth.

Roan felt Inca's undiluted pleasure over each morsel of the salmon. In no time, the fish was gone and only the foil package remained on her lap. There was a satiated look in her eyes as she stuck each of her fingers in her mouth to savor the taste of salmon there.

Sighing, Inca lifted her head and looked directly at him. "Your name. It has meaning, yes?"

Shocked at her friendly tone, Roan was taken aback. Maybe his manners had earned him further access to her. He hoped so. Clearing his throat, he said, "Yes, it does."

"Among our people, names carry energy and skills." Inca lifted her hand. "I was named Inca by a jaguar priestess who found me when I was one year old and living with a mother jaguar and her two cubs. She had been given a dream the night before as to where to find me. She kept me for one year and then took me to another village, where another priestess cared for me. When I was five years old I learned that my name meant I was tied to the Inca nation of Peru. Each year, I was passed to another priest or priestess in another village. At each stop, I was taught what each one knew. Each had different skills and talents. I learned English from one. I learned reading from another. Math from another. When I was ten, I was sent to Peru, up to Machu Picchu, to study with an Andean priest name Juan Nunez del Prado. He lived in Aqua Caliente and ran a hostel there for tourists. We would take the bus up to the temples of Machu Picchu and he would teach me many things. He told me the whole story, of what my name meant, and what it was possible to do with such a name.'' She lifted her hand in a graceful motion. ''What my name means, what my destiny is, is secret and known only to me and him. To speak of it is wrong.''

Roan understood. ''Yes, we have a similar belief, but about our vision quest, not about our name. I honor your sacredness, having such a beautiful name.'' Roan saw her fine, thin brows knit. ''With such an impressive history behind your name, I think you were destined for fame. For doing something special for Mother Earth and all her relations. The Incas were in power for a thousand years, and their base of operation was Cuzco, which is near Machu Picchu. In that time, they built an empire stretching the whole breadth and length of South America.'' Roan smiled at her. He saw that each time he met her gaze or shared a smile with her, she appeared uneasy. He wondered why. ''From what I understand from Mike, you have a name here in Amazonia that stretches the length and breadth of it, too.''

''I have lived up to my name and I continue to live the destiny of it every day,'' she agreed. Eyeing him, her head tilting slightly, Inca asked, ''Have you lived up to yours?''

Inca would never directly ask why he had been given his name, and Roan smiled to himself. She wanted to know about him, and he was more than willing to share in order to get her trust. They didn't have much time to create that bond.

''My family's name is Storm Walker. A long time ago, when my great-great-grandfather rode the plains as a Lakota medicine man, he acquired storm medicine. He had been struck by lightning while riding his horse. The horse died, and as he lay there on the plain afterward, he had a powerful vision. He woke up hours later with the name Storm Walker.

He was a great healer. People said lightning would leap from his fingers when he touched someone to heal them of their ills or wounds.''

''Yes?'' Inca leaned forward raptly. She liked his low, modulated tone. She knew he spoke quietly so that the captain could not overhear their conversation, for what they spoke of was sacred.

''One member of each succeeding generation on my mother's side of the family inherited this gift of lightning medicine. When our people were put on a reservation, the white men forced us to adopt a first and last name. So we chose Storm Walker in honor of my great-great-grandfather.''

''And what of Roan? What is a roan? It is a name I have never heard before.''

He quelled his immediate reaction to her sudden warm and animated look. Her face was alive with curiosity, her eyes wide and beautiful. Roan had one helluva time keeping his hands to himself. He wanted to see Inca like this all the time. This was the real her, he understood instinctively. Not the tough, don't-you-dare-touch-me warrior woman, although that was part and parcel of her, too. When there wasn't danger around, she was wide-open, vulnerable and childlike. It was innocence, he realized humbly. And the Great Spirit knew, he wanted to treat that part of her with the greatest of care.

''Roan is the color of a horse,'' he explained. ''Out on the plains, my people rode horses. Horses come in many colors, and a roan has red and white hairs all mixed together in its coat.'' He smiled a little and held her burning gaze. ''My mother was Lakota. A red-skinned woman. My father was a white man, a teacher who has white skin. When I was born, my mother had this vision of a roan horse, whose skin is half red and half white, running down a lane beneath a thunderstorm, with lightning bolts dancing all around it. She decided to call me Roan because I was part Indian and part white. Red and white.''

Inca stared at him. She saw the vulnerable man in him. He was not afraid of her, nor was he afraid to be who he was in front of her. That impressed her. It made her heart feel warm and good, too, which was something she'd never experienced before. ''That is why you are not darker than you are,'' she said, pointing to his skin.

''I got my mother's nose, high cheekbones, black hair and most of her skin coloring. I got my father's blue eyes.''

''Your heart, your spirit, though, belongs to your mother's red-skinned people.''

''Yes,'' Roan agreed softly.

''Are you glad of this?''

''Yes.''

''And did you inherit the gift of healing?''

Roan laughed a little and held up his hands. ''No, I'm afraid it didn't rub off on me, much to my mother's unhappiness.''

Shrugging, Inca said, ''Do not be so sure, Roan Storm Walker. Do not be so sure....''

Chapter 4

Roan had excused himself and went to the opposite side of the tug from where she stood. Once he felt sure they were safely motoring down the Amazon, the shooters nowhere in sight. His adrenaline had finally ebbed after the firefight. He'd noticed her hands were shaking for a little while afterward, too. It was nice to know she was human. It was also nice to know she was one cool-headed customer in a crisis. Not too many people that he knew, men or women, would have been so efficient and clear thinking in that rain of hot lead.

Absently, he touched the medicine piece at his throat and found the blue stone was so hot it felt like it was burning his skin. It wasn't, but the energy emanating from it made it feel that way. The stone always throbbed, hot and burning, anytime he was in danger. Roan knew without a doubt, from a lot of past experience, that the mysterious blue stone was a powerful talisman. There had been so many times in the past when it had heated up and warned him of forthcoming danger. One of his biggest mistakes had been not listening to his intuition the day his wife, Sarah, had gone climbing and died. On that morning, before she left, Roan had had a powerful urge to take off his amulet and place it around her slender neck. He knew she would have accepted the gift, but he'd never, ever entertained the thought of giving the stone to anyone. It had been ingrained by his mother and the tradition of his mother's tribe that the medicine piece should remain with one person until near the time he or she was to die, and then be passed on to the next deserving recipient. Still, the urge to give Sarah the stone had been overpowering, but he'd fought it because of his ancestral tradition. He told himself that it was wrong to take the stone off and give it away prematurely. Sadly, he now knew why his cougar guardian had urged him through his intuition to give Sarah the necklace to wear that day. It *might* have saved her life. He would never know. Rubbing his chest, Roan frowned, the guilt eating at him even to this day.

When he'd grabbed a cab at the airport to head to the dock, the blue stone had begun to throb with heat and energy. Roan had thought the stone was warning him about Inca, but he'd been wrong. She wasn't the one to fear; it was the gang that followed him to the dock that had brought danger.

He wanted to ask Inca a hundred questions now that things were calming down, but he knew Indian protocol, so he had to forego his personal, selfish desire to get nosy. Still, being in her company was like being surrounded by an incredible light of joy and freedom.

Moving to the other side of the tug, he dug deeply into his canvas carry-on bag. Because he was Indian, and because it was only proper to introduce himself to the spirits of this new land, Roan pulled out a large, rainbow-colored abalone shell, a stick of sacred white sage and a red-tailed hawk feather fan. Native Americans did not presume that the spirits of the water, land or air would automatically welcome them into their midst. A simple ceremony of lighting sage and asking for acceptance was traditional.

Once the flame was doused, Roan placed the smoldering smudge stick in the shell. Picking it up, he faced the north direction, the place where Tatanka, the great white buffalo spirit, resided. Leaning down until the shell was near his feet, Roan used the fan to gently waft the thick, purling smoke upward around his body. The smoke was purifying and signaled his sincerity in honoring the spirits of this land. Fanning the smoke about his head, he then placed the shell back on the deck. Sitting down, his back against the cockpit, Roan closed his eyes and prayed. He mentally asked permission to be allowed to walk this land, to be welcomed to it.

As he said his prayers, his arms resting comfortably on his drawn-up knees, Roan felt a burst of joy wash over him. He smiled a little in thanks. That was the spirits of the river, the land and air welcoming him to their territory. He knew the sign well and was relieved. Roan didn't want to go anywhere he wasn't welcomed by the local spirits. It would have been a bad choice, and bad things would have befallen him as a result.

Opening his eyes, he dug into his tobacco bag, which he always carried on a loop on his belt. The beaded bag, made out of tanned elk hide and decorated with a pink flower against a blue background, was very old. It had been his mother's tobacco bag. Digging into it, he held the proffered gift of thanks upward to the sky, and then to the four directions, to Mother Earth, before bringing it to his heart and giving thanks. Then, opening his hand, he threw the fragrant tobacco outward. He watched the dark brown flakes fly through the air and hit the muddy water, then quickly disappeared.

To his surprise, four river dolphins, sleek and dark, leaped within ten feet of the tug, splashing the peeling wood of the deck. Stunned, Roan watched the playful foursome race alongside the tug.

"The river spirit has taken your prayers and gifts to heart," Inca said in a low, serious voice as she approached him from the left.

Surprised, Roan tried to hide his pleasure that she was coming to speak to him. He would never gain her trust if he kept going to her and plying her with endless questions; she'd slam the door to herself tighter than Fort Knox.

The dolphins leaped again, their high-pitched cries mingling with the sound of the foaming, bubbling water. They arced high and splashed back into the river.

Roan smiled a little. "Helluva welcome. I didn't expect it."

Inca stopped and gazed at him critically. He looked relaxed, his large, scarred hands resting on his narrow hips. His profile was Indian; there was no question. Only the lightness of his copper skin revealed his other heritage, through his father. "The dolphin people don't often give such a welcome to strangers to their land, to their river," she murmured. She saw and felt his amazement and gratitude. Maybe Michael was right after all: Roan stood apart from all other men she'd known before. He was more like a Jaguar Clan member, knitted into the fabric of Mother Earth and all her relations. Roan understood that all things were connected, that they were not separate and never had been. Her heart lifted with hope. It was a strange, wonderful feeling, and automatically, Inca touched that region of her chest. She studied the medicine piece that hung around his thickly corded neck. With her clairvoyant vision she could see the power emanating from around that beautiful sky-blue stone he wore.

"You said your mother was a healer, yes?"

Roan nodded and squatted down. "Yes, she was." He saw that the smudge of sage had burned out. Tossing it into the river as an added gift, he took the abalone shell and placed it back into his bag.

"And did she heal by laying her hands on others, as we do in the Jaguar Clan?"

Roan wrapped the feather fan gently back into the red cotton cloth and placed it back into the bag as well, and then zipped it shut. He craned his neck upward and met her half-closed eyes. There was a thoughtful look on Inca's face now. She was so incredibly beautiful. Did she know how attractive she was? Instantly, he saw her brows dip. Was she reading his mind again? Frustrated, Roan figured she was, as he eased to his full height once again.

"My mother was a Yuwipi medicine woman. Her assistants would tie her wrists behind her back and tie up her ankles and then roll her up into a rug and tie the rug up as well. The lights would be doused, the singers and drummers would begin. The ceremony takes hours, usually starting at nightfall and ending at dawn. My mother, with the help of her spirit guides, was released from her bonds. She then prayed for the person whom the ceremony was for. Usually, that person was there in the room. There could be five, ten or fifty people sitting in that room, taking part in the ceremony. Lights would dance through the place. Horns would sound. The spirits brushed the attending people with their paws, their wings or tails. All prayers from everyone were directed to the person who was ill."

Inca nodded. "A powerful ceremony. And did the person get well?"

He smiled a little and put his hands in the pockets of his jeans. "They always did when my mother conducted the ceremony. She was very famous. People came to her from around the world." He glanced at Inca's shoulder, where the splinter had wounded her. "And your clan heals with touch?"

Inca nodded. "You could say that."

"And healing is your calling? Your vision?"

"It is my life," she said simply. Lifting her hand, she watched as the dolphins sped away from the tug, finished with their play. "I took a medicine vow when I became a woman at age twelve. The jaguar priestess who was training me at that time inducted me into the service of our mother, the earth. She then prepared me to go to the clan's village for training, which began at age sixteen."

Roan shook his head. "It sounds like you were passed around a lot, from person to person. Did you ever find out who your parents were?" Instantly, he saw her close up. Her eyes grew opaque with pain and her lips compressed. Roan mentally kicked himself. He'd asked the wrong damn question. "Forget it," he said quickly. "You don't have to answer. That's too personal...."

Touched by his sensitivity, Inca found herself opening up at his roughly spoken words. She saw so much in his large eyes, in those glinting black pupils. Normally, if someone broached a question regarding her past, she'd shut down, get angry and stalk off. Not this time. Inca couldn't explain why her heart felt warm in her breast, or why her pulse quickened when he gave her that special, tender look. Always, she felt that blanket of security and warmth automatically surround her when Roan met and held her gaze. She was unsure of how to react, for she'd never met a man quite like this before. She wanted to be wary of him, to remain on guard, but his demeanor, and the fact that he was Indian like her, made her feel safe. Safe! No one had ever given her that sense before.

"No, I will answer your question." Inca sat down and leaned against the bulkhead. The last of the shakiness that always inhabited her after a confrontation left her. Being with Roan was soothing to her hard-wired nervous system, which was always on high alert. She crossed her legs, her hands resting on her thighs. Roan did the same, keeping a good six feet of space between them. Inca sighed. There was always something soothing about the gentle rocking of a boat in the arms of the Amazon River. "At times like this, I feel like a babe in my mother's arms," she confided throatily. "The rocking motion...somewhere in my memory, a long time ago, I recall being rocked in the arms of a woman. I remember fragments of a song she sang to me."

"One of the priestesses?"

"No." Inca picked at a frayed thread of the fabric on her knee. "I remember part of the song. I have gone back and asked each woman who helped to raise me if she sang it, and none of them did. I know it was my real mother...."

Roan heard the pain in her low voice. He saw her brows dip, and her gaze move to her long, slender, scarred hands. "I was abandoned in the rain forest to die. As I told you before, a mother jaguar found me. I was told that she picked me up in her mouth and carried me back to where she hid her two cubs. When the first jaguar priestess found me, I was a year old and suckling from the mother jaguar. I have some memories of that time. A few...but good ones. I remember being warm and hearing her purr moving like a vibrating drum through my body. Her milk was sweet and good. The woman who found me was from a nearby village. In a dream, she was told where to go look for me. When she arrived, the mother jaguar got up and left me."

Inca smiled softly. "I do not want you to think that the people who raised me from that time on did not love me. They did. Each of them is like a mother and father to me— at least, those who are still alive, and there are not many now...."

"You were on a medicine path, there is no doubt," Roan said.

"Yes." Inca brightened. "It is good to talk to someone who understands my journey."

"My mother set me on a path to become a medicine man, but I'm afraid I disappointed her." Roan laughed a little and held up his hands for a moment. "I didn't have her gift."

"Humph. You have a spirit cougar, a female, who is at

your side. Medicine people always have powerful spirit guides. Perhaps you will wait until middle age to pick up your medicine and practice it. That is common down here in Amazonia. Most men and women do not even begin their training until their mid-forties.''

"You were trained from birth, which means you brought in a lot of power and skills with you," Roan said. He saw Inca smile sadly.

"There are days when I wish…'' Her voice trailed off. Shaking her head, she muttered, "To be hunted like an animal, with a price on my head…to be hated, feared and misunderstood." She glanced over at him. "At least the Indians of the basin understand. They know of my vow, know I am here to help protect them. The white men who want to destroy our rain forests want my life. The gold miners would kill me if they saw me. The *gaucqueros*, the gem hunters, would do the same. Anyone who wants to rape our land, to take without giving to it something equal in return, wants me dead.''

Roan felt her sadness. Quietly, he said, "It must be a heavy burden to carry. I hope you have friends with whom you can share your burdens and dreams.''

Rubbing her brow, Inca whispered, "I am all but thrown out of the Jaguar Clan. Grandfather Adaire has sentenced me and told me never to return to the village where all clan members train. I—I miss going there. Grandmother Alaria…well, I love her as I've loved no one else among those who have raised me. She is so kind, so gentle, all the things I am not…. I am like a rough-cut emerald compared to her. She is so old that no one knows how old she is. I miss talking to her. I miss the time we spent together.''

"Then you're an outcast?" Roan saw the incredible pain in every feature of Inca's face. In some part of his heart, he knew she was opening up to him in a way that she rarely did with anyone. The energy between them was tenuous…fragile, just like her. He found himself wanting to slide

his arm across her proud shoulders, draw her into his arms
and simply hold her. Hold her and comfort her against the
awful weight of pain she carried. In that moment, she was
more a hurting child to him than a warrior woman.

"No, not exactly an outcast... Oh, to be sure, some members have been cast permanently out of the clan." She gave
him a pained, one-cornered smile, and then quickly looked
away. "My sentence is an ongoing one. Grandfather Adaire
says I am walking on the dark side with some choices I have
made. And until I can walk in the light all the time, I am
not allowed to return to the village as a full member of it."

Roan frowned. "Light and dark? Familiar words and
themes to me." He opened his hands. "Where I come from,
in our belief system, light does not exist without darkness,
and vice versa. You can't have one without the other. And
no human being is ever all one or the other." He glanced
over at her. "Are they expecting you *not* to be human? Not
to make mistakes?"

She laughed abruptly. "The Jaguar Clan is an honorable
part of the Sisterhood of Light. There are rules that cannot
be broken...and I broke one of them. It was a very serious
thing. Life-and-death serious." Inca frowned and tugged at
the frayed thread on her knee until it broke off in her fingers.

"Mike Houston said you saved his life," Roan said. He
ached to reach out to her now. There were tears swimming
in her eyes, although Inca's head was bowed and slightly
turned away from his in an effort to hide them from him. In
her softened tone he could hear the wrenching heartache she
carried. She moved her hands restlessly.

"That is why I was asked to leave my own kind, my
home.... Michael was dying. I knew it. And yes, I broke the
rule and went into the light where the souls of all humans
who are dying go. I pulled him back from the Threshold. I
gave my life, my energy, my heart and love, and drew him
back. If not for Grandmother Alaria, who revived me be-

cause I was practically dead after saving Michael, I would not be here today.''

"So, you saved a life? And Grandfather Adaire kicked you out of the clan for that?'' Roan had a hard time understanding why.

"Do not be judgmental of Grandfather Adaire. He was only following the code of the clan. You see, we are trained in the art of life and death. Because we have the power, that means we must walk with it in strict accordance to the laws of the universe. I broke one of those laws. Michael had made his choice to die of his wound. I had been caring for him for a week, and for the first time in my life, I felt as if I had met my real brother. Oh, he was not, but that was the bond we had from the moment we met. It was wonderful....'' She sighed unhappily. "I saw him slipping away daily. My heart cried. I cried alone, where no one could see me. I knew he would die. I did not want it to happen. I knew I had the power to stop it. And I knew it was wrong to intervene.'' Inca smiled sadly as she looked at the shore, which was a half a mile away on either side of the chugging tug.

"I wanted a brother just like Michael. I'd been searching so long for a family—I was so starved to have one—that I did it. I broke the law. And I did it knowingly.'' Gravely, Inca turned her head and met his dark blue eyes. "And that is why I was asked to leave. What I did was a 'dark side' decision. It was selfish and self-serving.''

Roan choked as she finished the story. He felt anger over it. "Didn't Grandfather Adaire realize that, because you were abandoned, family would mean so much more to you than it would to others?''

She hitched one shoulder upward and looked out at the muddy river. "That is an excuse. It is not acceptable to the clan. I broke a law. It does not matter *why* I broke it.''

"Seems a little one-sided and unfair to me,'' he groused.

"Well,'' Inca said with a laugh, "my saving Michael's life, in the long term, had its positive side. He asked to

become my blood brother. And when he fell in love with
Dr. Ann, and she had his baby, Catherine, I became a godmother to their child.'' The tears in her eyes burned. Inca
looked away. She wanted to wipe them away, but she didn't
want Roan to know of her tears. No one ever saw her cry.
No one. Choking on the tears, she rasped, ''I have a family
now. Michael and Ann love me. They accept me despite
who I am, despite what I do for a living.'' She sniffed and
reached for a pouch on her right side. ''Look...here...let me
show you baby Catherine....''

Roan watched Inca eagerly fumble in the pouch. The joy
mirrored in her face was like sunlight. She valiantly tried to
force the tears out of her glimmering willow-green eyes as
she handed him a frayed color photo.

''This is Mike and his family,'' he said.

''Yes,'' Inca replied, and she leaned forward, her shoulder
nearly touching his as she pointed at the baby held between
them. ''And this is Catherine...I call her Cat. She has a male
jaguar spirit guide already! That is very special. She is special. Ann and Michael know it, too. Little Cat is my god-
daughter.''

The pride was unmistakable in Inca's passionate voice. It
took everything for Roan not to respond to her excitement.
She was so close he could smell her. There was a wonderful,
fragrant scent to Inca. It reminded him of the bright pink
Oriental lilies that grew behind his cabin, where Sarah had
planted them. Looking up, he smiled into Inca's glimmering
eyes as he handed her the photo.

''You should be proud of Catherine. She's lucky to have
you as a godmother. Very lucky.''

A sweet frisson of joy threaded through Inca's heart at
his huskily spoken words. When she met and held his dark
blue gaze, Inca's heart flew open. It caught her by surprise.
A little breathless, she quickly put the photo back into the
protective plastic and snapped the pouch shut.

''In my mind,'' she said, ''what I did to save Michael's

life was not wrong. It hurts to think I can never go home, but now my home is with him and his family, instead."

The sweet bitterness of Inca's past moved Roan deeply. "I don't know how you handle it all," he admitted. "I'd be lost without my family, my parents.... I don't know what it's like to be an orphan."

"Hard."

He nodded and saw that she was frowning. "I can't even begin to imagine...."

Inca found herself wanting to talk more to Roan. "You are a strange man."

He grinned. "Oh?"

"I find myself jabbering to you, making my life an open book to you. Father Titus was such a talker. He would tell me everything of what lay in his heart and feelings. Being Indian, we are normally quiet and reserved about such things. But not him. He made me laugh many times. I always thought he was a strange old man with his bird's nest of white hair."

"He was vulnerable and open with you."

Sobering, Inca nodded, "Yes, he was...and still is, even though I do not visit him as often as I would like because my duties are elsewhere."

"So..." Roan murmured, "am I like Father Titus?"

"No, I am! I blather on to you. As if I have known you lifetimes. I bare my soul to you, my heart—and I do not ever do that with anyone."

Wanting to reach out and touch her hand, Roan resisted. Instead he rasped, "Inca, your heart, your soul, are safe with me. Always and forever."

Regarding him gravely, Inca felt his words. She was afraid of him for some unknown reason, and yet, at the same time, drawn to him just as a moth is driven to dive into the open flame of a campfire. "You are of two worlds, Roan Storm Walker. One foot stands in the white man's world,

the other in the Indian world. Yet you are not a two-heart.
Your heart belongs to Mother Earth and all her relations.''

"Judge me by my actions," he cautioned her. "Not my
skin color."

Inca gazed at him raptly, before she suddenly felt the pull
of the jaguar's warning.

Danger!

"Something is wrong." Inca was on her feet in an instant.
When her spirit guide jaguar gave her such a warning, her
life was in danger. "Get up!" she ordered Roan. Running
around the stern of the tug, Inca grabbed her rifle.

Roan struggled to his feet. The soft, vulnerable Inca was
gone in a heartbeat. Shaken by her sudden change, he stared
at her. Secondarily, he felt the stinging, burning heat of the
blue stone at the base of his neck throbbing in warning—
only he hadn't felt it until now because he was so taken with
Inca.

"What's wrong? What is it?"

"My guardian has warned me. We are in danger."

Before Roan could say another word, he heard the heavy,
whapping sounds of a helicopter approaching them at high
speed. He turned on his heel. Coming up the river, directly
at them, was an olive-green, unmarked helicopter. It flew
low, maybe fifty feet off the water's surface. His eyes widened. This was no tourist helicopter like the one he'd seen
plying the skies of Manaus earlier. No, this was a helicopter,
heavily armed with machine guns and rockets. The lethal
look of the dark, swiftly moving aircraft made his heart rate
soar with fear.

"Captain Ernesto!" Roan called. Before he could say
anything, the blazing, winking lights on the guns carried by
the military helicopter roared to life. Roan cursed. He saw
two rows of bullets walking toward them like soldiers
marching in parallel lines. The tug was right in the middle
of the two rows.

"*Jump*, Ernesto!" Roan roared.

Inca positioned herself against the cockpit. She aimed her
rifle at the charging helicopter. The first bullets hit the tug,
which shuddered like a wounded bull. Wood splinters exploded. Crashing, whining sounds filled the air. The thick
thump, thump, thump of the blades blasted against her ears.
Still she held her ground. Aiming carefully, she squeezed
off a series of shots. To her dismay, she watched them hit
the helicopter and ricochet off.

"Inca! Jump!"

At the urgency of his tone, she jerked a look toward Roan.
Before she could say anything, he grabbed her by the arm
and threw her into the water.

Choking, Inca went under. She was heavily weighted
down with the bandoliers of ammunition she always carried.
Panicked, she gripped her rifle. Wild, zinging, whining bullets screamed past her as she floundered, trying to kick her
way back up to the surface. Impossible! She had to remain
cool. She had to think. Think! If she could not focus, if she
could not concentrate, she would drown and she knew it.

Kicking strongly, her booted feet also weighing her down,
Inca felt the current grab her. The water was murky and
opaque. She could see nothing. Bubbles streamed out her
open mouth as she lunged toward the surface.

Where was Inca? Roan looked around as he treaded water.
The helicopter was blasting the tug to bits. Ernesto had not
gotten off in time. Roan suspected the man did not know
how to swim, so he'd stayed with his tug. Jerking at his
boots, Roan quickly got rid of them. Inca? Where was she?
He saw some bubbles coming to the surface six feet away
from him. Taking a deep breath, he dove, knowing she was
in trouble. She was too weighted down by the ammo she
wore and she'd drown. Damn! Striking out in long, hard
strokes, he followed the line of bubbles. There! He saw Inca,
a vague shape in the dim, murky water.

Lunging forward, his hand outstretched, Roan gripped her

flailing arm. Jerking her hard, he shoved her up past him to the surface.

Inca shot up out of the water, gasping for air, but still holding on to her rifle. Roan surfaced next to her and immediately wound his arm around her waist.

"Get rid of the boots!" he yelled, and he took the rifle from her.

Struggling, Inca did as he ordered. She saw the tug in the distance, a blazing wreck. The helicopter was mercilessly pummeling it with bullets.

"Now the ammo!"

"No!" she cried. "Not the ammo!"

"You'll drown!"

"No, I will not." Inca flailed and pushed his hand away. "Swim for shore," she gasped.

Roan wasn't going to argue. He kept the rifle and slung it over his shoulder. They struck out together. The Amazon River might look smooth on the surface, but the currents were hell. He kept his eye on the chopper.

"It's turning!" he yelled at Inca, who was ten feet ahead of him. "It's coming for us! Dive!"

Inca saw the military helicopter turning, its lethal guns trained on them. She heard Roan's order. Taking a huge breath into her lungs, she dived deeply and quickly. It was easy with the extra weight of the ammo around her upper body. At least twenty bullets zinged around her. Roan? What about him?

Worried, Inca halted her dive and turned around. Roan? Where was he? She could hear the helicopter's shattering sound just above them, the reverberation pulsating all around her. It was hovering over the water, very near to where she treaded. Roan was wounded! She felt it. No!

Anxiety shattered Inca. She kicked out violently and moved in the direction she knew Roan to be, even though she could not see him. The helicopter moved away, the dark shadow leaving the area. Concentrating, her lungs bursting for air, Inca kicked hard and struck out strongly. Roan? Where was he? How badly was he shot?

Her heart beat in triple time. Inca didn't want to lose Roan. She'd just found him! He was so much like her blood brother, Michael. Men like Roan were so rare. And she wanted—no, demanded of Mother Earth—that he be saved. She was lonely, and he filled that lonely space within her.

Yes, it was selfish, but she didn't care. Inca struck out savagely. She felt Roan nearby now. Well, selfishness had landed her in hot water with the clan before. Inca knew she was being tested again, but she didn't care if she failed this test, too. She would not let Roan die!

Blood and muddy water moved by her in thin, crimson and brown strips. She saw a shadow up ahead, striking toward the surface. Roan! Inca followed and, with her hand, pushed him upward. She could see blood oozing around his lower leg. He must have taken a bullet to the calf. Was his leg broken? Could he swim?

Unsure, Inca moved up, slid her arm around his massive torso and urged him upward.

They broke water together, like two bobbins coming to the surface. Water leaked into her eyes. She shook her head to clear them. The helicopter was moving back down the river, leaving them. Relief shuddered through Inca.

"Roan! Roan, are you all right?" She held on to him as he twisted around. His lips were drawn back from his clenched teeth. His face was frozen with pain.

"My leg..." he gasped, floundering.

"Can you use it to swim?" Inca cried. Their bodies touched and glided together. She kicked strongly to keep his head above water.

"Yeah...not broke. Just hurts like hell... And the blood. We've got piranhas in this water...."

Inca tugged at his arm. "Do not worry about them. Just head toward that shore. Hurry!" Mentally, Inca sent out her guardian and told him to keep the bloodthirsty little piranha schools at bay. Once they got the scent of blood in the water, fifty to a hundred of them would attack and shred both of them in a matter of minutes. That was not how Inca wanted to die. Nor did she want the man who relied heavily on her now to die, either.

"Kick! Kick your good leg," she ordered. "I will help you...."

It seemed like hours to Roan before they made it to the sandy red shore. Gasping for breath, he crawled halfway out of the water before his strength gave out. He was weakened from the loss of blood. Looking over his shoulder, he could see his bloody pant leg.

Inca hurried out of the water, threw off her ammo belts and ran back to him. She urged him to roll onto his back, and then hooked her hands beneath his arms. Grunting and huffing, she managed to haul him completely out of the water and onto the bank. Positioning him beneath some overhanging trees, she stopped for a moment, panting heavily. Dropping to her knees, she took out her knife and quickly slit open his pant leg to reveal the extent of his wound.

"H-how bad is it?" Roan gasped. He quelled the urge to sit up and grip the wounded leg. He felt Inca's hands moving quickly across his lower extremity, checking it out.

"Bad..." she murmured.

Roan forced himself to sit up. The bullet had torn through the fleshy, muscled part of his lower leg. Fortunately, it had missed the bones. Unfortunately, the wound was still spurting blood.

"An artery's been cut. Put pressure on it," he muttered. Dizzy, he fell back, and felt blackness encroaching on his vision. His gaze was pinned on Inca. Her hair was wet and stuck to the sides of her face. Her expression was intense, her eyes narrowed as she reached out and placed her hand across the jagged wound.

"Close your eyes," she snapped. "Do nothing but rest. Clear you mind. I will help you."

He didn't have much choice in the matter. Her hand, the moment it touched his feverish leg, was hot. Hot like a branding iron. Her fingers closed across his leg, strong and calming. Groaning, he stopped struggling and lay beneath the shade of the overhanging trees, breathing hard. His heart was pounding violently in his chest. Sounds meshed and collided. He was dumping. His blood pressure was going through the floor and he knew it. *Damn.* He was going to die. Darkness closed over his opened eyes. Yes, he would die.

Just as he drifted off into unconsciousness, Roan saw something startling. He saw Inca kneeling over him, her hand gripping his leg, and the blood spurting violently between her fingers. He saw the tight concentration on her face, her eyes gleaming as she focused all her attention on his wound. Roan saw darkness begin to form above her head. It appeared to be a jaguar materializing. Was he seeing things? Was he out of his mind? Was the loss of blood pressure making him delirious? Roan gasped repeatedly and fought to remain conscious. The head and shoulders of a jaguar appeared above Inca. And then it slid, much like a glove onto a hand, down across her head and shoulders. Blinking rapidly, Roan saw a jaguar where Inca had once been. Sweat ran into his eyes. Then he saw Inca, and not the jaguar.

Simultaneously, he felt raw, radiating heat in his lower leg. He cried out, the burning sensation so intense that it made the pain he'd felt before feel minor in comparison. Automatically, his hand shot out, but he was weak and he fell back. In the next instant, he spiraled into a darkness so deep that he knew he was dying and whirling toward the rainbow bridge where a spirit went after death.

Chapter 5

Roan awoke slowly. The howl of monkeys impinged on his consciousness first. Secondly, he heard the raucous screech of parrots as they shrieked at one another in a nearby rubber tree. And then—he was fatigued and it was an effort to sense much of anything—he felt warmth against his back. At first he thought it was Sarah snuggled up beside him, because she would always lay with her back against his in the chill of the early morning hours. The sensation in his heart expanded. No, he wasn't imagining this; it was real. Very real.

As he pried his eyes open, the events of the night before came tumbling back to him in bits and pieces until he put it all together. He'd been shot...he'd been bleeding heavily and he distinctly remembered dumping and preparing himself to die.

Wait... Inca...

His eyes opened fully. Roan pushed himself up on his elbow and twisted to look over his shoulder. In the gray dawn light, a vague yellowish-white glow illuminating to the cottony clouds suspended over the rain forest, he saw Inca. She was curled up on her side, one arm beneath her head, the other hand wrapped protectively around the barrel of the rifle that paralleled her body.

He'd been dying. Inca had leaned over him and placed her strong, firm hand over the spurting, bloody wound on his leg. He glanced down to see the pant leg torn up to his knee, revealing his dark, hairy calf. Sitting up and frowning, Roan slid his fingers along the area that had been chewed up by the bullet. Nothing. There was no sign of a wound. And he was alive.

"I'll be damned."

Twisting to look over his shoulder again, he stared hard at Inca. She had healed him with her mystical powers. Now he recalled the burning heat of her hand on his flesh. He'd thought he was getting third-degree burns. He'd fainted from loss of blood. Scowling, he touched his brow. Yes, he was feeling tired, but not as weak as yesterday, when he'd lost at least a couple pints of blood.

Looking down at her, Roan's heart expanded wildly. In sleep, Inca looked vulnerable and approachable. Her hair, once in a thick braid, was now loose and free about her shoulders and face. Black tendrils softened the angularity of her cheeks. Her thick, ebony lashes rested on her golden skin. His gaze moved to her lips, which were softly parted in sleep. Instantly, his body tightened with desire.

Grinning haphazardly, Roan forced himself to sit up and look around. Running his fingers through his sand-encrusted hair, he realized he needed to clean himself up. Testing the leg, he was surprised to discover it felt fine, as if nothing had happened to it. A flock of scarlet ibis, with long, scimitarlike beaks, flew over them. Their squawks awakened Inca. He watched, somewhat saddened because he'd wanted more time to simply absorb her wild, ephemeral beauty into his heart.

As Inca opened her eyes, she met the penetrating blue

gaze of Roan Storm Walker. Lying on the sandy bank, the warmth of it keeping her from being chilled in the dawn hour, Inca felt her chest expanding like an orchid opening. The look in the man's eyes was like a tender, burning flame devouring her. She was most vulnerable upon awakening. Normally, Inca would shove herself out of this mode quickly and efficiently. Nearby, Topazio lay and yawned widely. There was no danger or her spirit guardian would have growled and jolted her out of her wonderful sleep.

Inca drowned in the cobalt blue of Roan's large eyes. She saw a soft hint of a smile tugging at his mouth. What a wonderful mouth he had! She had never considered men beautiful, or bothered to look at them in that light before. With Roan, gazing at him was a sensuous pleasure, like eating a luscious, juicy fruit.

Inca found herself wanting to reach out and slide her fingers along his flat lower lip and explore the texture of him. She wanted to absorb that lazy smile of welcome. Simultaneously, she felt that incredible warmth of an invisible blanket embracing her once more. This time she didn't fight it. This time, she absorbed it and knew it came from Roan to her—as a gift. Inca accepted his gift in her sleep-ridden state. Nothing had ever felt so good to her. It made her feel secure and cared for. That particular feeling was so new to her that it jolted her even more awake. Her eyes widened slightly as she considered the feelings that wrapped gently around her like a lover's arms.

Always, it was Inca who cared for others, who protected them, and not the other way around. The last time she'd had this feeling of care and protection was as a child growing up. After being asked to leave the village of the Jaguar Clan at age eighteen, she'd never felt it again. Not until now, and this sensation was different, better. She felt like a thirsty jaguar absorbing every bit of it.

As she studied Roan's shadowed features, the soft dawn light revealing the harsh lines around his mouth, the deeply embedded wrinkles at the corners of his eyes, she realized he laughed a lot. Father Titus had similar lines in similar places on his round, pudgy face, and he was always laughing and finding pleasure in the world around him, despite the fact that he was as poor as the Indians he cared for.

"You laugh a lot," she murmured drowsily, continuing to lie on her back observing him.

Roan's smile broadened boyishly, then faded. "I used to. I lost the ability to find much to laugh about two years ago."

Placing one arm behind her head, she gazed up at the soft, grayish-yellow clouds that hung silently above them, barely touching the canopy of the rain forest. "Why did you stop laughing two years ago?"

Roan lost his smile completely. He felt the tenuous intimacy strung between them, and realized he was starving for such intimacy. He'd had it once before and he missed it so very much. Now it was a gift growing between himself and Inca, and Roan was humbled by it.

"Two years ago, my wife, Sarah, died in a climbing accident." Roan felt old pain moving through his chest. He pulled his knees upward and wrapped his arms around them. He looked out at the silently flowing Amazon that stretched endlessly in front of him.

"You'd have liked Sarah," he told Inca in a low, intimate tone. "She had red hair, cut short. She was an artist who drew the most incredible flowers and landscapes. She was a hellion. She knew no boundaries except the ones she wanted to create for herself. She was a world-class mountain climber. And she laughed at danger...." Roan closed his eyes. Why was he telling Inca all of this? It had sat in his heart like an undigested stone, rubbing and grinding on almost a daily basis. Yet, by him speaking to Inca, it was as if that stone was finally dissolving away and not hurting him as much.

"She was a warrior woman."

Nodding, Roan answered, "Yes. In all ways. She was a

part of nature. More animal than human at times.'' He smiled fondly in remembrance. ''We lived in a small cabin up in the Rocky Mountains in Montana. Hurt birds and animals would show up on our porch, and Sarah would care for them, feed them, tend their injuries, and when they were well enough, she'd free them. She'd always cry....'' He shook his head and smiled gently. ''Sarah was so attuned to nature, to life, to her own heart. One moment she'd be laughing and rolling on the floor with me, and the next, she'd read a newspaper or magazine and begin to cry over something sad she'd read.''

Inca digested his hoarsely spoken words. She realized he was allowing her entrance into the deepest part of his heart. She had no experience with such things, but she sensed that she needed to be careful. Just as she offered comfort when she held a sick baby in her arms for healing, Roan needed that comfort from her right now. Pushing her fingers through her hair, Inca whispered, ''How did she die?''

''On the Fourth of July, a holiday in our country. She was climbing a tough mountain made of granite to get ready for her big climb on El Capitan a week after that. She had friends that climbed that mountain every year. But this time Sarah was alone. I knew where she was, and what time she was to come home....'' Roan felt his gut knotting. ''I was out back of the cabin, fixing my truck, when I felt her fall. I could hear her scream in my head...and I knew...''

Wincing, Inca said, ''You were in touch with her spirit. People who touch one another's hearts have this direct way of talking to one another.''

Roan nodded. ''Yes, we had some telepathy between us.''

''What did you do then?''

''I jumped in the truck and drove like a madman to the rock wall where she'd been climbing.'' His voice turned ragged. ''I found her dead at the bottom. She'd died instantly of a skull fracture.'' And if he'd given her his medicine piece to wear, she might still be alive today. But he didn't voice his guilt over that issue.

"A clean death."

"Yes," Roan said, understanding Inca's words. "At least she didn't feel any pain. She was gone in a heartbeat. I'm glad she didn't suffer."

Wryly, Inca looked up at him. He was suffering and she wanted to reach out and console him. Shocked by that, she curled up her fingers. "But you have been suffering."

"Sure. When you love someone like I loved her...well..."

Inca sat up. Her hair fell around her back, shoulders and arms, the ebony strands reaching well below her breasts. She opened her hands. "I do not know what love is. I have seen it between Michael and Ann. I have seen a mother's love of her child, a father's love of his children."

Giving her a look of shock, Roan tried to hide his reaction. "But...you're twenty-five years old. Isn't there someone in your life—a man—you love?"

Scowling, she skimmed the hair through her fingers and separated it into three long swatches. Expertly, she began to braid it, her fingers flying through the silky length. "Love? No, I do not know love like that."

Trying not to stare at her like an idiot, Roan quickly put some facts together about Inca. "Don't your clan members ever marry among themselves?"

Shrugging impatiently, Inca said, "Almost always. Only we understand each other's special skills and talents. People outside the clan are afraid of us. They are afraid of what they do not understand about us. Sometimes, a jaguar clan member will marry outside of it. Michael married Ann. There is no law as to who you marry. Of course, we would like the blessing of the elders."

"And does the person marrying a member of the Jaguar Clan know about his or her special skills?"

"Eventually, perhaps. And sometimes, no. It just depends.

I know that Ann knows everything about Michael and his skills. She accepts them because she loves him.'' Inca took a thin strip of leather, tied off the end of her braid and tossed it across her shoulder. She saw the amazement on Roan's features. Why was he so surprised she did not have a lover? Did he not realize that in her business she had no time for such things? Life and death situations took precedence over selfish pleasures such as love...or so she told herself.

''Does Ann have problems coping with Michael's unusual abilities?''

Inca smiled. ''I think so, but she tries very hard to accept what she does not understand about metaphysics. And their daughter has her father's skills, as well. Clan blood is carried on, generation after generation. One day my godchild, little Catherine, will be going up to the village for years of training.'' She smiled, satisfaction in her tone. ''Until then, I get to see her from time to time, whenever I am near Mike and Ann's house.''

Inca's family. It was all she had, really. Roan was beginning to understand her loneliness, the lack of a man in her life who could love her, care for her and give her safe harbor from a world that wanted her dead at any cost. Frowning, he rubbed his face, the feeling of his beard spiky against his fingers.

''Do you have any children by Sarah?''

The question caught him off guard. Roan eased his hands from his face and met her inquiring gaze. ''No...and I wish I did, now.''

''She did not want children?''

''We both wanted them. We'd been married only two years and wanted to wait a couple more before we settled down to having a family.''

Inca rose slowly to her feet. She wriggled her bare toes in the red sand. ''That is very sad. My heart goes out to you. Sarah was a warrior. She died loving what she loved to do, and in that there is great honor.'' Inca looked up at the clouds that now had a golden cast because the sun was going to rise shortly. "But it was her time to pass over. She had accomplished all that she set out to do in this lifetime." Giving Roan a dark look, she added, "We all have a time when we will die. When whatever we wanted to accomplish is complete. And when that happens, we leave. We walk over the Threshold to the other worlds."

He slowly got to his feet. He felt a little weak, but not bad, considering what had almost happened. "Speaking of dying…I owe you my life, Inca. Thanks." He stuck out his hand to shake hers. "My mother could heal by touching a person, too, so I'm no stranger to what you did."

Inca stared at his hand and then slowly lifted hers. She slid her slender fingers into his roughened ones. Trying to tell herself she did not enjoy making such contact with this tall, stalwart warrior, she avoided the sincerity of his burning blue gaze and whispered unsteadily, "I did nothing. My spirit guide did it. You should thank him, not me."

Roan closed his fingers gently over Inca's proffered hand. Her fingers were strong and yet, even as she gripped his hand, he felt her softness, her womanliness just waiting like a ripe peach to be lovingly chosen by the right man—a man who would honor her as an incredible woman and human being. He found himself wanting to be that man. The thought shook him deeply as he watched her hang her head and avoid his gaze. In some ways, she was so childlike, her innocence blinding him and making his heart open when he'd thought it impossible that anything could make him feel like this again.

"Thank *you* and thank your guide," he murmured, and released her hand. He saw relief in her features as she snatched it back. Inca wasn't used to being touched. At least, not by a man who had heartfelt intentions toward her.

"It was not your time to die," Inca said briskly. She looked down at his bare feet. "Ernesto died in the attack,"

Inca said sadly. "He was a good friend and helped me often."

Roan frowned. "I'm sorry, Inca."

Nodding, her throat tight with grief, she whispered, "I will pray for him." Lifting her head, she said, "We must go. There is much to do. I know where to get shoes for both of us. I always hide gear at different villages in the Basin in case I need replacements." She frowned, dropped her hands on her hips and looked up the Amazon to where they'd nearly gotten killed the day before. "Who attacked us? Marcellino? He hates me. He blames me for his son's death when I had nothing to do with him dying."

Brushing off the seat of his pants, Roan said, "Marcellino gave his word he wouldn't try and kill you. Could it be drug runners?"

A wry smile cut across her face as she hoisted the bandoliers back into place on her shoulders. "That is always possible. Drug lords hate me. For once, the country's government and they agree on one thing." She slung the rifle across her shoulder and gave him an imperious look. "They agree that I need to be dead."

"They'll have to come through me, first."

His voice was a dark growl. Shocked, Inca realized Roan meant it. She saw his brows draw down, his eyes narrow. And she felt his protection wrapping around her. Laughing with embarrassment, Inca said, "You are the first man who has said that to me. Usually, it is the other way around—I protect men, women and children. They do not protect me."

"Even you need a safe harbor, some quiet, some down time," Roan reminded her. He looked around and then back at her. She had an odd look on her expressive features—one of pleasure mixed with shock. It was about time she got used to the fact that a man could care for her. Even though Roan honored her abilities, he knew that no human being was impervious to all the world's hurts. Sarah had taught him that. Inca was a woman. A beautiful, naive and innocent woman. And with each passing moment, Roan found himself wanting more and more to draw her into his arms and protect her from a world gone mad around her. She was too beautiful, too alive to die at the hands of some drug lord or crazed government soldier who wanted the considerable bounty on her head. No, as long as he was here, he'd make damn sure she was protected.

"Your feet," Inca said, pointing to them. "You lost your boots in the river. Where we need to go, you cannot travel. Your feet are soft." She held up one of her feet and pointed to the thick calluses on the bottom. "I can make it to the village, but you cannot."

"What if I cut off my pants to here—" he gestured with his index finger "—and wrap the cloth around them? Could I make it then?"

"Yes." Inca moved to the trees along the shore. She took out her knife and cut several long, thin, flexible vines from around one tree. She held them out to him. "Here, use my knife, and tie the cloth with these onto your feet."

Thanking her, Roan took her knife and the vines. In no time, his feet were protectively wrapped in the material. As he stood up and tried his new "shoes," she laughed deeply.

"My people will gawk at you when you enter their village. They will wonder what kind of strange man wears material on his feet."

Chuckling, Roan said, "Let them laugh. I'll laugh with them. How far is this village where you have supplies?"

Shrugging, Inca said, "By my pace, it is an hour from here." She eyed him. "But I do not think you will keep up with me, so it may take longer."

Grinning, Roan said, "Let's see, shall we?"

"Stop here," Inca said, and held up her hand. They halted near the edge of the rain forest. Before them was a Yanomami village of around fifty people. The huts were round in shape and thatched with dried palm leaves. In the center of

the village were cooking pots hung on metal tripods. The
men and women wore little clothing. Around their necks
were seed and bead necklaces. Some wore feather necklaces
from brilliant and colorful parrots. Their black hair was sleek
and straight, cut in a bowl fashion around their heads. All
the women wore brightly colored material around their
waists, their upper bodies naked, save for the necklace
adornments. Naked children of all ages were playing among
the huts. Babies either sat on the yellow-and-red packed dirt,
or hung on their mother's back as she worked over a cooking
pot, stirring it with a stick.

Inca quickly divested herself of her bandoliers of ammunition, her knife and rifle. She laid them carefully beneath
some bushes so that they were well hidden from prying eyes.
She saw the question on Roan's face.

"I never enter any village with my weapons. I come in
peace to my people. They see enough warfare waged against
them, enough drug running soldiers brandishing weapons
and knives. I do not want them to ever be afraid of me."

"I understand."

She pursed her lips. "Just watch. The Yanomami know
very little Portuguese and no English. Say nothing. Be respectful."

Roan accepted her orders. She quickly moved out of the
rain forest and onto the hard-packed dirt paths of the village.
One of the first people to spot her was an old woman. Her
black-and-gray hair was cut short, the red fabric of her skirt
thin and worn around her crippled body. She gave a shrill
cry in her own language, and instantly, villagers came hurrying toward where the old woman sat, hovering over her
black kettle of bubbling monkey stew.

Roan stayed a good twenty paces behind Inca. The Yanomami looked at him, and then their expressions turned to
adoration, their dark eyes glittering with joy as they threw
open their arms, raised more cries of greeting and hurried
toward Inca.

Every person in the village rushed forward until they surrounded Inca. Roan was startled by the change in her. No longer was she the defensive warrior. Instead, she was smiling warmly as she reached out and touched each of them— a pat on a person's head here, a gentle caress along a child's cheek there. Surrounding her, they began to chant, the people locking arms with one another and beginning to sway back and forth. Their faces were illuminated with unabashed joy over Inca's unexpected arrival.

Inca hailed them by name, laughed and smiled often. The Indians then ceased their welcoming chant in her honor, stepped away and made a large, respectful circle around Inca. Someone hurried forward with a rough-hewn, three-legged stool. They set it down and excitedly ask her to sit on it. As they brought her gifts—fruit and brightly colored parrot feathers—she complied.

A mother with a baby hurried forward. Her singsong voice was high-pitched, and tears were running down her tobacco brown face as she held her sickly infant toward Inca.

Inca murmured to the mother soothingly, and took the baby, who was no more than two months old, into her arms. The mother fell at Inca's feet, burying her head in her hands, bowing before her and begging her to heal her baby.

From where he stood, Roan could see that the infant was starving, his small rib cage pronounced. Did the mother not have enough milk to feed him? More than likely. Roan stood very still, knowing he was privy to something that few people would ever see. Even thirty feet away, he felt a shift and change in energy. It was Inca. He watched as she closed her eyes. Tenderly, she shifted the weak infant in her hands and gently placed him against her breast.

The mother's wailing and sobbing continued unabated and she gripped the hem of Inca's trousered leg. The pleading in her voice didn't need any translation for Roan. Narrowing his eyes, he saw darkness begin to gather around and above Inca. Blinking, he wondered if he was seeing things. No, it was real. A dark grayish-black smoke was coming out of the ethers above Inca's head. Then, quickly, the smoky mist began to take on a shape as it eased down across Inca's form. Roan stared hard. It was the jaguar! Roan recalled seeing it seconds before he'd lost consciousness the day before.

This time he steadied himself. He saw the jaguar apparition completely engulf Inca's upper body. It was superimposed upon her and he could see both simultaneously. Instead of Inca, he saw the jaguar's massive flat head, sun-gold eyes and tiny black, constricted pupils. A wave of energy hit Roan, and it reminded him of standing out in knee-high surf in the ocean and being struck by a large, far more powerful wave. He rocked back on his heels and felt another pulsating wave of energy hit him, and then another, as if the jaguar's intense and powerful energy was causing tidal fluctuations that rocked him rhythmically.

Roan tried to keep his concentration on the baby Inca held gently to her breast. Her head was tipped forward. At one point, she turned the child on his back and blew gently into his opened mouth. The sobs of the mother continued. Her face was streaked with tears, her eyes filled with agony as she begged Inca to save her dying baby.

Blinking, unsure of what all he was perceiving, Roan saw golden light coming out of Inca's and the jaguar's mouth simultaneously. He saw the golden threads move into the infant's slack mouth and fill his tiny form, which began to sparkle and throb with life. What was once a grayish, murky cocoon around the infant suddenly became clearer and more distinct. The grayness left, replaced by the white and golden light of life that now enveloped the baby.

As Inca raised her head, her eyes still closed, Roan saw the jaguar disappear. Instantly it was gone, as was the smoky cloud the animal had come out of. All Roan saw now was Inca and the baby. Holding his breath, along with the rest of the villagers, he realized he was watching a miracle take place. As Inca slowly opened her willow-green eyes, the infant in her hands moved and gave a weak cry. And then the baby's cry no longer wavered, but was strong and lusty.

The mother breathed the infant's name, leaped to her feet and stretched out her arms. Inca smiled softly, murmured reassuring words and carefully passed the baby back to her.

The woman held her child to her breast and bowed repeatedly to Inca, thanking her through her sobs. She looked at the baby, noting his animation and the fact that he was thriving and not sickly any longer. Face wet with tears, she knelt down before Inca.

Inca stood and drew her to her feet. She embraced the mother and held her for just a moment. Then releasing her, Inca asked who was next. Who wanted to be healed?

Roan stood there for a good hour, witnessing one healing after another. First to come were babies and mothers. After they were cared for, young boys and girls came forward. Sometimes Inca would simply lay her hand on a child's head. Sometimes she would ease youngsters onto her lap and hold them for a few moments. In nearly every case there was improvement, Roan noted. When it was finally time for the elderly, Inca went to them. Some were crippled. Others were so sick that they lay on pallets inside their makeshift huts.

Roan didn't mind waiting. A part of him wished that people like Colonel Marcellino could see this side of Inca. This was not the warrior; this was the healer. He began to understand what Mike Houston had said to him earlier. It was clear now why the Indians of the Amazon basin worshipped Inca as the jaguar goddess. No wonder. She had the power to heal. The power to snatch people from death's door and bring them back.

Her spirit guide did, Roan realized, mentally correcting himself. Inca was humble and lacked any egotism about her healing skills. That was typical of Indians. His own mother was one of the humblest souls he'd ever met. She never took credit for the energy that came through her and flowed into her patient. No, she gave thanks to the Great Spirit and to her spirit guides—just as Inca did.

Roan found a log to sit down on near the edge of the village. He was in no hurry today. As a matter of fact, being able to find out more about Inca and create a bond of trust with her was far more important than hurrying downriver to Marcellino's awaiting company. Roan hoped Inca would want to stay here overnight. He still felt weak, but was getting stronger and stronger as each hour slid by.

The peacefulness of the village was infectious. The laughter of the children, the barking of the dogs, the happiness on the faces of the people relaxed Roan. Above them, the clouds parted and sunlight lanced down through the triple canopy of the rain forest surrounding the village. A squadron of blue-and-yellow macaws winged overhead. They reminded him of rainbows in flight. Looking around, he saw that Inca was emerging from the last hut at the end of the village. He heard wails and cries coming from that hut. Inca looked tired. No wonder. She must have worked on fifteen people, nonstop.

Rising to his feet, he walked across the village to meet her. Without thinking, he reached out and slid his fingers around her upper arm. He saw turmoil in her eyes. The way her lips were set, as if against pain, touched him deeply.

"Come on," he urged her quietly, "come and sit down. You need to rest...."

Chapter 6

Jaime Marcellino stifled his anger toward his son. He had had only two children, but now only one was left. Julian was just a young, shavetail lieutenant straight out of the military academy, and Jaime wished mightily that he was more like his older brother, Rafael, had been: bold, brash and confident. As Jaime sat at his makeshift aluminum desk in the canvas tent, which was open at both ends to allow the humid air to sluggishly crawl through, he gripped his black-and-gold pen tighter. Julian stood at strict attention in front of him.

Oh, how young and cherubic his son's face was! At twenty-two, he looked more like a little boy than a man. Rafael had had Jaime's own sharply etched, proud and aris-tocratic features. Julian took after his mother, who was soft, plump and dimpled. Scowling as he scribbled his signature on some of the orders in front of him, Jaime jammed them into his attaché's awaiting hands. Around him, he could hear the company of soldiers preparing for the coming trek. They had just disembarked from a number of tug boats, and the men were setting up camp in the muggy afternoon heat.

"Lieutenant," he muttered, "your request to lead point with that—that woman is denied."

Julian's large, cinnamon-colored eyes widened. He opened his mouth to speak. His father's face was livid with rage. He could see it as well as feel it. The colonel's attaché, Captain Humberto Braga, blanched and stood stiffly at attention next to his father's chair.

"Sir, with all due respect—"

"Enough!" Jaime smashed his closed fist down on his table. Everything on it jumped. Snapping his head up, he glared at his son. "Permission denied. Point is the most dangerous position! I will not allow you to risk your life. You have a platoon to take care of, *Tenente,* Lieutenant. I suggest you do so. You have tents to set up, food to be distributed, and make sure that the men's rifles are clean and without rust. You have *plenty* to do. *Dismissed.*"

The attaché glared at Julian and jerked his head to the left, indicating that he should get out of the tent. Julian knew his father's rage well. He'd been cuffed many times as a child growing up, though after Rafael had been murdered, his father was less inclined to deride him and not take him seriously. Rafael had been a huge, heroic figure to Julian. He'd always looked up to his older brother. He'd gone to the military academy to follow in his big brother's footsteps, which he felt he could never possibly fill. Julian had labored and struggled mightily through four years of academy training. He'd barely gotten passing marks, where Rafael had gotten straight A's. Rafael had been captain of the soccer team, while Julian couldn't even make second string.

"Yes, sir," he murmured, and he did an about-face and stepped smartly out of the tent.

"Damn youngster," Jaime muttered glumly to his attaché after his son was out of earshot. He scribbled his signature hurriedly on another set of orders. He hated the paperwork.

He was a field officer, not a paper pusher. Oh, that kind of attitude had garnered him many enemies among the army ranks, that was for sure, but Jaime didn't care. He loved the outdoors. He reveled in missions such as the upcoming one. The only fly in the ointment was that the jaguar goddess was going to lead the company. And what the hell was wrong with Julian wanting, of all things, to work side-by-side with her? Had his youngest son gone *louco*? Crazy?

"I think he's trying to behave as Rafael might have in this situation, sir," the attaché ventured gently. "To do something heroic, to get your attention. My opinion, of course, sir." Humberto steeled himself for an explosion from his superior.

Grunting, Jaime looked up. He folded his hands restlessly. Looking out the side of the tent where the flap was thrown upward, he growled, "He'll *never* be Rafael. I wish he'd quit trying. Ever since he was murdered, Julian has been trying to make up for it." With a shake of his head, he muttered, "And he never will. Julian will never be what Rafael was."

"I think he knows that, sir," Humberto said, some pity in his tone.

"He's soft. Look at his hands! No calluses. His face is soft and round. I doubt he'll even be able to keep up with his men on this mission," Jaime fumed in a whisper so no one else would overhear. "Rafael was tough—hard as a rock. He was an incredible athlete. Julian has trouble making the mandatory runs and hikes." Snorting, Jaime looked up at the thirty-year-old career officer. Humberto Braga was a trusted individual who had come from the poverty of Rio de Janeiro and worked his way through college and eventually joined the army. Jaime admired anyone with that kind of courage and guts. Humberto was someone he could trust and confide in, too.

"Yes, sir, he's not Rafael in those respects," Humberto said, "but his men like him. They listen to him."

Raising his thick, black brows, Jaime nodded. "Yes, thank goodness for that."

"Perhaps this mission will be good for the boy, sir. He needs to show you he's capable."

Leaning back in the metal chair, Jaime pondered the younger man's reflection. "Asking to work with Inca is like asking to work with a bushmaster snake."

Humberto chuckled indulgently. Bushmaster snakes were well known to be one of the most poisonous in the Amazon. Not only that, but when the snake was disturbed, it would literally chase an unfortunate person down, bite him and kill him. Not many snakes were aggressive like the bushmaster, and it was to be feared. It had earned its reputation by leaving bodies of people in its wake over the centuries. The legends about the snake had grown, and Humberto knew most of them were true. "I hear you, sir."

Looking at his watch, Jaime muttered, "Where the hell is Storm Walker? He said they'd meet us here this morning. It's already noon." Again Jaime snorted and went back to the necessary paperwork. "And Morgan Trayhern said he was punctual. Bah."

Humberto was about to speak when he saw a tall man, an Anglo dressed in cutoff pants, a burgundy polo shirt and sandals, approach the tent. He'd seen a picture of Roan Storm Walker, so he knew it was him. Surprised, he stammered, "Colonel, Senhor Storm Walker is here...."

"Eh?" Jaime glanced up. Humberto was pointing toward the tent entrance. Jaime turned his head and met Roan's narrowed eyes. Storm Walker had a two-day growth of beard on his hard face and it made him look even more dangerous.

"It's about time," Jaime snapped. "Enter!"

Roan moved into the tent. He glanced at the thirty-year-old captain, who curtly nodded a greeting in his direction. "Colonel, I'm a little late."

Jaime glared up at him. "More than a little. I'm not impressed, Storm Walker."

Roan stood more or less at ease in front of the colonel, whose face had flushed a dull red. He saw the anger banked in the officer's eyes.

"I think you know why, too."

"What? What are you talking about?"

Roan studied him. The officer seemed genuinely surprised. "That unmarked helicopter that came out of nowhere and blasted the tug we were on to pieces? Does that ring a bell, Colonel?" Roan tried to keep the sarcasm out of his voice. Who else but Marcellino knew of their plans to meet, as well as the place and the time? No one.

Chagrined, Marcellino put down the pen and gave Roan a deadly look. "I haven't the faintest of what you are talking about, Storm Walker. What helicopter? And what tug?"

"We were attacked yesterday," Roan said tightly, "first by thugs in two cars. We barely made it onto the tug before they started firing at us with military rifles. There were six of them. And an hour later we were attacked by a green, unmarked military helicopter. It rocketed the tug. We jumped off it and dove as deep as we could." Roan decided not to tell of his wounding and of Inca's healing. He wanted to stick to the point with the colonel. "We had to swim to shore. And if it weren't for Inca knowing the lay of the land, I wouldn't be here now. We were twenty miles northwest of your landing area when the attack happened."

Marcellino slowly rose. "I know nothing of this attack," he protested strongly.

"You were the only one who knew our itinerary," Roan retorted, barely hanging on to his temper. He rarely got angry, but the colonel's innocent look and remarks stung him. He'd had a restless night's sleep, and hiking through the humid rain forest for fifteen miles this morning hadn't helped his mood at all.

"Are you accusing *me* of those attacks?" Marcellino struck his chest with a fist. Then he placed his hands flat on the table, leaned forward and glared up into the *norte-*

americano's livid features. "I had *nothing* to do with either attack!"

"You hate Inca," Roan declared. "You'd do anything to kill her because you mistakenly believe she killed Rafael, your eldest son."

Rearing back, Jaime put his hands on his hips in a defiant stance, despite the fact that he wasn't anywhere near Roan's height. "I gave my word to Senhor Trayhern that I would *not* lay a hand on her. And I have not!" His nostrils flared and quivered. "You are gravely mistaken, *senhor.*"

"Inca's angry. She has a right to be. She thinks *you* were behind the attack."

Jaime laughed explosively. "Oh, how I wish I were, Senhor Storm Walker." He lost his smile and glared at him. "But if I had of been, believe me, you two would not be alive today. I'd have hung that helicopter over the water and put a hundred bullets through her body when she came up to get air." He jabbed a finger toward Storm Walker. "Captain Braga!"

Humberto snapped to attention. "Yes, sir!"

"Take Senhor Storm Walker to our quartermaster. Get him a set of army fatigues, a decent pair of boots and other gear. And loan him a razor. He needs to shave."

Roan looked at the colonel. Was he lying? Was he telling the truth? Roan wasn't sure. The colonel's response seemed genuine; he'd looked surprised when he'd learned of the attacks. "As soon as I get cleaned up, I need a copy of the map you're using. Inca will look at it with me and I'll get back to you about the route we'll take tomorrow morning at dawn."

"Fine." Marcellino looked out of the tent. "Where is she?"

"Nowhere that you or your men will ever find her," Roan growled.

Shrugging, Jaime said, "Make sure she stays out of my

way. I have ordered my men *not* to fire at her, or to make any overture toward her that she may read as harm.''

Turning on his heel, Roan ducked beneath the canvas of the tent and followed Captain Braga out into the main encampment. The hundred and eighty men of Macellino's company were loosely strung out for half a mile along the shore of the Amazon. He could tell that the contingent wasn't used to rain forest conditions. Tents were going up. Men were smoking cigarettes and talking as they dug in for the evening hours ahead. The odor of food cooking caught his attention.

''Hungry?'' Humberto asked with a slight smile.

Roan looked over at the officer who accompanied him. Humberto Braga sported a thin, black mustache. His face was square and he was built like a bulldog. He wasn't aristocratic in bearing or facial features; he had more of a peasant demeanor. Roan couldn't dislike the soft-voiced officer. ''Yeah, just a little.''

''You hiked fifteen miles this morning?''

Roan gave him a cutting smile. ''Yeah.'' Inca had taken the lead and moved effortlessly, hour after hour, through the rain forest. He'd known she was in superb shape, but her ability to move at a continued trot without rest had stunned him. She'd only rested when he needed to take a break. As she had pointed out to him, he was wearing sandals that one of the Indians had given him, and sandals were not best for that kind of march.

Humberto pointed to the quartermaster's large tent. ''Here we are. I'll help you with getting all the equipment you will need.'' He eyed Roan again. ''Fifteen miles in how many hours?''

''Three.''

Sighing, Humberto said with a grin, ''And I wonder how fast we can push this company starting tomorrow morning.''

Roan halted. ''That's a good question, Captain, and not one I can answer right off the top of my head.'' He eyed the struggling company entrenching its position. A number of soldiers were heading out to predestined points several hundred yards ahead of the encampment, he saw. They would be forward observers—the eyes and ears of the company—to protect it from possible attack by drug runners.

"I think we will need two or three days to get—how do you say—the hang of it?"

Roan nodded. His mind and his heart were elsewhere—with Inca. She'd agreed to stay out of sight. Worried that the FOs might surprise her, he wanted to get done with the clothes exchange as soon as possible and get back to where she was hiding.

Julian Marcellino took off his helmet and wiped his sweaty brow with the back of his arm. He'd stumbled over some exposed roots and nearly fallen. Looking back, he grinned a silly grin. As usual, he wasn't watching where he was going. Rafael would never have tripped. He'd have seen the twisted roots sticking above the damp layer of leaves on the rain forest floor, and avoided them completely.

Halting, Julian heard the noise of the encampment far behind him. He had chosen men from each platoon to serve as forward observers, had picked out stations for them and ordered them to begin digging their foxholes, where they would remain for a four-hour watch before another two men took over for them. Then he'd made an excuse and gone off on his own.

He didn't like the cacophony of noise that was ever-present at the camp. No, in his heart he longed for the pristine silence of nature. As he looked up admiringly at the towering trees, the brightly colored orchids hanging off the darkened limbs, the sunlight sifting through the canopy, he sighed softly in appreciation. Tucking his helmet beneath his left arm, he wandered on into the rain forest, glad to be relieved of his responsibilities for just a little while. The leaves were damp and there was a wonderful musty, sweet scent from their decay. The screech of monkeys in the distance made him turn in their direction. The floor of the forest wasn't flat, but undulating. He climbed up and over a hill, and the noise from the company abated even more. That was good. He loved the silence.

Wiping his sweaty brow again, he moved quickly down the hill. At one point, he slid because of the dampness. Here in this humid country the rains would come and go, keeping the ground beneath the fallen leaves slick and muddy. Landing on his butt, he slid down to the bottom of the hill, where there was a small, clean pool of water. Laughing out loud over his lack of athleticism, Julian was very glad his father hadn't seen his awkward, unmanly descent. Or his men. Julian knew they tolerated him because his father was a colonel. He saw the amused and disdainful looks they traded when they thought he wasn't looking.

Remaining in a sitting position, Julian raised up enough to push his helmet beneath him. At least his butt would stay dry. Drawn to the beauty of the deep blue oval pool, of the orchids suspended above it on branches, he sighed again. Most of the noise of the company had faded in the distance. Here there was peace. A peace he craved. Placing his elbows on his thighs, he rested his jaw against his hands and simply drank in the beauty of the landscape. Being in Amazonia was turning out to be a wonderful, surprising gift to him.

Inca watched the soldier. She sat very still against a tree, hidden by the extended roots that stretched out like flying buttresses. When he'd appeared at the top of the hill, she had focused in on the soldier instantly. She had been eating her lunch, her back against one of the sturdy roots, when her guardian had warned her of his approach.

He was young looking. No threat to her. His face was babyish, his lips full. His eyes were wide with awe as he slowly absorbed the scene around him. The pistol he carried at his side indicated he was an officer, not an enlisted soldier. Snorting softly, she finished her mango and wiped her glistening lips with the back of her hand. Rolling over onto her hands and knees, she continued to watch the man. There was a bright red bromeliad on a dead log near where he sat. She watched as he reached out, his gesture graceful, the tips of his fingers barely grazing one of the many bright red bracts, which were really leaves and not petals. The way he touched the plant piqued Inca's interest. Most men would not even pay attention to it, much less touch it with such respect and reverence.

His hair was black, short and close cropped like Roan's. His ears were large and stuck out from the sides of his head, which was probably why he looked more like a boy growing through an awkward stage than a man. Inca smiled mirthlessly. She felt no threat from this young whelp. He looked out of place in a uniform. The way he touched the bromeliad again and again, and raptly studied it, made her decide to reveal her presence.

Julian heard a sound across the pool. It wasn't loud, just enough to snag his attention. As he lifted his chin, he gasped reflexively. There on the other side of the pond was a woman in military gear. Her willow-green eyes ruthlessly captured and held his gaze. She stood with her head high, a challenging look on her face, her hands resting arrogantly on her hips. And then, just as quickly, he realized *who* she was.

Inca laughed, the sound carrying around the pool. She felt the young man's shock when he realized who she was.

Lifting her hands, she said, "I am unarmed, *Tenente.* I come in peace. Do you?"

He saw the laughter in her willow-green eyes. He heard the derision and challenge in her sultry tone. Her hair was unbound and flowed freely across her proud shoulders and the bandoliers of ammunition she wore crisscrossed on her chest. Swallowing hard, he leaped to his feet. The heel of his boot caught and he slipped hard to the ground once more. Julian felt a rush of shame and humiliation. He expected her to deride him for floundering around like a fish out of water.

But she did not. Scrambling to his feet, he spread his boots far enough apart to give him some stability on the soft, damp leaves near the lip of the pond. Breathing hard, he stared across the hundred feet that separated them.

"Y-you're Inca...the jaguar goddess...." he croaked. "Aren't you?"

Julian had seen rough sketches of the woman on Wanted posters. She was supposed to have murdered his brother. He had never believed it. In person, she was shockingly beautiful. Just looking at her Indian features, the light shining in her eyes and the way she smiled at him, he rejected even more strongly the possibility that she had murdered Rafael. She had the face of an angel. Never had he seen anyone as beautiful as her! Even his fiancée, Elizabeth, who was truly lovely, could not match Inca's wild, natural beauty.

"I am," Inca purred. She removed her hands from her hips. "So, you are from the company that I am to lead?"

Gulping, his heart pounding, Julian stammered, "Er, y-yes...we are. I mean, I am...."

Laughing, Inca watched as his face flushed crimson. "Do not worry. I will not harm you, *Tenente*." She held up her hands. "I was finishing my lunch. Would you care for a mango? I have one left."

Stunned by her pleasant demeanor, Julian found himself utterly tongue-tied. Maybe it was her beauty. Or maybe it was all the whispered legends about her filling his head in a jumble that made him cower before her obvious power and confident presence.

Inca leaned over, picked up the mango. "Here," she called, "catch!"

Julian's hands shot out. He caught the ripe mango.

"Good catch." Inca laughed. She watched the young officer roll the fruit nervously in his hands. "You are quick. That is good. We will need that kind of reaction where I am going to lead you."

"T-thank you, Inca...or do you want to be called jaguar goddess?"

Inca felt the shame and humiliation coming from him. Why? Her heart went out to this young man, who really didn't belong in the army. He belonged in a garden tending his vegetables. Or perhaps in a greenhouse tending beautiful orchids. That would make him happy. Still, Inca respected him. "Call me Inca. And you are?"

Holding the mango gently in his hands, he said, "Y-you may call me Julian." He hooked a thumb across his shoulder. "I'm a lieutenant with this company. I have a platoon that I'm responsible for. I was really looking forward to being here. I've never been out in the rain forest and I've always wanted to come...."

She smiled and said, "You are at home here."

Julian was dumbfounded. "Why, yes...yes, I am. But—how could you know?"

"I read minds when I want to."

Gulping, Julian nodded. "I believe you. I really do." His heart was pounding hard with the thrill of getting to see this legendary woman in person.

"And the other men," Inca called, "are they as friendly and unthreatening as you are toward me?" The corners of her mouth lifted in a barely disguised smile of sarcasm.

"Oh, them...well, they are all right, Inca. I mean...most of them have heard the legends about you. They are all hoping to see you, to get a glimpse of you—"

"Why? To put a bullet through my head?"

Wincing, Julian held up his hand. "Oh, no, no...not that. There's been so much speculation, even excitement, about you...the possibility of seeing you. That's all."

She moved slowly toward the edge of the pond and said, "What about Colonel Marcellino? Does he still want to see me dead?" Her voice was flat and hard.

Gulping, Julian raised his eyes. "That...my father has mixed feelings about you. I mean, it's understandable...I never believed you did it. Not ever. But he was so full of anguish and grief that he had to blame someone. I don't believe drug runners, and that is who said you killed Rafael.''

Inca froze. Her eyes narrowed to slits. The moment she heard Julian say "my father," her hand went to the pistol at her side. "Colonel Marcellino is *your* father?" she demanded.

"Y-yes, he is. I'm Julian Marcellino. I apologize. I should have told you my last name. It's just that…well, I'm a little shook up, afraid.…" His voice drifted off.

Looking at him, Inca growled, "You do not believe I killed Rafael?"

Shaking his head adamantly, Julian said, "No…and now, seeing you in person, even more I do not believe you killed my older brother."

Inca knew that something greater was at play here. What were the chances of the brother of Rafael showing up where she was hiding? Very slim. She understood the karma of the situation. The soldier was white-faced now, and stood stiffly, the fruit clutched in his hands. Buffeted by his tumultuous feelings, Inca ruthlessly entered his mind to see if he was, indeed, telling her the truth.

Julian winced. He took a step back, as if he'd been physically struck.

"Sorry," Inca called. She moved more gently into his mind. Julian staggered and sat down unceremoniously. As she moved through his psyche, she saw and felt many things. That was the problem with telepathy—it wasn't just about getting information, it meant feeling all the damnable emotions that came along with the information. It was so hard on her that she rarely read minds. She didn't want to deal with many emotions.

In her mind, she saw Julian as a baby, a youngster, a teenager during his time spent in the military academy. As she withdrew her energy from him, he uttered a sigh of relief. Inca squatted down on her haunches and stared at him across the pond. "You are not a soldier at heart. This is not a job you love. You are doing this to please your father, not yourself."

Rubbing his head, Julian felt a slight headache. The power that Inca possessed stunned him. "Yes, well, my father wanted me to carry on in Rafael's place. How could I say no? He put such importance on me carrying on the family name and tradition. All the firstborn men went into the army and distinguished themselves. It is expected."

Laughing harshly, Inca said, "Better that you go tend a garden, my young friend." She knew now that Julian bore her no grudge. He wasn't a killer. Inca seriously wondered if he could even pull the trigger of a rifle pointed toward an enemy. No, he was a peaceful, serene person who was not faring well in the military world. At all.

"I like gardening," Julian said, slowly getting to his feet. He retrieved his helmet and settled it awkwardly on his head. "Is there anything I can do for you? Do you need supplies? Food?"

Touched by his thoughtfulness, Inca said, "No...thank you. I am waiting for Roan Storm Walker to return with the map."

"Oh, to see which direction we go tomorrow morning?" Julian smiled a little. "I'd give *anything* to be with you two as you take us into the rain forest."

The eagerness in his voice was genuine. Inca slowly relaxed. "Your father would never let you near me and you know it. Go back. Go back to your men and say nothing of our encounter. If your father finds out, he will be very upset about it."

"Yes, he would," Julian admitted ruefully. He smiled a little hesitantly. "Thank you for the fruit. That was very kind of you, Inca. And if there is anything I can do to help you, please let me know?"

She lifted her hand. "I will, *Tenente*. Go now."

Inca watched the soldier clamber awkwardly up the incline. Shaking her head, she realized that the entire company would struggle like that on this slick, leafy terrain. Turning, she went back to her hiding spot between the roomy wings of the tree roots, more than adequate to protect her from prying eyes. Sitting back down, she leaned against the smooth gray bark and closed her eyes.

Missing Roan, Inca wondered if he was all right. She felt a connection to him, like an umbilical cord strung invisibly between them. She sighed. The fifteen-mile hike this morning had been hard on both of them. Wanting to take a nap now, but not daring to do so, Inca felt her jaguar guardian move around. Instantly, she sat up, her eyes flying open.

There on the edge of the hill above the pool was Roan. He carried a map in his hand. She smiled and felt heat rush through her. How handsome he was in her eyes. And this time he was dressed in jungle fatigues and had a good pair of black leather boots on his feet instead of the sandals. Standing, she left the tree to meet him halfway down the hillside.

"You look different." She grinned and pointed to his face.

Rubbing his jaw, Roan absorbed her teasing expression. "Yeah, the colonel wanted me clean shaven. Now I know why I got out of the Marine Corps." He chuckled. Holding up the map, he said, "We've got work to do. Are you up to it?"

Inca nodded and fell into step beside him. There was something wonderful about his height, and that feeling of warmth and protection that always surrounded her when he was near. "Of course. Are *you?*"

Giving her an intimate look, Roan said, "Of course." He saw she had some mangos for him in the small cotton knapsack tied to her web belt. It was spring in Amazonia, and far too early for such fruit to be ripe. When she'd reached into it and brought out fruit and nuts earlier, during one of the rests they had taken on their march, Roan had considered asking about them.

"Where do you get this fruit? It's out of season," he said now, sitting down against the tree with her.

Inca picked out a mango and handed it to him. "I will it into being."

Opening the map before her, he glanced up. "What do you mean?"

"We are taught how to move and use energy in the Jaguar Clan village. If I will a mango into existence, it occurs. Or nuts." With a shrug, Inca said, "Our will, our intent is pushed and ruled by our emotions. If I am in alignment with my feelings and really desire something, I can manifest it on a good day." She grinned mirthlessly. "And on a bad day, when my concentration is not good, or I am emotionally shredded, I forage on the rain forest floor like all the rest of our relations to find enough food to stop my stomach from growling."

Taking the mango, Roan bit into it. "It's real."

"Of course it is!"

The flesh was juicy and sweet. He pointed to the map. "This is the army's best attempt at defining the trails through Amazonia. We're here—" he tapped his finger on the map "—and this is where we have to go. Now, you tell me—is there a better way to get there? I don't see any trail marked between here and there."

Studying the map, Inca grimaced. "This map is wrong. I expected as much." She tapped her head. "I know how to get us there."

"At least draw it on the map for me? The colonel will want something concrete. He's not a man who can go on a wing and a prayer like you or I do."

"Humph." Inca took the map and placed it across her lap, her thin brows knitting.

Roan absorbed her thoughtful expression. The moments of silence strung gently between them. Her hair was loose, and he had the urge to thread his fingers through that thick silken mass. There was such sculpted beauty in Inca, from her long, graceful neck to her fine, delicate collarbones, prominent beneath the T-shirt she wore, to the clean lines of her face.

"You will not guess who I just ran into minutes before you came."

Frowning, Roan asked, "Who?"

Lifting her head, she met and held his dark blue gaze. "Tenente Julian Marcellino."

Eyes narrowing, Roan rasped, "What?"

Chuckling, Inca told him the entire story. When she was done, she said, "He is a sweet little boy in a man's body. He is not a warrior. He does this for his father, to try and fill in for his missing big brother."

Sucking air between his teeth, Roan said worriedly, "That was a little too synchronistic."

Shrugging, Inca said, "We got along well. He believes me to be innocent of Rafael's murder. That is good."

Saying nothing, Roan allowed her to continue to study the map. After Inca had traced a route in pencil and handed it back to him, he said, "Marcellino swears he didn't try and bushwhack us with that helicopter, or those men on shore."

Inca eyed him. She slid her long fingers through her dark hair and pushed it off her shoulders. The afternoon humidity was building and it was getting hotter. "Do you believe him?"

"I don't know," Roan murmured, studying the route she'd indicated on the map. "He seemed genuinely surprised when I told him."

"If not him, then drug runners," Inca said flatly.

"Maybe. How could they get the info on where we'd be going and the time we'd be at the dock?"

"They have their ways," Inca said. "They are part of the Dark Brotherhood, and have people who can read minds just as I can. They can travel in the other dimensions, look at information, maps, reports, and bring the information back to the drug lords.''

''I didn't know that.''

One corner of Inca's mouth pulled inward. ''Do you think I and my kind fight a battle only on this dimension you call reality? No. The battles occur on many other levels, simultaneously. The Dark Brotherhood works to see chaos replace the goodness of the Sisterhood of Light.'' She waved her hand above her head. ''If you think for a moment that the drug lords do not use every tool they can, think again.''

''Then…Colonel Marcellino could be telling the truth.''

She smiled a little at his thoughtful expression. The urge to reach out, slide her hand across his cleanly shaved jaw caught her by surprise. But then, Inca was finding that around Roan, she was spontaneous in ways that she'd never been with another man. Pulling her focus back from that unexpected urge, Inca whispered, ''Yes, the colonel could be telling the truth.''

Chapter 7

"**W**ell?" Marcellino snapped, as he mopped his perspiring brow with his white, linen handkerchief, "what do you have for us, Storm Walker?"

Roan stood before the colonel, who had decided to leave his stifling tent and continue to make plans at a makeshift table beneath the tangled, grotesque limbs of a rubber tree fifty feet from the bank of the Amazon.

"I've talked to Inca," Roan said, spreading the map before the colonel, his captain and lieutenants, who stood in a semicircle around the metal table. Dusk was coming and shadows had deepened. When he'd arrived back in camp, all the tents were up, in neat order. The men had eaten and were now cleaning their rifles for the coming march, which would take place at 0600 tomorrow morning.

Moving his large hands across the map of the area, Roan traced the route with his index finger for the colonel. The lamp was suspended precariously above them on a limb and drawing its fair share of insects. "This is the route that Inca feels we should go."

Scowling, Jaime squinted his aging eyes. At fifty-three, he had to wear bifocals now. Grudgingly, he pulled them from his blouse pocket and settled them on the end of his nose. The light was poor, but he could see the penciled line on the map. Leaning down, he studied it for a number of minutes.

"This takes us through some of the worst terrain in the basin!" he muttered, as he lifted his head and straightened up. Perspiration trickled down his ribs. The long-sleeved fatigues, which everyone wore as protection from biting insects, did not breathe well. Jaime was gulping water like a camel to stay hydrated. Wiping his wrinkled brow, he saw his son, Julian, standing among the four lieutenants across the table from him. The boy's expression was eager as he studied the route.

"Sir," Julian said respectfully, "I see why Inca is doing it." He tapped his finger on the map. "We avoid the swamp to the south of us. To the north, there is a major river to cross, and we do not have the capabilities to span it. By tackling the steep terrain, we take the safest route. Swamps are well known for their diseases, piranhas, snakes and other vermin."

Many other soldiers were crowding around, at a distance, to eavesdrop. They had nothing else to do in the twilight, and Julian's soft voice made them trudge a few inches closer to hear his words.

"That's exactly why she chose the route," Roan intoned. He saw the colonel's narrow face flash with annoyance. The glare he gave his hesitant son made Roan angry. The young man was diplomatic, yet had the guts to take on his father, who everyone tiptoed around.

Captain Braga leaned down and studied the map. "The swamp is too large to try and march around, sir. But at this time of year, in spring, there is the chance of heavy rains, flooding, and that is lowland area. If we get too much rain, that swamp will rise five or ten feet in a hurry. Men could drown in such a scenario." He frowned and looked closely at the suggested route. "Yet I see why you don't like the other route, Colonel. It is very steep, hilly terrain."

"Exactly," Marcellino snapped. "It will increase our time to the valley by another week. Besides, men will fall, slip, and we'll have injuries—sprained ankles and perhaps broken legs." Marcellino looked down at the damp leaves beneath his shining boots. "This is slippery footage at best."

"Colonel, Inca strongly suggests you do not choose the swamp route," Roan said. "Even though spring signals the end of the wet season here, that doesn't guarantee it won't rain. If your men get out in the swamp and the river floods its banks, they could drown. We have no quick, sure way of rescuing a company that's stuck on one of the islands in that swamp. It's too far from any base, and helicopters, unless they refuel in flight, couldn't manage a rescue attempt."

"The swamp is the fastest route to the valley," Marcellino growled. "We can send point men ahead to test the terrain where we're going to march."

Julian compressed his lips. His father remained ramrod straight, his mouth thinned, hands resting imperiously on his hips. He was going to take the swamp route, Julian knew. He opened his mouth to say something when, from the back of the large group of men, there came a shout of surprise. And then another. And another. Because he was short, barely five foot ten inches tall, he stood on tiptoe to find out what all the excitement was about.

Roan turned on his heel when he heard a number of men calling loudly to one another and moving rapidly aside at the rear of the assemblage. It was Inca! She was striding toward them like she owned the place. Didn't she? Roan turned sharply and pinned the colonel with his eyes.

"It's Inca," he warned him tightly.

Instantly, Marcellino's hand went to the holster hanging at his right hip.

Roan nailed him with a glare. "Don't even think about it," he rasped.

Julian smiled in greeting as he saw Inca, who strode, tall and proud, up to the table. The crowd parted for her, the men's mouths hanging open in awe, their stares all trained on her. They gave Inca plenty of room. When she swung her cool, imperious gaze toward him, Julian bowed his head slightly in honor of her unexpected presence. She was, indeed, a goddess! Every man, with the exception of his father, looked up at her in admiration, respect and fear. She was afraid of no one and nothing. Marching bravely into their camp only made her more untouchable, in Julian's eyes.

Roan met and held Inca's laughter-filled eyes. The half smile on her mouth, the way she held herself as she halted at the table, opposite the frozen colonel, made him go on alert. Inca was in danger. Marcellino's face darkened like a savage thunderstorm approaching. His eyes flashed with hatred as he met and held her challenging look.

"If I were you, Colonel, I would listen to your son and your other officer, here." Inca flicked a hand lazily in Braga's direction, who stood staring at her in awe. "If you go the swamp route, you are guaranteeing the death of a number of your men. Is that what you want? A high body count before you even reach that valley where the Valentino Brothers hold my countrymen as slaves?" she demanded, her husky voice quieting the throng.

Roan moved to Inca's side, standing slightly behind her to protect her back. He trusted no one here. Marcellino had given his word that he and his men would not harm her, but he believed none of them. Cursing to himself, he wished Inca hadn't marched into camp like she owned the damn place. Keeping his eye on the men who were gawking like slobbering teenage boys at Inca, and the colonel, whose face was turning a dusky red with rage, Roan geared himself to take action.

"What you say has nothing to do with anything!" Marcellino hissed in a low, quavering tone. ''You promised to stay out of my encampment.''

Shrugging easily, Inca growled in return, ''I am in the business of saving lives, Colonel, unlike you, who considers your soldiers nothing more than cannon fodder on the road to reaching your own objectives.''

As she stared him down, beads of sweat popped out on the colonel's wrinkled brow. His hatred spilled over her, like tidal waves smashing against her. Because she was innocent, she did not connect emotionally into the colonel's rage, grief and loss. She had no compassion for the man whose fingers itched to pull the pistol at his hip out of that black, highly polished leather holster, and fire off round after round into her head and heart.

Marcellino cursed. ''You bitch! You murdering bitch. Get out of here before I kill you!''

Roan stepped forward. ''Colonel—''

It was too late. Marcellino unsnapped his holster, clawing at the pistol resting there.

Just as Roan moved to step in front of Inca to protect her, he felt the energy around her change drastically. It felt as if someone had sucker punched him with a lightning bolt. Roan staggered backward, off balance. Braga made a choking sound and backed away, too. Julian uttered a cry and fell back many feet. The energy sizzling around Inca was like an electric substation that had just been jolted with fifty thousand watts of electricity.

Roan heard Marcellino give a cry. Jerking his head around, he saw the colonel drop the pistol from his hand. Grabbing at his throat, he squawked and took two steps back, his face going white and then a gray-blue color. His eyeballs bulged from their sockets. His mouth contorted in a soundless scream.

''Do not presume you can kill me, Colonel,'' Inca snarled.

Roan blinked. Something invisible had the colonel by the throat, strangling him. He cried out and crashed to his knees, wrestling with the invisible force. He cried out again and began to choke.

Julian grabbed the tent pole to steady himself. When he saw what was happening, he leaped forward. "Papa!"

Roan turned, his back against Inca's. His narrowed gaze swept the men, who were now mesmerized and frightened by the unfolding spectacle. Automatically, he drew his pistol and held it in readiness, should any one of them try to shoot Inca.

Jaime choked. Slobber sputtered from the corners of his gaping mouth. He felt as if some large, powerful animal had gripped him by the throat with its invisible jaws. He was dying! Unable to draw in a breath of air, he fell, writhing, to the damp ground. All he saw were Inca's willow-green eyes, thoughtful and concentrated upon him. Devastated and shocked by her power, he kicked out. The table went flying.

Julian fell to his side, sobbing for breath. "Stop! Stop!" he begged Inca. "Don't kill him! He's my father!"

Inca lifted her chin slightly. She ordered her spirit guardian, Topazio, to release the white-faced colonel from his massive jaws. The army officer, now semiconscious, fell into his son's arms. "Very well, Julian. For you, I do this," she stated.

Marcellino gasped and then gagged. He rolled onto his side and vomited. Julian pulled out his handkerchief and cleaned around his father's mouth, then held him protectively in his arms.

Gripping his neck weakly, Jaime swore he could still feel the invisible force, though the sensation was dissipating rapidly. Head hanging down, he lay in his son's arms, breathing harshly. How good it felt to have air in his lungs again!

Julian's hand fluttered nervously over his shoulders. "Leave me!" he ordered his son hoarsely. "I'll be fine!" And Jaime forced himself to sit up on his own. Angrily, he shoved his son away from him, embarrassed that his men had seen him in such a compromising position.

Julian winced and staggered to his feet. Trying to hide his hurt over his father's rejection, he sought out and found Inca's gaze. "T-thank you...."

"Everyone stand down," Roan ordered, his voice carrying across the assemblage. "Inca came in peace and she's going to leave that way. If I see anyone lift a weapon, I'll fire first and ask questions later." He held up the pistol as a reminder.

Rage fueled Marcellino. He staggered to his hands and knees, and sat down unceremoniously, still dizzied. Spitting out the acid taste in his mouth, he twisted his head and glared up at the cool, collected woman warrior at whose boots he sat at like a pet dog.

"You promised not to hurt me," Inca reminded him in a dark tone. "You went back on your word. You are not to be trusted. I came here to help you."

"And you will," Jaime rasped as he staggered to his feet. Gripping the edge of the table with one hand, he wiped his other hand across his mouth. "The great Green Warrior will go back on her word, eh? So now you refuse to lead us?"

Inca smiled a deadly smile. "I will lead you, Colonel. My word is my bond. The only thing that will break it is death. But I am warning you—do not go through the swamp. It is too dangerous at this time of year as we move from wet to dry season."

"Inca, you'd better leave," Roan warned over his shoulder.

She smiled laconically and slid her fingers beneath the leather strap of her rifle, which rested on her right shoulder. "I am leaving now."

Julian rushed forward. He gripped Inca's arm.

Inca froze momentarily. She looked down at the lieutenant.

"Thank you," he whispered unsteadily, giving her arm an awkward pat. "For your compassion, your understanding..."

There was something heart-wrenchingly innocent and vulnerable about Julian. Inca reached over and placed her hand across his. "I did it for you, *Tenente*. Not for *him*." And she glared at the colonel. "Your son needs you as a father. I hope you realize that someday. You treat him like a mongrel dog come late to your family, and that is wrong."

Marcellino stared in shock at Inca as she turned on her booted feet and imperiously marched off the same way she'd come. He hated her. She had murdered Rafael. In the twilight, as she reached the rain forest beyond his gaping soldiers, Inca seemed to disappear into thin air. Rubbing his eyes angrily, Marcellino told himself it was the poor light of the coming dusk that tricked him. Gently touching his aching throat, he tried to explain away the pain that still throbbed where invisible hands—or jaws—had wrapped powerfully around his throat and damn near choked him to death.

"Pick up my pistol," he ordered Braga in a scratchy voice that warbled with fear. Irritated, humiliated in front of his men, Marcellino turned on all of them. They looked as if they'd seen a ghost. "All of you!" he roared, his voice breaking. "Get back to your quarters and your posts. We rise at 0500. Get some sleep!"

The men quickly departed. Marcellino saw Roan holster his pistol and come back to the table, his black brows drawn down with displeasure. Too bad. Grabbing the map, Marcellino threw it at his attaché.

"We go through the swamp, Captain."

Braga blanched, but took the map and gently folded it up. "Yes, sir, Colonel."

Roan stood there in shock. Was the man crazy? And then it dawned on him that whatever Inca said, Marcellino was going to do the exact opposite. Fuming, he turned away.

"I'll see you at 0600, Colonel."

Nodding brusquely, Marcellino turned and hurried back to his tent.

* * *

Roan moved back into the darkening rain forest. Very little light trickled down through the canopy as, with monkeys screaming and chattering, the cape of night was drawn across Amazonia. Being careful where he walked, he allowed his eyes to adjust to the gloom. What the hell had prompted Inca to make that kind of entrance? What was going through her mind? She was a proud woman. And she probably couldn't stand not being in on the planning of the march. In some ways, Roan didn't blame her.

He moved along the trail back to their hiding place. A sound—someone crying possibly—drifted into earshot. Halting, Roan keyed his hearing. Yes…there is was again: a soft, halting sobbing. Where? He turned and slowly allowed his ears to become his eyes. Turning off the trail, he moved quietly down a slight incline. Below were six silk-cotton trees, their winged roots splaying out around them. The grove looked like a darkened fortress in the twilight. The sound was coming from there.

Scowling, Roan lightened his step. It *was* someone crying. A woman weeping. Who? Frowning, he stepped down into the clearing among the trees. As he rounded one of the huge, winglike roots, he stopped. Shock jolted through him. It was Inca! Crouched there, her head bowed upon her arms, she was crying hard. Taken aback, Roan stood, unsure of what to do. He felt embarrassed for her, for coming upon her without her knowledge. Why was she weeping? Stymied, he cleared his throat on purpose to let her know he was there. Every particle of him wanted to rush over and embrace her and hold her. He felt her pain.

Sniffing, Inca jerked up her head. Roan stood no more than five feet away from her. Shaken and surprised, she quickly wiped her face free of tears. Why hadn't her guardian warned her that he was coming? Feeling broken and distraught, Inca knew emotionally she was out of balance with herself. When she was in this state, her guardian often had a tough time trying to get her attention. She was, after all, painfully human, and when she allowed her emotions to get the better of her, she was as vulnerable as any other person.

"What do you want?" she muttered, humiliated that he'd seen her crying.

"Stay where you are," Roan urged softly. Taking a chance, a helluva big one, he moved over to her. He slowly crouched down in front of her, their knees barely touching. "I don't care if you are the jaguar goddess," he whispered as he lifted his hand and reached out to her. His fingers grazed her head, the thick braid hanging across her left shoulder. Her hair felt crinkly from the high humidity.

Inca wasn't expecting Roan's gesture and she stiffened momentarily as his long, scarred fingers brushed the crown of her head. Warmth flowed down through Inca. She was shaken by his continued, soothing stroking of her hair. At first she wanted to jerk away, but the energy in his touch was something she desperately needed. Forcing herself to remain still, Inca leaned back against the trunk of the tree and closed her eyes. An unwilling sob rose in her. She swallowed hard and tried to ignore her tumultuous feelings.

Roan moved closer, sensing her capitulation to his grazing touches. He saw the suffering in her face, the way the corners of her mouth were pulled in with pain. "I'm glad to see you this way," he said wryly. "It's nice to know you are human, that you can cry, that you can let someone else help you...." And it was. Each time his fingers stroked her soft, thick hair, a burning fire scalded his lower body. Roan wanted to lean down and brush her parted lips with his, to soothe the trembling of her lower lip with the touch of his mouth. More tears squeezed from beneath her thick, black lashes.

"I cry for Julian," she managed to whisper hoarsely, in explanation of her tears. "I felt his pain so sharply. Julian adores his father, and yet his father does not even realize he exists." Sniffing, Inca wiped her nose with the back of her hand. She looked up at Roan's dark, heavy features. His eyes were tender as he leaned over her. She felt safe. Truly safe. It was such an unusual feeling for Inca. Her whole life was one of being on the run, being hunted, with no place to let down her guard. Yet she felt safe with Roan.

Smiling gently, Roan settled down next to Inca. It was a bold move, and yet he listened to his heart, not his head. He eased himself behind her, placing his legs on either side of her.

"You're crying for Julian. Tears for the boy who needs a father." Roan whispered. He allowed his fingers to caress the back of Inca's neck. Her muscles were tight. As he slowly began to massage her long, slender form, he felt her relax trustingly.

Everything was so tenuous. So fragile between them. As if an internal thunderstorm was ready to let loose within him, Roan felt driven to hold her, to comfort her, to be man to her woman.

Inca trembled. Roan's fingers worked a magic all their own on her tight, tense neck muscles. She leaned forward, her head bowed, resting her arms on her drawn-up knees so that he could continue to ease the tension from her.

More tears dribbled from her tightly shut eyes as he massaged her neck. "Julian is sweet. He is innocent, like the children I try to help and heal. He tries so hard to please his father. Back there, I watched him. He was a man. More of a man than his father. And he is right about the path. I was surprised he accepted my route."

Roan could smell her sweet, musky odor and inhaled it. She was like a rare, fragrant orchid in that moment. It would be so easy to pull her into an embrace, but his heart warned him that it would be rushing Inca and could destroy her growing trust in him. No, one small step at a time.

"If Julian knew you were crying for him, I think he would cry, too."

Choking on a sob and laughter, Inca nodded. "I like him. He is a kind man. He reminds me of Father Titus, the old Catholic priest who raised me for a while."

"You don't see many of those kind of men down here, do you?" Roan moved his hand tentatively from her neck to her shoulders and began to ease the tension from them.

Inca moaned. "You have hands like no one else."

"Feel good?" He smiled a little, heartened by her unexpected response.

"Wonderful…"

"You let me know when you've had enough, okay?" Roan knew it was important for Inca to set her own emotional boundaries with him. She trusted him, if only a little. His heart soared wildly. He was close enough to press a warm, moist kiss on her exposed neck. What would her flesh feel like? Taste like? And how would she respond, being such a wild, natural woman?

Lifting her head, Inca gave him an apologetic look. "Much touches my heart."

"You just don't let others know that about you," Roan murmured as he moved his hand firmly against her shoulders. "Why?"

"Because the miners, those who steal the timber and those who put my people in bondage will think it is a sign of weakness." Inca wrinkled her nose. "What do you think Colonel Marcellino would do if he saw me crying over how he treated his devoted and loving son? He would put that pistol to my head faster than he tried to today."

"I can't argue with you," Roan said heavily. "How do your neck and shoulders feel now?" He gave her a slight smile as she turned sideways and regarded him from beneath tear-matted lashes.

"Better." Inca managed a broken, trembling smile. "Thank you…" She shyly reached out and slid her fingers across his large hand, which rested on his thigh. It was an exhilarating and bold move on her part and she could see

Roan invited her touch. She'd never had the urges she felt around him. And right now her heart was crying out for his continued touch, but she felt too shamed and embarrassed to ask him to do more.

"Anytime."

"Really?"

He grinned a little. "Really."

She lifted her hand from his, her fingertips tingling pleasantly from the contact. The back of his hand was hairy. She felt the inherent strength of him, as a man, in that hand. Yet he'd been so incredibly gentle with her that she felt like melting into the earth.

"I think you are a healer and do not know it yet."

Roan lifted his hands. "My mother wished that her medicine had moved through me, my blood, but it didn't. Sorry." Giving Inca a humorous look, he told her conspiratorially, "If I can ease a little of your pain, or massage away some tight muscles, then I'm a happy man."

She snorted softly and wiped the last of her tears from her cheeks. "It takes very little to make you happy, then, Storm Walker."

"I don't consider what we share as little or unimportant," he told her seriously. "I like touching you, helping you. You carry the weight of the world on those proud shoulders of yours. If I can ease a little of that load, then it does make me happy."

Inca considered his words, which fell like a warming blanket around her. She craved Roan's continued closeness. She liked the way his bulk fit next to her. In some ways, he was like a giant tree whose limbs stretched gently overhead, protecting her. She smiled brokenly at the thought. The warmth of his body was pleasant, too, with the humidity so high and the sun gone away for the night. The night hours were always chilly to her. What would Roan think if she moved just a few inches and leaned her back against his body? Frightened and unsure, Inca did nothing. But she wanted to.

"What is it about you that makes me feel as I do?" she demanded suddenly, her voice strong and challenging.

Eyebrows raising, Roan stared down at her. The way her petulant lips were set, the spark of challenge in her eyes, made him smile a little at her boldness. "What do you mean? Do I make you feel bad? Uncomfortable?"

"No...just the opposite. I like being close to you. You remind me of a big tree with large, spreading branches—arms that reach out and protect people."

"That's my nature," Roan said in a low tone. He saw her eyes narrow with confusion for a moment. Her tentative feelings for him were genuine and his heart soared wildly with that knowledge. Roan knew instinctively that Inca was an innocent. He realized she was a virgin, in more ways than one. Her relationship skills were not honed. Yet the honest way she had reached out to him touched his heart as nothing else ever could.

"You make me feel safe in my world—and in my world there is no safety." Inca's lips twisted wryly. "How can that be?"

"Sometimes," Roan told her gravely, "certain men and women can give one another that gift. It is about trust, too."

Inca sighed. "Oh, trust...yes, that. Grandfather Adaire said until I could trust someone else with my life, that I would never grow. That I was stuck." She frowned and leaned her head back, looking up at the silhouettes of the trees in the darkness surrounding them.

"And what did Grandmother Alaria say?"

Surprised, Inca twisted to look up at him. His eyes gleamed in the darkness, rich with irony and humor. "How do you know she said anything to me?"

"She's the leader of the village, isn't she? I'd think that she'd have something positive to say to you while you're working on the emotional blocks that were created by your being abandoned at birth."

His insight was startling. Inca found herself not feeling

alarmed about it as she normally would. Raising her hands, she said, "Grandmother Alaria said my heart wound was stopping me from trusting, but that, at some point when I was a little older, more mature, I would work on this blockage. She said she had faith in me to do it."

"Because you have a magnificent heart, Inca. That's why she said those words to you."

Deeply touched by his praise, she said, "I am a bad person, Roan. Grandfather Adaire has said that of me many times. A bad person trying to fulfill the Sisterhood of Light's plan to help all my relations here in Amazonia."

Reaching out, Roan captured some errant, crinkled strands of her hair and gently tucked them behind her ear. He saw her eyes mirror surprise and then pleasure. Good, she was beginning to see his touch as something positive in her life. Tonight Inca had opened her heart to him. The trust in him that inspired that made him feel like he was walking on air. The joy that thrummed through him was new and made him breathless.

"You're a good person, Inca. Don't listen to Grandfather Adaire. Good people make mistakes." He frowned and thought of how he hadn't given Sarah his medicine necklace to wear on that fateful climb. Why, oh why, hadn't he followed his instincts? "Guaranteed, they do. Sometimes really disastrous mistakes. But that doesn't make them bad." Just sorry for an eternity, but he didn't mouth those words to Inca. She was suffering enough and didn't need to know from what experience his words came.

Inca gave him a flat look, her mouth twitching. "Then what? If I am not bad, what am I?"

"Human. A terribly vulnerable and beautiful human being…just like me. Like the rest of us.…"

Chapter 8

"They are going to have many of their men injured or killed going through the swamp," Inca said the next morning as she stood beside Roan on a hill that overlooked the thin, straggling column of men a good half mile away. They were well camouflaged by the rain forest. Luckily, the floor of the forest was clear of a lot of thick bushes and ferns, due to the fact that the triple canopy overhead prevented sunlight from reaching the ground. It made marching faster and easier.

"The colonel is bullheaded," he said, turning and looking at her. This morning he felt a change in Inca. Oh, it was nothing obvious, but Roan felt that she was much more at ease with him. It was because of the trust he was building with her. "I wish he'd listen to his son."

Snorting, Inca adjusted the sling of the rifle on her right shoulder. "Julian has more intelligence than his father ever will."

"You like him, don't you?"

With a shrug, Inca said, "He is a gentle person in a machine of war. He does not fit in it. I like his energy. He is a man of peace. My heart aches for him, for all he wants from his father. The colonel is lucky to have Julian. But he does not know that.''

"You don't find many men like that," Roan said, partly teasing. "The peaceful type, that is."

"You are like that."

"Yeah?" He baited her with a growing grin. Just being next to her was making him feel happier than he had a right to be. Roan recalled that Sarah had made him feel that way, too. There was something magical about Inca. She was completely naive to the fact that she was a beautiful young woman. Not many of the men of the company had missed her beauty. Roan had seen them staring openmouthed at her, like wolves salivating after an innocent lamb.

Inca liked the warm smile he turned on her. "Sometimes I think you have been trained by the Jaguar Clan. You handle yourself, your energy, carefully. You do not give it away. You conserve it. You know when to use it and when not to." She found herself wanting to reach out and touch Roan. That act was foreign to her, until now. He stood there in his fatigues, the shirt dampened with sweat and emphasizing his powerful chest and broad shoulders. Recalling his touch, Inca felt warmth stir in her lower body like sunlight warming the chill of the night. An ache centered in her heart as she lifted her gaze to his mouth, which was crooked with that slight, teasing smile. She liked the way Roan looked. His face was strong and uncompromising, like him. When he'd moved to her back and drawn his pistol to protect her from possible harm by the soldiers as she confronted the colonel, she'd been grateful. Not many men would stand their ground like that. Though badly outnumbered, he'd been good at his word; he had protected and cared for her when it counted. He *could* be trusted.

She smiled a little as she watched the army column below. The men were slipping and falling on the damp, leaf-strewn rain forest floor. Inca wanted the colonel to make twenty miles a day, but the men of this company were too soft. They'd be lucky to make ten miles this first day.

"With the way they are crawling along, the Valentinos will be well prepared for them when we finally make it to that valley."

Roan nodded. "The troops aren't in good shape. It will take at least five days to toughen them up. We'll lose a lot of time doing that."

Inca's eyes flashed with anger. "And Colonel Marcellino said these were his *best* troops. Bah. My people would embarrass and shame them. The Indians are tough and have the kind of endurance it takes to move quickly through the forest."

"Well," Roan sighed, his gaze brushing her upturned features, "we'll just have to be patient with them. I'm more worried about what's going to happen when we hit the edge of that swamp two days from now."

Giving the column a look of derision, Inca growled, "Marcellino is going to have many of his men injured. The swamp is nothing but predators waiting for food."

Roan reached out and briefly touched her shoulder. Instantly, he saw her features soften. It was split seconds before she rearranged her face so that he could not see her true feelings. "Do you want to move ahead of the column?"

"Humph. They are many at the pace of a snail," Inca complained as she started gingerly down the slope. "I think I will move ahead to where I think they will straggle to a stop at dusk. We need meat. I will sing a snake song and ask one of the snakes to give its life for us as a meal tonight."

Roan nodded. "You'll find us, I'm sure."

She flashed him a grin as she trotted down the last stretch of slope to the forest floor below. "I will find you," she promised, and took off at a slow jog, weaving among the trees.

Roan smiled to himself. Inca moved with a bonelessness that defied description, her thick braid swinging between her shoulder blades. He thought he saw a black-and-gold jaguar for a moment, trotting near her side. When he blinked again, the image was gone, but Roan knew he wasn't seeing things. His mother had been clairvoyant and he'd managed to inherit some of that gift himself.

Moving along at a brisk walk, Roan opened the blouse of his fatigues, his chest shining with sweat. The humidity was high, and the cooling breeze felt good on his flesh. Planning on moving ahead and remaining with the point guards out in front of the column, he already missed Inca's considerable presence. Yes, he liked her. A lot. More than he should. His heart blossomed with such fierce longing that it caught him by surprise. Inca was like a drug to his system, an addiction. Roan had thought his heart had died when Sarah left him. But that wasn't so, he was discovering. And for the first time in two years, he felt hope. He felt like living once more, but squashed that feeling instantly. The thought of ever falling in love again terrified Roan. The fear of losing someone he loved held him in its icy clutches. He fought his feelings for Inca. He didn't dare fall for her. She lived her life moment to moment. Hers was not a world where one was guaranteed to live to a ripe old age. And compared to Sarah's love of climbing, Inca's career was even more dangerous.

Inca squatted down in front of the open fire. She had found Roan at dusk. He was in the midst of making sure the colonel's column was getting set up for the coming night. As he left the company, she met him near one of the mound-like hills and led him to her chosen hiding spot for the night, in a grove of towering kapok trees. It was easy to hide among the huge, six-to-eight-foot tall, winglike roots. There were smaller trees nearby, and she'd already hung out two hammocks for them to sleep in.

Just seeing Roan made her heart soar. Inca had found that

as she traveled the rest of the day without Roan at her side, she had missed him more than she should. His quiet, powerful presence somehow made her feel more stable. Protected. And that scared her. In her panic, she had left him with the troops instead of staying with him. She was afraid of herself more than him, of the new and uneasy feelings she was now experiencing. No man had made her feel like he did, and Inca simply didn't know what to do with that—or herself.

Inca had called a snake to give its life so that they could eat. It had come and she had killed it, and after praying for the release of the spirit, she had skinned it and placed it on a spit. As it cooked, she looked across the fire at Roan. The shadows carved out every hard line in his angular, narrow face. "I thought about you a lot today after we split up," she said. "It feels odd to me to work with someone." She squarely met his blue eyes, which were hooded and thoughtful looking after she tossed the bombastic comment his way.

"You're used to working alone," he agreed. "My job here is to be your partner." Roan lifted his chin and looked down at the clearing where the Brazilian Army continued to set up camp for the night. They could see the company, but the men there could not see them.

Snorting, Inca tried to ignore his deep, husky baritone voice. Fear ate at her. She decided to bluff him, to scare him off. "I told you before—I was abandoned to die at birth and I will die alone. I work alone. My path is one of being alone." But she knew, whether she liked it or not, she had felt a thrill race through her that Roan had chosen to be at her campsite and not remain with the colonel's company. Pursing her full lips, she concentrated on keeping the four-foot-long snake turning so it would not burn in the low flames. She liked the warmth of the fire against her body as she worked near it. "I do not need you. Go back to the company. That is where you belong, with the other men."

Roan swallowed his shock. Where was this coming from?

Until now, Inca had seemed happy with his presence. What had changed? Had he said something to her this morning? Roan wasn't sure. Seeing the fear in Inca's eyes, he realized she was pushing him away. If he didn't have the directive from Morgan Trayhern, he'd respect her request, but leaving her alone was not an option. Roan had given Mike Houston his word to protect Inca, and he sure couldn't do that if he was half a mile from her campsite at night. Clearing his throat, he said softly, "Everyone needs someone at some point in their life."

Inca scowled as she continued to deftly turn the meat over the fire. Her heart thudded with fear. Her bluff was not working. "That is not my experience. Jaguars, for the most part, live alone. The only time they see one of their own kind is during mating season, and they split shortly thereafter. The female jaguar goes through her pregnancy and birthing alone, and raises her cubs—alone." She lifted her head and glared across the fire at Roan. "I do not need a partner to do what I do here in Amazonia."

"Because?"

Anger riffled through Inca. The expression on Roan's face told her he wasn't going to budge on this issue. Her black brows dipped. "You have an annoying habit of asking too many questions."

"How else am I to know how you feel?" Roan decided to meet her head-on. He found himself unwilling to give up her hard-earned trust so easily.

"I am not used to showing my feelings to anyone." She raised her voice to a low, warning growl. Usually, such an action was enough to scare off even the bravest of men. Inca recalled vividly how Roan had found her weeping yesterday and how his touch had been soothing and healing to her. When she looked up again, she saw his blue eyes had softened with interest—in her. That set her back two paces and she felt panicky inside. Roan was not scared off like the male idiots she'd had the sorry misfortune to encounter thus far in her life. And maybe that was the problem: Roan Walker was *not* the usual male she was used to dealing with. That thought was highly unsettling.

"I'm not either, so I know how you feel," Roan murmured. "Sometimes, when we're in so much pain, we need another person there just to hold us, rock us and let us know that we're loved, anyway, despite how we're feeling."

Love? Where had that word come from? Reaching out, Roan placed two more small sticks of wood on the fire. Light and shadows danced across her pain-filled face. A flash of annoyance and then fear laced with curiosity haunted her lovely willow-green eyes. He smiled to himself. Roan felt her powerful and intense curiosity in him as a man. He sensed her uneasiness around him and also her yearning.

More than anything, Roan needed to continue to cultivate her trust of him. Unless he could keep her trust, she would do as she damned well pleased and would leave him behind in an instant—which was exactly what Mike Houston and Morgan Trayhern didn't want to happen. Especially with that trigger-happy Brazilian colonel looking for Inca's head on a platter and the multimillion dollar reward he'd collect once he had it. And then the colonel would have his revenge for his eldest son's death at Inca's hands. No, it was important Roan be able to act as her shield—another set of eyes and ears to keep danger at bay, and Inca safe.

The snake meat began to sizzle and pop as the juices leaked out. With a swipe of her index finger, Inca quickly began to catch them before they fell into the fire. Each time she put her finger into her mouth and sucked on it, making a growling sound of pleasure.

"This is good...."

Roan smiled a little, enjoying her obvious enjoyment of such small but important things in her life. "So tell me," he began conversationally as he watched her sit back on her heels and continue to expertly turn the meat, "why do you distrust men so much?"

Inca laughed harshly. "Why *should* I trust them? Many of them are pigs. Brazilian men think they *own* their wives like slaves." She glared up at him. "No man owns a woman. No man has the right to slap or strike a woman or child, and yet they do it all the time in Brazil. A woman cannot speak up. If she risks it, her husband can strike her. If she so much as looks at another man, the husband, by law, has the right to murder her on the spot. Of course, any married man is allowed to have all the affairs he wants without any reprisal. To other men, he has machismo. Pah." Her voice deepened to a snarl. "I see nothing good in that kind of man. All they can do is dominate or destroy children and women. I will not be touched by them. I will not allow one to think that he can so much as lift a hand in my direction. I will not allow any man to dictate what I should or should not say. And if I want to look at a man, that is my right to do so, for the men here stare at women all the time."

"That's called a double standard in North American."

Curling her upper lip, she rasped, "Call it what you want. Men like that mean destruction. They manipulate others, and they want power *over* someone else. I see it all the time. I walk through one of my villages, and I see what drug dealers have done to those who will not bend to their threats and violence. I see children dead. I see women shot in the head because they refuse to give these men their bodies in payment for whatever they need."

"That's not right," Roan agreed quietly. He heard her stridency, saw the rage in her eyes. It was righteous rage, he acknowledged. And while he was a stranger to Brazil, he had heard of the laws condoning the shooting of a wife who looked at another man. And he'd also heard from Mike Houston that husbands here often had a mistress on the side, as a matter of course.

"Many men are not *right*." She pointed to her breasts beneath the thin olive-green tank top she wore. Earlier, she'd taken off her bandoliers and hung them on a low branch nearby. "All they can do is stare here—" she jabbed at her breasts "—and slobber like dogs in heat. You would think they had never seen a woman's breasts before! Their tongues hang out. It is disgusting! Yesterday, the soldiers stared at me when I walked into camp to challenge Colonel Marcellino."

Raising his brows, Roan nodded. With the bandoliers of ammo set aside, he had to admit that the thin cotton did outline her small, firm breasts beautifully.

"I have watched you," Inca said, slowly rising to her full height, the skewer in hand. "And not once have you stared at my breasts like they always do. Why not?"

Chuckling to himself, Roan reveled in Inca's naive honesty. He watched as she walked over to her pack. There was an old, beat-up tin plate beside it. She squatted down and, sliding the huge knife from its scabbard at her hip, cut the meat into segments and removed them from the skewer. Putting the skewer aside, she picked up the plate and stood up.

"Well?" she demanded as she walked back to him, "why do you not stare at me like they do?"

Roan nodded his thanks as she set the tin plate between them. Inca squatted nearby and quickly picked up a steaming hot chunk of meat with her fingers. There was such a natural grace to her. She was a wild thing, more animal than woman with that feral glint in her eyes.

Reaching for a piece of the roast white meat, he murmured, "Where I come from, it's impolite to stare at a woman like that."

"Impolite?" Inca exploded with laughter, her lips pulling away from her strong, white teeth. "Rude! Piglike! Even in nature—" she swept her arm dramatically around the jungle that enclosed them "—male pigs do not salivate like that over a female pig!"

Roan looked at her as he popped a piece of meat into his mouth. It tasted good, almost like chicken, he thought as he relaxed and watched the firelight lovingly caress her profile.

Her hair was frayed and it softened the angularity of her thin, high cheekbones. She was more sinew and bone than flesh. There was no fat whatsoever on Inca. She was slender like a willow, and each hand or finger movement she made reminded him of a ballet dancer.

"So the men from your tribe do not stare at a woman's breasts?"

He shook his head and took a second chunk of snake meat from the plate. "Let's just say that men of my nation consider women their equals in every way. They aren't..." he paused, searching for the right words "...sexual objects to be stared at, abused or hurt in any way."

She gave him a sizzling sidelong look. "Pity that you cannot teach these Brazilian soldiers a thing or two! I would just as soon put a boot between their legs when they stare and slobber like that, to remind them of the manners they do not possess."

"Try and refrain from that," Roan suggested dryly, hiding a grin desperately trying to tug at one corner of his mouth. "We need their cooperation. I can't have you injuring them like that. We wouldn't make twenty miles a day in this jungle if you did."

Throwing back her head, Inca laughed deeply, the juice of the meat glistening along her lower lip. With the back of her hand, she wiped her mouth clean. "These men, with kicks between their legs or not, will *never* make ten miles a day. They are out of shape. Unfit weaklings."

Roan didn't disagree. "You're right. We'll be lucky to make ten miles a day until they get their legs under them."

With a snort, Inca wiped her long fingers across her jungle fatigues. "They are city boys. They are not hard. They cannot take this hill climbing and humidity. They pant like old dogs with weak, trembling hind legs."

Chuckling, Roan motioned to the last piece of meat in the tin. "It's yours. Eat it."

Inca shook her head. "You have eaten too little today.

You are larger and heavier than me. If you are to keep up with me again tomorrow, this will give you strength." She jabbed with her finger. "Eat it." Rising, she stretched fitfully. "You were the only one to keep my pace." She eyed him with respect and acknowledged that although he towered over her, he was lean, tight and hard muscled. There was a litheness to him that reminded her of a jaguar fit for territorial combat. She liked the humor she saw glinting in his eyes as he took the last piece of meat and bit into it. Pleased that he would take directions from her, Inca walked slowly around the fire as she peered out into the darkness that now surrounded them.

"So how does your tribe see women, then? I am curious."

Roan nearly choked on the meat as he looked up at her. She stood proudly, her shoulders thrown back, the thick braid lying across one shoulder, her chin lifted at an imperious, confident angle once again. Her green eyes glimmered as her gaze caught and held him captive. Her hands rested comfortably on her hips as she stared down at him waiting for him to answer. Swallowing the meat, he rasped, "We see a woman like a fruit tree filled with gifts of beauty and bounty."

"Fruit tree?" Inca saw the sudden seriousness in his eyes and knew he was not joking with her. Why was he so different? And intriguing? Allowing her hands to slip gracefully from her hips, she moved back to where he remained in a squatting position. Taking a seat on a nearby log, she held her hands out toward the fire and savored the heat from it.

Wiping his hands on his fatigues, Roan twisted to look in Inca's direction. He saw that she was genuinely interested and that made him feel good. He hungered for deep, searching conversation with her and about her. "All life comes from Mother Earth," he began, and he patted the damp, fallen leaves on the soil next to where he was crouching. "We see women as a natural extension of Mother Earth.

They are the only ones who are fertile, who can carry and birth a baby. I was taught a long time ago that a fruit tree, which can bear blossoms, be impregnated by a honeybee and then bear fruit, is a good symbol for women. Women are the fruit of our earth. For me, as a man, a woman is a gift. I do not assume that a fruit tree or a woman wants to share her fruit with me. We always give a gift and then ask if the tree—or the woman—wants to share her bounty with us. If she or the tree says yes, then that's fine. If she says no, that's fine, also.''

Inca rested her chin on her closed hands. She planted her elbows on her thighs and pondered his explanation. "Women and trees being one and the same..."

"Symbolically speaking, yes." Roan saw the pensive expression on her face, the pouting of her lower lip as she considered his words. The firelight danced and flickered across her smooth, golden features, highlighting her cheekbones and wrinkled brow. She was part child, part wise woman, part animal. And at any given moment, any one of those facets could emerge to speak with him. He found her exciting and had to contain the thrill he felt. But, Roan also felt her hatred and distrust of the Brazilian military, and he couldn't blame her at all for her defensive stance around them. After all, they had a high bounty on her head—dead or alive.

As she stared into the fire, lost in thought, Roan tore his gaze from Inca. She was too easy to savor, as if she were a priceless, rare flower. Too easy to emotionally gorge himself. If he took too much, it would destroy her pristine, one-of-a-kind beauty. Besides, he knew Inca did not like to be stared at; but then again, he didn't like it either. He wondered if it was their Indian blood that made them feel that their energy was being stolen when someone stared. Anglos certainly didn't get it, but he understood Inca's unhappiness. Still, she was incredibly beautiful and there wasn't a man in that military contingent that wasn't smitten by her drop-dead-gorgeous looks. Inca was as natural and wild as the rain forest that surrounded them with its humid embrace. Roan had seen more than a few looks of lust in those soldiers' eyes today as they marched and talked animatedly about her dramatic entrance to their camp the night before. And he knew Inca sensed their lust and was completely disgusted by it.

Inca's husky voice intruded upon his reverie.

"Then, if you see women as fruit trees—" she turned and stared at him fully "—how do you see their breasts?"

She asked the damnedest questions. Roan understood it was innocent curiosity, her obvious naïveté of men and the world outside this rain forest. Opening his hands, he said, "I can only speak for myself on this, Inca."

"Yes?" she demanded, goading him impatiently.

"A woman's breasts remind me of warm, sun-ripe peaches."

Her brows knitted. "Peaches? What is a peach? Do they grow here in South America?"

Shrugging, he said, "I don't know. They do where I live."

"Tell me about this peach. Describe it. Does it look like a breast?"

A slight smile curved his mouth. Staring into the fire in order not to make the mistake of looking at her too long, he murmured, "A peach is about the size of my palm," and he held it up for her to look at. "It's an incredible fruit. It's round in shape and when you lean close and smell it, well, it has the sweetest fragrance. When it's ripe, it's firm and has a soft fine fuzz all over it. The colors take your breath away. It's often a clear pinkish gold, but that graduates into red-orange, and orange, or to apricot or a bright sun-gold." He closed his eyes, picturing the fruit. "When I see a ripe, sun-warmed peach on the branch of a tree, all I want to do is reach out and cup my fingers around it, feel those soft, nubby hairs sliding against my fingertips. I want to test the firmness, the roundness and the heat of it as I continue to encircle it...."

Inca felt her breasts tighten and she sat up, surprised. What was going on? She gave him a disgruntled look. Roan sat there, his hands clasped between his opened thighs, his head lifted slightly and his eyes closed. What would it be like to feel him slide those long, large-knuckled, work-worn fingers around her breasts? Instantly, her skin tingled wildly. She felt her nipples harden and pucker beneath her shirt. A wonderful, molten ache began to pool through her lower body as she continued to stare at his hard, angular profile. It was as if her body had a life of its own! And worse, it was responding on its own to his husky, melting words, which seemed to reach out and caress her like a lover.

Scowling, Inca sat there. She'd never had a lover. She couldn't describe what having one was like. Yet his deep, rumbling words continued to touch her almost physically. Her breasts felt hot, felt achy, and she wanted Roan to reach out and caress them! The thought was so foreign to her that Inca gasped.

Roan opened his eyes and slowly turned his head in Inca's direction. He saw a pink stain on her cheeks. He saw her startled expression, and the way her lips parted provocatively, looking so very, very damn kissable. What would it be like to kiss that wild, untamed mouth of hers? How would she feel beneath his mouth? Hot? Strong? Fierce? Hungry? Or starving, like he felt for her? As Inca turned to meet and hold his gaze, Roan sensed her chagrin, her embarrassment and—something else he couldn't quite put his finger on. If he wasn't mistaken, the gold flecks in her willow-green eyes hinted of desire—for him. The impression he received from her was that she wanted him to reach out with his fingers, touch the sides of her breasts, caress them and... With a shake of his head, he wondered what the hell was happening.

It was as if he was reading Inca's thoughts and feelings in her wide, vulnerable-looking eyes during that fragile moment. He saw that her nipples were pressed urgently against the material of her shirt and he could see the outline of the proud, firm breasts that he ached to encircle, tease and then suckle until she twisted with utterly, wanton pleasure in his arms. Roan wanted to be the man to introduce Inca to the realm of love. It was a molten thought. She had never been touched by any man, he knew. A virgin in her mid-twenties, she was a wild woman who would never entertain the touch of a mere mortal, that was for sure.

Inca tore her gaze from Roan's dark, hooded stare. She felt a lush, provocative heat radiating from him toward her. Because she was of the Jaguar Clan, her six senses were acutely honed. For a moment, she'd allowed her mind and heart to touch his. When it had, she'd seen the flare of surprise and then his smoldering, very male look in return. Inca understood in that split second that Roan could touch her in a way she'd never before experienced...and the sensation was galvanizing, aching, filled with promise—yet it scared her.

Heart palpitating wildly in her chest, Inca stared, disgruntled, into the fire. Suddenly breathless beneath that glittering look in his blue eyes—one that reminded her of lightning striking the earth—she was at a loss for words. Her skin tightened deliciously around her breasts. She felt needy. She felt hungry for *his* touch. A man's touch. Of all things! Inca could not reconcile that within herself. Her mind railed against it. Her heart was wide-open, crying out for the intimate touch he promised her in that one look, in that one touch with his mind and heart. Closing her eyes, she hid her face in her hands momentarily.

"I am tired," she muttered. "I must sleep now." Getting up quickly, she moved around the massive root to where she had placed her hammock.

Roan heard the turmoil in her tone. He sat very still because she appeared to be poised like a wild horse ready to spook and hightail it. What had happened? He swore he'd felt her very real presence inside his head—and even more so, in his expanding heart. For an instant, Inca had been *in* him, somehow—attached to or connected to his thoughts and feelings as if… Stymied, Roan wished he could talk to Houston about this experience.

Something had happened, because when Inca had lifted her face and her hands fell away, he'd seen the fear in her eyes. Fear and…did he dare put the name desire to it, also? Was that smoldering, banked desire in her cloudy gaze aimed at him? Very unsure, Roan muttered, "Yeah, we both need to turn in and get some sleep. Tomorrow is going to be a rough day."

In more ways than one, he thought as he rose to his feet. *In more ways than one…*

Chapter 9

Inca halted in her tracks and gulped. It was the third morning of the march into the swamp, and she had gone down a hill to wash herself before the day's activities began. Only, Roan had beat her to the enchanting place. He stood out in the middle of a shallow pool that had been created by the seasonal winter rains. Though the pool was small now, it was just large enough for a person to be able to grasp the white sand surrounding it, and scrub his flesh clean before rinsing off in the knee-deep waters. Hiding behind a tree, her hand resting tentatively against the smooth, gray bark, Inca found herself unable to resist watching Roan's magnificent nakedness as he bathed. Surprise and then pleasurable, molten heat flowed through her.

Inca was torn. She *should* leave. Oh, she knew what men looked like, but an unbidden curiosity and something else was tempting her to remain hidden and devour Roan with her eyes. His clothes were hung on the limb of a nearby rubber tree. He was sluicing the clear, cooling water across his thick, broad shoulders and well-sprung chest, which was covered with a dark carpet of black hair. Gulping unsteadily, she dropped her gaze lower…and lower…then just as quickly, Inca looked away. Disgusted with herself, she spun around and placed her back against the tree, her arms wrapped tightly across against her chest. Nostrils flaring, she told herself she shouldn't be doing this.

Heart pounding, Inca felt that warm, uncoiling sensation deep in her body. It was a wonderful, new feeling that seemed to blossom within her when she was around Roan. She had not been able to bully or scare him off. He'd stayed at her side like a faithful dog would its master, and Inca had grudgingly given up on trying to get him to go back to the company of men. The last two days had cemented their relationship to the point where Inca felt the last of her defenses toward him dissolving. Oh, it was nothing he did directly, just those smoldering looks he gave her from time to time, that crooked smile that heated her spirit and made it fly, his sense of humor and ability to laugh.

She heard him singing, his voice an engaging baritone. The forest around the pool area absorbed most of the sound as he chanted in a language that was foreign to her. Understanding it was a ceremonial song of his people, to greet the rising sun, she slowly turned around and peeked from behind the tree. Both hands on the trunk to steady herself, Inca watched as he leaned down, grabbed some sand from the bottom of the pool and briskly began to scrub his chest. There was something vulnerable and boyish about Roan in that molten moment. Gulping hard, Inca found herself wondering what it would be like to slide her fingers through that dark hair splayed out across his broad, well-developed chest. Or to allow her hands to range downward in exploration.…

Making a strangled sound, Inca jerked away and dug the toe of her boot into the soft, muddy earth. She had to get out of here! Hurrying silently up the hill in a line that would hide her from his view, she wiped her lips with the back of her hand. Her whole world was crumbling because of Roan.

She could not keep him at bay. She melted a little more each time he shared an intimate glance with her, or smiled at her.... So many little things were unraveling her mighty defenses!

Panicked by all that she was feeling, because she'd never felt it before, Inca had no one to turn to to ask what was going on inside her. She wished one of the Jaguar Clan mothers who had raised her were still alive. They'd been old women when they nursed her from babyhood to girlhood. They were all gone now, having long ago walked across the Threshold to the other worlds. Again the biting reminder that she was alone, abandoned by everyone, sank into her.

Back in their makeshift camp, Inca hurriedly removed her dark green nylon hammock from between two trees and stuffed it in the bag she would carry across her shoulders. If only she hadn't been banished from the Jaguar Clan village. Inca yearned to talk to Grandmother Alaria. Yes, Grandmother Alaria would understand what was going on inside her. Grandfather Adaire, however, would block her entrance to the village and tell her to leave—or else deliver the worst punishment of all: ban her forever not just from the village but from the Jaguar Clan. Inca couldn't tolerate the thought of being forced to give up the one thing that she'd been raised to do all her life—work as a healer for her people.

"Your turn."

Inca gasped. She dropped the hammock and spun around, caught off guard. Roan stood behind her, dressed in his fatigues, his upper chest naked, the towel draped over his head as he casually dried his dark hair. She saw the sparkle in his blue eyes. Gulping, she realized he knew she'd seen him bathing. Heat rolled up her neck and into her face. She avoided his tender look. There was no laughter, no censure in his eyes. Indeed, he seemed to understand what she'd done and why. Inca wished she did.

"I—it was an accident," she stammered, nervously picking up her hammock and rapidly jamming it into her small canvas pack.

"Of course," Roan murmured. The rosy flush in her cheeks made Inca unbearably beautiful to him. He saw the surprise, the shame and humiliation in her darkening eyes. "Accidents happen. I wasn't upset."

Lifting her head, she twisted to look in his direction. "You weren't?" She would be.

Wiping his brow dry, Roan hung the small, dark green towel on a branch to dry. Not that it would dry much in this humidity. Shrugging on his fatigue blouse, he rolled up the arms on each sleeve to his elbow. "No."

"I would not like someone coming upon me as I washed."

"That's different." He smiled as she straightened. Inca was not the confident warrior now. Instead she was a young woman, unsure of herself, of her relationship to him, and possibly, Roan ruminated, of what she was feeling toward him. He knew, without question, that Inca was drawn to him like a bee to sweet honey. And he was no less smitten with her even though he was trying desperately to ignore his feelings toward her. Constantly, Roan had to harshly remind himself that they had a mission to complete. He refused to fall in love with another woman. He would not indulge in his growing, powerful feelings for her. Having to cap them, sit on them and ignore them was becoming a daily hell for him. It was a sweet hell, however. Inca was precious to him in all ways—from the smallest gesture to her great unselfishness toward others who were less fortunate than her.

"Humph," Inca said as she grabbed her towel and moved quickly toward the pool. "I will return."

Buttoning his shirt, Roan grinned to himself. When he heard the snap and crackle of boots crushing small sticks that had fallen from the canopy above, he knew someone was coming. Moving out from behind a tree, he saw it was

Julian. The young officer's face was flushed and he had a worried look.

"Good morning," Roan greeted him, placing the towel on top of his pack.

"*Bom dia*, good morning," Julian said, breathing hard. "I just wanted to tell Inca that she was right. Coming into this swamp is creating a disaster of unexpected proportions." He stopped, removed his cap and wiped his brow with his arm. Looking back toward where the company was preparing to march, he continued. "I tried to talk to my father this morning. We have ten men down with malaria symptoms. We have another five with dysentery. And six from yesterday that have assorted sprained ankles or knees from falling and slipping." He shook his head. "I don't know what to do...."

Roan patted the shorter man on the shoulder. "There isn't much you can do, Julian. We're halfway through the swamp." Looking up, he saw a patch of bright blue sky. It looked as if the weather was going to be sunny. That meant it would be very hot today, and with the humidity around ninety-five percent at all times, the stress on the men would be great. "How about heat exhaustion? How many cases?"

"My *médico*, Sargento Salvador, says we have fifteen men who are down. We need to get a helicopter in here, but we are too far into the jungle for them to land. One of the other officers is taking all the injured and sick back to the edge of the swamp. From there, they will march to the river, where the helicopters will fly in and take them to the nearest hospital, which is located in Manaus."

"A lot of technical problems," Roan agreed somberly. He reached down and removed his tin cup, which had coffee in it that had been warming over the last of the coals of their morning campfire. He offered some to Julian, who shook his head.

"Does Inca know any *quick* way out of this swamp? Is there any way we can get out of it now?"

Roan shrugged and sipped his coffee. "She said there is none. That was the problem. Once you committed to this route, there was no way out except back or straight ahead."

"Damn," Julian rasped. "Very well. I am lead point with my squad today. We will be working with you and Inca." He smiled a little, his eyes dark with worry. "I'm afraid we'll lose many more men today to this heat. There's no cloud cover...."

"Just keep them drinking a lot of water, with frequent rests," Roan advised solemnly.

"My father wants out of the swamp. He's pushing the men beyond their physical limits. I can try, but he's in command...."

Roan nodded grimly. "Then we will just have to do the best we can to get through this."

Inca moved silently. It was dusk and she was watching the weary soldiers of the company erect their tents and reluctantly dig in for the coming night. Perspiration covered her. It had been a hot, humid, brutal day. She saw Colonel Marcellino in the distance. He was shouting at Julian, who stood stiffly at attention. Her heart broke for the young officer. She liked Julian. Why did his father have to treat him so cruelly? Did he not realize how fragile life was? They could all die in a minute in this deadly swamp.

She felt Roan coming, and leaned against a tree trunk and waited for him. The day had been hard on everyone. Even he, with his athleticism and strength, looked fatigued tonight. She nodded to him as he saw her. When he gave her a tired smile in return, her heart opened. Crossing her arms, she leaned languidly against the tree. Roan halted about a foot away from her, his hands coming to rest on his hips.

"They look pretty exhausted," he muttered.

"They are. How many men went down today?"

"Twenty more to various things—malaria, dysentery and heat exhaustion."

"Humph." Brows knitting, Inca watched as Julian was dismissed. He disappeared quickly between the tents that were being raised. "The colonel is an old man and a fool. He will lose as many tomorrow, before we get out of this place."

Scratching his head, Roan studied her in the soft dusk light. She had discarded her bandoliers and her rifle back at their recently made camp. Tendrils of hair stuck to her temples, and her long, thick braid was badly frayed by the high humidity. The soft pout of her lips, her half-closed eyes, made Roan want her as he'd never wanted another woman. He hoped she wasn't reading his mind. Inca had told him she rarely read other people's thoughts because it took much energy and focus. Most people's thoughts were garbage anyway, she told him wryly. Roan sighed. Well, Inca was tired, there was no doubt. There were faint shadows beneath her large eyes. The heat had been brutal even on her, and she lived here year-round.

There was a sudden scream, and then a hail of gunfire within the camp. A number of men were running around, screaming, yelling and brandishing their weapons. More shots were fired.

Inca stood up, suddenly on guard. "What...?"

Roan moved protectively close, his hand on her shoulder, his eyes narrowed. The company of men looked like a disturbed beehive. There were more screams. More shouts. More gunfire. "I don't know...."

Keying her hearing, Inca heard someone shout, *"Médico! Médico!"*

"Someone is hurt," Inca said, her voice rising with concern. "Who, I do not know. There are no drug runners around, so what is going on?"

Before Roan could speak, he saw one of the point soldiers they'd worked with today, Ramone, come racing toward them. The point patrol always knew where they had their camp for the night. The look of terror etched on his young

Get 2

HOW TO GET YOUR
2 FREE BOOKS AND FREE GIFT

1. Peel off the 2 FREE BOOKS seal from the front cover. Place it in the space provided at right. This automatically entitles you to receive two free books and an exciting mystery gift.

2. Send back this card and you'll get 2 "The Best of the Best™" novels. These books have a combined cover price of $11.00 or more in the U.S. and $13.00 or more in Canada, but they are yours to keep absolutely FREE!

3. There's <u>no</u> catch. You're under <u>no</u> obligation to buy anything. We charge nothing – ZERO – for your first shipment. And you don't have to make any minimum number of purchases – not even one!

4. We call this line "The Best of the Best" because each month you'll receive the best books by the world's hottest authors. These authors show up time and time again on all the major bestseller lists and their books sell out as soon as they hit the stores. You'll like the convenience of getting them delivered to your home at our discount prices…and you'll love your subscriber newsletter featuring author news, horoscopes, recipes, book reviews and much more!

5. We hope that after receiving your free books you'll want to remain a subscriber. But the choice is yours – to continue or cancel, anytime at all! So why not take us up on our invitation, with no risk of any kind. You'll be glad you did!

6. And remember…we'll send you a mystery gift ABSOLUTELY FREE just for giving "The Best of the Best" a try!

®

MIRA

SPECIAL FREE GIFT!

We'll send you a fabulous mystery gift, absolutely FREE, simply for accepting our no-risk offer!

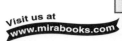

Visit us at
www.mirabooks.com

Books FREE!

DETACH AND MAIL CARD TODAY!

HURRY! Return this card
promptly to get
2 FREE Books
and a
FREE Gift!

The Best of the Best™

YES! Please send me the
2 FREE "The Best of the Best" novels
and FREE gift for which I qualify. I
understand that I am under no
obligation to purchase anything
further, as explained on the
opposite page.

Affix
peel-off
2 FREE BOOKS
sticker here.

P-BB1-00
385 MDL CY2W

185 MDL CY2X

| | | | | | | | | | | | | | | | | | | | |

NAME   (PLEASE PRINT CLEARLY)

ADDRESS

APT.#   CITY

STATE/PROV.   ZIP/POSTAL CODE

The Best of the Best™—Here's How it Works

Accepting your 2 free books and gift places you under no obligation to buy anything. You may keep the books and gift and return the shipping statement marked "cancel." If you do not cancel, about a month later we will send you 4 additional novels and bill you just $4.24 each in the U.S., or $4.74 each in Canada, plus 25¢ delivery per book and applicable sales tax, if any.* That's the complete price, and — compared to cover prices of $5.50 or more each in the U.S. and $6.50 or more each in Canada — it's quite a bargain! You may cancel at any time, but if you choose to continue, every month we'll send you 4 more books, which you may either purchase at the discount price…or return to us and cancel your subscription.
*Terms and prices subject to change without notice. Sales tax applicable in N.Y. Canadian residents will be charged applicable provincial taxes and GST.

face made Roan grip Inca a little more securely. "Let's see what's going on."

Inca agreed. She liked the touch of his hand on her shoulder. He stood like a protective guard, his body close and warm, and she hungrily absorbed his nearness.

Both of them stepped out into the path of the running, panting soldier. He cried out their names.

"Inca! We need you! Tenente Marcellino! A bushmaster snake bit him! Hurry! He will die!"

Stunned, Inca tore from beneath Roan's hand. She knew she wasn't supposed to enter the colonel's camp. She was unarmed, and risking her own life because the colonel was capable of killing her.

"Inca!" Too late. Roan cursed. He saw her sprint down the trail, heading directly for where the men were running around and shouting. *Damn.* Roan gripped the soldier by the arm. "Let's go. Show me where he's lying." Roan was a paramedic, but he didn't have antivenin in his medical pack. He wasn't even sure there was antivenin for the poison of a bushmaster. As he ran with Ramone, who was stumbling badly, he mentally went over the procedure for snakebite. This particular snake was deadly, he knew. No one survived a bite. No one. He saw Inca disappear between two tents. Digging in his toes, Roan plunged past the faltering and gasping soldier.

Julian Marcellino was lying on the ground near his tent, next to the brackish water of the swamp, and gripping his thigh. Blood oozed from between his white fingers. No more than three feet away lay a dead bushmaster snake that he'd killed with his pistol. Julian's eyes were glazing over as Inca leaned over him. The *médico,* Sargento Salvador, had tears in his eyes as he knelt on the other side of the semiconscious officer.

"I can't save him!" Salvador cried as Inca dropped to her knees opposite him.

"Be quiet!" Inca snarled. Out of the corner of her eye,

she saw Roan running up to her at the same time Jaime Marcellino did. "Move away!" she shouted. "Give me room. Be quiet! All of you!"

The men quickly hushed and made a wide semicircle around Julian. All eyes riveted upon Inca, who studied the two fang punctures as she gently removed Julian's hand from his thigh.

"Uhh," Julian gasped. His eyes rolled in his head. He saw darkness approaching. Inca was watching him intently through her slitted gaze. Her mouth was compressed. "I—I'm going to die...." he told her in a rasping tone.

"Julian," Inca growled, "be still! Close your eyes. Whatever you do, do *not* cross the Threshold! Do you understand me? It is important not to walk across it."

"Stop!" Jaime screamed as he ran toward them. "Do not touch my son!" He saw Inca place one hand over Julian's heart and the other on the top of his head. His son lay prostrate and unmoving. His flesh, once golden, was now leached out like the color of bones found in the high desert of Peru.

Roan jerked the colonel's arm back as he reached out to haul Inca away from where she knelt over Julian.

"No, Colonel! Let Inca try and help him," Roan ordered tightly.

Glaring, the colonel fought to free himself from Roan's grip. "Let me go, damn you! She'll murder him, too! She's a murderer!" His voice carried in the sudden eerie calm of the camp as the men stood watching the exchange.

Breathing hard, Roan pulled the pistol from his holster and pressed the barrel against the colonel's sweaty temple. "Damn you, stand still or I'll take you down here and now. Inca isn't going to kill Julian. If anything, she's the only thing standing between him and death right now. Let her try and heal him!"

Jaime felt the cold metal pressed against his temple. He saw Storm Walker's eyes narrow with deadly earnestness.

Yes, this man would shoot him. Sobbing, he looked down at Julian, who was unconscious now, his mouth slack, his eyes rolled back in his head.

Roan looked around. "No one move!" he roared. "Let Inca do her work."

Taking a deep, steadying breath, Inca leaned close to Julian. With one hand on his heart, the other on top of his head, she silently asked her guardian to come over her. She felt the incredible power of her guide as he did so. The moment he was in place, much like a glove fitting over a hand, she could see through his eyes. A powerful, whirling motion took place, and she felt herself being sucked down counterclockwise into a vortex of energy. In seconds, she stood in the tunnel of light. They were at the Threshold. Breathing hard and trying to hold her focus and not allow outside sounds to disrupt her necessary concentration, Inca saw Julian standing nearby. Two light beings, his guardians, were on the other side of the Threshold. Moving to them directly, she asked, "May I bring him back?"

Under Jaguar Clan laws, if the light beings said no, then she must allow his spirit to cross over, and he would die, physically. Inca had only once in her life made the mistake of disobeying that directive when she'd brought Michael Houston back from this place. He should have died. But she'd decided to take things into her own hands. And because she was young and only partly trained, she had died physically doing it. Only Grandmother Alaria's power and persuasion had brought her back to life that fateful day so long ago.

Inca waited patiently. She saw the light beings convene. Julian was looking at them. She saw the yearning on his face to walk across that golden area that served as the border between the dimensions.

"If you decide to bring him back to your world," one of the light beings warned, "you may die in the process. He is full of poison. You must run it quickly through your own body, or you will die. Do you understand?''

Inca nodded. ''Yes, I do.'' In her business as a healer, she had to take on the symptoms, in this case, the deadly snake venom, and run it through her own body in order to get rid of it. She would certainly perish if not for the power of her jaguar guardian, who would assist her with his energy in the process, draining it back into Mother Earth, who could absorb it. If it was done fast enough, she might survive.

''Then ask him to return. His tasks are not yet complete.''

Inca held out her hand to Julian. ''Come, Julian. I will bring you home. You have work to do, my young friend.''

''I don't want to return.''

Inca saw the tears in the young officer's eyes. ''I know,'' she quavered unsteadily. ''It is because of your father.''

''He doesn't love me!'' Julian cried out, the tears splattering down his face. ''I am so distraught. I drew the snake to me, to bite me. I can't stand the pain any longer!''

Inca knew that when things in life were very tough on a person, they sometimes drew an accident to them in order to break the pattern, the energy block they were wrestling with. By creating an accident, the gridlock was released and the person was allowed to work, in a new way, on the problem they'd chosen to learn from and work through. ''I understand,'' she told Julian in a soothing voice. Stretching out her fingertips, Inca moved slowly toward him. ''Come, Julian, take my hand. I will bring you back. Your father loves you.''

''No, he doesn't!'' Julian sobbed. He turned toward the light beings on the other side. ''I want to go. I want to cross. He's never loved me! He only loved Rafael. I tried so hard, Inca…so hard to have him love me. To say he loved me, or to show me he cares just a fraction of how he cared for Rafael. But he treats me as if I'm not there. That is why I want to leave.''

Inca took another, deliberate step forward. ''You cannot.

You *must* come back with me, Julian. Now." Once he touched her outstretched fingers, he had committed to coming back. Julian didn't know that, but Inca did. It was a cosmic law. Halfheartedly, he took her hand.

"I don't know…" he sobbed.

"I do." And Inca forced the darkness she saw inhabiting his body to funnel up through her hand and into her body. She was literally willing the snake venom into herself. Instantly, she groaned. She felt the deadly power of the poison. Losing sight of Julian, of the light, Inca felt as if someone had smashed into her chest with a huge fist. Gasping, she tightened her grip around Julian's hand. She knew if she lost him at this critical phase, that his spirit would wander the earth plane forever without a physical body. *Hold on!*

Roan heard Inca groan. She sagged against Julian, her head resting on his chest, her eyes tightly shut. Her mouth was contorted in a soundless cry. Worriedly, he sensed something was wrong. Marcellino moved, and Roan tightened his grip on the officer's arm. "Stay right where you are," he snarled, the pistol still cocked at his temple.

"My son!" Jaime suddenly cried, hope in his voice. He reached out toward Julian. "Look! Look! My God! Color is returning to his face! It is a *miracle!*"

Roan shot a glance toward Julian. Yes, it was true. Color was flooding back into Julian's once pasty face. The men whispered. They collectively made a sound of awe as Julian's lashes fluttered and he opened his eyes slightly.

But something else was wrong. Terribly wrong. Inca was limp against Julian. Her skin tone went from gold to an alarming white, pasty color. Roan felt a tremendous shift in energy—a wrenching sensation that was almost palpable, as if a lightning bolt had struck them. The soldiers blanched and reacted to the mighty wave of invisible energy.

As Julian weakly lifted his arm, opened up his mouth and croaked, "Father…" Inca moaned and fell unconscious to the ground beside him.

Roan released the colonel. Jamming the pistol into the holster, he went to Inca's side. She lay with one arm above her head, the other beside her still body. Was she breathing? Anxiously, he dropped to his knees, all of his paramedic abilities coming to the forefront.

"Salvador! Get me a stethoscope! A blood pressure cuff!"

The *médico* leaped to his feet.

Jaime fell to Julian's side, crying out his name over and over again. He gripped his son by the shoulders and shook him gently.

"Julian! Julian? Are you all right? My son, speak to me! Oh, please, speak to me!" And he pulled him up and into his arms.

A sob tore from Jaime as he crushed his son against him. He looked down to see that Julian's color was almost normal. His lashes fluttered. When he opened his eyes again, Jaime saw that they were clear once more.

"Father?"

Jaime reacted as if struck by a thunderclap. A sob tore from him and he clasped his son tightly to him. "Thank God, you are alive. I could not bear losing you, too."

Roan cursed under his breath. He took Inca's blood pressure. It was dumping. She was dying. Heart pounding with anxiety, he threw the blood pressure cuff down and held her limp, clammy wrist. He could barely discern a pulse.

The men crowded closer, in awe. In terror. They all watched without a sound.

"Inca, don't die on me, dammit!" Roan rasped as he slid his arm beneath her neck. He understood what she had done: used her own body to run the venom through. That was the nature of healing. Could she get rid of it soon enough? Could her jaguar spirit guide help her do it? Roan wasn't sure, and he felt his heart bursting with anguish so devastating that all he could do was take her in his arms and hold her.

As he pressed her limp body against his, and held her tightly, he blocked out Jaime's sobs and Julian's stammered words. He blocked out everything. Intuitively, Roan knew that if he held Inca, if he willed his life energy, his heart, his love, into her, that it would help her survive this terrible tragedy. He'd seen his mother do this countless times— gather the one who was ill into her arms. She had told him what she was doing, and he now utilized that knowledge.

The instant Roan pressed her hard against him, her heart against his heart, his world shattered. It took every ounce of strength he'd ever had to withstand the energy exploding violently through him. Eyes closed, his brow against her cheek, he felt her limpness, felt her life slipping away.

No! It can't happen! Breathing hard, Roan tried to take deep, steadying breaths of air into his lungs as he held her. Behind his eyes, he saw murky, turgid green and yellow colors. Out of the murkiness came his cougar. He'd seen her many times before in his dreams and in the vision quest he took yearly upon his mother's reservation. The cougar ran toward him full tilt in huge striding leaps. Roan didn't understand what she was doing. He thought she would slam into him. Instead, as she took a mighty leap directly at him, he felt her warm, powerful body hit and absorb into his. The effect was so surprising that Roan felt himself tremble violently from it.

The yellowish-green colors began to fade. He felt the cougar in him, around him, covering him. It was the oddest sensation he'd ever experienced. He felt the cougar's incredible endurance and energy. It was as if fifty thousand volts of electricity were coursing through him, vibrating him and flowing out of him and into Inca. Dizzy, Roan felt himself sit down unceremoniously on the damp ground with Inca in his arms. He heard the concerned murmurs of soldier's voices. But his concentration, his focus, belonged inside his head, inside this inner world where the drama between life and death was taking place.

Instinctively, Roan held Inca with all his strength. He saw and felt the cougar's energy moving vibrantly into Inca. He saw the gold color, rich and clean, moving like an energy transfusion into her body. The murky colors disappeared and in their place came darkness. But it wasn't a frightening darkness, rather, one of warmth and nurturance. Roan knew only to hold Inca. That in holding her, he was somehow helping her to live, not die.

When Inca moaned softly, Roan felt himself torn out of the drama of the inner worlds. His eyes flew open. Anxiously, he looked down at the woman in his arms. Her flesh had returning color. And when her lashes fluttered weakly to reveal drowsy willow-green eyes, his heart soared with the knowledge that she was not going to die. Hot tears funneled through him and he rapidly blinked them away.

He felt Salvador's hand on his shoulder. "How can we help?" he asked.

Slightly weakened, Roan roused himself and looked up. "Just let me sit here with her. She's going to be okay...." he rasped to the soldiers who stood near, their faces filled with genuine concern.

Looking down at Inca, Roan gave her a broken smile. "Welcome back to the land of the living, sweetheart."

Though incredible weakness stalked Inca, she heard Roan's huskily spoken words and they touched her pounding heart. She was too tired to even try to lift her hand and touch his face. How wonderful it felt to be held by him! Inca had wanted to experience this, but not like this.

"Roan...take me home...out of here. I need rest...." Her voice was a whisper. Gone was her husky, confident tone. She felt like she was a drifting cloud, at the whim of the winds.

"I'll take you home," he promised.

Roan eased Inca into a sitting position. Many hands, the hands of the soldiers who had witnessed this drama, came to help. Inca sat with her head down on her knees. She was very weak and incapable of walking anywhere on her own. Getting to his feet, Roan felt the last of the dizziness leave him. Looking over, he saw Julian sitting up, too, his father's arm around his shoulder. And he saw Jaime's face covered with tears, his once hard eyes now soft with love for his son.

Several of the soldiers lifted Inca into Roan's awaiting arms. He reassured them all that she would be fine, that all she needed now was a little rest. Julian looked up, his eyes still dull from the event. Roan nodded to him and turned and left. Right now, all he wanted to do was get Inca to their camp to tend to her needs.

The soup tasted salty and life-giving to Inca as she sat propped up against a tree at their camp, and accepted another spoonful from Roan. He had opened up a packet of soup and made it for her and the chicken broth was revitalizing. He stood up and moved to the fire to place more wood on it, the flames dancing gaily and highlighting his hard, carved face. Inca was covered with only a thin blanket and was chilled to the bone. Though the soup warmed her, she wished, more than anything, that Roan would come and sit next to her, embrace her and warm her with his powerful body.

"More soup?" Roan asked as he came back to her and knelt down beside her.

"No...thank you...." Inca sighed deeply.

"You almost died," Roan said as he sat down.

Inca avoided his hooded look. She felt terribly vulnerable right now. "Yes. Thanks to you and your spirit guide, I will live."

His heart told him to move closer and take her into his arms. After almost losing her, he no longer tried to shield himself from Inca. Roan wasn't sure when his guard had come down, only that the crisis earlier had slammed that fact home to him. "Come here," he murmured, and eased her against him. She came without a fight, relieved that he was going to hold her. Her flesh was goose pimpled. As Roan settled his bulk against the tree with Inca at his side, her head resting wearily on his shoulder, he'd never felt happier.

"Okay?" he asked, his lips pressed to her long, flowing hair. She felt good in his arms, fitting against him perfectly, as if they had always been matched puzzle pieces just waiting to be put together.

Sighing softly, Inca nuzzled her face into the crook of his neck. "Yes…" And she closed her eyes. Risking everything, she lifted her hand and placed it on his chest. The moment was so warm, so full of life. She could hear the insects singing around them, the howl of some monkeys in the distance. All that mattered right now was Roan.

"You are so brave," she whispered unsteadily. "I needed help and you knew it. I was told before I took Julian's hand to help him return that it might kill me."

Roan frowned. "And you did it anyway?"

Barely opening her eyes, she absorbed Roan's warmth, felt his hand moving gently across her shoulders. "What choice did I have? He had not finished his life's mission on this side. He had to come back. He drew the snake to him to create a crisis that would overcome his father's reserve."

"Well," Roan muttered, "that certainly did the trick. The man was crying like a baby when Julian returned."

"Good," Inca purred. She nuzzled against his shoulder and jaw, a soft smile on her lips. She felt the caress of Roan's fingers along her neck and across her cheek and temple. How wonderful it felt to be touched by him! All these years, Inca had been missing something. She couldn't verbalize it. She hadn't known what it was until now. It was the natural intimacy that Roan had effortlessly established with her. The warmth, the love she felt pouring from him brought tears to her eyes. Was this what love felt like? Inca had no way of knowing for sure. She'd read many books by famous authors and many poems about love. To read it was one thing. To experience it was something new to her.

"Do you often get into this kind of a predicament with someone you're going to heal?"

Inca shook her head. "No."

"Good."

She smiled a little. Roan's fingers settled over the hand she had pressed to his heart. She could feel the thudding, drumlike pounding of it beneath her sensitive palm. "Someday you must go with me to the Jaguar Clan village. I would like you to meet the elders. I think you have powerful medicine. All you need is some training to understand it and work with it more clearly."

Roan nodded. He lay there in the darkness, near the dancing fire, and told her what he'd felt and seen when he'd taken her into his arms. When he was done, he felt Inca reach up, her fingertips trailing along his jaw.

"You are a very brave warrior," she told him. Lifting her head so that she could look up at him, she saw the smoldering longing in his eyes—for her. Because she was weak and feeling defenseless, or perhaps because she'd nearly died and she was more vulnerable than usual, Inca leaned up...up to press her lips to his. It wasn't something she thought about first, for she was completely instinctual, in touch with her primal urges. As her lips grazed the hard line of his mouth, she saw his eyes turn predatory. Something hot and swift moved through her, stirring her, and she yearned for a more complete union with the softening line of his mouth.

Surprised at first, Roan felt her tentative, searching lips touching his like a butterfly. Her actions were completely unexpected. It took precious seconds for him to respond— appropriately. Primally, his lower body hardened instantly. He wanted to take her savagely and mate with her and claim and brand her. But his heart cautioned him not to, and in-

stead of devouring her with a searing kiss, Roan hauled back
on his white-hot desires.

If anything, he needed to be gentle with Inca. As her lips
tentatively grazed his once more, he felt the tenuousness of
her exploration of him, as a man to her woman. He understood on a very deep level that people did odd things after
they almost died. Making love was one of them. It confirmed
life over death. All those thoughts collided within his whirling mind as her lips slid softly across his. She did not know
how to kiss.

The simple reminder of her virginal innocence forced
Roan to tightly control his violent male reaction. Instead, he
lifted his hands and gently framed her face. He saw her eyes
go wide at first, and then grow drowsy with desire—for him.
That discovery just tightened the knot of pain in his lower
body even more so. Swallowing a groan, Roan repositioned
her face slightly, leaned over and captured her parted lips.
The pleasure of just feeling her full mouth beneath his sent
shock waves of heat cascading through him. He felt her gasp
a little, her hands wrapping around his thick, hairy wrists.
Easing back, Roan tried to read Inca and what her reaction
meant.

He saw her eyes turn golden-green. The heat in them
burned him. She trembled violently as he leaned down and
once more tasted her lips. This time, he captured her firmly
beneath his mouth. He felt her hesitantly return his kiss.
Smiling to himself, he broke it off and moved his tongue
slowly across her lower lip. Again, surprise and pleasure
shone in her half-closed eyes. Smiling tenderly, he leaned
over and moved his mouth against hers once more. This time
her lips blossomed strongly beneath his. She caught on fast.

Inca purred with pleasure as Roan's mouth settled against
hers. This was a kiss. The type she'd seen other people give
to one another. And now she understood the beauty and
sensual pleasure of it, too. Now she knew why people kissed
one another so often. A flood of heat flowed through her.

She felt the caresses of his mouth upon her lips, the gliding heat created by their touching one another. Her heart was skipping beats. Lightning settled in her lower body, and like a hot, uncoiling snake, she felt a burning, scalding sensation flowing through her. The feeling was startling. Intensely pleasurable.

Shocked by all that she was feeling, Inca tore her mouth from his. She blinked. Breath ragged, she whispered, "Enough... I feel as if I will explode...."

He gave her a lazy, knowing smile. Brushing several strands of hair from her cheek, he rasped, "That's good. A kiss should make you feel that way." Indeed, the flush in Inca's cheeks, the golden light dancing in her widening eyes told Roan just how much she'd enjoyed their first, tentative kiss. Exploration with her was going to be hell on earth for him. He felt tied in painful knots. Inca could not know that, however. She was a child in the adult world of hot love-making and boiling desire. It would be up to him to be her teacher and not a selfish pig, taking her in lust. If nothing else, today had taught Roan that he felt far more toward Inca than lust, but because of his past, he had denied it. He told himself their relationship was only temporary, that when the mission was over, their torrid longing for one another would come to an end.

Inca shyly looked up at him, and then looked away. Her lips were throbbing in pleasure. She touched them in awe. "I did not know a kiss could do all this. Now I know why people kiss so much...."

Laughter rolled through Roan's chest. He embraced her a little more tightly and then released her. "I'm not laughing at you, Inca. I agree with your observation."

She smiled a little tentatively. Touching her lips once more, she looked up at him. "I liked it."

He grinned. "So did I."

"The feelings..." she sighed and touched her heart and

her abdomen with her hand "…are so different, so wonderful…as if a fire is bursting to life within me."

"Oh," Roan said wryly, "it is. But it's a fire of a different kind."

"And it will not burn me?"

He shook his head solemnly. He would burn in the fires of hell while she explored her sensual nature, but he was more than willing to sacrifice himself for her. "No, it won't hurt you. It will feel good. Better than anything you can imagine."

Stymied, Inca lay content in his arms. "Being like this with you is natural," she whispered. "It feels good to me. Does it for you?"

"You feel good in my arms," Roan told her, pressing a small kiss to her hair. "Like you've always belonged here…." And she did as far as he was concerned. He was old enough, experienced enough to realize that Inca owed him nothing. He was her first man, and he understood that it didn't mean she would stay with him. No, he expected nothing from her in that regard. Inca was the kind of wild spirit no man could capture and keep to himself. She had to be free to come and go as her wild heart bade her. Selfishly, he wanted to keep her forever. But Inca's life was a day-by-day affair. And in his own philosophy of life, Roan tried to live in the moment, not in the past and not trying to see what the future might bring him.

Inca nuzzled beneath his hard jaw. She closed her eyes. "You saved my life today. And you gave me life tonight. I do not know how to thank you."

Grazing her shoulder, Roan whispered, "Just keep being who you are, sweetheart. That's more than enough of a gift to me."

Chapter 10

"Inca...you've come...." Julian weakly raised up on the pallet where he lay. Shortly, two soldiers were going to carry him out of the swamp and back to the Amazon, where a helicopter would take him to a hospital in Manaus for recovery. He smiled shyly and lifted his hand to her as she drew near.

Inca ignored the soldiers who stood agape as she approached the *tenente*'s litter. There was admiration and wariness in their eyes. They didn't know what to make of her, and that was fine; she liked keeping people off balance where she was concerned. She'd known intuitively that Julian would be gone as the sun rose this morning, and she wanted to say goodbye to him. In her usual garb, she removed the rifle from her shoulder and knelt down beside the young officer, who was still looking pale. Inca knew that the colonel didn't want her in camp with weapons, but that was too bad.

"*Bom dia,* good day," she said, reaching out and gripping his fingers. "You are better, eh?"

Julian's mouth moved with emotion. His lower lip trembled. The strength in Inca's hand surprised him. He held her hand as if it were a cherished gift. "Yes, much… I owe you everything, Inca." His eyes grew soft with gratefulness. "I understand from talking to the men earlier that you risked your life to save mine. I don't recall much…just bits and pieces. I was so shocked when I walked out of my tent. The snake was waiting for me at the flap. I never saw him until it was too late. After he sank his fangs into my leg, I screamed. I remember pulling my pistol and firing off a lot of shots at it. And then…I fell. I don't remember much more." His eyes narrowed on hers. "But I do remember being in the light, and you were there." His voice lowered. "And so was your jaguar. I saw him."

Julian glanced about, wanting to make sure the men of his platoon couldn't hear his whispered words. "I felt myself on the brink, Inca. I wanted to leave, and you brought me back." He squeezed her hand gently and closed his eyes. "I'm glad you did. Don't think for a moment that I wasn't glad to open my eyes and find myself in my father's arms." He looked at her, the words filled with emotion. "He was holding me, Inca. Me. And I owe it all to you, to your strength and goodness."

She saw the tears well up in his eyes. Touched to the point of tears herself, she whispered, "Yours was a life worth saving, my friend."

Julian pressed a soft kiss to the back of her scarred hand and then reluctantly released her strong fingers. Sighing, he self-consciously wiped the tears from the corners of his eyes. "I shouldn't be crying. I feel very emotional right now."

Inca nodded. "That always happens after a near death event. Let your tears fall." She smiled a little. "I see you and your father have connected again?"

Julian's eyes grew watery. "Yes…and again, I have you to thank."

Shaking her head, Inca sensed the crush of soldiers who

had begun to crowd around to get a closer look at her and to try and hear what they were talking about. "No, Julian, I had nothing to do with that. I am glad that it happened, though."

Julian kept his voice down. "Yes, we are really talking to one another for the first time since Rafael's death." Choking up, he rasped, "Last night, my father told me he loved me. It's the first time I can recall him saying that to me. It's a miracle, Inca."

Smiling tenderly, Inca nodded. "That is wonderful. And so, you go to Manaus to recover, my friend?"

Nodding, Julian said unhappily, "Yes. I want to stay.... I want to lead my men into that valley, but my father says I must go." With a wry movement of his mouth, he said, "I shouldn't complain. He cares openly for me, and he wants to see me safe. He told me that I was their only son and now it is my turn to carry the family's honor and heritage forward."

"A wise man," she murmured. Patting Julian's hand, she rose. "I wish you an uneventful journey, Julian. Because where we go, it will be dangerous and interesting."

Julian's gaze clung to hers. "I'll never forget you, Inca. The legend about you being the jaguar goddess is true. I'll speak your name with blessings. People will know of your goodness. Your generous heart..."

She felt heat tunnel up her neck and into her face. Praise was something she could never get used to. "Just keep what you have with your father alive and well. That is all the thanks I need. Family is important. More than most people realize. Goodbye..." She lifted her hand.

The men parted automatically for her exit. Inca looked at them with disdain as she strode through the crowd toward Roan, who stood waiting for her at the rear of the crowd. Her heart pounded briefly beneath the smoldering look of welcome he gave her. When his gaze moved to her mouth, her lips parted in memory of that scorching, life-changing kiss they'd shared last night. She had left camp early this morning to bathe and then find Julian. At that time, Roan had still been asleep in his hammock as she moved silently around their camp.

The warm connection between her heart and his was so strong and beautiful. Inca felt as if she were not walking on Mother Earth but rather on air. Just the way he looked at her made her joyful. A slight smile curved her lips as she drew near.

"I see what you are thinking," she teased in a husky voice meant for his ears only.

Roan's mouth moved wryly upward. He slid his hand around her shoulder and turned her in another direction. "And feeling," he murmured. His gesture was not missed by the soldiers, for they watched Inca as if mesmerized by her presence and power. "Come on, Colonel Marcellino wants to see you—personally and privately."

Instantly, Inca was on guard. She resisted his hand.

Roan felt her go rigid. He saw the distrust in her eyes, and the wariness. "It's not what you think, Inca. The man has changed since yesterday. What you did for Julian has made the difference. He's no longer out to kill you."

"Humph, we will see." She shouldered the rifle and moved with Roan through the stirring camp. There were a hundred and twenty men left in the company, thanks to the colonel's poor judgment in taking them through this infested swamp. Inca was angry about that. Julian would not have been bitten by the bushmaster had they gone around the swamp.

Inca tried to steady her pounding heart as they approached the opened tent, where Colonel Marcellino sat at his make-shift desk. His attaché, Captain Braga, bowed his head in greeting to Inca.

"Colonel Marcellino would speak privately with you," he said with great deference, and he lifted his hand to indicate she was to step forward. Inca looked over at Roan, a question in her eyes.

"I'm staying here."

"Coward."

Roan grinned. "This isn't what you think it is. Trust me."

Flashing a disdainful look at him, Inca muttered, "I will. And I will see where it leads me."

Chuckling, Roan touched her proud shoulder. "Sweetheart, this isn't going to be painful. It's not that bad."

Inca thrilled to the endearment that rolled off his tongue. She liked the way it made her feel, as if physically embraced. Roan was not aware of his power at all, but she was, and Inca indulged herself in allowing the wonderful feelings that came with that word to wrap around her softly beating heart.

Turning, she scowled and pushed forward. Might as well get this confrontation with the colonel out of the way so they could get out of this dreaded swamp today.

Jaime Marcellino looked up. He felt Inca's considerable presence long before she ducked beneath the open tent flaps to face him. She stood expectantly, her hands tense on her hips, her chin lifted with pride and her eyes narrowed with distrust.

"You wanted to see me?" Inca demanded in a dark voice. She steeled herself, for she knew Marcellino was her enemy.

With great deliberation, Jaime placed the gold pen aside, folded his hands in front of him and looked up at her. "Yes, I asked for you to come so that we may talk." Flexing his thin mouth, he said with great effort, "Most important, I need to thank you for saving my son's life. I saw firsthand what you did. I cannot explain *how* you saved him. I only know that you did."

Inca held herself at rigid attention. She did not trust the colonel. Yet she saw the older man's face, which was gray this morning and much older looking, lose some of its authoritarian expression. His dark brown eyes were watery with tears, and she heard him choking them back. It had to be hard for him to thank her, since he accused her of murdering his eldest son.

Her flat look of surprise cut through him. Her facial expression was one of continued distrust. Jaime wanted to reach inside that hard armor she wore. What could he expect? He'd treated her badly. Lifting his hands in a gesture of peace and understanding, he whispered, "I wish to table my earlier words to you, my earlier accusations that you murdered my eldest son. Because of what has happened here, I intend, when this mission is over, to go back to Brasilia and interrogate the drug runner who accused you of shooting Rafael. And I will use a lie detector test on him to see if indeed he is telling the truth or not." His brows drew downward and he held Inca's surprised gaze.

"I owe you that much," he said unsteadily. "My logic says that if you saved Julian, why would you have murdered my firstborn? All that I hear about you, from the gossip of my soldiers, as well as the villagers we have passed on this march, is that you heal, you do not kill."

Inca slid her fingers along the smooth leather sling of her rifle. "Oh, I kill, Colonel," she whispered rawly. "But I do it in self-defense. It is a law of my clan that we never attack. We only defend. Do you really think I *enjoy* killing? No. Does it make me feel good? Never. I see these men's faces in my sleep."

"You are a warrior as I am," he replied. "Killing is not a pleasure for any of us. It is a duty. A terrible, terrible duty. Our sleep is not peaceful, is it?" He cleared his throat nervously. "I have heard legends surrounding you, of the lives you have taken." Jaime rose, his fingers barely touching the table in front of him. "And judging from what I've seen, you do *not* enjoy killing, any more than I do."

Inca's nostrils flared. Her voice quavered. "What sane human being would?" She waved her hand toward the encampment. "Do any of us *enjoy* killing another human being? Only if you are insane, Colonel. And believe me, I have paid dearly…and will continue paying for the rest of my life, for each person's life I have taken. Do you not see those you have killed in your sleep at night? Do you not hear their last, choking cries as blood rushes up their throat to suffocate them?" Eyes turning hard, Inca felt the rage of injustice move strongly through her. "Even the idea that I would murder anyone in cold blood is beyond my comprehension. Yet you believed it of me." She jabbed her finger at him. "I told you I did not kill your other son, Rafael. Father Titus has an affidavit, which is in your possession, that tells you I was nowhere near that part of Brasil on that day."

The colonel hung his head and moved a soiled and damp sheet of paper to the center of his desk. "Yes…I have it here.…"

"Since when did you think priests of your own faith would lie about such a thing?"

Wincing, Jaime rasped, "You are right, Inca.…" He touched the crinkled, creased paper that held Father Titus's trembling signature. "I have much to do to clear your name of my eldest son's death. And I give you my word, as an officer and a gentleman, that once I return home, I will do exactly that."

Inca felt her rage dissolving. Before her stood an old man worn down by grief and years of hatred aimed wrongly at her. "I will take your words with me. Is that all?"

Nodding, Jaime said wearily, "Yes, that is all. And I also want to let you know that you were right about this swamp. I'm afraid my arrogance, my anger toward you, got the better of me. From now on I will listen to you. You know this land, I do not. Fair enough?"

Inca hesitated at the tent opening, her fingers clenching the strap of the rifle on her shoulder. "Yes, Colonel. Fair enough. In five more days we will reach the valley, if we follow my route through the jungle."

* * *

Inca lay on her belly, the dampness feeling good against her flesh in the midday heat as she studied the valley below. Roan lay beside her, and his elbow brushed hers as he took the binoculars from her and swept the narrow, steeply walled valley.

"Do you see the factory?"

Roan kept his voice low. "Yes, I see it."

Inca watched as the colonel's company spread out in a long, thin line along the rim of the valley. They had a hundred men ready to march against the Valentino Brothers' factory, which was half a mile away, nestled at one end of the valley. The factory was large, the tin roof painted dark green and tan so that it would not be easily spotted from the air. They had positioned it beneath the jungle canopy to further hide its whereabouts from prying satellite cameras.

Eyes narrowing, Inca watched as her Indian friends moved ceaselessly in and out of the opened doors of the huge factory. A dirt road led out of the area and down the center of the valley, more than likely to a well-hidden villa up the steep valley slopes. They carried bushel baskets of coca leaves, which would be boiled down to extract the cocaine. Other Indians were carrying large white blocks wrapped in plastic to awaiting trucks just outside the gates. That was the processed cocaine, ready for worldwide distribution. Guards would yell at any Indians who moved too slowly for them. She saw one guard lift his boot and kick out savagely at a young boy. Her rage soared at the bondage of her people.

"It looks like an airplane hangar," Roan muttered, adjusting the sights on the binoculars. "Big enough to house a C-130 Hercules cargo plane."

"I estimate there are over a hundred Indians in chains down there," she said, anger tinging her quavering tone.

"There's a lot of guards with military weapons watching every move they make," Roan stated. "A high fence, maybe ten feet tall, with concertina wire on top to discourage any of them from trying to escape."

"At night, the Indians are forced to live within the fence. Sebastian and Faro Valentino are down there. Look near that black Mercedes at the gate." She jabbed her index finger down at them. "That is them."

Roan saw two short men, one with a potbelly and the other looking like a trim, fit athlete. Both were dressed in short-sleeved white shirts and dark blue trousers, and they were talking with someone in charge of the guards, a man in military jungle fatigues. "Got 'em."

"They look pitifully harmless," Inca growled. "But they are murderers of my people—hundreds of them over the last four years. The one with the pig's belly is Sebastian. Faro is the thin one, a pilot. His helicopter is over there." She pointed to the machine sitting off in the grass near the compound. "He has a fleet of military helicopters that he bought from foreign countries, and he uses them to ferry the cocaine out of the area. He has also used his helicopters to shoot down Brazilian Air Force helicopters that have tried to penetrate this area. He is dangerous. He is here to pick up a load of cocaine and fly it to Peru. The Indians are carrying it to the machine right now."

Roan heard the grating in her voice. Faro had a military helicopter, dark green in color and without markings. "I've read up on these two. Sebastian is the lazy one of the family. He stays put in Brazil, which is his territory. He's satisfied with doing business from here. Faro has his own military air force, with choppers in nearly every South American country. He wants to dominate not only all of South America, but eventually Central America, as well. We're lucky to catch the brothers together. I was hoping we'd get Sebastian." His voice lowered with feeling. "I'd like to take 'em both down."

"Do not be fooled by the piglike expressions on their faces. They are as smart as jaguars."

"And you think the best time to attack is at night?"

"Yes, under cover of darkness. The guards go inside the factory at night to package the cocaine into blocks and wrap them, while the Indians sleep outside. I will go down, contact the chief who leads all the people there, and they will spread the word quickly and quietly as to the coming attack. I will break open the chain around the gate and open it. They will run. That is when the colonel will attack."

Roan nodded and counted the guards. "I see twenty guards."

"There are more inside the factory. Perhaps an equal number."

"Forty men total. Against our hundred."

Snorting, Inca gave him a cutting glance. "Do not think forty men cannot kill all of us, because they can." She glared at the line of Brazilian soldiers hunkering down on their bellies along the rim to observe their coming target of attack. "While these soldiers have gotten stronger over the last ten days, no one says that they are battle hardened or can think in the middle of bullets flying around them. The Valentinos' men are cold, ruthless killers. Nothing distracts them from the shots they want to take. Nothing."

"I understand," Roan said. He reached out and touched Inca's cheek. Time was at a premium between them. And as much as he wanted to kiss her, he knew that she had to come to him. Inca had shyly kissed him two more times. The enjoyment was mutual. He could almost feel what she was thinking now, as if that invisible connection between them was working with amazing accuracy. Inca had told him that because a bond of trust was forged between them, he would easily pick up on her thoughts and feelings—just as she would his.

Roan watched her eyes close slightly as he touched her cheek. "I worry about you. You're the one taking all the chances. What if the guards spot you at the fence?"

Inca captured his large hand and boldly pressed a kiss

into the palm of it. Smiling widely, she watched his eyes turn a dark, smoky blue, which indicated he liked what she had done. The last five days had been a wonderful exploration for her. She felt safe enough, trusting enough of Roan to experiment, to test her newfound feminine instincts. He made her happy. Deliriously so.

"Do not worry. They will not see me coming. I will use the cover of my spirit guide to reach the fence. Only then will I unveil myself." She released his hand and turned over on her back, her gaze drifting up through the canopy. Above her, a flock of red-and-yellow parrots skittered among the limbs of the trees. "You worry too much, man of my heart."

Roan gave her a careless smile in return. He lay on his back, slid his arm beneath her neck and moved closer to her. When she pressed her cheek against him, he knew she enjoyed his touch. "I like where we're going, Inca," he told her quietly as they enjoyed one of the few private moments they'd been able to steal during the march. "I don't know where that is, but it doesn't matter."

Inca laughed softly. She closed her eyes and fiercely enjoyed his closeness, the way he nurtured her with his touch, with his hard, protective body. "I do not know, either, but I want to find out."

A sweet happiness flowed through Roan. "So do I." And he did. In the last five days they had bonded so closely. Despite his fear, Inca had somehow surmounted that wall within him. Roan was scared. But he was more frightened of losing Inca to the danger of her livelihood. Did she love him? Was there hope for their love? There were many obstacles in their path. Was what she felt for him puppy love? A first love rather than a lasting love built upon a foundation of friendship and mutual respect? Roan wasn't sure, and he knew the only way to find out was to surrender his heart over to her, to the gift Inca had given to him alone.

Inca opened her eyes and looked at Roan, a playful smile on her face. "You are the first man to open my heart. I do not know how you did it, only that it has happened." She lightly touched the area between her breasts where the bandoliers of ammo met and crossed.

More serious, Roan held her softened willow-green eyes. "What we have…I hope, Inca…is something lasting. That's what I want—what I hope for out of this."

"Mmm, like Grandfather Adaire and Grandmother Alaria have? You know, there is gossip that they are a thousand years old, that they fell in love on an island off the coast of England. They were druids on the Isle of Mona, where they were charged with keeping the knowledge of druid culture alive for the next generation. When the Romans came and set fire to the island, destroying the druid temples and thousands of scrolls that had their people's knowledge recorded on them, they fled. It is said they came by boat over here, to Peru, and helped to create the Village of the Clouds."

"And they're husband and wife?"

Chuckling, Inca said, "Oh, yes. But Grandmother Alaria is the head elder of the village. Grandfather Adaire is one of eight other elders who comprise the counsel that makes decisions on how to teach jaguar medicine and train students from around the world."

"A thousand years," Roan murmured. "That's a long time. How could they live so long?"

Inca shrugged and gazed up through the trees. "I do not know. It is said that when humans have a pure heart, they may live forever or until such time that they desire to leave their earthly body." She laughed sharply. "I do not have a pure heart. I will die much, much sooner!"

Roan moved onto his side, his body touching hers. He placed his hand on her waist and looked deeply into her eyes. "You have the purest heart I've ever seen," he rasped. Reaching out, he brushed several strands of hair away from her brow. "The unselfish love you have for your people, the way you share with others…if that isn't pure of heart, I don't know what is."

Just the touch of his fingers made her skin tingle pleasantly. Reaching up, Inca caressed his unshaved jaw. "Roan Storm Walker, you hold my heart in your hands, as I hold yours. You think only good of me. Those of the Jaguar Clan are charged with seeing us without such feelings in the way." She smiled gently.

Leaning down, he whispered, "Yes, you hold my heart in your hands, my woman—"

"Excuse me.…"

Roan heard the apologetic voice just moments before he was going to kiss Inca. Instead, he lifted his head and sat up. Captain Braga stood uncertainly before them, clearly embarrassed for intruding upon their private moment. "Yes?"

Clearing his throat, Captain Braga said, "A thousand pardons to you both."

Inca felt heat in her face as she sat up. She picked several tiny leaves out of her braid. "What is it?" she demanded. More than anything, she'd wanted Roan's kiss, that commanding, wonderfully male mouth settling against her hungry lips.

"The colonel…he asks you to come and help him with the attack plans. Er, can you?"

Inca was on her feet first. She held out her hand to Roan, who took it, and she pulled him to his feet. "Yes, we will come.…"

Roan tried to quell his fear for Inca's safety. He'd followed her down the steep, slippery wall of the narrow valley in the darkness, but Inca had disdained his offer of a flak jacket and headphone gear. Roan adjusted the microphone near his mouth. He was in contact with the officers of the company, who also wore communication gear. He wished Inca had agreed to the headset and protective vest. She had told him it would hamper her abilities to shape-shift and he'd reluctantly given in. The one thing he did do, however, was take off his medicine necklace and give it to her—for protection. The urge to give it to her had overwhelmed him, and this time he'd followed the demand.

Inca's eyes had filled with tears as he'd hung it around her neck, the beautiful blue stone resting at the bottom of her slender throat. She'd smiled, kissed his hand, knowing instinctively the importance of his gesture.

The clouds were thick and a recent shower made the leaves gleam. The rain had muffled their approach to their target which was fortunate. The factory was less than two hundred yards away. The road to it was deeply rutted, and now muddy. Trees had been cleared from the edge of the road, but otherwise the valley was thickly covered by rain forest. Faro's helicopter sat tethered near the factory. He and his brother had disappeared inside the main facility hours earlier.

Roan's heart beat painfully in his chest for Inca as he followed her, for her raw courage under such dangerous circumstances. She didn't seem fazed by her duties, and if she felt fear, he didn't see it in her eyes or gestures. How brave she was in the name of her people.

Inca carefully removed her bandoliers and put her rifle aside. She took off the web belt. There was a guard outside the gate, his military weapon on his shoulder as he walked back and forth in front of it. Hidden in the forest above and around the factory were the Brazilian soldiers, who had crept carefully into position. The attack would take place in a U-shaped area. The only escape for the Indians would be down the road. Inca would urge them to run and then take cover in the rain forest. There was a squad of Brazilian soldiers half a mile from the front gate, their machine gun set up to stop any guards from driving away from the factory once the battle began.

Roan said nothing. His heart hammered with worry and anxiety for her. What was Inca going to do? Just walk up to the guard and knock him out? The guard would see her coming. Though his mouth was dry, Roan wiped it with the back of his hand. She slowly stood up, only a foot away from him.

"It is time," she said. Looking up at him, her mouth pulled slightly upward. "Now you and all of them will see why they call me the jaguar goddess."

Roan reached out and gripped her hand. "Don't do anything foolish. I'm here. I can help you...."

She squeezed his fingers. "You just gave me the greatest gift of all, my man." She gently touched the medicine necklace. "Your heart, your care, will keep me safe." Stepping forward, she followed her wild instincts. Her mouth fitted hotly against his. She slid her fingers through his damp hair, and hungrily met and matched his returning ardor. Pulling away, her heart pounding, Inca whispered, "I will return. You have captured my heart...." Then she quickly moved down the last stretch of slope to a position near the road.

Roan's lips tingled hotly from her swift, unexpected kiss. He watched through the lazy light filtering through the clouds from the moon above them. Inca's form seemed to melt into the surrounding grayness. For a moment, Roan lost sight of her. And then his heart thudded. Farther down, something else moved. Not a human...what, then?

Eyes slitting, he lifted the light-sensitive binoculars to try and pinpoint the dark, shadowy movement. He was looking for Inca's tall, proud form. It was nowhere to be found. *There!* Roan scowled. His hands wrapped more strongly around the binoculars. He saw the shadowy outline of a jaguar moving stealthily toward the guard in the distance. His black-and-gold coat blended perfectly into the shadows and darkness surrounding him. Was that Inca? The jaguar was trotting steadily now toward his intended target—the guard walking past the gate. She had told him of her shape-shifting ability, of being able to allow her jaguar spirit guardian to envelope her so that she appeared in his shape and form.

Roan didn't know how it was done, exactly, but he recalled his own experience with his cougar recently. Among his own people, there were medicine men and women who were known to change shape into a cat or wolf. In this altered form, Inca had told him, she possessed all the jaguar's powerful abilities, including sneaking up on her intended target without ever being noticed.

Roan's breath hitched. The guard had turned and was coming back toward the corner of the fence closest to the jungle. Compressing his lips, Roan hunted anxiously for the cat. Where was it? It seemed to have disappeared. Instead, he watched the guard, who was lazily smoking a cigarette, a bored look on his face. Just as the guard reached the corner and was going to turn around, something caught his attention. Startled, he dropped the cigarette from his lips, jerked his rifle off his shoulder and started to raise it to fire.

Out of the darkness of the rain forest, a jaguar leaped toward the man. In an instant, the stunned guard was knocked on his back, the rifle flying out of his hand. In seconds, the cat had strangled the soldier by grabbing hold of his neck in his jaws and suffocating him into unconsciousness, not death though that was how a jaguar killed.

Roan stood, the binoculars dropping to his chest. He picked up his rifle and moved rapidly down the hill. In the distance, he could barely see the soldier lying motionless on the ground. A number of Indians had run to that area of the fence. All hell was going to break loose in a few seconds. Running hard, Roan hit the muddy road and sprinted toward the front gate. The other guards would be making their rounds. Inca would have only moments to open that front gate and release her people.

Inca moved soundlessly. It took precious seconds for her spirit guardian to release her. Shaking off the dizziness that always occurred afterward, she blinked several times to clear her head. Then, breathing hard, she picked up the machete the soldier had strapped to his belt.

The Indian factory workers pressed their faces to the fence, clenching the wire. Their expressions were filled with joy as they whispered, "the jaguar goddess." Inca hissed to them in their language to be silent. Digging her feet into the muddy red soil, she lunged toward the gates. Gripping the handle of the deadly three-foot-long machete, Inca raced to where a chain and padlock kept the two gates locked together.

The Indians followed her, as if understanding exactly what she was going to do to free them. Men, women and children all ran toward her without a sound, without any talking. They knew the danger they were all in. Their collective gazes were fixed on the woman they called the jaguar goddess. The thin crescent moon on her left shoulder blade—the mark of the jaguar—was visible as her sleeveless top moved to reveal it. There was no question in their eyes that she was going to save them. She was going to free them!

Breathing hard, perspiration running down the sides of her face, Inca skidded to a halt in the slimy clay. She aimed the machete carefully at the thick iron links that held the Indians enslaved. Fierce, white-hot anger roared through her. She heard a sound. *There!* To her left, she saw a guard saunter lazily to the end of his prescribed beat. He'd seen her! His eyes widened in disbelief.

Lifting the machete, Inca brought it down not only with all her own strength, but with that of her guardian as well, the combined power fueled by the outrage that her people were slaves instead of free human beings. Sparks leaped skyward as the thick blade bit savagely into the chain. There was a sharp, grating sound. The chains swung apart.

Yes! Inca threw the machete down and jerked opened the gates. She saw the guard snap out of his stupor at seeing her.

"Come!" she commanded, jerking her arm toward the Indians. "Run! Run down the road! Hurry! Go into the forest and hide there!"

They needed no more urging. Inca leaped aside and allowed them to run to freedom. She jerked her head to the left and remained on the outside perimeter of the fence. The soldier was croaking out an alarm, fumbling with his rifle. Yanking at it with shaky hands, he managed to get it off his shoulder. He raised his rifle—at her. With a snarling growl, Inca spun around on her heels and ran directly at the drug runner guard. It was the last thing he would expect her to do, and she wagered on her surprising move to slow his reaction time.

The man was shocked by her attack; he had expected her to run away. He yelped in surprise, his eyes widening enormously as Inca leaped at him. She knocked the rifle back against his jaw, and there was a loud, cracking sound. As the guard fell backward, unconscious, Inca tumbled and landed on all fours. Breathing hard, she saw the soldier crumple into a heap. Grinning savagely, she scrambled to her feet, grabbed his rifle and sprinted down the fence to find the third guard. By now there was pandemonium. Gunfire began to erupt here and there.

Breathless, Inca slid to a halt in the mud near the corner of the compound. She nearly collided with another guard, who was barreling down the fence from the opposite direction after hearing his compatriot's shout of warning. This man was big, over two hundred pounds of muscle and flab. He saw Inca and jerked to a stop. And then his lips lifted in a snarl as he pulled his rifle to his shoulder and aimed it at her. As he moved to solidify his position, one foot slipped in the mud. The first bullet whined near her head, but missed.

Firing from the hip, Inca got off two shots. The bullets tore into the legs of the guard. He screamed, dropped his rifle and crumpled like a rag doll into the mud. Writhing and screaming, he clawed wildly at his bleeding legs.

Inca leaped past him and began her hunt for the fourth and last guard outside the gate. If she could render him harmless, the colonel's men would have less to worry about. Jogging through the slippery mud, she ran down the fence line. Glancing to her left, she saw that the Indians had all escaped. *Good!* Her heart soared with elation. She heard the Brazilian soldiers coming down the slopes of the valley. They were good men, with good intent, but nowhere physically fit for such a battle.

Turning the corner, Inca spotted the last soldier outside the gate. She shouted to him and raised her rifle. He turned, surprised. Rage filled his shadowed face as he saw her. Lifting his own weapon, he fired several shots at her.

Inca knew to stand very still and draw a bead on the man who fired wildly in her direction. She heard the bullets whine and sing very close by her head. Most men in the heat of battle fired thoughtlessly and without concentration. Inca harnessed her adrenaline, took aim at the man's knee and fired. Instantly, he went down like a felled ox. His screams joined the many others. From the corner of her eye, she saw a shadow. Who?

Twisting to face the shadow that moved from behind the building inside the fence, Inca sensed trouble. When the figure emerged, his pistol aimed directly at her head, her eyes narrowed. It was Faro Valentino. His small, piggish eyes were alive with hatred—toward her. He was grinning confidently.

At the same instant, through a flash of light in the darkness, she saw Roan. He shouted a warning at her and raised his rifle at Valentino.

Her boots slipped in the mud as she spun around to get off a shot at the murderer of so many of her people. And just as she did, she saw the pistol he carried buck. She saw the flicker of the shot being fired. She heard Roan roar her name above the loud noise of gunfire. And in the next second, Inca felt her head explode. White-hot pain and a burst of light went off within her. She was knocked off her feet. Darkness swallowed her.

Chapter 11

"**S**he's down! Inca's down!" Roan cried into the microphone. Scrambling, he leaped down the slope to the muddy ground near the compound. "I need a *médico!* Now!" He slipped badly. Throwing out his hands, he caught his balance. *Run! Run!* his mind screamed, *she needs you! Inca needs you!*

No! No! This can't be happening! Roan cried out Inca's name again. He ran hard down the fence line toward her. He fired off shots in the direction of Faro Valentino, who was standing there smiling, a pleased expression on his face he eyed Inca's prone, motionless form. The drug runner scowled suddenly and jerked his attention to Roan's swift approach. He took careful aim and fired once, the pistol bucking in his hand.

Roan threw himself to the ground just in time. The bullet screamed past his head, missing him by inches. Mud splashed up, splattering him.

Faro cursed loudly. He turned on his heel and hightailed

it down the fence to where his helicopter was revving up for takeoff.

Cursing, Roan realized he faced a decision: he could either go after Faro or go to Inca's side. It was an easy choice to make. Getting awkwardly to his feet, he sprinted the last hundred yards to her.

Roan sank into the mud next to where Inca lay on her back, her arms flung outward. "Inca!" His voice cracked with terror.

The gunfire was intense between drug runners and soldiers as the Brazilian army closed in around the compound. Several nearby explosions—from grenades—blew skyward and rocked him. The drug dealers were putting up a fierce fight. Faro's helicopter took off, the air vibrating heavily from the whapping blades in the high humidity. He was getting away! Hands trembling badly, Roan dropped the rifle at his side.

"Inca. Can you hear me?"

His heart pounded with dread. Automatically, because he was a paramedic, Roan began to examine her from head to toe with shaking hands. It was so dark! He needed light! Light to see with. *Where is she wounded? Where?* Gasps tore from his mouth. In the flashes of nearby explosions, he saw how pale Inca was. *Is she dead? Oh, Great Spirit, No! No, she can't be! She can't! I love her. I've just found her....* His hands moved carefully along the back of her head in careful examination.

Roan froze. His fingers encountered a mass of warm, sticky blood. After precious seconds, his worst fears were realized. Inca had taken a bullet to the back of her skull. *Oh, no. No!* He could feel where the base of her skull protruded outward slightly, indicating the bones had been broken. Lifting his fingers from beneath her neck, he screamed into the mouthpiece, "*Médico! Médico!* Dammit, I need a doctor!"

Médico Salvador came charging up to him moments later.

Panting, he slid awkwardly to a halt. Mud splattered everywhere. His eyes widened in disbelief.

"*Deus!* No!" he whispered, dropping to his knees opposite Roan. "Not Inca!"

"It's a basal skull fracture," Roan rasped. Sweat stung his eyes. He crouched as gunfire whined very close to where they knelt over Inca. Automatically, he kept his body close to hers to shield her.

Salvador gasped. "Oh, *Deus...*" He tore into his medical pack like a wild man. "Here! Help me! Put a dressing on her wound. *Rápido!*"

Roan took the dressing, tore open the sterilized paper packet, pulled the thick gauze out and placed it gently beneath Inca's neck and head. He took her pulse. It was barely perceptible. Roan shut his eyes and fought back tears.

"Pulse?" Salvador demanded hoarsely, jerking out gauze with which to wrap the dressing tightly about her head.

"Thready."

"Get the blood pressure cuff...."

More bullets whined nearby. Both men cringed, but kept on working feverishly over Inca.

Roan went through the motions like a robot. He was numb with shock. Inca was badly wounded. She could die.... He knew her work was dangerous. Somehow, her larger-than-life confidence made him believe she wasn't mortal. Could he hold her as he did before? Could he heal her? Another grenade exploded nearby, and flattening himself across Inca's inert form, Roan cursed. She *was* mortal. Terribly so. The battle raged, hot and heavy around them, but his mind, his heart, centered on her. *Great Spirit, don't let Inca die...don't let her die. Oh, no... I love her. She can't die— not now. She's too precious to you...to all of us....*

Salvador cursed richly as he pumped up the blood pressure cuff. "This is bad—90 over 60. Damn! We have no way to get her to a hospital for emergency surgery." He gave Roan a sad, frustrated look.

Just then, Roan heard another noise. *No! How could it be?* Lifting his head to the dark heavens, he held his breath. Did he dare believe what he heard? "Do you hear that?" he rasped thickly to Salvador.

The Brazilian blinked, then twisted in the direction of the noise, a roaring sound coming from the end of the valley. Within moments, it turned deafening and blotted out the gunfire around them. "*Deus,* it's helicopters! But…how? They cannot travel this far without refueling. Colonel Marcellino said none were available. Is it Faro coming back with reinforcements? We saw him take off earlier. He's got a chopper loaded with ordnance. What if it's him?" Frightened, Salvador searched the ebony heavens, which seemed heavy with humidity—rain that would fall at any moment.

Out of the night sky, to Roan's surprise, at least three black, unmarked gunships sank below the low cloud cover and came racing up the narrow valley toward them. He croaked, "No, it isn't Faro. They're Apache helicopters! At least two of them are, from what I can make out from here. They must be friendlies! I'll be damned!" Roan had no idea how they'd gotten here. Or who they were. There was still a chance they were drug runners. He knew from Morgan's top-secret files that Faro Valentino had a fleet of military helicopters stationed in Peru. And according to their best intelligence from satellites, there were no enemy helicopters in this immediate area. So who were these people? Brazilian Air Force? Roan wasn't sure. Even if they were, they would have had to have refueled midair to penetrate this deeply into the Amazon basin. Colonel Marcellino had never said anything about possible air support. Roan was positive he would have told his officers if it was an option. Besides, the Valentinos were known to have refuelling capabilities to get in and out of areas like this one.

"Captain Braga!" Roan yelled into his microphone. "Are these approaching Apaches ours? Over!"

Roan waited impatiently, his eyes wary slits as he watched

the aircraft rapidly draw near. If the copters were the enemy, they were all dead. Apaches could wreak hell on earth in five minutes flat. Roan's heart thudded with anxiety. He jerked a look down at Inca. Her mouth was slack, her flesh white as death. Her skin felt cool to his probing touch. Looking up, he saw Salvador's awed expression, his gaze locked to the sky. Flares were fired. The sky lit up like daylight as the helicopters approached the compound area.

Roan scowled. Of the three helos, two were Apache and one was a Vietnam era Cobra gunship. Surprised, he didn't know *what* to make of that. The valley echoed and reechoed with the heavy, flat drumming of their turning blades. Who the hell were they? Friend or enemy? Roan was almost ready to yell for Braga again when Braga's winded voice came over his headset.

"We don't know *whose* they are! They're not Brazilian! They're not drug runners. Colonel Marcellino is making a call to headquarters to try and find out more. Stand by! Over."

"Roger, I copy," Roan rasped. Blinking away the perspiration, he saw the Cobra flying hell-bent-for-leather between the two heavily armed Apaches. There was a fifty-caliber machine gun located at the opened door. He saw the gunner firing—at the drug runners!

"They're friendly!" Salvador shouted. *"Amigos!"*

The gunships all had blinking red and green lights on them. The two Apache helicopters suddenly peeled off from the Cobra; one went to the right side of the valley, the other to the left side. The Cobra barreled in toward the compound, low and fast, obviously attempting to land. The valley shook beneath their combined buffeting.

Roan suddenly put it all together. Whoever they were, they were here to help turn the tide against the savagely fighting drug runners! The Cobra began hovering a hundred feet above them, an indication that it was going to land very close to the compound. Sliding his hands beneath Inca, Roan growled to Salvador, "Come on! That chopper is going to land right in front of this factory. We can get Inca outta here! She has a chance if we can get her to the hospital in Manaus. Let's move!" Inca weighed next to nothing in his arms as Roan lifted her gently and pressed her against him. He made sure her head was secure against his neck and jaw. Every second counted. Every one.

The sound of powerful Apache gunships attacking began in the distance. Hellfire missiles were released, lighting up the entire valley. The missiles arced out of the sky toward the main concentration of drug runners, many of whom began to flee down the road toward the other end of the valley. Brutal noise, like that of a violent thunderstorm, pounded savagely against Roan's eardrums.

Salvador jerked up his medical pack and ran, slipping and stumbling, after Roan as he hurried in a long, striding walk to the compound entrance. The rain forest was alive with shouts from excited Brazilian soldiers. Hand-to-hand combat ensued. Out of the corner of his eye, Roan saw Captain Braga running down the slope with a squad of men. In the flashes of light, he saw triumph etched across the captain's sweaty, strained face.

Gripping Inca more tightly, Roan rounded the corner of the compound fence, heading directly to the Cobra, which had just landed just outside the gates. Neither he nor Salvador had weapons. Salvador was a medic and they never carried armament. Roan had left his rifle behind in order to carry Inca. Out of the darkness came two drug runners, weapons up and aimed directly at them.

Roan croaked out a cry of warning. "Salvador! Look out!" He started to turn, prepared to take the bullets he knew were coming, in order to protect Inca, who sagged limply in his arms.

Just then another figure, dressed in body-fitting black flight suit and flak jacket, helmet on his head, appeared almost as if by magic behind the drug runners who had Roan in their gunsites. The black helmet and visor covered the upper half of his face, but his pursed lips and the way he halted, spread his booted feet and lifted his arms, told Roan he was there for a reason.

Roan stared in horror and amazement as whoever it was— the pilot of the landed Cobra helicopter?—lifted his pistol in both hands and coolly fired off four shots. All four hit the drug runners, who crumpled to the muddy earth. The man then gestured for Roan and Salvador to make a run for it. He stood tensely and kept looking around for more enemy fire.

"Come on!" Roan roared, and he dug his boots into the mud. He saw the pilot turn and yell at him, his voice drowned out by the machine gun fire of the nearby Cobra. The pilot lifted his arm in hard, chopping motions, urging them to hightail it.

Roan's breath came in huge, gulping sobs as he steadied himself in the mud. *Hurry! Hurry!*

Salvador slipped. He cried out and smashed headlong into the ground and onto his belly. His medical pack went flying.

Roan jerked a look in his direction.

"Go on!" Salvador screamed. "*Corra!* Run! Get to the chopper! Don't worry about me!"

Roan hesitated only fractionally. He surged forward. Barely able to see the six-foot-tall pilot except in flashes of gunfire, Roan saw him reach toward him. The grip of his hand on his arm was steadying.

"Stay close!" the pilot yelled, his voice muffled by the shelling.

Roan's only protection for Inca as he ran along the compound fence was the wary pilot, who moved like a jaguar, lithe and boneless, the gun held ready in his gloved hand. Roan followed him toward the front corner of the barbed-wire barrier.

As Roan rounded the corner, he saw the helicopter, an antique Huey Cobra gunship from the Vietnam War, sitting on high idle waiting for them, its blades whirling. Roan followed the swiftly moving pilot back to the opening where the machine gunner was continuing to fire at drug runners. More than once, the pilot fired on the run, to the left, to the right, to protect them. Bullets whined past Roan's head like angry hornets. Slugs were smattering and striking all around them. Mud popped up in two-foot geysers around his feet. Roan saw the copilot in the aircraft making sharp gestures out the opened window, urging them to hurry up and get on board. The gunfire increased. The drug runners were going to try and kill them all so they couldn't take off.

Hurry! Roan's muscles strained. They screamed out in pain as he ran, holding Inca tightly against him. Only a hundred feet more! The pilot dived through the helicopter's open door, landed flat on his belly on the aluminum deck and quickly scrambled to his knees and lunged forward into the cockpit. The gunner at the door stopped firing. He stood crouched in the doorway, arms opened wide, yelling at Roan to hurry. All of them were dressed in black flight suits, with no insignias on their uniforms. Their helmets were black, the visors drawn down so Roan couldn't make out their faces. They looked brown skinned. Indians? Brazilians? He wasn't sure. Roan thought they must be from some secret government agency. The real military always wore patches and insignias identifying their country and squadron.

The blast of the rotor wash just about knocked him off his feet. His arms tightened around Inca. The pilot was powering up for a swift takeoff. The violent rush of air slapped and slammed Roam repeatedly as he ducked low to avoid getting hit by the whirling blades. The gunner held on to the frame of the door, the other hand stretched outward toward them. He was screaming at Roan to get on board. An explosion on the hill rocked him from behind. Fire and flame shot up a hundred feet into the air. One of the attack choppers must have found an ammo dump! Thunder rolled through the narrow valley, blotting out every other sound for moments.

By the time Roan made it to the doorway, his arms were burning weights. The gunner wrapped a strong hand under his biceps and hefted him upward, then moved aside and made a sharp gesture for Roan to place Inca on an awaiting litter right behind him in the rear of the small helicopter. Wind whipped through the craft. As Roan gently lay Inca on the stretcher and quickly shoved several protective, warm covers over her, the gunner placed a pair of earphones across Roan's head so he could have immediate contact with everyone else in the helicopter.

"Get us to the nearest hospital!" he gasped to the pilot as he knelt over Inca. "She's got a basal skull fracture. Time's something we don't have. She's gonna die if we can't get her stabilized. Let's get the hell outta here! Lift off! Lift off!"

The gunner went back to his station, and in seconds, the machine gun was firing with deep, throaty sounds once again. Red-and-yellow muzzle light flashed across the cabin with each round fired. Roan heard bullets striking the helo's thin skin as the craft wrenched off from the ground and shot skyward like a pogo stick out of control. He bracketed Inca with his own body, the gravity and power of the takeoff a surprise. This old machine had a lot more juice in it than he'd thought. The ride was violent and choppy. Everyone got bounced around. The pilot took evasive maneuvers, steering the aircraft in sharp zigzag turns until they could get out of the range of gunfire from below, moving swiftly up the valley, to gain altitude and head for Manaus.

The instant they were out of rifle range, the gunner stopped firing. He slid shut the doors on each side of the Cobra so that the wind ceased blasting through the aircraft. The helicopter shook and shuddered as it strained to gain altitude in the black abyss surrounding them. Before Roan could ask, a small, dull light illuminated the rear cabin where they were sitting on the bare metal deck, allowing him to see in order to take care of Inca. Quickly, he tied the green nylon straps of the litter snugly around her blanketed form so she couldn't be tossed about by the motion of the chopper.

"Give him the medical supplies," came the husky order from the pilot over his earphones.

Roan was in such shock over Inca's condition that it took him precious seconds to realize the ragged voice he heard was a woman's—not a man's. Surprised, he jerked a look toward the cockpit. He saw the pilot, the one who had shot the two drug runners and saved their lives, twist around in her seat and look at him for a moment. She pushed the visor up with her black glove and gazed directly at him and then down at Inca, the expression on her face one of raw emotion. Her eyes were alive with anger and worry as she stared at Inca.

His mouth dropped open. Even with the helmet and military gear, Roan swore she was nearly a carbon copy of Inca! How could that be? The light was bad and her sweaty face deeply shadowed, so he couldn't be sure. The shape of her face was more square than Inca's, but their nose and eyes looked the same. The pilot's expression was fierce. Her eyes were slitted. There were tears running down the sides of her cheeks. She was breathing heavily, her chest heaving beneath the flak jacket she wore.

"How's Inca doing?"

Roan blinked. Clearly this woman knew Inca. His mind tilted. He opened his mouth. "Not good. She's stable for now, but she could dump at any time."

Nodding, the woman wiped her eyes free of the tears. "She couldn't be in better hands right now."

Stymied, Roan saw the depth of emotion in her teary eyes. Tears? Why? The stress of combat? Possibly.

"I know you have a lot of questions, Senhor Storm Walker. In time, they'll be answered. Welcome aboard the black

jaguar express.'' She made a poor attempt to smile. ''I'm
Captain Maya Stevenson. My copilot is Lieutenant Klein.
Take care of my sister, Inca, will you? We're heading for
Manaus. My copilot's already in touch with the nearest hospital. There'll be an emergency team waiting for us once we
land. We brought some help along.'' She jerked a thumb in
the direction of her door gunner. ''Sergeant Angel Paredes
has a lot of other skills you can use. We call her the Angel
of Death. She pulls our people from death's door.'' Her lips
lifted, showing strong white teeth. ''Get to work.'' She
turned back to her duties.

''Here,'' the door gunner said, ''IV with glucose solu-
tion.'' She pushed up the visor into her helmet, her round
Indian face in full view beneath the low lighting.

Stunned, Roan looked at her. Paredes grinned a little.
''This is a woman's flight, *senhor*. Tell me what else you
need for Inca.'' She gestured toward a large medical bag
nearby. ''I'm a paramedic also. How may I assist you?''

Shaking his head in stunned shock, Roan had a hundred
questions. But nothing mattered right now except Inca and
her deteriorating condition. ''Put the IV in her right arm,''
he rasped. Leaning out, he pulled the IV bag over to him
and hung it on a hook so that the fluid would drip steadily
into her arm. ''You got ice on board?''

Paredes nodded as she knelt down and wiped Inca's arm
with an alcohol swab. ''Yes, sir.'' She pointed to it with her
black, gloved hand, then took off her gloves and dropped
them to the deck. ''In there, *senhor*. In that thick plastic
container.'' She skillfully prepped Inca's arm to insert the
IV needle.

Roan found the containers and jammed his hand into the
pack. This was no ordinary paramedic's pack, he realized.
No, it was like a well-stocked ambulance pack. It had everything he could ever want to help save Inca's life. The
helicopter shook around him. His ears popped. He heard
constant, tense exchanges between the pilot and copilot.

Both women's voices. A three-woman air crew. What country were they from? He picked up the plastic bag of ice and struck it hard against his thigh, then waited a moment before gently placing it beneath Inca's neck. It was an instant ice pack, which, when struck, mixed chemicals that created coolness. The door gunner handed him some wide, thick gauze.

"To hold the ice pack in place," she instructed.

Nodding his thanks, Roan began to feel his adrenaline letdown make him shaky. Inca lay beneath the warming blankets, her beautiful golden skin washed out and gray looking. Reaching for the blood pressure cuff, he took a reading on Inca. To his relief, her pressure was holding steady. Ordinarily, on a wound like this, the person dumped and died within minutes because the brain had been bruised by the broken skull plates and began to swell at a swift rate. So far, her blood pressure was remaining steady, and that was a small sign of hope.

"How's Inca doing?" Stevenson demanded.

Roan glanced forward. The captain was flying the helicopter as if the hounds of hell were on her tail. They needed all the speed this old chopper could give them. Time was of the essence, and she seemed to share his sense of haste. The aircraft shook and vibrated wildly as the pilot pushed it to maximum acceleration, tunneling through the clouds.

"Stable," he croaked. "She's remaining stable. That's a good sign."

"I could use some good news," Stevenson growled.

And then Roan noticed that the helicopter was following another one, at less than one rotor length. Stymied, Roan saw the red and green, flashing lights on the underbelly of the copter in front of them.

"What's that chopper doing so close?" he demanded, terror in his tone.

Stevenson gave a bark of laughter. "This old bag of bones doesn't have any IFR, instrument flight rules, equipment on board to get us through the clouds or for night flight, Senhor Storm Walker. The chopper ahead of us is a state-of-the-art Apache gunship. She's equipped with everything we need to get the hell out of here and get Inca to Manaus. I'm following it. If I lose visual contact with it, we're all screwed. I'll lose my sense of direction in this soup and we'll crash.''

Roan's eyes narrowed. She was doing more than following it, for there was barely a hundred feet between them. One wrong move and they'd crash into one another. That kind of flying took incredible skill and bravery. No wonder the Cobra was shaking like this; it was in direct line of the rotor wash of the far more powerful Apache. Yet he knew the gunship was a two-seater and had no room for passengers.

''Shove this old crone into the redline range,'' the pilot ordered the copilot. ''Tell them to put the peddle to the metal up there. Squeeze *every* ounce of power outta her.''

''Roger.''

Roan shook his head disbelievingly. He looked down at Inca. Her face was covered on one side with mud. Taking a dressing, he tried to clean her up a little. He loved her. He didn't want her to die. Moving his hand over Inca's limp one, he felt the coolness of her flesh.

''Pray for her, *senhor*. Prayer by those who love someone is the most powerful,'' the door gunner said as she got up and crawled forward toward the cockpit.

Roan touched Inca's unmarred brow with trembling fingertips. She looked so beautiful. So untouched. And yet a bullet had found her. Why hadn't he realized she was vulnerable just like any other human being? Why hadn't her spirit guide protected her? Squeezing his eyes shut, Roan ruthlessly berated himself. Why hadn't he shot first before Faro Valentino had fired at her? His heart ached with guilt. With unanswered questions. Again he stroked Inca's cheek and felt her softness. Gone was her bright animation. Inca's spirit hung between worlds right now. Roan didn't fool himself. She could die. The chances of it happening were almost guaranteed.

"Another hour, Senhor Walker," the pilot murmured. "We'll be there in an hour...."

How could *that* be? Roan twisted to look toward the gunner, who was crouched in a kneeling position, her hands gripping the metal beams on either side of her as she hung between the seats of the two pilots. They were a helluva lot farther from Manaus than an hour! What was going on? Roan felt dizzy. He felt out of sync with everything that was going on around him. He realized he was in shock over Inca's being wounded. He was unraveling and everything felt like a nightmare.

"An hour?" he rasped. "That can't be."

The pilot laughed. "In our business, *anything* is possible, Senhor Walker. Just keep tending Inca. Be with her. I'll take care of my part in this deal. Okay?"

Who are these women? The question begged to be asked. Roan watched through the cockpit Plexiglas as they rose higher and higher. Suddenly they broke through the soup of thick clouds. He gasped. The Apache gunship was just ahead of them, and he felt the hard, jarring movement from being in the air pockets and rotor wash behind it. Captain Stevenson was within inches of the Apache's rotors. Marveling at her flying skills, Roan turned away. He couldn't watch; he thought they'd crash into one another for sure. The woman was certifiable, in his opinion. She had to be crazy to fly like this.

His world was torn apart and tumbling out of his control. Roan felt stripped and helpless. He leaned close to Inca and placed a kiss on her cool cheek. All he could do now was monitor her blood pressure, her pulse, and simply be with her. And pray hard to the Great Spirit to save her life. She was too young to die. Too vital. Too important to Amazonia. Oh, why hadn't he taken out that drug runner first? Roan hung his head, and hot tears squeezed beneath his tightly shut lids.

He felt a hand on his shoulder. "You did all you could, *senhor,*" Paredes said gently. "Don't be hard on yourself. Some things are meant to be…and all we can do is be there to pick up the pieces afterward. Just hang in there. Manaus is nearby…."

Roan couldn't look up. All he could do was remain sitting next to Inca, his bulk buttressing the litter against the rear wall of the aircraft so that she had a somewhat stable and stationary ride. He felt Paredes remove her hand from his shoulder.

His world revolved around Inca. Never had he loved someone as he loved her. And now their collective worlds were shattered. All the secret hopes and dreams he'd begun to harbor were now smashed. Closing his eyes, Roan took Inca's hand between his and prayed as he'd never prayed before. If only they could be at Manaus right away. If only they could get her into emergency surgery. If only…

Roan sat tensely in the waiting room on the surgery floor of the hospital in Manaus. There was nothing else he could do while Inca was being operated on. Forlornly, he looked around at the red plastic sofas and chairs. The place was deserted. It was one in the morning. The antiseptic smells were familiar to him, almost soothing to his razor-blade tenseness. An emergency team had been waiting for them when the woman pilot landed the Cobra on the roof of the Angel of Mercy Hospital. And just as soon as Inca was disembarked by the swift-moving surgery team, Captain Stevenson had taken off, her Cobra absorbed into the night sky once again. He hadn't even had time to thank her or her brave crew. Instead, Roan's attention had been centered on Inca, and on the team who rushed her on a wheeled gurney into the hospital. He gave the information on Inca's condition to the woman neurosurgeon who was to do the surgery.

Her team hurried Inca into the prepping room, while he was asked to go and wait in the lobby area.

Reluctantly, Roan had agreed. He'd paced for nearly two hours, alone and overwhelmed with grief and anger. Life wasn't fair, that he knew. But to take Inca's life, a woman whose energy supported so many, who held the threadbare fabric of the old Amazonia together, was too unfair. Rubbing his smarting, reddened eyes, Roan had finally sat down, feeling the fingers of exhaustion creeping through him. He was filthy with mud that had encrusted and dried on his uniform. Inca's blood was smeared across it as well. He didn't care. He stank. He could smell his own fear sweat. The fear of losing Inca.

Nothing mattered except Inca, her survival. He heard a sound at the doorway and snapped up his head. The neurosurgeon, Dr. Louisa Sanchez, appeared in her green medical garb. Her expression was serious.

"Inca?" Roan voice rang hollowly in the lobby. He stood up and held his breath as the somber surgeon approached.

"Senhor Storm Walker," she began in a low tone, "Inca is stable. I've repaired the fracture. The bullet did not impact her brain, which is the good news. It ricocheted off the skull and broke the bone, instead. What we must worry about now is her brain swelling because of the trauma of the bone fracture. It is very bad, *senhor*."

Roan blinked. He felt hot tears jam into his eyes. "You've packed her skull in ice?"

"Yes, she is ice packed right now."

"And put an anti-inflammatory in her IV to reduce the swelling of her brain tissue?"

Dr. Sanchez nodded grimly. "*Sim*. I've given her the highest amount possible, *senhor*. If I give her any more, it will kill her." The surgeon reached out. "I'm sorry. We must wait. Right now, she's being wheeled into a special room that is outside of ICU. She will be monitored by all the latest equipment, but it is not glass-enclosed. It is a private room."

Roan felt his world tilting. He understood all too well what the doctor was saying without saying it. The private room was reserved for those who were going to die, anyway. This just gave the family of the person the privacy they needed to say their goodbyes and to weep without the world watching them.

"I—see...." he croaked.

Sadly, Dr. Sanchez whispered, "She's in the hands of God, now, *senhor*. We've done all we could. I anticipate that in the next forty-eight hours her fate will be decided.... I suggest you get cleaned up. And then you can stay with her, yes?"

The doctor's kindness was more than Roan had expected. Inca was going to die. Blinking back the tears, he rasped unsteadily, "No, I want to stay with her, Doctor. Thank you...."

The beeps and sighs of ICU equipment filled the white room where Inca lay. Normally, Roan felt a sense of security with all these machines. Inca was breathing on her own, which was good. As he stood at her bedside, he saw how pale she had become. Her head was swathed in a white dressing and bandage. The ice packs were changed hourly. And every hour, her blood pressure was moving downward, a sign of impending death. Miserably, Roan stood at her bedside, her cool hand clutched within his. Dawn was peeking through the venetian blinds. The pale rose color did not even register with him, only as a reminder that Inca would enjoy seeing the beauty of the colors that washed the dawn sky. So many conversations with her played back to him. Each one twinged his aching heart. He had tried to heal her as he had once before, but it didn't work. He was too exhausted, too emotionally torn to gather the necessary amount of laser-like concentration. Never had he felt so helpless.

Leaning down, Roan pressed his lips to her forehead. Easing back a little, he studied Inca's peaceful face. She looked as if she were asleep, that was all; not fighting a losing battle for her life. Roan knew that the brain could continue to swell despite whatever efforts doctors made, and that if it swelled too much, it would block the necessary messages to the rest of the body and she'd stop breathing. Her blood pressure dropping was a bad sign that her brain was continuing to swell despite everything. A very bad sign.

"I love you, Inca. Do you hear me, sweetheart?" His voice broke the stillness of the room. His tone was deep and unsteady. Hot tears spilled from his eyes. "Do you hear me? I love you. I don't know when it happened, it just did." He brushed the soft skin of her cheek. "At first, I was afraid to fall for you, Inca. But now I'm glad I did. I want you to fight, Inca. Fight to come back to me. To what we might have. This isn't fair. None of it. I've just found you…loved you.… Please—" he squeezed her fingers gently "—fight back. Fight for our love, fight for yourself, because there are so many people who need you. Who rely on you…"

The door quietly opened and closed. Roan choked back a sob, straightened up and twisted to look in that direction. He'd expected the nurse, who would take Inca's vitals and replace the old ice pack for a new one. His eyes widened. It was Captain Stevenson. She was still dressed in the clinging black nylon uniform, her flak jacket open. Beneath her left arm was her helmet. His gaze ranged upward to her face. His heart pounded hard. She looked drawn and exhausted as she stepped into the room.

He met her slightly tilted emerald-green eyes as they locked on his. Blinking, Roan again saw the powerful resemblance between her and Inca. They almost looked like— twins! But how could that be? His mind spun. She had her black hair, tightly gathered in a chignon at the nape of her long neck. The pride and confidence in her square face was unmistakable. But there was grief in her eyes, and her full lips twisted slightly in greeting.

She moved soundlessly to the other side of Inca's bed. Glancing down at Inca, she quietly placed her helmet on the bedstand. "You're right, Senhor Storm Walker. I *am* her twin." She smiled tenderly down at Inca and ran her fingers along her arm. "Fraternal twin."

"But...how...? Inca never told me about you."

Maya shrugged. Her expression softened more as she leaned down and placed a kiss on Inca's damp brow. Straightening, her voice hoarse, she said, "Inca never knew I existed. So she couldn't tell you about me. I was told of her being my sister a year ago by the elders of the Jaguar Clan. Once I knew, I was told I would meet her." She grimaced. "They didn't tell me how I would meet her until a week ago. That's why I'm here...."

Stunned into silence, Roan stared at the woman. She was a warrior, no doubt. She was as tall as Inca, and he could see the black leather holster on her thigh.

"My poor sister," Maya whispered in a choked tone as she continued to stroke Inca's hair in a gentle motion. "Our fate has been one made in darkness. I'm so sorry this happened. I wished I could've stopped it, but I couldn't. You have one more bridge to cross, my loving sister. Just one..." And Maya straightened and looked directly at Roan.

"She's going to die," Maya told him in a low tone.

Roan rocked back. He gripped Inca's hand and tried to deal with the truth.

Maya sighed as the pain moved through her heart. She held Inca's other hand in hers.

"I tried to save her like I did once before," he told Maya.

She shook her head. "You don't have the kind of training it takes to be able to heal in the middle of a battle." She gave him an understanding look. "It takes years of training to do it, so don't blame yourself."

"It worked once...I hoped...wanted it to work again...."

"You're lucky it happened once. There's a huge difference between a snake bite and a firefight. You just didn't have the emotional composure to pull it off when she got shot."

Roan stared at her. "Earlier you said 'black jaguar express.' I thought you were kidding. But if you're Inca's sister, then you're from the Jaguar Clan, too?"

She smiled tightly. "The *Black* Jaguar Clan, *senhor*. Very few know about us. Let's just say we do the dirty work for the Sisterhood of Light. The Jaguar Clan you know of, Inca's people, work in good, positive ways. The Black Jaguar Clan...well, let's just put it this way—someone has to clean up the ugliness in life." Her mouth was grim. There was a glitter in her eyes that said she was committed to what her life was about.

"You—work for the Brazilian government, then?" His mind spun. His heart ached. Inca was going to die.

Maya shook her head and gave a low growl as she continued to devote her attention to Inca. "What an insult. We work for a much higher power than that. But enough of this. You need to listen to me carefully, *senhor*. Inca has one shot at living. That's why I'm here. I've been told that she can have her life back. There's only one possibility for her to live, however."

Eagerly, Roan listened. "How? What can I do?"

Maya studied him fiercely. "You are a credit to the human race, *senhor*. Yes, you can help." She pointed toward the ceiling. "In the laws of the Sisterhood of Light, it's said that if a person willingly gives up her or his life for another, the one who is dying may survive. But—" Maya gave him a hard, uncompromising look "—in order for that to occur, that person must *willingly* give her or his life in exchange. It must be someone who loves the dying person unselfishly."

The silence swirled between them.

Roan looked down at Inca. He would have to die in order

for her to live. His hand tightened around hers. He felt Maya's stare cutting straight through him. It was clear she possessed a power equal to Inca's, and then some.

Inca's life for his own. His heart shattered with the finality of the her words.

"You know," Roan whispered in a broken tone, "I've been a lucky man. I never thought I'd know what love was in this lifetime until I met Sarah. And then she was torn from me. After that—" he looked up at Maya, tears in his eyes "—I never expected to fall in love again, until Inca crashed into my life. I'd given up hope. I was just surviving, not living life, until she came along." Gently, he brushed Inca's arm with his fingertips. "My life for hers. There's no question of who's more important here. She is."

Roan lifted his chin and met and held Maya's hard emerald gaze. Her expression was uncompromising as she stood there, the silence deepening in the room.

"Yes. Take my life for hers. Inca is far more important than me. I love her...."

Maya regarded him gravely. "In order for this exchange to occur, you must love her enough to not be afraid of dying."

Shaking his head, Roan rasped, "There's no question of my love for Inca. If you're as powerful metaphysically as she is, then you already know that. You knew the answer before coming here, didn't you?"

Giving him a mirthless smile, Maya whispered, "Yes, I knew. But you see, my brave friend, there's always free will in such matters." She glided her hand across Inca's unbound hair. "If I could give my life for hers, I'd do it in a heartbeat. But the laws state that I can't; we're twin souls, and therefore, it's unacceptable."

Roan looked at one monitor. He saw Inca's blood pressure dipping steeply. "She's dumping," he growled, and pointed at the screen. "She's dying. Just do it. Get it over with. Just tell her when she wakes up that I loved her with all my heart and soul.''

Maya took a deep breath and gave him a warm, sad look. "Yes, I promise she'll know. And…thank you. You've given me my sister, whom I've never been allowed to approach or to know. Now we'll have the time we need to get to know one another…and *be* sisters.…''

Roan nodded. "More than anything, she wanted a family, Maya. I'm glad she has one. I know she's going to be happy to see you when she wakes up."

Blinking hard, Maya whispered, "Place your hand over her heart and your other hand over the top of her head. Keep your knees slightly bent and flexed. It will allow the energy to run more smoothly. If you lock your knees, you'll block it and cause problems. And whatever happens, keep your eyes closed and keep a hold on her. Me and my black jaguar spirit guide will do the rest.''

Roan leaned down. One last kiss. A goodbye kiss. His mouth touched and glided against Inca's, whose lips were slightly parted. Her lips were chapped and cool beneath his. He kissed her tenderly, and with all the love that he felt for her. He breathed his breath into her mouth—one last parting gift. His breath, his life entering into her body, into her soul. As he eased away, he whispered, "I'll see you on the other side, sweetheart. I love you.…''

"Prepare!'' Maya growled. "She's leaving us!''

Roan did exactly as Maya asked. He stood at Inca's bedside and braced himself against the metal railing for support. He had no idea what would happen next. Well, he'd had one hell of a life. He'd been privileged to love two extraordinary women—two more than he deserved. The moment his hands were in place, he felt Maya's strong, warm hands move over his. It felt like a lightning bolt had struck him. He groaned. The darkness behind his lids exploded into what could only be described as sparks and explosions of color and light. In seconds, Roan was whirling and spinning as if caught in a tornado's grip. He lost all sense of time, direction and of being in his body.

And then he lost consciousness as he spun into a darkened void. The only thing he felt, the last thing he remembered, was his undying, tender love for Inca....

Chapter 12

An intense, gutting pain ripped through Roan and made him groan out loud. His voice reverberated around him like a drum sounding. Was he dead? He felt out of breath, gasps tearing raggedly from of his mouth, as if he'd run ten miles without resting. Everything was dark. His body felt as if a steel weight was resting on him. It was impossible to move.

"Lie still, lie still, and soon the pressure will lift. Be patient, my son...."

Roan didn't know the woman, but her voice was remarkably soothing to his panicked state. Had he died? Struggling to see, he groaned.

"Shh, my son, just relax. No, you are not dead. You've just been teleported from Manaus to here. In a few moments your eyes will open."

He felt her hand on his shoulder, warm and anchoring. His head hurt like hell, a hot, throbbing sensation. What of Inca? What had happened to her? He opened his mouth to speak, but only a croak came out of it.

He heard the woman chuckle. She patted his shoulder.

"Young people are so impatient. Try to take a deep breath, Roan. Just one."

Struggling to do as the woman asked, he concentrated hard on taking a breath. His mind was scattered; he felt like he was in five or six major pieces, floating out of body in a dark vacuum.

"Good," she praised. "And again…"

Roan was able to take the second breath even more deeply into his chest. He was hyperventilating, but by honing in on her voice, he was able to slow his breathing down considerably.

"Excellent. My name is Alaria. When you open your eyes, you will find yourself in a large hut here at the Village of the Clouds. You and Inca are welcome here."

Roan felt a surge of electricity move from her hand into his shoulder. The jolt was warm and mild, but he was very aware of the energy moving quickly through him. "My son, when Inca returns from the Threshold, she will want to see your face first…." He felt the gentle pat of Grandmother Alaria's hand on his shoulder.

And then, almost without effort, he lifted his lids. Bright light made him squint, and he turned his head briefly to one side to avoid it. Shafts of sunlight lanced through an open window. Blinking several times, Roan managed to roll onto his side and then slowly sit up. Dizziness assailed him. All the while, Alaria's hand remained on his arm to steady him. That electrical charge was still flowing out of her hand and into him. Shaking his head, he rubbed his face wearily.

"Take your time. You've been through a great deal," she said quietly. "Inca is fine. She is lying next to you, there." She pointed to the other side of the mat where he sat. "Inca will recover fully, so do not fret. I need you to come back, into your body, and become grounded. Then the dizziness will leave and you will no longer feel as if you're in pieces, floating around in space."

Next to him, on a soft, comfortable pallet on the hard dirt

floor, was Inca, who was asleep or unconscious. She lay beneath several blankets. Her skin tone was normal and no longer washed out. Most of all, the peaceful look on her unmarred features made Roan's fast-beating heart soar with hope. Looking up, he saw the woman named Alaria for the first time. Relief flooded him that Inca was here and she was all right. He didn't know *how* she could be; but having been around Inca, he knew that miracles were everyday occurrences in the life of Jaguar Clan members.

And perhaps a miracle had just occurred for both of them. He felt better just looking into Alaria's aged but beautiful face. Her eyes sparkled with tenderness, her hand firm and steady on his shoulder. She had her silver hair plaited into two thick braids, which hung over her shoulders, and she was dressed in a pale pink blouse and a dark brown cotton skirt, her feet bare and thickly callused. His mind spun. With her parchmentlike hands, she continued to send him stabilizing energy, reassuring him that he wasn't dead.

"I know you have many questions," Alaria soothed. "Just rest. You are still coming out of the teleport state that Maya initiated with our help. All questions will be answered once Inca has returned to us." She brushed his dampened hair with aged fingers. "You are a courageous and unselfish warrior, Roan Storm Walker. We have been watching you for some time. Be at peace. There is safety here in the Village of the Clouds for you and Inca." Pouring some liquid into a carved wooden cup, she handed it to him. "Drink this warm tea. It contains a healing herb."

He was thirsty. His mouth was dry. Eagerly, he drank the contents of the mug. There was a slightly sweet and astringent taste to the tea. Roan opened his mouth to speak, then closed it. He watched Alaria slowly get to her feet. She straightened and gave him a grandmotherly smile.

"Inca will be awakening soon, and she will be disoriented and dizzy just like you for a while. Be with her. We are monitoring her energy levels at all times. Her wound has been healed. There is no more swelling of her brain.'' A slight smile crossed her lips. ''And you are not dead. You are both alive. I'll return later. Give Inca the herbal drink when she's ready for it.''

''T-thank you,'' Roan said, his voice sounding like sandpaper.

Alaria nodded, folded her thin hands and moved serenely out of the roomy thatched hut. Outside, thunder caromed in the distance, and he saw an arc of lightning brighten the turbulent blue-and-black sky. It was going to rain shortly. The beam of sunlight that had blinded him earlier was gone, snuffed out by the approaching cumulus clouds, which were dark and pregnant with water.

Turning his attention to Inca, Roan moved his trembling fingers along her right arm. She wasn't dead. She was alive. Her flesh was warm, not cool and deathlike as before. Dizziness assailed him once more, and he shut his eyes tightly and clung to her hand. He still felt fragmented. He felt as if pieces of him were still spinning wildly here and there in space. It was an uncomfortable sensation, one he'd never experienced before.

Opening his eyes, Roan studied Inca's soft, peaceful features. Her lips, once chapped, were now softly parted and had regained their natural pomegranate color. Her hair was combed and free flowing, an ebony halo about her head and shoulders. And his medicine piece now lay around her neck, resting on her fine, thin collarbones. The last thing he remembered was placing the amulet between their hands—a last gift, a prayer for her, for her life. Someone must have put the necklace back in place around Inca's neck, but he didn't know who had done it. Roan gently touched the opalescent blue stone which felt warm and looked as if it was glowing.

So much had happened. Roan couldn't explain any of it. One moment he was in the hospital room in Manaus, following Maya's orders to save Inca's life. And the next, it felt as if fifty thousand volts of lightning had struck him squarely. Roan remembered spinning down into a dark abyss, but that was all. And then he'd groggily regained consciousness here, in this hut.

Frowning, he felt a wave of emotion. Inca was here with him. He loved her. His heart swelled fiercely with such feeling that tears automatically wet his lashes. Not caring if anyone saw him cry, Roan didn't try to stop the tears that were now moving down his unshaved face.

"Come back, sweetheart. They said you would live...." he rasped thickly, as he moved his fingers up her arm in a comforting motion. She should have had needle imprints and a little bruising around where the IVs had been placed in her arms, but there was no sign of them on her beautiful, soft flesh. And when he examined the back of her head, the wound was gone. Gone! Her skull bone no longer protruded. There was no tissue swelling. It was as if the injury had never occurred.

How could this be? Roan couldn't stop touching Inca. His heart was wide-open and pounding with anguish one second, giddy with joy the next. Her skin was warm and firm. Her thick, black lashes rested across her golden, high cheekbones. Moving his fingers through her lush, silky hair, he marveled at her wild, untamed beauty.

The rain began, pelting softly at first on the thatched roof. Lightning shattered across the area and illuminated the rain forest at the edge of the village, its power shaking the hut. Thunder caromed like a hundred kettledrums being struck simultaneously. Cringing slightly, Roan waited tensely.

Inca stirred.

His hand tightened around hers. He held his breath. Did he dare hope? Was she coming out of the coma? Would she be whole or brain damaged? Would she have amnesia and not recognize him? Roan leaned down, his eyes narrowing, his heart pounding wildly.

"Inca? Sweetheart? It's me, Roan. You're not dying.

You're alive. Open your eyes. You're here with me. You're safe. Do you hear me?'' His fingers tightened again about hers. Once more her lashes fluttered. And then her parted lips compressed. One corner of her mouth pulled inward, as if she were in pain. Was she? Anxiety tunneled through him. Roan wished mightily for Alaria to be here right now. He had no idea what to expect, what to do in case Inca was in pain. It was his nature, as a paramedic, to relieve suffering, and right now he felt damned useless.

"Inca?"

Roan felt her fingers twitch, then curve around his. He smiled a little. "That's it, come on out of it. You're coming back from a long journey, my woman. You're my heart, Inca. I don't know if you can hear me or understand me, but I love you...." He choked on a sob. Roan watched in amazement as color began to flood back into her face. He felt a powerful shift of energy around her and himself. Her cheeks took on a rosy hue. Life was flowing back into her.

A second bolt of lightning slammed into the earth, far too close to the hut. Roan cringed as the power and tumult of the flash shook the ground. Rain was now slashing down, the wind howling unabated. The wide, sloping roof kept the pummeling rain from coming into the open windows. Instead, cooling and soothing breezes drifted throughout the clean, airy hut.

Inca's brows moved downward. Roan's breath caught in this throat as her lashes swept upward and he saw her drowsy looking, willow-green eyes. Anxiously, he searched them. Her pupils were huge and black as she gazed up at him. Was she seeing him? Or was she still caught in the coma? Roan knew that it took days and sometimes weeks or even months for a person who was in a coma to come out of it and be coherent. She stared up at him. Her pupils constricted and became more focused. His heart pounded with anxiety.

"Inca? It's Roan. I'm here." He lifted her hand and

pressed it against his heart. Leaning down, he caressed her cheek. "I love you. Do you hear me? I'm never going to leave you. You're coming out of a coma. Everything's all right. You're safe…and you're here with me…." He managed a wobbling smile of hope for both of them.

A third bolt of lightning struck, even closer to the hut than the last one, it seemed. This strike made the hut shudder like a wounded beast. Automatically, Roan leaned forward, his body providing protection for Inca. As the thunder rolled mightily around them, Roan eased back. It was then that he recalled that Inca had been born in an eclipse of the moon and during a raging thunderstorm. Sitting up, he watched her eyes become less sleepy looking and more alive, as if her spirit were moving back inside her physical form and flooding her with life once again. The symbolism of the storm was not lost on him. Mike Houston had told him she'd been born in a storm it would make sense that her rebirth would take place during another storm.

He smiled a little, heartened by that knowledge. Indians saw the world as a latticework of symbols and cosmology that were all intertwined. As he gently pressed her hand against his heart, he saw her lashes lift even more. Inca's eyes were now clearer and far more focused. Her gaze clung to his. Roan felt her returning; with each heartbeat, he felt Inca coming home, to him, to what he prayed would be a lifetime with her if the Great Spirit so ordained it.

"Where…?" Inca croaked, her voice rough from disuse.

"You're here at the Village of the Clouds, sweetheart. With me. Alaria said we were teleported by her from the hospital in Manaus." Roan didn't care if his voice wobbled with tears. With joy. Inca was here. And she was alive! He reached down and tenderly caressed her cheek. Her pupils changed in diameter, so he knew she was seeing him and that her brain was not damaged as he feared.

"Welcome back," he rasped. "You're home, with me…where you belong…."

The words fell like a soft, warm blanket around Inca. The sensation of vertigo was slowly leaving her. She felt her spirit sliding fully and locking powerfully into her physical body. Roan's large, scarred hand held hers. She closed her eyes, took in a deep, shaky breath and whispered, "I can feel your heartbeat in my hand...." And she could. Inca opened her eyes and drowned in his dark, smoky-blue gaze. There was no question that she loved him. None. Just that little-boy smile lurking hesitantly at the corner of his mouth, and the hope and love burning in his eyes, made a powerful river of joy flow through her opening heart.

"Are you thirsty? Alaria said you should drink this herbal tea. It will help you."

As Inca became more aware of her surroundings, she frowned. Alaria? Yes, Roan had mentioned Grandmother Alaria. Inca's heart bounded with hope. She had been here with her? Could it be they were *really* at the Village of the Clouds? Her head spun. She had been banned from her real home. So why was she here now? Nothing made sense to Inca. Her hope soared. "Y-yes..."

Roan reached for a pitcher and poured some of the contents into a mug carved out of a coconut shell. "Hold on," he murmured, "and I'll help you sit up enough to drink this."

Inca heard the wind howling around them. It was a powerful storm. She felt it in her bones, felt it stirring her spirit back to life within her body. As a metaphysician, she had experienced many strange sensations, but this one was new to her. She'd teleported once or twice before and was familiar with the process. But this was different. When Roan leaned over and slid his thick arm behind her neck and shoulders and gently lifted her into his arms, Inca became alarmed at how weak she was.

"Don't fight," he soothed as he angled her carefully, cradling her against his body. He watched as Inca tried to lift her hand. It fell limply back to her side. Seeing the surprise in her eyes, he raised the mug to her lips.

"Drink all you want," he urged. "Alaria said you would be weak coming out of the teleportation journey."

He held her like he might hold a newborn infant. The sense of protection, of love, overwhelmed Inca, and she drank thirstily. The warm herbal tea tasted sweet and energizing to her. She was a lot thirstier than she'd first realized. She drank from the mug four times more before her thirst was sated.

The medicinal tea brought renewed strength to her. This time when she forced her arm to move it moved. As Roan placed the mug on the mat beside him, Inca looked up at him with pleading eyes. "Just hold me? I need you...." And she weakly placed her hand against his thick biceps. Roan was dressed in his fatigues, spattered with dried mud, with blackish-red blood stains on his left shoulder. She realized it was *her* blood. From her wound. And yet she felt whole, not wounded. So much had happened. Inca was unable to sort it out. Later, she knew, the memories would trickle back to her.

Roan smiled down at her. "Anytime you want, sweetheart, I'll hold you." And he slid his other arm around her and brought her close to him. A ragged sigh issued from her lips as she rested her head against his shoulder, her brow against his hard, sandpapery jaw.

Closing her eyes, Inca whispered, "I almost died, didn't I? I feel as if I've just returned from the Threshold. You saved me, Roan. You gave your life willingly for me—I remember that. But that's all. I recall nothing more...."

Rocking her gently in his arms, he took one of the blankets from the pallet and eased it around Inca's shoulders and back to ensure her continued warmth. The fierce thunderstorm was dropping the temperature and there was a slight chill in the hut now. He smiled, closed his eyes and gave her a very gentle squeeze.

"Between the two of us, Inca, you're the one that should've had the chance to live, not me." She felt so good in his arms—weak and in need of his protection. That was something he could give her right now, and it made him feel good and strong. Gone was the fierce woman warrior. Right now, Inca was completely vulnerable, open and accessible to him, and it was such a gift. Roan knew that when a person had a near death experience, he or she came back changed—forever. Sliding his arm across her blanketed back, he caressed her.

"I love you. I never told you that before you were shot and went into a coma."

Inca lifted her head and met his stormy blue gaze. She saw the anguish in his eyes and felt it radiating out from him. Roan's love for her was so strong and pure that it rocked her returning senses. "I did not think anyone would find me worth loving," she whispered brokenly. Lifting her hand, Inca added hoarsely, "I am not a good person. I have a dark heart. That is why I was told to leave the village and never return."

"Well," Roan said in a fierce whisper, "I think all that's changed, sweetheart." He caressed her loose, flowing hair. "And your heart is one of the purest and finest I've ever seen. So stop believing that about yourself."

A sad smile pulled at her mouth. "I am so tired, Roan. I want to sleep...."

Roan eased Inca to the pallet. "Go ahead. Sleep will be healing for you. I'm going to close the windows. There's too much breeze coming in on you." He got to his feet, groping for the wall of the hut to support himself. The dizziness was gone and his legs felt pretty solid beneath him. He shut the windows to stop the wind from filtering into the hut. Turning, he saw Inca watching him from half-closed eyes. She opened her hand.

"Will you sleep with me? I need you near...."

Touched, Roan nodded. "There's nothing I'd like better."

He expected nothing from Inca. He had shared his love with her. Even if she never loved him, she would know the truth of what lay in his heart. As he knelt down upon his pallet, which was next to hers, he heard the storm receding. The pounding rain was lessening now. Father Sky had loved Mother Earth. That was how Indians saw the dance of the storms that moved across the heavens—as a way of the sky people and spirits caressing and loving their mother, the earth.

Inca sighed, her lashes feeling like weights. Her heart was throbbing with so much emotion, feelings she'd never experienced before. Just the way Roan cared for her told her of his love for her, and quenched and soothed her thirsty heart. She could no longer say she did not know what love was for she had experienced it with him—on the highest and most refined level. He had given his life so that she could return and continue her work in Amazonia. And through whatever mechanism and for whatever reasons, Roan's life had been spared. Joy filtered through her sleepy state. Inca knew she was still weak from having nearly died. It would take days for her to recover fully. The fact they were here in the Village of the Clouds surprised her, but she was too exhausted, and too in need of Roan's steady and loving presence to find out why.

Inca nuzzled Roan unconsciously as she awoke from the wings of sleep. She felt his large, strong body next to hers. She had one leg woven between his, and his arms were around her, holding her close to him. The masculine odor of him drifted into her flaring nostrils. The scent was heady, like an aphrodisiac to her awakening senses as a woman. Automatically, she began to feel heat purl languidly between her legs. Her belly felt warm and soft and hungry—for him. All these sensations were new to her and she reveled in them. Around her, she heard the screech of monkeys, the sharp calls of parrots in nearby trees, and the pleasant, gurgling sound of a nearby creek behind the hut.

She was alive...and Roan loved her. Stretching like a cat, Inca gloried in the movement of her strong, firm body against his. One of her arms was trapped between them, the other wrapped behind his thick neck. Savoring their closeness, Inca sighed, leaned forward and pressed a small kiss on his roughened jaw. How good it felt to be alive! And how dizzying and glorious to know that someone loved her—despite her darkness. Roan loved her as a woman—not as a goddess to be worshipped, as her Indian friends did, but as an ordinary human being. Opening her eyes, Inca absorbed the sight of Roan's sleeping features. His breath was like a warm caress against her cheek and neck. Wondering at all the small, beautiful things that a man and woman could share, Inca welcomed this new world of love he'd opened to her. No wonder being in love was written about so much throughout literature. Now she knew why.

Roan stirred. He felt Inca move. Automatically, his arm tightened and his eyes groggily opened. He felt her pull away, to sit up. Drowsily, he watched as her dark, shining hair cascaded about her shoulders. She wore a soft cotton shift of the palest pink color. As she eased her fingers through her hair, he watched in sheer enjoyment of her femininity. Her profile, that proud nose and chin, and her soft lips, grazed his pounding heart. Today was a new day. A better day, he realized.

Rousing himself, he eased into a sitting position beside Inca. The covers fell away. Through the open doorway, Roan saw a bright patch of sunlight slanting into their hut. Moving his gaze back to Inca, he smiled tenderly at her.

"You look more like your old self. How are you feeling?"

She brushed her hair back and drowned in his sleepy blue gaze. "I feel human again." She leaned forward and placed her hand on his shoulder. He had taken off the soiled shirt and was bare chested. Moving her fingers through the dark hair there, Inca murmured, "I feel alive, Roan, and I know it is because of you...because of your heart and mine being one...." And she pressed herself against him and placed her lips against his mouth.

Pleasantly shocked by her boldness and honesty, he felt her small, ripe breasts grazing his chest, the surgery gown a thin barrier between them. Roan knew Inca's innocence of the world of love and respected it. She was reaching out to him as never before, and he gratefully accepted her bold approach as normal and primal. Sliding his hands upward, he framed her face and looked deeply into her shining willow-green eyes, which seem to absorb him to his very soul. Her pupils were huge and dark, filled with sparkling life once more. And with returning love for him. Oh, she'd never said the words, but that didn't matter to Roan as he smiled deeply into her eyes. The fierce, proud warrior woman had now shifted to her soft and vulnerable side with him. It was an unparalleled gift for Roan. He thanked the Great Spirit for her love, for her courage in reaching out boldly to him despite her own abandonment.

He wasn't about to destroy the new, tenuous love strung delicately between them. Inca needed to explore him at her own pace. As her lips grazed his curiously, he kissed her gently and warmly. She growled pleasantly over his actions, her arms moving sinuously up across his and folding behind his neck as she pressed herself more insistently against his upper body. Roan smiled to himself. He loved her boldness. She tasted sweet and innocent to him as her lips glided tentatively against his. Rocking her lips open, he took her more deeply, his hands firm against her face. He felt her purr, the sound trembling throughout her. Her fingers slid provocatively along his neck and tunneled sinuously into his hair and across his skull. Fire exploded deep within Roan. She was sharing herself with wild abandon, not realizing how powerfully her presence, her innocence, was affecting him.

It didn't matter, he told himself savagely. Inca needed the room to explore him and what they had in her own timing. Roan wanted to ignite the deep fires of her as a woman, passions she was just being introduced to through his love for her.

"Ahem...excuse me, children. Might I have a moment with you?"

Roan tore his mouth from Inca's. Grandmother Alaria stood in the doorway of their room, her face alight with humor. In her hands was a tray filled with steaming hot cereal, fresh fruit, a pitcher and two glasses.

Inca gasped. "Grandmother!" She blushed deeply and avoided the older woman's shining eyes, which were filled with understanding and kindness.

"Welcome home, my child," Alaria murmured. With a sprightly air, she moved into the large room and said, "I felt you awaken. You are both weak from your experiences. I thought that a good hot cereal would bring you back to life." She grinned as she placed the tray across Roan's lap. "But I see that life has returned of its own accord to both of you in another way, and I'm joyful."

Inca stared up at the old woman, who was dressed in a long-sleeved white blouse and dark blue skirt that fell to her thin ankles. "But—how—how did I get here?" she stammered.

"Tut, tut, child. Come eat. Eat. Both of you. I'll just make myself at home on this stool here in the corner. While you eat, I'll talk. Fair enough?" Her eyes glimmered as she slowly settled herself on the rough-hewn stool in the corner.

Shaken, Inca looked at Roan, who had a silly, pleased smile on his face. He, too, was blushing. She touched her cheek in embarrassment. It felt like fire. And then she stole a look at the village elder. Alaria had the same kind of silly grin on her mouth that Roan had. What did they know that she did not? Roan handed her a bowl made of red clay pottery, and a hand-carved wooden spoon. The cereal looked nourishing and good. The tempting nutlike flavor drifted up to her nostrils.

"I took the liberty of putting some honey in it for you," Alaria told Inca. "This was always your favorite meal when you were with us."

Inca thanked Roan and held the bowl in her hands. Much of her weakness was gone, but she was still not back to her old self. "Thank you, Grandmother." As always, she prayed over her food before she consumed it. The spirits who had given their lives so that she might live needed such thanks. Lifting the wooden spoon, she dug hungrily into the fare. Her heart was still pounding with desire, her senses flooded from the swift, hot kiss Roan had given her. Her body felt like lightning, energized and unsettled. She wanted something, but could not name what it was.

Alaria nodded approvingly as they both began to eat. "Food for your spirits," she murmured, "and a gift to your physical body." She lifted her hands from her lap. "I know you both have many questions. Let me try to answer them in part. Some other answers will come later, when you are prepared properly for them."

Inca discovered she was starving, and gratefully spooned more of the thick, warm cereal into her mouth. Grandmother Alaria had doted upon her when she was at the village in training. At one time she had been a favorite of Alaria's and Adaire's. Once, Alaria had admitted that Inca was like the child they'd always wished to have, but never did. In some ways she'd been like a daughter to them, until she'd gravely disappointed them by breaking the laws of the clan.

"I do not understand why you have allowed me to come back here," Inca said, waving the spoon at the ceiling of the hut.

"I know," Alaria whispered gently, her face changing to one of compassion. "There was a meeting of the elder council after you were wounded and dying."

Inca frowned. "A meeting? What for?"

Roan looked at her. "You don't have a memory of Faro Valentino shooting you, do you?"

Inca solemnly shook her head. "All I remember is that I was dying, Roan, and you traded your life for mine. That is all."

"She will recall it," Alaria counseled. "All things will come back to you in time, my child, as your heart and emotions can handle the experiences."

"I was wounded by Faro Valentino?" She looked down at the cereal bowl in her hand, deep in thought. She aggressively tried to recall it, but could not. Frustration ate at her.

"In the valley…" Roan began awkwardly. He knew that victims of brain trauma often wouldn't remember much of anything for weeks, months or years after the experience. "We were with Colonel Marcellino's company. You had freed the Indians who were slaves in the cocaine compound of the Valentino Brothers. You were working your way around the outside of the compound, getting rid of the guards, so that Marcellino's men wouldn't be in such danger when they attacked from the walls of the valley." He looked to Alaria, who nodded for him to continue the explanation. "One drug runner—"

"Faro Valentino," Alaria interjected unhappily.

Roan nodded, trying to handle his anger toward the man. "Yes, him."

Gravely, Alaria said, "He has murder in his heart. He is one of the darkest members of the Brotherhood of Darkness." She turned to Inca. "Faro shot at you before you could turn and get a shot at him. Roan was behind you, and shouted at you, but you slipped in the mud, and that is what doomed you. At the angle Roan was standing, he couldn't get a bead on Faro to stop him before he fired at you. A bullet grazed the back of your head, my child, and broke your skull, and you dropped unconscious to the ground." Alaria gestured toward Roan, tears in her eyes. "He saved you later, by giving permission to give his life so that you might return from the Threshold to us. There are few men of Roan's courage and heart on the face of Mother Earth. Without his unselfish surrendering, you would not be with us today."

Inca lost her appetite. She set the bowl aside and looked deeply into Roan's eyes. "I remember only part of being on the Threshold. I remember him calling me back…. That is when I knew I was dying."

"And you took his hand, which you had to do in order to decide to stay here instead of moving on to the other dimensions in spirit form." Alaria smiled gently and wiped the tears from the corners of her eyes. "His unselfish act of love did more than just save your life, my child."

Inca reached out and threaded her fingers through Roan's. He squeezed gently and smiled at her. "What else did it do?" Inca asked.

Alaria looked at her for a long time, the silence thickening in the hut. She placed her hands on her thighs. Her mouth turned inward, as if in pain. "You were told not to come back to the Village of the Clouds because you broke a cardinal rule of the Jaguar Clan."

"Yes," Inca said haltingly. "I did."

"And when a clan member knowingly breaks a rule, the council must act on it. You were told to leave and never return."

Hanging her head, Inca closed her eyes. She felt all those awful feelings of the day she'd been asked to leave. Roan held her hand a little more tightly and tried to assuage some of her grief. Choking, Inca whispered, "I had been abandoned once without choice. By coming to Michael's rescue, I knowingly gave up my family, and it was my choice. I have no one to blame for my actions but me. I knew better, but I did it anyhow."

"Yes," Alaria murmured sadly. "But we, the council, have been watching you the last seven years since you left us. We have watched you grow, and become less selfish, living more in accordance with the laws of the Sisterhood of Light." She gestured toward the rain forest behind the village. "For seven years you have followed every law. We have watched and noted this, Inca. You have turned into a wonderful healer for the sick and the aging. This is part of your blood, your heritage. But it is also part of your life to protect and defend the people of Amazonia. And this you have done willingly, without any help from us at any time. You have been completely on your own. You could have gone over to the Brotherhood of Darkness, but you did not. You struggled, grew and transformed all on your own into a proud member of the Jaguar Clan."

Inca blinked. "But I am not of the clan. I stand in the in-between world, neither dark nor light. That is what you said at my judgment."

"That was then." Alaria spoke quietly. She held Inca's unsure and fearful gaze, feeling the pain of her abandonment and loss. "You came to us without family. Without relatives. We loved you like the daughter we never had. Adaire and I cherished you. We tried to give you what you had been denied all those years, without a true mother and father."

Hot tears moved into Inca's eyes. She felt emotionally vulnerable because of all that she'd just experienced, and could not hide how she felt, or hold back the tears that now ran down her cheeks. "And I hurt both of you so very much. I am sorry for that—sorrier than you will ever know. Grandfather Adaire and you loved me. You gave me so much of what I was hungry for and never had before I came here." Self-consciously, Inca wiped her cheeks. "And I ruined it. I did not respect the love that you gave to me. I abused the privilege. I will be forever sorry for the hurt I have caused you, Grandmother. You *must* believe me on that."

"We know how sorry you are, Inca. We have always loved you, child. That never changed throughout the years while you were away." Alaria's face grew tender. "Inca, you could have chosen so many other ways to lead your life when you left the village. No one but Adaire and I had hope that you would turn out to be the wonderful human being you are now. You care for the poor, you protect them, you heal them when it is within the laws, and you think nothing of yourself, your pain or your suffering. You have put others before yourself. This is one of the great lessons a clan member must learn and embrace. And you have done that.''

Inca sniffed and wiped her eyes. "T-thank you, Grandmother.''

"You're more than welcome, child. But here is the best news yet. The council has decided, unanimously, that you are to be allowed back into the Jaguar Clan with full privileges and support.'' She smiled as she saw the shock of their community decision register fully on Inca's face. She gasped. Roan placed his arm around her and gave her a hug of joy. He was grinning broadly.

Alaria held up her hand. "Not only that, Inca, but when you are fully recovered, the council wants to publicly commend and honor you for what you have accomplished in Amazonia, thus far. *That* is why you are here, child. Your banishment is over. You have earned the right to be among us once again.'' She smiled a little, her eyes glimmering with tears. "And I hope this time that you honor the laws and never break any of them ever again.''

Inca sobbed. She threw her arms around Roan and clung to him as she buried her face against his shoulder.

Roan felt tears in his own eyes. He understood what this meant to Inca. Moving his hand through her thick, dark hair, he rasped against her ear, "You have your family back, sweetheart. You're home...you're really home...''

Chapter 13

Roan found Inca wandering in a field near the village. Since it was nearly noon, he had made them lunch. Swinging the white cotton cloth that held their meal in his left hand, he stepped out into the field. It was alive with wildflowers, the colors vibrant against the soft green of the grasses, which were ankle- to knee-high. The meadow was bordered on three sides by old, magnificent kapok trees, their buttressing roots looking like welcoming arms to Roan.

Above him, as always, were the large, slowly rolling clouds that seemed to always surround the village. He'd been here seven days and he had more questions than answers about this very special place. All his focus, however, was on Inca and her continued rehabilitation from her near death experience. From the day that Grandmother Alaria had told her she was part of the Jaguar Clan once more, Inca had become more solemn, more introspective. She was holding a lot of feelings inside her; Roan could sense it. He saw his part in her adjustment as simply being on hand if she wanted to talk about it and a needed, sympathetic ear, a shoulder to lean on. So far she hadn't, and he honored her own sense of healing. At some point, he knew, Inca would talk with him at length. All he had to do was be patient. Fortunately, his Native American heritage gave him that gift. The other good news was that the mission led by Colonel Marcellino had been successful.

As he crossed the field, the sunlight was warm and pleasant. The village seemed to be climate controlled at a balmy seventy-five degrees during the day and sixty-five degrees at night—neither too hot nor too cold. Even the temperature reflected the harmony and peace that infused the village and its transient inhabitants. The white-and-gray clouds that slowly churned in mighty, unending circles around the village had something to do with it, he suspected. He could see the steep, sharp granite peaks of the Andes in the distance. On the other side of the village the rain forest spread out in a living green blanket. They were literally living between the icy cold of the mountains and the hot, humid air arising from the rain forest below. No wonder there were always clouds present around the village, hiding it from prying, outsiders' eyes like a snug, protective blanket.

Inca was bending over a flower and smelling it, not yet aware of his presence. Since her accident, she seemed much more at ease, not jumpy and tense like before. As Grandfather Adaire had told him, this was a place of complete safety. Nothing could harm the inhabitants who lived and studied in the village. Maybe that was why he was seeing her relaxed for the first time. The change was startling and telling for Roan. Here Inca wore soft cotton, pastel shifts and went barefoot, her hair loose and free about her proud shoulders. Gone was the warrior and her military garb. There were no weapons of any kind allowed in the village. All the people Roan saw—and there were many from around the world—were dressed in loose fitting clothing made of natural fibers.

Inca lifted her head in his direction, her eyes narrowing.

Roan smiled as he felt her warm welcome embrace him, an invisible "hug" he knew came from Inca. The serious look on her face changed to one of joy upon seeing him. This morning he'd gone with Grandfather Adaire on an exploratory trip around the village. The elder had shown him many of the new and interesting sites that surrounded them. No wonder Inca had loved living and studying here. Roan understood more than ever how devastating it had been when she was told to leave. The way she had sobbed that morning when Grandmother Alaria told her she was welcomed back had been telling, pulled from the depths of her hurting, wounded soul. Roan had held her, rocked her and let her cry out all her past hurt and abandonment, the relief that she was once more welcomed back to her spiritual family. And they had told him not to mention anything about Maya to her yet. Inca was still reeling emotionally and Grandmother Alaria said that at the right time, Inca would meet her sister. Roan could hardly wait for that to happen. He knew how much Inca needed her real family.

Waving his hand, he quickened his stride toward her. The breeze lifted strands of her shining ebony hair. How soft and vulnerable Inca appeared as she stood expectantly waiting for him. In her hand were several wildflowers that she'd picked. He grinned. Gone, indeed, was the warrior. In her place was the woman who had resided deeply in Inca until she could be released in the safety of such a place as the village. Roan liked the change, but he also honored her ability to use her masculine energy as a warrior. Every woman had a warrior within her, whether she knew it or not. He was at ease with a woman who could use all the strength within herself.

Every woman had to deal with the myriad of issues life threw at them. They were far stronger emotionally and mentally than men, and Roan had no problem acknowledging that fact. He'd seen too many women squash that latent primal warrior, that survival ability within themselves, never tap into it because society said it was wrong for a woman to be strong and powerful. At least Inca had not allowed that to happen to her. She had carried her warrior side to an extreme, but her life mission asked that of her. Still, it was good that she had the village to come to, to rest up. To let go of that role she played.

Lifting the cloth bag with a grin, he called out, "Lunchtime. Interested?" His heart seemed to burst open as he heard her light, lilting laughter bubbling up through her long, slender throat. The gold flecks dancing in her willow-green eyes made him ache to love Inca fully and completely.

"I'm starving!" she called, and eagerly moved toward him, the hem of her dress catching now and then on taller flowers and grass blades.

How Roan loved her! A fierce need swept through him, and as Inca leaped forward, her hair flying behind her shoulders like a dark banner, he laughed deeply and appreciatively. Suddenly, life was good. Better than he could ever recall. Sarah, his wife, would always have a part of his heart. But Inca owned the rest of it.

Every day, Inca surrendered a little more to her own curiosity and feminine instincts to touch him, kiss him. Someday, he hoped, she would ask him to love her fully and completely. Right now, Roan knew she was processing a lot of old emotions and traumas, and working through them. Her heart was shifting constantly between healing herself and reaching out to him, woman to his man. He was more than content to wait, although it was wreaking havoc on him physically.

Inca reached him and threw her arms around his neck.

Laughing, Roan caught her in midair and pressed her body warmly against his. Her arms tightened around his neck. He saw the mischievous glint in her eye and dipped his head to take her offered, smiling mouth.

Her lips tasted of sunlight and warmth. Staggering backward from her spontaneous leap into his arms, he caught

himself, stopped and then held her tightly against him. She
had such a young, strong, supple body. Like a bow curved
just right, Roan thought as he held her against him.

"Mmm…this is my dessert," Inca purred wickedly as she
eased her lips from his. Looking up into Roan's eyes, she
saw his hunger for her. She felt it through every yearning
cell in her body, and in every beat of her giddy heart. How
handsome Roan looked to her. That scowl he'd perpetually
worn in Brazil was gone here in the village, which lay within
Peru's border. Today he dressed in a pair of cream-colored
cotton trousers, sandals on his huge feet, and a loose, pale
blue shirt, the sleeves rolled up to his elbows. The warrior
in both of them had been left behind when they came to the
village.

Chuckling, Roan eased her to the ground. "Still hungry,
or do I finish off this feast by myself?" he teased. Sliding
his arm around her waist, Roan led her to the edge of the
meadow. Sitting down in the shade of a towering tree, his
back against one of the buttressing roots, he pulled Inca
down beside him. She nestled between his legs, her back
curved against him.

"No, I am hungry. Starved like a jaguar…." And Inca
quickly opened the cloth bag.

Roan leaned back, content to have her within his loose
embrace. He heard her gasp in delight.

"Pineapple with rice!" She grinned with triumph. "You
must have begged Grandmother Alaria to make this for us.
It is my favorite recipe. She used to make this for me when
I was training here in the village."

Tunneling his fingers through her dark hair, Roan watched
the breeze catch it as it sifted softly down upon her shoulders. "Yep, I bribed her."

"Oh!" Inca held up a container, her face alight with surprise. "Cocoa pudding!"

"Your second favorite, Grandmother said. I asked her to

make you something special, and she said you used to hang around her hut every day and beg her to make it for you."

Inca gloated as she tore the lid off and grabbed a spoon. "Hah! And more times than not, Grandmother gave in to my pleadings."

"Hey, that's dessert! You're suppose to eat your other food first."

Inca twisted around and gave him a crooked grin of triumph. "Who said so?" She pointed to her belly. "It is all going to the same place. It does not care what comes first, second or third!" And she laughed gaily.

Watching her spoon the still-warm pudding into her mouth, Roan picked up a sandwich of cheese and lettuce liberally sprinkled with hot chilies. "Now I know why you like this place so much. You can do exactly what you want to do here."

Chuckling indulgently, Inca leaned back and quickly consumed half of the pudding with gusto. When she'd finished, she set the container aside. "Your half," she instructed him primly.

"That's big of you. I thought you were going to wolf the whole thing down in one gulp."

"Jaguars do such things," she agreed wryly, meeting his smiling eyes as she picked up the other cheese sandwich. Munching on it, she announced, "Today, I feel magnanimous in spirit. I will share with you my favorite dessert."

"I like it when you can smile and tease. Here you have a sense of humor and you're playful. I never saw that side of you in Brazil. It's nice."

Inca nodded and eagerly finished off the sandwich. The bread, too, was still warm from the oven. Licking her fingers one at a time, she murmured, "Here I do not have to be anything but myself. I do not have to be a warrior constantly. I can relax."

Sobering, Roan wiped his hands on another cloth and reached for the bowl of chocolate pudding. "I'm glad you have this place to return to, Inca. You were worn down. You needed someplace to heal." He gazed around. In the distance he saw a great blue heron flying toward what he knew was the waterfall area. The day was incredibly beautiful. But every day in this village was like being in a secret, hidden Shangri-La.

Inca turned around and crossed her bare legs beneath the thin fabric of her dress. Taking one of the mangoes, she began to methodically peel it with her long, slender fingers. "I feel better today than ever before, Roan. More..." she searched for the right word "...whole."

"Yes," he murmured. "You've had a long, hard journey for seven years, sweetheart. You've more than earned this place, this down time." He looked fondly toward the village. "All of it."

"I have my family back," Inca said as she bit into the ripe mango.

Roan nodded, understanding the implications of her softly spoken, emotion-filled words. There was so much more he wanted to say, but he was under strict orders by Grandmother Alaria to say nothing of Maya, who had helped to save Inca's life. A part of him chaffed under that stern order. He wanted to share his discovery of Maya, and the fact she was Inca's twin sister, but Alaria had warned him sufficiently that he backed off from saying anything. Inca needed time and space to heal. She would know the truth when Maya chose to appear and break the news to her, Alaria had told him.

Roan watched Inca through half-closed eyes, the afternoon heat, the good food and her company all conspiring to make him feel regally satisfied in ways he'd never experienced.

Wiping her hands on the damp cloth, Inca looked at him. "You look like a fat, old happy jaguar who has just eaten more than his fill and is going to go sleep it off."

His mouth lifted. "That's exactly how I feel." Roan

reached out and grazed her cheek. "Only I have my jaguar mate here with me. That's what makes this special."

"I put you to sleep?" Inca demanded archly, unmercifully teasing him.

The fire in her eyes, the indignation, wasn't real, and Roan chuckled. "You would put no man to sleep, believe me," he rasped as he eased her around so that her back fit beautifully against him once more. "Come here, wild woman. My woman…"

Sighing contentedly, Inca settled against Roan. He took her hands in his, and they rested against her slightly rounded abdomen. A small but warming thought of someday carrying his child in her belly moved through Inca's mind. As she laid her head back on his broad, capable shoulder and closed her eyes, she sighed languidly. "I have never been happier, Roan. I did not know that love could make me feel this way." She felt the warmth of the breeze gently caressing her as she lay in his arms, his massive thighs like riverbanks on either side of her slender form. "You make me feel safe when I have never felt safe before. Did you know that?" She opened her eyes slightly and looked up at him, and felt him chuckle, the sound rolling like a drumbeat through his massive chest.

"I know," he replied as he moved his fingers in a stroking motion down her slim, golden arm. He saw many old scars here and there across her firm flesh. It hurt him to think of her being in pain, for Inca had lived with not only physical pain, but the sorrowful loss of her family, from the time she was born. In a way, it had made her stronger and self-reliant. She was able to move mountains, literally, because of the strength this one event had given her in life. Roan tangled his fingers with hers. "I love you, my woman," he whispered next to her ear. Her hair was soft against his lips. "Just know that you own my heart forever."

Her fingers tightened around his. Nuzzling his jaw, she whispered huskily, "And you hold my heart in your hands.

You did from the beginning, even if I was not aware of it at first."

"When I saw you," Roan said in a low, deep tone as he caressed her hair, "I fell in love with you on the spot."

"Is that possible?"

"Sure. Why not?"

Inca shrugged. "When I first saw you, I felt safe. Safe in a way I never had before. I knew you would protect me."

"That's a part of love," Roan said, smiling lazily.

"I do not know much of what all love is about," she began, frowning. "This is new to me." She touched her heart. "I see others who are married. I see them touch one another, as we touch one another now. I see them kiss." She pulled away and met his hooded eyes. "I think our kisses are more active than others I have seen. Yes?"

Grinning, Roan said, "*Passionate* is the word I think you're searching for."

"Mmm, yes... And I see married couples touch each other's hands and hold them...and we do that, too."

"Loving a person, Inca, means loving them in many ways. There's no one way to tell that special person that you love them. You love them in many, many ways every day."

"And you brought me flowers that morning after Grandmother Alaria told me I was a member of the clan once again." Inca smiled up at him. "I was deeply touched. I did not expect such a gift from you."

"I wish I could have done more. I know what it meant to you, to be allowed to come home." Roan caught several dark strands of hair that moved with the breeze across her cheek, and tucked them behind her ear.

"I must understand more of this love that we hold for one another. I try to learn by watching what others do." Her eyes lit up with laughter. "And then I try it out on you to see if it works or not."

He chuckled. "No one can accuse you of not being an astute observer," he said dryly. "I like discovering love with you. Just give yourself time and permission to explore when it feels right to you, Inca.''

Sliding her hand across his dark, hairy one, she said, "My body is on fire sometimes. I ache. I want something…but I do not know what it is, how to get it, how to satisfy that burning within me.''

"I do.''

"Yes?''

"Yes.'' Roan looked down at her animated features.

"Will you show me? I feel as if I will explode at times when you kiss me, or touch me, or graze my breasts with your hand. I ache. I feel…unfulfilled, as if needing something and I do not know what it is. I feel frustrated. I know something is missing…but what?''

Roan kept his face serious. Caressing her cheek, he said, "All you have to do is ask me, Inca, and I'll show you. It's something I can teach you. Something that is beautiful and intimate, to be shared only by those who love one another.''

Nodding, she sighed. "Yes. I'd like that.''

"A woman should always be in control of her own body, her own feelings,'' he told her seriously, and pressed a kiss to her hair near her ear. "You tell me what you want, next time you feel like that—where you want me to touch you, where you want my hand placed. Making love to another person is one of the most sacred acts there is between human beings.''

"It is more than the mating frenzy,'' Inca said. "I have watched many animals couple. It is because they want to make babies. I understand that. But…'' She hesitated. "This is different, yes? Between people? Do they always want to make a baby when they couple?''

He felt her searching. Having lived her life in a rain forest, without any education about her own sexuality, about how a man and woman pursued intimacy, Inca was truly innocent. Gently, Roan took her hands into his. "Maybe we're lucky, sweetheart. Humans don't have to couple for the express purpose of having a baby. We can do it because it feels right, and it feels good for both of us. It's the ultimate way to tell the other person how you feel about them.''

Inca smiled and closed her eyes. ''Grandmother Alaria said I should go to the Pool of Life and bathe there. She said I need the healing water to help me. Right now I want to have a nap with you. After I wake up, it feels right for me to do that.''

Roan held her gently. Closing his eyes, he murmured, ''Go to sleep, my woman. When you wake, go to the pool.''

Inca lay in the soft grass beside the Pool of Life, where she had bathed and swum for nearly an hour. Now she understood as never before the healing qualities of the sparkling, clear water. The glade sheltering the oval pool was filled with flowering bushes and trees. As she lay on her back, arms behind her head, watching the lazy, late afternoon clouds move across the deep blue sky, she sighed. Never had she felt so whole or so much in balance. Her errant thoughts centered on Roan and how much he meant to her. She loved him. Yes, she knew now as never before that she loved him. When she left this wonderful place, she would search him out and tell him that to his face. A tender smile pulled at her lips as she lay there, enjoying the fragrance of the wildflowers and the warmth of the sun.

Dressed once again in her pale pink shift, her skin still damp from the pool, Inca dug her toes joyfully into the grass that tickled the soles of her feet. Birds were singing, and she could hear monkeys screaming and chattering in the distance. Life had never felt as good as it did now.

Inca suddenly sat up, alert and on guard. She felt a vibration—something powerful that distinctly reminded her of someone teleporting in to see her. Who? The energy was very different, like none she was familiar with. Turning, Inca looked toward where the energy seemed to be originating. She saw a woman—a stranger—standing near the bushes, no more than twenty feet away from her. She was dressed in a black military flight suit and black, polished boots. As her gaze flew upward, Inca gasped. Instantly, she was on her feet in a crouched position, her hands opened, as if prepared for an attack by the unexpected intruder to her reverie.

Shock bolted through her, made her freeze. Her eyes widened enormously as she met and held the dark emerald gaze of the intruder. Her gasp echoed around the flowery glade. The woman looked almost exactly like her! Head spinning, Inca slowly came out of her crouched position. All her primal senses were switched on and operational—those instinctual senses that had saved her life so many times before. The woman who stood relaxed before her had black hair, just as she had. Only it was caught and tamed in a chignon at the base of her slender neck.

Breathing hard, Inca shouted, "State your name!"

The woman gave her a slight smile and lifted her hand. She took off her black flight gloves. "Be at ease, Inca. I'm Captain Maya Stevenson. And I come in peace." Her smile disappeared and she took a step forward. "I'm unarmed and I'm not an enemy. I'm here to fulfill a prophecy...." Tears glittered in her narrowed eyes.

Gulping, her heart pounding, Inca was assimilating all kinds of mixed messages from this tall, darkly clad woman warrior whose face was filled with emotion. "Y-you look like me! Almost..." She took a step back, not understanding what was going on. Her pulse continued to race wildly and she had to gasp for air. She felt like crying as a sharp, jolting joy ripped though her heart. Inca understood none of these wild, untrammeled feelings as the woman walked slowly down the slope toward her, and halted less than six feet away.

Searching her face, Inca saw that there were minute differences between them. This woman—Maya—had a square face. Though her eyes were slightly tilted like Inca's, Maya's were a different color—emerald and not willow-green. Her mouth was full and her cheekbones high, but her face was broader. Her bone structure was different, too; while Inca was slender, Maya was of a larger, heavier build, and more curved than she. Still, the woman in black warrior garb stood equally tall, with that same look of confidence, her shoulders thrown back with unconscious pride.

"I—I do not understand this. You look like me. A mirror image. What is going on? What prophecy?"

Maya wiped her eyes. She tucked the gloves, out of habit, into the belt of her flight suit. "I think you'd better sit down, Inca. What I have to tell you might make you faint, anyway." And she gestured to the ground.

"No. Whatever you have to say I will take standing."

"Okay...have it your way. You always did have one helluva stubborn streak. Me? I need to sit down to say this to you." Maya grinned a little and sat down in front of her. She pulled her knees up and placed her arms around them, hooking her fingers together. "Of course, your stubbornness also gave you the guts to survive and flourish."

Breathing hard, Inca stared down at Maya. "What do you speak of? Who *are* you?"

Maya looked up, her emerald eyes dark and thoughtful. Her voice lowered, soft and strained. "I'm your fraternal twin sister, Inca. Our mother birthed us minutes apart. I came out first, and you, followed. We're sisters, you and I. I was finally given permission by the elder counsel to come and meet you, face-to-face, to initiate contact with you." She shook her head sadly. "And I've waited a long time for this day to come...."

Inca staggered backward. Her eyes flared and her lips parted. When she felt her knees go wobbly, she dropped to the grass on her hands and knees. Staring at Maya, who sat calmly watching her, she could not believe her ears. She saw the compassion in Maya's strong face, the tears running freely down her cheeks. In the next moment, Inca felt a shift of energy taking place between them, and she swallowed, unable to speak. Indeed, Maya was almost a carbon copy of her. Shaking her head, Inca clenched her fist.

"I do not understand!" she cried in desperation. "How can you be my sister? I was abandoned by my parents at birth! I was left for dead until a jaguar mother came and carried me back to her den to raise me." Inca's nostrils flared. Her breathing was chaotic. Her heart was bursting with pain and anguish.

Maya leaned forward, her hand extended. Gently, she said, "I'm sorry you had to suffer so much, Inca. You were so alone for so long. And for that, I'm sorry. We agreed to this plan long before we ever entered human forms. We each did," she stated with a grimace. Looking up, she took a deep breath and held Inca's anguished gaze. "I have a story to tell you. Listen to me not only with your ears, but with your heart. Sit down, close your eyes and let me show you what happened—and why. Please?"

Unable to catch her breath, Inca sat down and faced Maya. She had a sister? *She* was her sister? Maya looked so much like her. How could this be? Tears escaped from Inca's eyes. "Is this a trick? A horrible trick you have come to play on me?"

"No, my loving sister," Maya said in a choked tone, tears filling her eyes again, "it isn't. Please...try to gather yourself. Close your eyes. Take some deep breaths...that's it. Let me tell you telepathically what happened to us...."

Inca rocked slightly as she felt the energy from Maya encircle and embrace her. It was a loving, warm sensation and it soothed some of the ragged feelings bursting out of her hurting heart. Transferring her full focus to her brow, between her eyes, Inca began to see the darkness shift and change. Like all clairvoyants, Inca could literally see or perceive with her third eye. Her brow became a movie screen, in color. What she saw now made her cry out.

She saw her mother and father for the first time. Her mother was breathing in gasps, squatting on the ground, her hands gripping two small trees on either side of her to stay upright. She saw her father, a very tall, golden-skinned man with black hair, kneeling at her side, talking in a soothing, calming tone to her. His hands opened to receive the baby that slid from his wife's swollen body. Within moments, the child was wrapped snuggly in a black blanket made of soft alpaca wool. To Inca's shock, she saw a second baby being delivered shortly thereafter. The infant was wrapped in a gold blanket with black spots woven into it. Inca knew at once that it was she—the second baby born from her mother's body. Twins…she had a twin! And she'd never known it before this moment.

Heart pounding, Inca zeroed in on her mother's gleaming face as she slowly sat down on another blanket with the help of her husband, and then reached out for her babies. She had a broad, square face and her eyes were the deep green color of tourmaline gemstones. Her hair was long, black and slightly curly as it hung around her shoulders. She was smiling through her tears as her husband knelt and placed each baby into her awaiting arms. Both parents were crying for joy over the births of their children. The exultation that enveloped Inca made her injured heart burst open with such fierceness that she cried out sharply, pressing her hand against her chest. She felt her heart breaking.

For so long she'd thought her parents did not want her, did not love her. That that was why they had abandoned her, to die alone.

But she was not alone! No, she had an older sister! Inca watched with anxious anticipation as her father, whom she most closely resembled, put his arm around his wife and his babies. He held them all, crying with joy, kissing his wife's hair, her cheek, and finally, her smiling mouth. It was a birth filled with joy, an incredible celebration. That realization flowed like a healing wave of warmth through Inca's pounding heart. She was loved! She was wanted! And she had a sister!

Staggered by all the information, Inca could no longer stand the rush of powerful emotions that overwhelmed her. She opened her eyes, her gaze fixed on Maya's serious, dark features.

"Enough!" she whispered raggedly. "It is so much...too much...." And she held up her hand in protest.

Maya nodded and stopped sending the telepathic information. She threw her shoulders back, as if to shake herself out of the trancelike state. When she looked up, she saw Inca's face contorted with so many conflicting emotions that she whispered, "I'm sorry it had to be revealed to you like this. You've been through a helluva lot...almost dying...but they said you needed this information now, not later."

Staring at Maya, Inca whispered unsteadily, "Who are 'they'?"

Smiling a little, Maya lifted her hand. "The Black Jaguar Clan. The clan I come from."

More shock thrummed through Inca. She sat there feeling dizzy, as if a bomb had exploded right next to her. She'd heard talk of this mysterious clan, and of those who volunteered their lives to work on the dark side knowingly, in the service of the Sisterhood of Light. Blinking, she looked strangely at Maya. Hundreds of memories came cascading through her mind. For several minutes, she sat there trying to absorb them all. Finally, Inca rasped, "I remember you now.... You saved my life, didn't you? I was shot in the back of the head and Roan was carrying me to your helicopter. You came around the end of the compound fence and shot two drug runners who were taking aim at us."

With a slight nod of her head, Maya said, "Your memories of that night are coming back. Yes, that's right. I couldn't let them kill my little sister, could I?"

Maya's teasing threaded through Inca's continuing shock. The rest of her rescue avalanched upon her, the memories engulfing her one after another. She saw the helicopter she was flying in, with Maya at the controls. She felt the urgency of Maya, her worry for her life as it slowly slipped away. And then she saw Maya standing at her bedside, opposite Roan. "Y-you saved me...."

Maya shook her head. "No, I can't take credit for that one, Inca. Roan saved you. I was under orders to tell him that he had to give up his life in order to save yours. Of course, that was a lie. It was really a test for him. And you know how tough our tests are." Her mouth pulled downward in a grimace. "He didn't know it was a test, of course, but in order to get you back, it had to be played that way. Those were the rules of the Sisterhood of Light. I told him the truth—that he had to love you enough to surrender his life. The elders of this village set up the conditions for him, not me or my clan. If Roan could pass this test, they knew he was worthy of being trained here, at the village. Of course, he willingly said yes. I had him place his hands on your heart and the top of your head, just as we do when we transmit a catalytic healing energy into a patient with the help of our jaguar spirit guide."

Her smile was gentle. "He did it. It was his love for you that brought you back. All I did was facilitate it by sending him to the Threshold to retrieve you. Then I teleported all of us here, to the Village of the Clouds. Helluva job, I gotta say. I did good work." She flexed her fist, pleased with her efforts. "I don't have many metaphysical talents, unlike you. But I'm a damn good teleporter when I set my mind—and heart—to it."

Maya shrugged, her eyes brimming with tears. "In my business, I work in the underbelly of darkness. It was something else to see Roan's pure, undiluted love for you pull you back from the Threshold. He doesn't have memory of this—yet. He will when it's right for him to know. Right now, *you* need to know that I'm your sister and that our parents loved us—fiercely. They surrendered their lives for us, so that we could come into being, to help a lot of other people. Our destiny was ordained long before our births. We agreed to come, to fight for the light, to fight for the under-dogs and protect them. And we both do this in our own way.''

Gulping back tears, Inca whispered, ''Tell me more about our parents. I *have* to know, Maya…please….''

Wiping her eyes, Maya said, ''Our parents knew who we were, spiritually speaking, and why we were coming into a body for this lifetime. Our mother was a member of the Jaguar Clan. Our father, a member of the Black Jaguar Clan. They met, fell in love and married. The elders who married them here, at the village, twenty-seven years ago, told them of their destiny—that they were to give each of us up. To trust the Great Mother Goddess and surrender their two children over to her. They were told they would then be killed by drug runners shortly after our births.'' Maya frowned. ''They accepted their fate, as we all do as clan members. We know we're here for a reason. They knew ahead of time what those reasons were. They had two wonderful years to-gether, before we came. They were very happy, Inca. Very. After we were born, they kissed us goodbye, and our mother took you and went east. My father took me and went off in a westerly direction. They were told where to leave each of us.''

Shaken, Inca moved a little closer. Close enough to reach out and touch Maya, if she chose. ''Who killed them?'' she rasped thickly. ''I want to know.''

''Juan Valentino. The father of the two Valentino sons, Sebastian and Faro. And Faro damn near added you to his coup belt,'' Maya said grimly. ''We're in a death spiral dance with the Valentinos, Inca. They murdered our parents. And now Sebastian has been captured and faces a life in prison in Brazil. That's one down, and one bastard to go. Faro nearly took your life.'' She flexed her fist again, her voice grim with revenge. ''And shortly, I'll move into a death spiral dance with him. He's fled to Peru in his gunship. He thinks he's safe there. But now the bastard's on *my* territory…and I promise you, dear sister of my heart, I'll find him and avenge what he did to you…."

Staring disbelievingly at Maya, Inca whispered, "This is all too much. Too much…" She dropped her head in her hands.

Gently, Maya reached out and slid her strong fingers along the curve of Inca's shaking shoulders. She was crying, too. "I know," she said in a choked voice. "You don't know how long I've waited to finally get to meet you in person. To tell you that you weren't ever alone, Inca. That you weren't really abandoned. That you were loved by our parents—and by me…." Smoothing the cotton material across Inca's shoulders, Maya inched a little closer to her. Sniffing, she whispered brokenly, "And how long I've dreamed of this day, of being here with you…with my own blood sister…."

Inca heard the pain in Maya's husky voice. Turning, she allowed her hands to drop to her sides. Tears ran freely down her cheeks as she stared into the marred darkness of Maya's gaze. "You really *are* my sister, aren't you?"

Maya nodded almost shyly. "Yes…yes, I am, Inca. We came from our mother's body. Greatly loved. Given over to a destiny that needed us for a higher calling." Reaching out, she slid her hands once more over Inca's shoulders. "And all I want to do right now is hug the hell out of you. I want to hold my sister. It's been so long a time in coming…."

Inca moved forward into her twin's arms. The moment they embraced, her heart rocked open as never before. When Maya tightened her arms around her, Inca understood for the first time in her life what family connection truly meant. She wept unashamedly on her sister's shoulder, and so did Maya. They cried together at the Pool of Life, locked in one another's embrace, saying hello for the first time since they had been separated at birth.

Chapter 14

Inca gripped Maya's hand after her tears abated. She felt that if she released her, Maya would disappear into thin air and she'd never see her again. Oh, that was foolish, Inca realized, but her heart was so raw from learning she had *real* family that she couldn't stand the thought of Maya being ripped away from her again.

Squeezing her fingers in a gesture meant to comfort Inca and allay her worries, Maya said, "Listen, from now on you'll see so much of me you'll be sick of me." And she gave a wobbly smile as she brushed the last of her tears from her cheeks. The clouds parted for just a moment and sent golden, dappling sunlight glinting upon the quiet surface of the pool at their feet.

Inca laughed a little, embarrassed by her sudden clinginess, and released Maya's hand. "I know my response is not logical. And I will *never* tire of seeing you, Maya. Not ever."

Maya reached out and patted Inca's arm. "Well, you're stuck with me, little sister. And I only found out about you and our past a year ago. Grandmother Alaria told me. I wanted to see you right then, but she said no, that you had the last of your karma to work through.'' Maya frowned. "She said you must experience death, but that I could be there to help save you. That's why we were waiting at a nearby secret base we use. I didn't know how your life might be threatened. When the time drew near, Grandmother Alaria told me when to go and where to fly in order to help you through all this.''

"It must have been very hard for you to wait and say nothing," Inca whispered painfully.

Maya sighed and held her compassionate gaze. "I gotta tell you, Inca, it was hell. Pure torture. I wasn't sure I could abide by the rules of the clan and stay away from you.''

"You are stronger than I am," Inca acknowledged.

"Not by much." And Maya smiled a little.

She turned and looked over her shoulder. "Hey, I think Grandmother Alaria and Roan are coming our way. I know Grandmother had more to tell us after we got over our introductions. Are you ready for them?''

Inca realized that she was so torn up emotionally—in shock, in fact—that she hadn't even felt their energy approaching the secluded glen. Her jaguar guardian had manifested and was lying near the pool, his head on his paws, asleep. She looked up. "Roan is coming?" Her heart beat harder. With love. With the anticipation of sharing her joy over her newfound sister. A sister!

Grinning, Maya said, "And Grandmother Alaria, too." She reached out and playfully ruffled Inca's hair. "I can tell you're head over heels in love with that hunk of man." She smiled knowingly. "Wish that I could get so lucky. All I know is Neanderthal types from the last Ice Age who are out to squash me under their thumb because I'm a woman. I envy you, but you deserve someone like Roan. I like him a *lot*. He definitely has my seal of approval." She winked wickedly. "Not that you need my okay on anything. You've got excellent taste, Inca!"

Blushing fiercely, Inca absorbed her sister's playful touch and teasing. It felt so good! Almost as good as having Roan in her life. As Inca impatiently waited for him to appear on the well-worn dirt path that led to the pool, she realized that there were different kinds of love—what she felt for her sister, what she felt for Roan. And for Grandmother Alaria. All were different, yet vitally important to her.

Grandmother Alaria appeared first. There was a soft smile on her face and tears sparkled in her eyes. Roan appeared next, an unsure expression on his face. He hung back at the entrance to the grove.

"Come on in," Maya invited with a wave of her hand. "You're supposed to be here, too, for this confab."

Roan looked over at Inca. Her eyes were red and she'd been crying. Not wanting to assume anything with her, he looked to her for permission to join them. Even though Grandmother Alaria had coaxed him into coming with her, he felt like an outsider to this group of powerful women.

"Sit by me?" Inca asked, and she stretched out her hand toward him.

Roan nodded and held her tender willow-green gaze. He felt such incredible love encircling him and knew it was Inca's invisible embrace surrounding him. Carefully moving around the group, he sat down next to her. She smiled raggedly at him.

"I have a sister, Roan. A sister! Maya, meet Roan. He holds my heart in his hands."

Maya grinned broadly. She reached across the small circle they had made as they all sat cross-legged on the earth. "Yes, we've met. But official introductions are in order. Hi, Roan. It's good to meet you—again." And she gripped his proffered hand strongly, shook it and released it.

"Same here," he said. "I never got to thank you for saving our lives when those two drug runners had a bead on us. Nice shooting.'' He liked Maya's easygoing nature. She was very different in personality from Inca.

Maya nodded and grimaced. ''We knew there was going to be danger for you two. I'm just glad I got there in time.''

Grandmother Alaria settled her voluminous cotton skirt across her knees. ''Children,'' she remonstrated, ''let me pick up the threads of why you are here. Inca, I've come to tell you all that happened, and why. I know some memories are returning to you, my child.''

Inca felt Roan's arm go around her shoulders, and she leaned against his strong, stalwart body. ''I have many questions,'' she said.

Inca listened as the elder told her everything, from beginning to end, about that night she'd nearly died. Alaria smiled kindly as she finished. ''It was Maya who was able to teleport you, herself and Roan here, from that hospital in Manaus. Members of the Black Jaguar Clan are the most powerful spiritual beings among our kind. She had our permission to transport.'' Alaria gave Roan a gentle look. ''And it could not have been accomplished without Roan. His heart is large and open. Maya needed to tell him to give his life for yours, Inca, because it required that kind of surrendering of his energy, his being, in order to try and affect this transport. If the heart is not engaged in such an activity, teleportation will not work for all concerned.''

Maya laughed softly. ''And I've gotta tell you, folks, it wasn't easy. Oh, I've teleported when I managed to get my ducks in a row, but nothing like this…not when it was my *sister* involved. I've never had to overcome so many fears as I did that day, Inca. I was crying inside. I was afraid of losing you. Roan here helped keep the stability of the energy pattern, whether he knew it or not. His love for you was so pure, so untainted, that it held this paper bag on wheels together so I could affect the transfer.''

Inca nodded and felt his arm tighten slightly around her

waist. "His heart is pure," she whispered, and she gave him a tender look. "I was saved by people who love me."

"I thought I was going to die," Roan admitted quietly. "I was ready to give up my life for Inca. She was far more important than I was. The things she was doing in the Amazon far outweighed anything I'd ever done in my life."

Grandmother Alaria looked at him for a long moment, the silence warming. "My son, you are far more powerful than you know. Your mother was a great and well-known medicine woman among us."

Roan gave her a startled look. "What do you mean?"

Alaria reached out and touched his arm in a kindly manner. "She was a member of the northern clan, the Cougar Clan, which is related to the Jaguar Clan here in South America. When she died, she sent her chief spirit guide, a female cougar, to you. What you did not know was that this cougar was in constant contact with us." She patted his arm in a motherly fashion. "We were watching, waiting and hoping that you would make the right decisions to come down here, to meet Inca and, hopefully, fall in love with her, as she is beloved by us."

Inca nodded, overwhelmed. "When I met Roan, I knew it was not an accident, Grandmother. I knew it was important. I just did not know *how* important."

"We're faced with many, many freewill choices," Alaria told them gravely. "Roan could have chosen not to come down here. He could have hardened his heart, because of the loss of his wife, and not given his love to you. You also had choices, Inca."

"I know," Inca whispered, and she looked down pensively at the green grass before her. "From the moment I met Roan I felt this powerful attraction between us. It scared me—badly. I did not know what love was then."

"You do now," Maya said gently, and she gave them a proud look. "You made all the right moves, Inca. Believe me, it was hell on me waiting, hoping, praying and watching you from afar.''

Inca looked over at her. "You knew all along that if I made the right choices, I would be wounded out there in that valley that night, did you not?"

Glumly, Maya nodded, then gave Grandmother Alaria a pained look. "Yeah, I knew. And it was hell on me. I didn't want you hurt. I was told that you would have to go through a life-death crisis. I didn't know the details. I was able to get permission from both clans to fly my helos into the area and be ready to help you when it happened. I was told when I could fly into the valley, and that was shortly after you were shot by Faro Valentino. It took all my training, all my belief and trust and faith, to stand back and let it happen. It was one of those times when I seriously considered breaking a clan law. I didn't *want* to have you go through all that stuff." She managed a crooked smile. "But I was told in no uncertain terms that if I didn't abide by the laws in your karma, I'd *never* get to see you, and that's something I didn't want to happen." Maya reached out and gripped Inca's fingers briefly, tears glimmering in her eyes.

Inca gave her a sad look. "I know how you feel. I have been placed in such a position before—and failed."

Maya made a strangled sound. "Well, I damn near did, too, with you. It's different when it's someone you love. It's real easy to let a stranger go through whatever they need to experience, but it's a whole 'nother stripe of the tiger when it's your family involved." Maya shook her head and gave Grandmother Alaria a rueful look. "I hope I *never* have to go through this kind of thing again with Inca."

"You will not, my child."

Roan frowned. "What I want to know is how you got those helicopters into that valley. Did you teleport in? There's no known airport or military facility close enough to give you the fuel you needed to reach us."

Maya laughed and slapped her knee in delight. "Hey,

teleporting *one* person, much less three, is a helluva big deal. But a bunch of helicopters? No way. I don't know of anyone who can facilitate that kind of energy change. No, we knew ahead of time what could possibly happen, so we flew in days earlier. Trust me, there are hundreds of small bases of operation that we've laid out all over South America. We've been fighting the drug trade in all these countries for a long, long time on our own—long before any governments got involved, or the U.S. started providing training support for the troops and air forces.''

Roan nodded. "Colonel Marcellino mentioned that he's seen unmarked, black helicopters from time to time. And he said he didn't know where they were from, or who they represented.''

"Not the druggies, that's for sure," Maya chuckled derisively. Humor danced in her emerald eyes. "Like I said before, the Black Jaguar Clan is the underbelly, the dark side of the Sisterhood of Light. We aren't constrained by certain laws and protocols that Inca and her people are. We're out there on the front lines doing battle with the bad guys— what Inca knows as the Brotherhood of Darkness—no matter what dimension they are in. To answer your question, we have a base near that valley. We were simply waiting." Maya lost her humor and reached out and gripped Inca's hand momentarily. "And I'm sorry as hell it had to happen to you, but in nearly dying and being saved with Roan's love, you were able to spiritually transcend your past and move to a higher level of ability. It gave you the second chance you wanted so badly. When I was told by the elders what could happen to help you, I stood back. Before that, I was more than prepared to interfere to save you from being hurt, law or no laws.''

"I understand," Inca whispered. "Sometimes it takes a near death experience to break open the door to the next level on our path." She gave Roan a wry look. "And thanks to you, I made it."

Roan shrugged, embarrassed. He looked around the circle at the three women. "I think," he told her huskily, "that this happened because of a lot of people who love you."

"Yes," Grandmother Alaria said, "you are correct. Anytime people of one mind, one heart, gather together, miracles will happen. It's inevitable." She turned her attention to Inca. "And we've got a wonderful gift to give you, my child, because of all that's happened." She smiled knowingly over at Roan and then met Inca's curious gaze. "The elders have voted to have you remain at the village for the next year for advanced spiritual training. And—" she looked at Roan, a pleased expression on her features "—we are also extending an invitation to you, Roan Storm Walker, as your mother once was invited, to come and study with us. You may stay to perfect your heritage—the abilities that pulse in your veins because of your mother's blood."

Gasping, Inca gripped Roan's hand. "Yes! Oh, yes, Grandmother, I would be honored to remain here! Roan?"

Stunned, he looked down at Inca. "Well…sure. But I'm not a trained medicine person, Grandmother. I don't know what I can offer you."

Chuckling indulgently, Alaria slowly got to her feet. Her knee joints popped and cracked as she stretched to her full height. She slowly smoothed her skirt with her wrinkled hands. "My son, people are invited to come here to the Village of the Clouds and they haven't a clue of their own heritage or traditions—or the innate skills that they may access for the betterment of all life here on Mother Earth." She gave him an amused look and gestured toward the village. "You see every nationality represented in our community, don't you?"

"Well, yes…" There were people from Africa, from Mongolia, Russia, the European countries and from North America, as well. Roan thought he was at a United Nations meeting; every skin color, every nationality seemed to be represented at the Village of the Clouds. It was one huge training facility to teach people how to use their intuition, healing and psychic abilities positively for all of humanity, as well as for Mother Earth and her other children.

"Our normal way of contacting an individual is through the dream state. We appear and offer them an invitation, and if they want to come, they are led here through a series of synchronistic circumstances. We talk to them, educate them about themselves and their potential. It is then up to them if they want to walk the path of the Jaguar Clan or not." She smiled softly. "Do you want to walk it?"

Roan felt the strong grip of Inca's fingers around his own. He looked over and saw the pleading in her eyes. "I'll give it a try, Grandmother. I still don't understand what you see in me, though...."

Maya cackled and stood up, dusting off her black flight suit. "Men! Love or hate 'em. I don't know which I'd rather do at times. The Neanderthals I know would be telling the elders they *deserved* to be here, and then there's guys like you, who are harder to find than hen's teeth—and you wonder why you're here." Maya threw up her hands and rolled her eyes. "Great Mother Goddess, let me find a man like you, Roan!" And she chuckled.

Inca frowned. "Do not worry about this, Roan. I came to this village when I was sixteen without knowing anything. They will teach you and show you. You will be taught certain exercises to develop what you already have within you."

"And," Alaria said, "it is always heart-centered work, Roan. The people who are invited to come here have good hearts. They are terribly human. They have made many mistakes, but above all, they have the courage to keep trying, and they treat people as they would like to be treated. Two of the biggest things we demand are that people have compassion for all life and respect for one another. You have both those qualities. That is not something you find often. You are either born with it or you are not. One's spirit must have grown into the heart, developed compassion for all our relations, in order to train here with us. And you are such a person. We'd be honored to have you stay with us."

Roan felt heat in his cheeks and knew he was blushing. Giving the elder a humorous look, he said, "I'll give it a go, Grandmother. Thanks for the invitation." He saw Inca's eyes light up with joy over his decision. She pressed her brow against his shoulder in thanks.

"I have to go, Inca," Maya said reluctantly as she looked at her military watch on her left wrist. She glanced apologetically over at Grandmother Alaria. "Duty calls. My women are telling me it's time to saddle up." She hooked her thumb across her shoulder. "I've got my squadron of black helicopters winding up outside the gates of the village back in real time. We've got a drug factory to bust."

Scrambling to her feet, Inca threw her arms around her sister. "Be safe?"

Maya hugged her fiercely and then released her. "Don't worry. I watch my six, Inca. Six is a military term that means we watch behind our backs. The bad guys are the ones who are in trouble when I and my force of women are around. In our business, I'm known to hang ten over the surfboard of life. I scare my copilots to death when I fly, but I guarantee you that drug runner is going to be out of business when I get done with him." She chuckled indulgently. Reaching over, Maya gripped Roan's hand. "Take care of my little sister? She's all the family I've got, and now that we have each other, I don't want to lose her a second time."

Roan gripped her strong hand. "That's a promise, Maya. Be safe."

Inca stood with Roan's arm around her waist as Maya hurried up the path and disappeared behind the wall of ferns and bushes. "She is so different from me in some ways, and yet so much like me."

Grandmother Alaria moved to Inca and gently embraced her. "You and Maya have twenty-five years to catch up on.

She was raised very differently from you. Now you have time to explore one another's lives. Don't be in a rush, Inca. Right now, Maya is entering a death spiral dance with Faro Valentino. She will not get to see you very much until her own fate can be decided.''

Roan frowned. ''A death spiral dance? What's that?''

''Faro tried to kill Inca. Maya had freewill choice in this karmic situation, Roan. She promised that if Faro decided to try and kill Inca, she would take it upon herself to even out the karma of his actions toward her sister. She will be his judge and jury in this, provided all things work the way she desires.'' Alaria shrugged her thin shoulders and looked up at Inca. ''You know from your own death spiral dance that things often do not go as planned. And many times, both parties die in the process.''

''I wish she had not taken the challenge against Faro,'' Inca whispered. ''I do not want to lose Maya.''

Alaria held up her hand. ''Child, your sister knew what she was getting into when she promised revenge against Faro Valentino. Right now, she and her squadron of helicopters are working to free the Indians at those five other factories that Colonel Marcellino never got to in Brazil. Be at ease. She and her women warriors know what they're doing. Maya is highly trained for military warfare. But more about that at another time. You need to trust your sister in the choices she's made. And not worry so much.''

Roan squeezed Inca's tense shoulders. ''I think it's only natural, Grandmother,'' he murmured.

''Of course it is,'' the elder replied as she moved up the path. ''Come, it's time for siesta. I know you're both tired. You need to sleep and continue your own, individual healing processes.''

As they followed her out of the glade, Roan asked, ''You said Maya is going to free the Indians at those other factories we had targeted?''

''Yes.'' Alaria turned and stopped on the trail back to the

village. "Colonel Marcellino was completely successful in his attack on the first compound. His men captured forty drug runners who worked with the Valentino Brothers. Sebastian was captured, too. They marched them back to the Amazon River, where Brazilian military helicopters took the company and the prisoners back to Brasilia. Of course, the colonel was worried about his young son, Julian, so he called off the rest of the attack. And he didn't have Inca to lead him or his men."

"I see...." Roan murmured, relieved. At least one of the Valentino Brothers was out of commission.

"Does he know that Maya and her helicopter squadron are going to take over the assaults?"

"Of course not. In our business, Roan, we are like jaguars—you see us only when we *want* you to see us." She smiled mischievously. "Maya is going to continue to clean up Inca's territory for her. That way, Inca won't have to worry about drug runners putting her people into bondage during the year she's with us. By the time you're both done with your education here, you'll return to the Amazon to live out your lives. You'll be caretakers of the basin, and of its people and relations. The difference is, this time you'll have our help and intervention, when asked for. Previously, when Inca was banished, she had no support from us whatsoever." Alaria eyed Inca. "Now it's different, and I think the drug barons are going to find it much harder to carry on business as usual in Brazil."

Roan moved down the path that led to the rainbow waterfalls, a small cloth in his right hand. The morning was beautiful, with cobbled apricot-colored clouds strewn like corn rows in the sky above. Inca had left much earlier to go down and wash her jaguar, Topazio, in the pool below the waterfalls. It was a particularly beautiful place, one of Roan's personal favorites. As he stepped gingerly down the well-trodden path, away from the busy village, his heart expanded with anticipation. With hope.

He knew that time at the village was not really based upon twenty-four-hour days, as it was in the rest of the world. Still, it had been three months, by his reckoning, since they'd arrived here. And today, he felt, was the day. Inca knew nothing of the surprise he had for her.

As he moved along the narrow, red clay path, he watched as a squadron of blue-yellow-and-white parrots winged above him. The lingering, honeyed fragrance of orchids filled the air. Early mornings were his favorite time because the air was pregnant with wonderful scents. What would Inca say? His heart skittered over the possibility that she'd turn him down. How could she? They had drawn even closer together over the months. And although it was a personal, daily hell for Roan, he patiently waited for Inca to ask him to love her fully. Completely. They had time, he told himself. But he had long waited for the day he could physically love her, fulfill her and please her in all ways.

More than once, Roan had talked to Grandmother Alaria about the situation, and she'd counseled time and patience.

"Don't forget," the elder would remonstrate, "that Inca was a wild, primal child without parental guidance or direction. She was loved and cared for by the priests and priestesses who raised her, but she never experienced love between a man and woman before you stepped into her life. Let her initiate. Let her curiosity overwhelm her hesitancy. I know it's challenging for you, but you are older, and therefore responsible for your actions toward her. Wait, and her heart will open to you, I promise."

Today was the day. Roan could feel it in his heart. His soul. As the path opened up and he left the ferns and bushes, he spotted Inca down at the pool. Her male jaguar was standing knee-deep in water and she was sluicing the cooling liquid lazily across his back. Her laughter, deep and husky, melted into the musical sounds of the waterfall splashing behind them. Because of the sun's angle, a rainbow formed and arced across the pool. Yes, Inca was his rainbow woman, and made his life deliriously happy.

"Roan!"

He smiled and halted at the edge of the water. "Hi. Looks like Topazio is getting a good washing."

Laughing, Inca pushed several strands of damp hair behind her shoulder. "We have been playing." She straightened and gestured to her wet clothes, which clung to her slender, straight form. "Can you tell?"

Roan grinned. Inca was dressed in an apricot-colored blouse and loose, white cotton slacks that revealed her golden skin beneath them. "Yes, I can. When you want to come out, I have something for you."

Instantly, Inca's brows lifted. "A gift? For me?" She was already turning and wading out of the clear depths of the pool.

Roan laughed heartily. "Yes, something just for you, sweetheart." Inca had changed so much in the last three months. She was no longer guarded, with that hard, warriorlike shield raised to protect herself. No, now she was part playful child, part sensuous woman and all his...he hoped.

As she hurried up the sandy bank, Roan gestured for her to join him on a flat, triangular rock. It was their favorite place to come and sit in one another's arms, and talk for hours. Often they shared a lunch at the waterfall on this rock, as their guardians leaped and played in the water. Of course, her jaguar loved the water, and Roan's cougar did not; but she would run back and forth on the bank as the jaguar leaped and played in the shallows.

Breathing hard, Inca approached and sat down next to him. She spied a red cotton cloth in his hands. Reaching out, she said, "Is that for me?"

Chuckling, Roan avoided her outstretched hand and said, "Yes, it is. But first, you have to hear me out, okay?"

Pouting playfully, Inca caressed his recently shaved cheek. Because the weather was warm and humid, all he wore was a set of dark blue cotton slacks. He went barefoot, choosing to no longer wear sandals. His feet were becoming hard and callused. Sifting her fingers through the dark hair on his powerful chest, she teased, "Can I not open it first and then hear what you say?"

As he sat on the rock, his legs spread across it, Inca sat facing him, her legs draped casually across his. "No," he chided playfully. He warded off her hand as she reached for the gift lying in his palm. "It's not a speech, so be patient, my woman."

A wonderful sense of love overwhelmed Inca as he called her "my woman." It always did when that husky endearment rolled off his tongue. Sitting back, she folded her hands in her lap. "Very well. I will behave—for a little while."

Smiling, he met and held her gaze. "I love that you are a big kid at heart. Don't ever lose that precious quality, Inca. Anyway—" Roan cleared his throat nervously "—I've been thinking…for a long time, actually…that I want to complete what we share. With your permission." He saw her eyes darken a little. His heart skittered in terror. "Among my people, when we love another person, Inca, we give them a gift of something to show our love for them. In my nation, if we love someone, we want to make a home with them. We want to live with them—forever. And if it's agreed on by both the man and the woman, children may follow."

She tilted her head. "Yes?"

Fear choked him. Roan knew she could turn him down. "In the old days of my people, a warrior would bring horses to the family of the woman he loved. The more horses, the more he loved her. The horses were a gift to the family, to show the warrior's intent of honoring the daughter he'd fallen in love with, wanted to marry and keep a home and family with for the rest of his life."

"I see...." Inca murmured, feeling the seriousness of his words.

Clearing his throat again, Roan said, "I don't have horses to give your parents, Inca. But if I could, I would. I have to shift to a white man's way of asking for your hand in marriage." He opened his fingers and gave her the neatly tied red cloth. "Open it," he told her thickly. "It's for you—a symbol of what I hope for between us...."

Roan held his breath as Inca gently set the cloth down between them and quickly untied it. As the folds fell away, they revealed a slender gold ring set with seven cabochon gemstones.

Gasping, Inca picked up the ring and marveled at it. "Oh, Roan, the stones are the color of my eyes!" She touched the ring with her fingertips, watching it sparkle in the sunlight. "It is beautiful!" She sent him a brilliant smile. "And this is a gift to me?"

"Yes." He tried to steady his voice. He saw the surprise and pleasure in Inca's expression, the way her lips curved in joy as she held up the ring. "It symbolizes our engagement to one another. An agreement that you will marry me...become my wife and I'll be your husband...." His throat became choked. He saw Inca's eyes flare as she cradled the ring in her palm.

"You are my beloved," she whispered softly, reaching out and gently touching his cheek. "You have always held my heart...."

"Is that a yes?"

Inca looked down at the ring, her eyes welling with tears. "For so long, I thought no one loved me. That I was too dark, too bad of a person, to love," she said brokenly. "You came along—so strong and proud, so confident and caring of me that I began to think I was not as bad as I thought I was, or as others have said of me...." Sniffing, Inca wiped the tears from her eyes and looked up at Roan. She saw the anguish, the unsureness, in his eyes, but she also felt his love blanketing her just as the sun embraced Mother Earth. "I understand what love is now…and I have had these months to take it into my heart." She pressed her hand against her chest.

"You were never a bad person, Inca. Not ever. Enemies will always say you're bad—but that's to be expected. You shouldn't listen to them. And I know you thought you were bad because you were banished from the village."

Inca hung her head and closed her eyes. "Yes," she admitted hoarsely. Reaching out, she gripped his hand, which was resting on her knee. "But you showed me I was a good person. That I was worthy of care, of protection, of being loved." Opening her hand, Inca stared down at the ring through blurry eyes. Tears splashed onto her palm and across the delicately wrought ring.

"If I accept this gift from you, it means you will be my husband? That you love me enough to want me as your partner?"

Tenderly, Roan framed Inca's face with his hands, marveling in her beauty. Tears beaded on her thick, black lashes. He saw the joy and suffering in her eyes. "Yes, my woman. Yes, I want you as my partner and wife. You're my best friend, too. And if the Great Spirit blesses us, I want the children you'll grow with love in your belly."

Sniffing, Inca placed her hands over his. "I love you so much, Roan…. You have always held my heart safely in your hands. I want to be your wife. I want Grandmother Alaria to marry us."

Gently, he leaned down and placed a soft, searching kiss on her lips. He tasted the salt of her tears. He felt her hands fall away from his and glide across his shoulders. Her mouth was hot with promise, sliding slickly across his. She moved to her knees and pressed her body against his in an artless gesture that spoke of her need for him.

Slowly, Roan eased his mouth from hers. He took the ring from her hand. "Here," he whispered roughly, "let me put it on your finger to make it official." His heart soared with such joy that Roan wondered if he was going to die of a heart attack at that moment. Inca was smiling through her tears and extending her long, slender fingers toward him. How easy it was to slip that small gold ring onto her hand. She wanted to marry him! She was willing to be his partner for life....

Sighing, Inca admired the ring. "What are the stones in the ring?" She marveled at their yellow-green, translucent beauty.

"They're called peridot," Roan said. "And they came from a mine on an Apache reservation in North America."

Murmuring with pleasure, Inca ran her finger across them. "Indian. That is good. It comes from their land, their heart."

"You like it?"

She nodded. "I like it, yes." Lifting her head, she looked at him through her lashes. "But I love the man who gave it to me even more...."

Chapter 15

The time was ripe. Inca sighed as Roan pulled her into his arms after he'd moved off the large, flat rock.

"There's a special place I found," he rasped as he lifted her easily. "I want to share it with you. It was made for us...."

"Yes...show me?" Inca pressed a kiss to his bristly jaw. The ferns gently swatted against her bare feet and legs as he carried her away from the waterfall and deep into the rain forest. Eventually the path opened up into a small, sunlit meadow ringed with trees. Bromeliads and orchids of many colors clustered in their gnarled limbs.

There was a shaded area beneath one rubber tree, and Inca smiled as Roan set her down upon the dark green grass. Looking up into his stormy eyes, she whispered, "Teach me how to love you. I *want* to love you, Roan, in all the ways a woman can love her man."

Nodding, he squeezed her hands and released them. She sat there, chin lifted, her innocence touching his heart as never before. "We'll teach one another," he told her as he began to unbutton his pants. "But you'll take the lead, Inca. You tell me what you want me to do. Where you want me to place my hands on you. I want you to enjoy this, not be in pain or discomfort."

Nodding, she watched as he eased out of his pants and dropped them to one side. He stood naked before her, and she thrilled at seeing him this way. There was no fat on him anywhere. His body was tightly muscled. The dark hair on his chest funneled down across his hard, flat stomach, and she gulped. Unable to tear her gaze from him, she felt her mouth go a dry. Oh, she'd seen animals mate, but this was different. This was a sacred moment, holding a promise of such beauty and wonder. Her mind dissolved and her feelings rushed like powerful ocean waves throughout her.

Just looking at Roan in the power of his nakedness as he knelt in front of her, his knee brushing hers, made her smile uncertainly. "I am shaking, Roan," she whispered. "But not from fear…"

Roan smiled in turn as he eased the buttons of her blouse open. "Yes, that's the way it should feel," he told her in a low, roughened tone. "Anticipation, wanting…needing one another."

Inca felt the material brush her sensitized breasts, her nipples hardening as the cloth was pulled away to expose them. She felt no shame in her nakedness with Roan. As he eased the blouse off her shoulders, she gloried in the primal look in his narrowed eyes as he absorbed the sight of her. His hands were trembling, too. Elated that he wanted her as badly as she wanted him, Inca stood. In moments, she'd followed his lead and divested herself of her damp cotton slacks. Standing naked in front of him, she felt a sense of her power as a woman. The darkening, hooded look in his eyes stirred her, making her bold and very sure of herself. She took his hand and knelt down opposite him. Acting on instinct, she lifted her hands and drew Roan's head down between her breasts.

Closing her eyes as their skin met and melded, Inca sighed and swayed unsurely as his hands, large and scarred, moved around her hips to draw her between his opened thighs and press her fully against him. The feel of his warm, hard flesh was exciting. The wiry hair on his chest made her breasts tingle, the nipples tighten, and she felt dampness collecting between her legs. Inca uttered another sigh of pleasure at the sensual delights assaulting her. The sounds of the rain forest were like music to her ears, the waterfall in the distance only heightening her reeling emotions, which clamored for more of Roan's touch.

As he lifted his head away, his hands ranged upward from her hips to graze the rounded curve of her breasts. A gasp of pleasure tore from her and she shut her eyes. Moaning, she guided his hands so that her breasts were resting in his large palms. Her skin tingled, grew even more tight and heated.

"Feel good?" he rasped.

Inca could not speak, she was so caught up in delicious sensations as his thumbs lazily circled her hard, expectant nipples. Oh! She wanted something…and she moaned and dug her fingers into his thick, muscular shoulders.

Understanding what she needed, Roan leaned over and licked one hardened, awaiting peak.

Uttering a cry of surprise, of pleasure, Inca dug her fingers more deeply into his flesh. She tipped her head back, her slender throat gleaming.

Seeing the deep rose flush across her cheeks, her lips parted in a soundless cry of pleasure, Roan captured the other erect nipple between his lips and suckled her. Inca moaned wildly, her hands opening and closing spasmodically against his shoulders. Trembling and breathing in ragged gasps, she moved sinuously in his embrace as he lavished the second nipple equally. A sheen of perspiration made her body gleam like gold in the dappled shade and sunlight beneath the tree where they knelt.

Inca collapsed against him, her head pressed against his, her soft, ragged breath caressing him. Roan was glad for the experience he had, so he could lead Inca to the precipice of desire. When the right moment came, she would gladly step off the ledge with him, he had no doubt. Gathering her into his arms, he moved to a grassy hummock, a few feet away from the tree and sat down, leaning his back against the firm, sloping earth. He smiled darkly up at Inca as he guided her so that she straddled him with her long, curved thighs. His hands settled on her hips and he gently positioned her above his hard, throbbing flesh.

Inca's eyes widened as she opened her legs to move across him. Never had she been close to a man like this! But she trusted Roan. Besides, her mind was so much mush that she could no longer think coherently. He lifted her into place, and her hands came to rest on his thick, massive shoulders. And as he slowly lowered her against his hard, warm length, she gasped, but it was a cry of utter surprise and growing pleasure. Her own feminine dampness connected and slid provocatively against him. She heard and felt him groan, as if a drum thrummed deeply in his body. A tremble went through him as if a bolt of lightning had connected them invisibly to one another.

The utter pleasure of sliding against him, the delightful heat purling between her legs made her shudder and grip him more surely with her thighs. What wonderful sensations! Inca wanted more and she wasn't disappointed. As if sensing her needs, Roan tightened his grip around her hips and dragged her forward across his rigid, pressing form. A little cry escaped her. More sensations shot jaggedly up through her boiling, womanly core as he slid partially into her throbbing confines. Her belly felt like a bed of burning, glowing coals. Her hands moved spasmodically against his chest. Her breath was coming in gasps.

Lost in the building heat as he moved her slowly back and forth against him, Inca felt him tremble each time. There was something timeless, something rhythmic and wild about this, and she wanted more, much more. Leaning forward, she brushed her breasts against his chest. Capturing his mouth, she kissed him with fierce abandon. He gently teethed her lower lip in the exchange, and she felt him lift and reposition her slightly. The sensation of something hot, hard and large pressed more deeply into her feminine core. The pressure remained, and heat swirled deeply within her and between her tensed thighs.

Gasping, Inca pressed downward and drew him more deeply into herself. Instantly, she heard Roan growl. Oh, yes, she recognized that growl. She'd heard it many times when two jaguars were in the throes of mating. He felt large and throbbing as she eased herself fully down upon him. The pleasure doubled. Then tripled as she slowly sat up, her hands tentatively resting against his hard abdomen. He was guiding her, monitoring her exploratory movements. Eyes closed, Inca marveled at all the exploding feelings, the wildness pumping through her bloodstream, and her heart pounded with a fierce, singular love for the man with whom she was coupling—for the first time in her life.

Moving her hips, she moaned and eased forward, then back. The oldest rhythm in the world took over within her. She was moving with the waves that pummeled the shore of her being, a movement so pure and necessary to life that she gripped his arms and pushed more deeply against him. Again he groaned. His body was tense, like a bow drawn too tightly. She could hear him breathing raggedly. His hands were tight around her hips, guiding her, helping her to establish that harmony, that wild rhythm between them.

Somewhere deep within Inca, something primal exploded. The savagery, the vibrant, throbbing pleasure, rolled scaldingly through her. She gripped Roan hard with her thighs and pushed rhythmically against him. The moment he lifted his hips to meet and match her hot, liquid stride, another powerful explosion rocked her, catching her off guard and tearing her breath from her lungs. For a long, amazing moment Inca sat frozen upon him, her hands lifting, her fingers flexing in a pleasure she had never before experienced. She could not move, the shower of hot ecstasy was so intense within her. When Roan eased her forward, the sensation was intensified tenfold. Inca threw her head back as a growl, as deep as her unfettered spirit, rolled up and out of her parted lips.

Roan could no longer control himself. As Inca moved wildly against him, lost in the throes of pleasure pulsing through her slender, damp form, he found his own pleasure explode in turn. Thrusting his hips upward, Roan took her deeply and continuously. White-hot heat mushroomed within him, and he groaned raggedly. He gripped her hips. Tensing, he felt himself spilling into her sacred confines.

Unable to move after the intensity of his release, he lay there panting for endless moments, his eyes open barely. Instinctively, Inca moved her hips in order to prolong the incredible sensations for him. A fierce love for her overtook him, and Roan lifted his hands and placed them on her shoulders.

Drawing her down upon him, their bodies slick against one another, Roan eased Inca off him and to his side. The grass welcomed them, cool against their hot flesh as he slid one arm beneath her neck and rolled her to her back. Pushing up on one elbow, he raised himself above her, their body's touching from hip to feet. Beads of sweat trickled down the sides of his face. His heart was beating erratically in his chest as he smoothed several dark, damp strands from her brow and temple. Inca's mouth was soft and parted, her lips well kissed and her eyes closed. Breathing raggedly, Roan studied her intently. It had been wonderful for both of them and he was thankful.

Her hands were still restless, wanting to touch him, feel him and absorb him. Her flesh was like a hot iron against him as her fingers tunneled through the damp hair on his chest. Inca dragged open her eyes. Her body vibrated with such joy and pleasure that she could only stare up through her lashes at Roan in wonder. His mouth was crooked with pride. She could feel his pleasure, his love for her and she sighed, then gulped to try and steady her breathing.

"I—I never knew…never imagined it felt like *this!* Why did we wait so long if it felt like this?"

Leaning over, Roan slid his mouth against her lips. She was soft and available. Although he knew the warrior side of her was still within her, he was privileged to meet, love and hold the woman within her, too. Lifting his mouth from her wet lips, he rasped, "There's a time for all things, sweet woman of mine. And it will get better every time we do it."

Gasping, Inca whispered, "I do not know how I can stand it, then." She slid her fingers across his damp face and into his thick black hair. "I feel like I am floating! As if the storm gods have come into my body." She gestured to her belly. "I still feel small lightning bolts of pleasure within me, even now. This is wonderful to share with you."

"Good," Roan whispered raggedly. Lying down, he drew Inca against him once more. She rested her head wearily in the crook of his shoulder, her arm languidly draped across his chest. The warmth of the day, the slight breeze, all conspired to slowly cool them off. Closing his eyes, Roan murmured, "I love you, Inca. I will until the day I die, and after that.…"

Touched, Inca tightened her arm around his chest. Lying next to Roan was the most natural place in the world for her to be. "Our love created this," she whispered unsteadily. "How I feel now, in my heart, is because of you—your patience and understanding of me." She lifted her head and gazed deeply into his half-opened eyes. There was such peace in Roan's features now. Gone was that tension she'd always seen around his mouth. "I understand what love is, at last. You have shown me the way."

As her fingertips trailed across his lower lip, he smiled

lazily up at her. Her hair was slightly disheveled, a beautiful ebony frame around her flushed face and widening, beautiful eyes. There was such awe and love shining in her gaze. It made him feel good and strong in ways he'd never felt before.

"Love is a two-way street, sweetheart. It takes two to make it work. We love one another and so the rest of easy." He trailed his fingers across the high slope of her cheek. "And best of all, you're going to be my partner, my wife. It doesn't get any better than that...."

Inca nodded and playfully leaned over and gave him a swift kiss, feeling bold and more confident about herself as a woman. "I never thought I would have anyone, Roan. I thought I was born into this life alone, and that I would die alone."

"No," he said thickly, catching her hand and placing a kiss into her palm, "you changed that, remember? You made a mistake, but you proved to everyone after making it that you were cut from a piece of good cloth. You worked long, hard years alone, to show the elders you were worthy of reconsideration." Using his tongue, he traced a slow, wet circle across her open palm. She moaned and shut her eyes for an instant. How easy it was going to be to give Inca all the pleasure he knew how to share with her. She was wide-open and vulnerable to him. She'd given the gift of herself to him, her innocence, and he cherished her for that. He hoped he would never hurt her in the coming weeks or months—that he would always honor the sacredness of the wild, primal woman she was.

"My jaguar woman," he teased gently. "I just hope I can keep up with you." As he moved his hand across her left shoulder, he felt the small crescent of jaguar fur that would always remind him she was uniquely different from most human beings. But that didn't mean she wasn't human, because she was.

Laughing delightedly, Inca said, "You are of the Cougar

Clan! Why should you not be my equal? The cougar is the symbol of the north, just as the jaguar is of the south. One is not stronger or better than the other.''

Roan sat up and took Inca into his arms. It felt damned good to be naked against one another. She threw her arms around his neck and kissed him spontaneously on the cheek.

"Let us go to the Pool of Life,'' she whispered excitedly. "I will wash you, my beloved. And you will wash me.''

Grinning, Roan said, "I like your take-charge attitude, Inca.'' He helped her to her feet and then holding her hand, gathered up her clothes and his.

"Let's go, sweetheart.''

Inca was standing beneath a rubber tree near their hut, at the round table where they took their meals, when she felt a disturbance in the energy around her. She was preparing lunch for her and Roan when it happened. Roan was out in the field with the rest of the men, tending their large, beautiful vegetable gardens beyond the meadow in the distance. Soon he would arrive, and she wanted to have a meal prepared for him.

Looking around, she saw that other inhabitants of the village were going about their noontime business. Shaking her head, she wondered what she'd felt. It was vaguely familiar, but nothing she could put her finger on right away. Sunlight glanced off the peridot ring on her left hand. Holding it up, she smiled happily. How had three months flown by? Grandmother Alaria had married them shortly after they had loved one another in that wonderful, private glade near the Pool of Life. Inca had never known what happiness was until now. She had been slogging through life alone, and suddenly life had taken on wonderful shades and hues of joy—ever since Roan entered her world. Yes, love made the difference. That and the fact she had family now.

Placing bowls on the table, Inca straightened. Maya, her sister...she had seen her only four times in the last three months, and only for an hour or two at the most. Maya was busier than Inca was. Yet they utilized every scrap of every moment to talk, share and search one another's separate lives, to understand how life had shaped them and made them into what they were today.

Inca always marveled at how alike they were. It was a joy to connect telepathically with her sister, to share, openly all her emotions with Maya. To have a sister was as great a gift as having Roan as her husband. And after talking it over with Roan, she had gifted Maya with the medicine necklace that Roan had bestowed on her. Somehow, Inca knew that the blue stone in the center of it was a great protection. How or why, she couldn't explain, but that didn't matter.

Roan had approved of her giving Maya the very ancient and powerful amulet. And Maya had received it with tears of thanks in her eyes. She told them that, as a pilot, she wasn't supposed to wear any jewelry when flying her daily, dangerous missions against the drug runners. Maya had tucked it gently beneath her flight suit, a grin of pride playing on her wide mouth. She thanked both of them for it, for she knew it had originally come from Roan's family and that sacred articles were always passed down through family.

Yes, Inca was truly blessed. She knew now that she had been in a dark tunnel for the last twenty-five years. She was out of that tunnel now, and in the light. It felt good. Very good. And Maya was now protected with the mysterious necklace that held that incredible blue, opalescent stone. That made Inca sleep better at night, knowing that the stone's amazing powers were supporting her sister's best interests.

"How are you today, child?"

Inca turned and saw Grandmother Alaria moving slowly toward her. She wore her hair in thick braids, her shift a dark pink color and her feet bare and thick with calluses. The gentle smile on her face made Inca smile in turn and eagerly pull out one of the rough-hewn stools for the old woman to sit upon.

"I have coffee perking. Would you like some, Grandmother?"

Sighing, Alaria nodded. "Yes, that sounds perfect, thank you." Settling down carefully on the stool beneath the shade of the rubber tree, Alaria painstakingly arranged the shift over her crossed legs. "The day is beautiful," she mused as Inca handed her a mug with steaming black coffee in it. "Thank you, child. Come, sit down near me."

Inca sensed the change in the air. Over the months, as she'd gone into training with her, she knew when Alaria had something of importance to say to her. Taking the other stool, she sat opposite her. Today she wore a sleeveless, white cotton tunic and dark red slacks that barely reached her slender ankles.

"Something is going on, is it not?" Inca asked.

Alaria sipped the coffee. "Yes. I have asked Roan to come in early from the fields. He'll be here shortly."

Frowning, Inca sensed that all was not well. She knew better than to ask, because if she was to know, Grandmother Alaria would tell her at the appropriate time.

"Did you sense a shift in the force field around the village?"

Raising her brows, Inca said, "Was that what it was? I sensed something but I could not identify it directly."

"Your sister just landed her helicopter outside the village. That is what you felt."

Gasping with joy, Inca said, "Oh! Maya's coming?"

Smiling, Alaria said, "Yes, and she's bringing Michael Houston with her."

"Really?" Inca clapped her hands in joy. She shot off the stool and craned her neck to look down the path toward where the clouds met the earth. That was one of two entrances in and out of the highly protected village. She saw no one—yet.

"Yes, you will have much of your family here in a few minutes," Alaria told her with a soft smile.

Unable to sit in her excitement, Inca saw Roan coming across the meadow. He had a rake propped on his shoulder as he walked in sure, steady strides toward the village center.

Joy thrummed briefly through Inca. She stopped her restless pacing and looked down at the elder, who sipped her coffee with obvious relish. "This is unusual, for Michael to be here, yes?"

"Yes."

"Are Ann and the baby coming, also?"

Alaria shook her head. "No, my child. I'm afraid this is a business visit."

A warning flickered though Inca's gut. She halted and scowled. Placing her hand against her stomach, where she felt the fear, she whispered, "Business?"

Setting the coffee on the table, Alaria nodded. "I'm afraid so."

Inca's heart pounded briefly with dread. She didn't want her perfect world shattered. She knew it was a childish reaction and not mature at all. Still, her love with Roan was so new, so wonderful and expanding, that she wanted nothing to taint what they had. Knowing that the grandmother could easily read her thoughts and emotions, Inca glumly sat down, all her joy snuffed out like a candle in a brisk breeze.

"I feel fear."

Reaching out, Alaria patted Inca's sloped shoulder. "Take courage, my child. You are of the Jaguar Clan. We face and work through our fears—together."

Just as Roan put his rake up against the hut and arrived at the table, Inca saw Maya and Mike Houston appear out of the gauzy, white cloud wall and walk toward them. Inca gave Roan a quick hug of hello, turned on her heel and ran through the center of the village toward them, her arms open, her hair flying behind her like a banner.

Roan chuckled, poured himself some coffee and sat down next to Alaria. "Looks like family week around here for Inca."

"It is," Alaria said, returning his smile and greeting.

Resting his elbows on the table, Roan watched with undisguised pleasure as Inca threw her arms first around her sister, who was dressed in her black flight suit, and then Mike Houston, giving him a puppylike smooch on his cheek. Then, nestled between the two, she slid her arms around their waists and walked with them. Roan couldn't hear their animated words, but the laughter and joking among the three of them made him grin. He was so happy for Inca. She had family now. People who loved her, who wanted her in their lives. He shifted a glance to Alaria, who was also watching them, with kindness in her eyes.

"She deserves this," he told the old woman in a low tone.

"Yes, she does, my son."

"All I want to do is keep that smile on her face, Grandmother. Inca's been deprived of so much for so long."

Patting his sun-darkened hand, Alaria said, "All you need do is continue to love her and allow her to grow into all of what she can become. I will warn you that Maya and Mike coming today is not good news. Inca will be distraught."

"Forewarned is forearmed. I'll take care of her afterward." Roan was grateful for the warning. At least he could hold Inca, console her, and be there for her. It was more than she'd had before, and Roan wanted to serve in that capacity. Being married meant being many things, wearing different hats at different times for his partner, and it was something he could do well. The years he'd spent with Sarah had prepared him for Inca. And he was grateful.

After everyone had shaken hands or embraced, they sat around the table. Coffee was poured and Inca brought out a dish of fresh fruit and cheese, plus a warm loaf of wheat bread and butter. Then she sat close to Roan, anxiety written in her features. Maya sat across from her. She'd placed her helmet on the table and thrown her black gloves into it. Her hair, as usual, was drawn back into a chignon at the base of her neck. Mike Houston was in military fatigues, his face grave. Inca threaded her fingers under the table nervously.

Alaria spoke quietly. "Inca, your sister is going to be working directly with Michael for the government of Peru. As you know, Maya and her band of pilots and mechanics have hidden bases in every country here in South America. When we want them to lend their considerable support in a situation, they fly in and help. Maya's main staging area is a Black Jaguar base near the Machu Pichu reserve in Peru. The Peruvian government has requested aid from Morgan Trayhern, and he's asked Michael to coordinate a plan to do so. Michael has spent most of his life in Peru, and he knows the land and its people well."

Inca nodded. She felt her mouth going dry. "This has to do with the death spiral dance between Maya and Faro Valentino, does it not?" The words came out low, filled with concern and trepidation. Seeing her sister's green eyes narrow slightly, Inca glanced back at Grandmother Alaria, for she was the authority at the table.

"It does, my child."

Inca's heart dropped, then froze with fear. She stared at Maya, who sat looking completely unconcerned about it all. Oh, perhaps there was a time in Inca's past that she'd behaved similarly, but not now. Not in the last three months. Compressing her lips, she struggled to keep quiet and let the elder do the talking. It was so hard, because Inca's love for Maya was just taking root. She'd just met her. They'd had so little time together. Inca acknowledged her selfishness, but still she wanted more. Much more. And a death spiral dance meant that only one of the two people involved would come out alive—with luck. Too many times, Inca had seen both people die as they circled one another like wary jaguars fighting over turf and territory. Fights to the death in the spiral dance were common—the death of both protagonists.

Dipping her head, Inca shut her eyes tightly, the tears feeling hot behind her lids. "I—I see...." The words came out brokenly. When Roan's hand moved gently across her drooping shoulders, Inca felt his concern and love. It stopped some of the fierce anguish and pain from assaulting her wide-open heart.

"Inca," Maya pleaded gently, "don't worry so much about me. This isn't any different from what I do out there every day. I'm always in the line of fire. And I *want* to take down Faro Valentino, more than anything."

Inca lifted her head and opened her eyes. She saw the fury burning in Maya's narrowed gaze. "I do not want you in a death spiral dance on my behalf, Maya. I want you alive. I—need you...."

Reaching across the table, Maya gripped Inca's proffered hand. "Silly goose. You have me. Don't worry, okay? I've been around this block many, many times. Mike will tell you that."

Mike leaned forward, his voice low and cajoling. "Inca, I've worked off and on with Maya for years. Now, I didn't know who she was, or what her relationship was to you. We called those black helicopters the 'ghosts of the rain forest.' Sometimes, during a hot firefight, when I and my men were tangling with drug runners or a drug lord, she and her colleagues would show up out of the blue. Many times, they made the difference between us living or dying, the battle moving in our favor and not the enemies. I never got to meet Maya personally to thank her. I had no idea it was a woman-run operation, or that they were part of the Black Jaguar Clan. Not until recently."

Inca saw the challenging sparkle in Maya's eyes as she released her hand and straightened up. There was no doubt that Maya was a leader in every sense of the word. It was clear in her defiant and confident expression; in the way she walked with military precision, her shoulders thrown back;

in that sense of absolute power and authority exuding from her.

"Inca," Maya pleaded, "we have a chance to not only get Faro, but close down his main factories in Peru in this sweep. Mike is going to coordinate the whole thing from Lima. He'll be buying us new Boeing D model Apaches to compete with Valentino's Kamov gunships. He's our contact. Morgan Trayhern is assigning people from Fort Rucker, Alabama—Apache helicopter instructors—to teach us the characteristics of the D model. I haven't met them yet, but Mike says Morgan is borrowing the best instructors from the U.S. Army, and they're considered the cream of the crop. The best! So you see, you have nothing to worry about. I'm in the best of hands." She flashed a triumphant grin.

Alaria looked from one sister to the other. "Inca can feel many possible outcomes of this death spiral dance," she stated quietly.

Maya lost her smile. "I'm prepared to die, little sister, if that's what it takes." Shrugging, she said, "I was born to die. We all were. My life is lived in the now, the present. That is how the Jaguar Clan operates, as you know." And then she eased the blue medicine piece from the neck of her flight suit. "See? I wear it twenty-four hours a day. It keeps me safe."

Nodding, Inca whispered brokenly, "Yes, yes, I know all that." She lifted her hand, searching Maya's grave features. "Suddenly, taking revenge on Faro does not feel right to me. Not if it puts you at risk, Maya." She looked pleadingly at Alaria. "Must the Jaguar Clan always even each score against it? Is there not another, better way?"

"My child, each member of the clan must walk through this lesson. Yes, it is much better not to seek revenge for hurt against one you love. Each of us learns this truth individually, however. One day, you and Maya will come to realize that surrendering over the hurt to a higher authority is better than trying to settle the score directly. Inca, you are at that place where you can see and understand this. Maya is not.'' Alaria held up her hands. ''You can't stop Maya. Nor should you. I suggest you pray daily for her, for her life. That is all you can do. Just because you love someone does not mean that love protects them always.''

Roan slid his arm around Inca. He could feel her tensing up with fear and anxiety, see it written clearly across her face. He wished he had the words to soothe her, to quell her anxiety, but he didn't.

Mike sighed and gave Inca a half smile. ''Listen to me. Maya is in the best of hands. These army instructors will be the best— They will be there to make the difference, to give her and her squadron even more of an edge. We've got some incredible technology for the gunship she flies. That will help her in finding and locating the drug runners and their facilities in northern Peru. So stop worrying so much.''

''Are these other instructors members of the Jaguar Clan?''

Maya shook her head. ''No...they don't know a thing about us, our skills and other talents. They're walking into this cold. I don't intend for them to know about our closet abilities, either.'' She flexed her hands. ''Besides, compared to you, I'm nothing. The only thing I can do is teleport when I'm in a good mood.'' Maya grinned. ''You, on the other hand, can heal, teleport, read minds...the list goes on. I'm blind, deaf and dumb compared to you.'' She laughed good-naturedly and reached over and gripped her sister's hand again. ''Whoever these pilot instructors are, I'm not about to tell them about us, either. So far as they know, we're a spook ops comprised of women pilots who are crazy enough to fly the best damned helicopter gunships in the world where they aren't supposed to be able to go.''

Inca nodded. ''I see....''

''Anyway,'' Maya said with a quick grin, ''I'm starving to death! Inca, I'm gonna help myself to this bread you just made.'' And she reached for a thick slice of it. Rising from the stool, she grabbed a knife. ''Mind if I dig in?''

Everyone chuckled.

''Just like a black jaguar,'' Mike intoned, trying not to smile. ''Take no prisoners...''

Alaria cackled. ''Black jaguars aren't known for their diplomacy or subtleties. Did you notice?''

Inca snapped out of her self-pity. She should savor the time she had with her family, not wallow in worry over their unknown futures. Live today for today. Expect nothing; receive everything. Those were Jaguar Clan Maxims. Well, she had to continue to learn how to do that. Rising, she reached out and gripped her sister's arm.

''Manners, please. Sit down. I will serve all of you.''

Mike chuckled. He pulled a wrapped gift out of a duffel bag he'd brought with him. ''Hey, Inca, this is for you— from Ann, the baby and me.''

How quickly the energy shifted, Roan thought as he saw Inca rally. She snapped out of her funk and her expression brightened. How much he loved her. She was at such a precarious point in her growth. Finding her sister, being allowed back into the clan and getting married all in three months was asking a lot of anyone. But especially someone with her background.

''What is it?'' Inca gasped, as she reached out for the bright red foil wrapped gift topped with a yellow ribbon.

''Open it,'' Mike said with a laugh. ''You'll see....''

Like a child, she eagerly pulled the paper from around it. ''Oh! Smoked salmon!''

Pleased, Mike winked at Roan. ''In case you don't know, she's a real jaguar when it comes to fish.''

Roan grinned. ''Jaguars eat fish. At least, that's what she told me.''

''Humph,'' Maya growled, sinking her teeth into the warm, buttered bread, ''they'll eat *anything* that isn't moving.''

"And even if it is moving, we'll freeze it, jump it and make it our own," Mike added, grinning broadly. Jaguars killed their quarry by freezing its movement. What few knew outside of those in metaphysics was that the jaguar pulled the spirit out of the body of its victim. Without the spirit, the victim cannot move.

Again, laughter filled the air. Roan watched as Inca quickly opened up the package and placed the salmon on the table so that everyone could partake. A fierce appreciation of her natural generosity rolled through him. He saw Inca trying to release her fear about Maya's coming mission. As always, she was putting others ahead of herself.

Rising, Alaria bestowed a warm smile upon them all. "Enjoy your lunch together, my children. I've already eaten and I'm being called to a counsel meeting. Blessings upon you…" And she turned and slowly walked away.

Mike dug into his bag again. "Hey, I brought something else for us, too." He grinned and lifted a bottle of champagne up for all to see.

Maya clapped her hands. "Yes! Perfect! What else have you got in that bag of tricks of yours, Houston?"

"Oh," he crowed coyly, "some other things." And he shifted the bag to the other side of his stool, out of Maya's reach—just in case.

Laughing, Inca quickly set wooden plates on the table and passed around the large platter of fresh fruit. Roan got up and handed everyone a mug so that the champagne could be uncorked and passed around. He then went to work on slicing the cheese.

Maya took the dark green bottle and, with her thumbs, popped the cork. It made a loud sound. The cork went sailing past Roan, struck the wall of the hut and bounced harmlessly to the ground. "One of the few times I've missed my intended target!" she exclaimed.

"You have to do better than that," Roan told her dryly. "I duck fast."

Laughing deeply, Maya stood and poured champagne into each cup. As Inca placed the sliced cheese on a large plate, she passed the first cup to her.

"Here, little sister, taste this stuff. You're gonna like it. You're a greenhorn when it comes to modern society, and this is one of the nice things about it. Go on, try it."

Sniffing the champagne cautiously, Inca sat down next to Roan. As the others began to reach for the sliced bread, fruit and cheese, she pulled her cup away and rubbed her nose. "It tickles!"

"You've been out in the bush too long," Maya said with a giggle. "That's champagne. It's supposed to bubble and fizz. Here, lift your mug in a toast with us." Maya raised her mug over the center of the small, circular table. "Here's to my sister, Inca, who I'm proud as hell of. For her guts, her moxie and never giving up—this toast is to her!"

Everyone shouted and raised their mugs. Inca hesitantly lifted hers. "This is a strange custom, Sister."

Roaring with laughter, Maya said, "Just wait. You've been sequestered in a rain forest all your life. I wasn't. So, each time I visit you, from now on, I'm gonna share a little of my partying life-style with you."

Inca watched as everyone grinned and took a drink of the champagne. Unsure, she sniffed it again. Lifting the mug to her lips, she tasted it. "Ugh!"

Roan smiled when Inca's upper lip curled in distaste. Brushing her cheek with a finger, he said, "Champagne is an acquired taste. The more you drink it, the more you like it over time."

"I do not think so." Inca frowned and set the mug on the table.

Giggling, Maya said, "Jungle girl! You've been too long out in the boonies, Inca. Come on, take another little sip. It will taste better the second time around. Go ahead...."

Giving Maya a dark, distrustful look, Inca did as she was

bid. To her surprise, Maya was right. Staring down at the mug, Inca muttered, "It tastes sweeter this time...."

"Yep. After a couple more sips, you'll see why we like it so much." Maya reached for the champagne bottle, which sat in the middle of the table. "Come on, Houston, drink up. I'm not polishing this bottle off by myself." She wiggled her eyebrows comically. "Of course, I *have* been known to do that—but not this time."

Inca sat back and laughed, the mug between her hands. She couldn't believe that Maya could drink a whole bottle by herself! Her sister was so funny, so playful and joking compared to her. Inca looked forward to Maya's visits so she could absorb every tiny detail of her sister's life. Compared to her, Inca felt as though she had been raised in a bubble.

Inca shared a loving look with Roan. Warming beneath his tender gaze, she felt a lot of her worry dissolving. Maya was a woman of the world. She knew and understood life outside the rain forest and how it worked, while Inca did not. Perhaps Maya *would* be safe. Inca prayed that would be true. With Michael working with her sister, Inca felt some assurance of that. However, she also knew that no Jaguar Clan member was impervious to death. They died just as quickly and easily as any other human being if the circumstances were right. She knew that from her own dire experience.

Epilogue

Inca sighed, nestling deeply into Roan's arms. They had just settled down for the night in their own hut, which to her delight was situated near the bubbling creek. Inhaling Roan's scent, she gloried in it as she moved her fingers languidly across his chest. Feeling his arms clasp her in a tender embrace, she closed her eyes.

"Each day, I become more happy," she confessed.

Smiling in the darkness, his eyes shut, Roan savored Inca's warm naked body pressed against his. He lay on his back, the pallet soft and comfortable beneath them. A cool breeze moved through the windows and brought down the temperature to a pleasant range for sleeping.

"I never thought I would have the kind of happiness I have now," he murmured near her ear. Sliding a strand of her soft, recently washed hair through his fingers, he pressed a kiss to the silky mass.

Snuggling more deeply into his arms, Inca lay there a long time, her eyes partly open, just staring into the darkness.

"What is it?" Roan asked as he trailed his hand across

her shoulder. "You're worrying. About Maya? Her mission?"

"I cannot keep my thoughts from you, can I?"

Chuckling indulgently, Roan said, "No."

"I am glad you allowed me to give her the necklace you gifted me with. Did you see Maya's eyes light up when she saw that blue stone?"

"Mmm, yes I did. She seemed to know a lot about that rock. One day, when the time's right, maybe she'll tell us about it. At least we know it comes from one seam in a copper mine north of Lima."

"And she held it as if it were precious beyond life."

Nodding, Roan continued to move his fingers down the supple curve of Inca's spine. Gradually, he felt the fine tension in her body dissolving beneath his touch. Love could do that. And he loved her with a fierceness and passion he'd never known before. "That stone has been passed down through my family for untold generations. My mother gave it to me after my vision quest at age fourteen—at the ceremony when I turned into a man. She told me then that it came from the south. I thought she might have meant the southwest—perhaps Arizona or New Mexico. Now I realize she meant South America, and specifically, Peru. It's had an amazing journey, and now it seems like it's come home to where it started so long ago."

Sliding her hand across his massive chest, Inca absorbed his warmth and strength. How wonderful it felt to be able to touch him whenever she pleased. It was a heady gift. "Maya said there is only one mine in the world that has a seam of this stone. It is so rare. She said men kill to steal it from miners who look for it."

"Yes, and that it possesses certain powers." He smiled a little. "I'd sure like to know more about what they are."

"I think Maya knows, but sometimes, because we are in the clan, information is given only when it is appropriate. Otherwise, we are not told."

Roan nodded and quirked the corner of his mouth. "Still, I'm curious. I'm beginning to think that maybe one of my ancestors was South American, but I have no way to prove it. Our people pass on traditions verbally, so nothing's written on paper to verify it one way or another."

Pressing a kiss against the thick column of his neck, Inca murmured, "I believe you are right. Why else would you have come back? Our spiritual path always makes a circle of completion. Perhaps one of your ancestors walked north and met and fell in love with one of your Lakota relatives, and remained and lived there. That would explain your twin path between the two Americas, yes?"

It made a lot of sense to Roan. "I like the idea of living in the Amazon basin with you and helping the Indian people to keep their land as the hordes flee the cities of Brazil. I'm looking forward to making a life for us there."

"I am content that our people are safe without us being there."

Roan knew Inca had worried about that. She was driven and responsible in the care and protection of the Indians in Amazonia. Maya's reassurances that they had reduced the number of cocaine-producing factories and, therefore, the ability of drug lords to enslave the Indians, lessened her anxiety about it.

"I want to use this next nine months here in the village as a well-deserved rest for you," Roan said, turning onto his side and pressing her gently against him. He felt Inca make that deep-throated purr that moved through him like promising, provocative fingers of heat. "See this as a vacation."

Laughing throatily, Inca eased back and looked up into his dark, carved features. She melted beneath his smoldering blue eyes, which regarded her through dark, spiky lashes. Mouth drawing upward, she whispered, "We are here for training. And the elders are pleased with your progress."

"I think they're pleased with both of us," he said, tracing

the outline of her broad, smooth forehead with his fingertips. "And I also think they're very glad you're back home here, with them. You're a powerful person, Inca. They need warriors with hearts like yours. People like you don't grow on trees, and they know that. Best of all, Grandfather Adaire has made amends to you. He's no longer the enemy you thought he was, and I'm glad to see that rift between you healed."

She nodded, her eyes softening. "He has always been the father I did not have, and now he is that again for me." Inca caught Roan's hand and placed a soft, searching kiss into his palm. She felt him tense. Lifting her head, she said, "In our business, there are not always happy endings, Roan. I was glad to hear of Julian, and his father, Colonel Marcellino, from Michael."

"Yes," Roan murmured, "the colonel embraced Julian and finally came to realize that his second son is just as worthy of all the praise and attention his first son had received. I'm sure it's made a difference in their family dynamic."

"So perhaps getting bitten by the bushmaster was a good thing." Inca sighed. "So often I see bad things happen to good people. At the time, I know they think they are being cursed, but it is often a blessing. They just do not realize it yet."

"No argument there," Roan said as he leaned down and nibbled on her bare shoulder. She tasted clean, of mango soap with a glycerin base that someone in the village had made days earlier. "I had a lot of bad things happen to me, and look now. Look who is in my arms and who loves me, warts and all." And he chuckled.

Laughter filled the hut, then Inca said petulantly, "You are not a frog! You have no warts, my husband."

"It's slang," he assured her, grinning at her impertinence. "In time, I'll have you talking just like Maya does."

"Humph. Maya was educated in North America. She

picked up all those funny words and sayings there. Many times, I do not understand what she talks about."

"Slang is a language of its own," he agreed, absorbing Inca's pensive features. Her eyes were half closed, shining with love—for him. "But next time Maya visits us, you'll be able to understand her better. I'll teach you American slang."

"Good, because half of what she says, I do not grasp."

"Like?"

"Well," Inca said, frustrated, "words such as *fire bird*."

"That's slang for an Apache helicopter gunship. They're called fire birds because of all the firepower they pack on board. They've got rockets, machine guns and look-down, shoot-down capabilities. A fire bird is one awesome piece of machinery. And in the right hands, it's a deadly adversary."

"Oh. I thought she meant a bird that had caught its tail on fire."

Roan swallowed a chuckle. "What other slang?"

Rolling her eyes toward the darkened ceiling, she thought. The chirping of crickets and croaking of frogs was a musical chorus against the gurgling creek. "Herks."

"That's a C-130 Hercules—a cargo plane. I think she's referring to the Herks that provide her helicopters with fuel in midair. The Apache can be refueled in flight to extend its range of operation. The Herk carries aviation fuel in special bladders within the cargo bay." He lifted his hand above her to illustrate his point. "The Herk plays out a long fuel line from its fuselage, like a rope, and the helicopter has a long, extended pipe on its nose. There's a cone at the end of the fuel line, and when the helo connects with that, gas is pumped on board, so the helo can continue to fly and do surveillance to find the bad guys."

"I see...." Inca sighed. "Her world is so different from mine. She was adopted and taken north and educated there. She is a pilot. She flies like a bird." Inca shook her head.

"I am on the ground, like a four-legged, and she is the winged one."

"Both of you carry very heavy responsibilities in the jobs you've agreed to take on," Roan reminded her. "Maya's role might appear more glamorous to outsiders, but the ground pounder—the person in the trenches, doing what you do every day—is of equal importance. Winning sky battles is only part of it. If people such as yourself were not on the ground doing the rest of the work, the air war would be futile."

"She has told me of the sky fights she's had with drug lords. She said they have helicopters that can shoot her out of the air." Inca frowned up at him. "Is this so?"

Groaning, Roan gathered her up and held her tightly to him. "My little worrywart," he murmured, pressing small kisses against her wrinkled brow. "Over the next few months, I'll try to outline what Maya does for a living. Mike Houston told me a lot about her background and education. I think once you know and understand more about her, you'll stop worrying so much. Maya is considered the best Apache helicopter pilot in this hemisphere. That's why the army is sending their best instructor pilots here. The army's hoping to map out a long-term strategy to eradicate drug lords from the highland villages, destroy all the little, hidden airports so that they can't ship their drugs out so easily. Maya's been trained for this, Inca. She's just as good at what she does as you are."

Satisfied, Inca sighed and surrendered to the warmth and strength of his arms. Lifting her hand, she looked at the two rings glittering on her finger. One of the gifts Michael had brought with him in that sack of his was a plain gold wedding band. Unknown to her, Roan had asked the major to furnish him with one to compliment her peridot engagement ring. Roan had given her the second ring when they were alone in their hut that very evening. Its beauty and symbolism touched her heart and soul deeply.

"I love you, man of my heart...." she said softly near his ear.

Roan smiled tenderly and stroked her hair. "And I'll love you forever, Inca. Forever..."

* * * * *

Attention Lindsay McKenna fans!
Look for next book in

MORGAN'S MERCENARIES:
MAVERICK HEARTS

in November 2000!
Available from Silhouette Special Edition.

Here's a sneak preview...

Chapter One

The next time Thane woke up, he found himself in a pale pink room. It took him a few minutes to realize that he was in a hospital, more than likely, Red Rock Hospital in Sedona, Arizona. To his left was a huge set of windows. There were shiny-leafed pyracantha bushes as a hedge along the bottom edge of the window. Beyond that, he saw the gorgeous spires and buttes of Sedona.

New emotions filtered through him as he gazed upon the red rock country that he'd grown up in.

The door to his room cautiously opened. Thane turned. His heart thudded hard in his chest. A young woman, dressed in a pale blue smock and loosely fitting dark blue slacks, a stethoscope around her neck and a chart in her hands, moved quietly into the room. She gave him a shy, hesitant smile.

Thane recognized her at once. It was Paige Black. How had she grown so beautiful? Her eyes were large and damp looking, as if she'd been crying earlier. But the look in them welcomed him with undeniable warmth and recognition.

"Hi, Captain Hamilton. I'm Paige Black. I was just coming to check on you to see if you were awake yet. Your mother wanted to know so she could drive over and welcome you home." As his intense gaze moved from her head down to her toes and back up to her face, Paige could feel a burning sensation through her like a fire suddenly out of control. Inwardly, she trembled with joy as well as trepidation.

Thane swallowed convulsively. Paige was more than beautiful. He remembered her in high school and she hadn't been half as pretty as she was now. Her shining ebony hair was drawn back with a large silver and turquoise studded comb. Her thick, arched eyebrows formed a frame over her large, cinnamon-colored eyes. Perhaps it was her height that gave her such a magnetic presence. Thane wasn't sure. When he saw her dip her head and avoid his eyes, he realized belatedly that Navajo's did not like to make eye contact—they felt it was disrespectful. And he'd been staring at her like a starving wolf!

Clearing his throat nervously, Thane lifted his hand in greeting. "Call me Thane, Paige. It's good to see you again." And it was. He greedily absorbed her soft features. Her skin was golden-colored, her cheekbones high, her eyes slightly tilted to give her a look of mystery and intrigue. More than anything, her mouth was delicious looking to him. But her lips had parted in surprise when he talked to her in such a friendly tone. Why?

"Y-you…remember me?"

Just the soft, husky tone of her voice soothed his jangled nerves and raw emotional state. He managed a brief, hoarse laugh. "Remember you? Sure I do. Why wouldn't I?" And indeed, why wouldn't he? Thane felt his heart beating rapidly in his chest. He was helplessly drawn to the quiet Paige Black. Everything about her spoke of peace and calmness. She was so unlike him, who felt like a tornado was ripping him apart inwardly.

Paige smiled gently and touched her cheek, which felt hot. "You have a wonderful memory, Captain…I mean…Thane…" How handsome he was! Paige tried to stop the old pain in her heart from leaking through her joy at seeing him once more. She'd never expected to see Thane Hamilton again after he'd left for Annapolis. If he knew that she'd had a crush on him all those years ago in high school, he'd laugh himself silly. Now he was back—here—with her. And not of his own free will.

Thane lay back. "I never forgot you, Paige."

The huskily spoken words rifled across her aching heart. Paige tried to sternly tell herself that Thane was her patient, someone she was to care for during his convalescence, and that was all. More heat rolled into her face. She placed her hands against her cheeks and looked away.

"I'm blushing like a teenager," she said, and laughed breathlessly. "I guess our school days follow us around after all."

As his eyes narrowed speculatively, Paige was caught in his gaze. How, oh, how was she going to care for Thane Hamilton when she was still so powerfully attracted to him?

The hours between dusk and dawn are filled with mystery, danger...and romance.

On sale September...

#1 *New York Times* bestselling author

NORA ROBERTS

brings you four dark and dazzling tales of passion and peril in

NIGHT TALES

a special 4-in-1 collector's edition containing 4 stories from her Night series from Silhouette Books.

And also in September

NIGHT SHIELD

a brand-new book in the exciting Night Tales series, from Silhouette Intimate Moments.

Silhouette
Where love comes alive

USA *Today* Bestselling Author

SHARON SALA

has won readers' hearts with thrilling tales
of romantic suspense. Now Silhouette Books
is proud to present five passionate stories from
this beloved author.

Available in August 2000:
ALWAYS A LADY
A beauty queen whose dreams have been dashed in a
tragic twist of fate seeks shelter for her wounded spirit
in the arms of a rough-edged cowboy....

Available in September 2000:
GENTLE PERSUASION
A brooding detective risks everything to protect the
woman he once let walk away from him....

Available in October 2000:
SARA'S ANGEL
A woman on the run searches desperately for a reclusive
Native American secret agent—the only man who can save
her from the danger that stalks her!

Available in November 2000:
HONOR'S PROMISE
A struggling waitress discovers she is really a rich heiress—
and must enter a powerful new world of wealth and
privilege on the arm of a handsome stranger....

Available in December 2000:
KING'S RANSOM
A lone woman returns home to the ranch where she was
raised, and discovers danger—as well as the man she once
loved with all her heart....

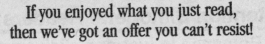

If you enjoyed what you just read,
then we've got an offer you can't resist!

Take 2
bestselling novels FREE!
Plus get a FREE surprise gift!

Clip this page and mail it to The Best of the Best™

IN U.S.A.	IN CANADA
3010 Walden Ave.	P.O. Box 609
P.O. Box 1867	Fort Erie, Ontario
Buffalo, N.Y. 14240-1867	L2A 5X3

YES! Please send me 2 free Best of the Best™ novels and my free surprise gift. Then send me 4 brand-new novels every month, which I will receive before they're available in stores. In the U.S.A., bill me at the bargain price of $4.24 plus 25¢ delivery per book and applicable sales tax, if any*. In Canada, bill me at the bargain price of $4.74 plus 25¢ delivery per book and applicable taxes**. That's the complete price and a savings of over 15% off the cover prices—what a great deal! I understand that accepting the 2 free books and gift places me under no obligation ever to buy any books. I can always return a shipment and cancel at any time. Even if I never buy another book from The Best of the Best™, the 2 free books and gift are mine to keep forever. So why not take us up on our invitation. You'll be glad you did!

185 MEN C229
385 MEN C23A

Name	(PLEASE PRINT)	
Address	Apt.#	
City	State/Prov.	Zip/Postal Code

* Terms and prices subject to change without notice. Sales tax applicable in N.Y.
** Canadian residents will be charged applicable provincial taxes and GST.
   All orders subject to approval. Offer limited to one per household.
   ® are registered trademarks of Harlequin Enterprises Limited.

BOB00   ©1998 Harlequin Enterprises Limited

In celebration of our 20th anniversary,
Silhouette Books proudly presents
the first three Silhouette Desire novels
by bestselling author

ANNETTE BROADRICK

in a landmark 3-in-1 collection!

**Three magnetic men, brimming with sex
appeal, have held a tight rein on their volcanic
desires—until now. For they are born to claim,
cherish and protect the women fated
to be theirs.**

Maximum Marriage:
Men on a Mission
(on sale 10/00)

Then, in November, watch for
MARRIAGE PREY
in Silhouette Desire.
This unforgettable love story is a brand-new sequel to
MAXIMUM MARRIAGE: MEN ON A MISSION.

Available at your favorite retail outlet.

Silhouette ®
Where love comes alive ™

MONTANA MAVERICKS

WED IN WHITEHORN

The legend lives on...as bold as before!

M-M

Coming in September...

THE MARRIAGE BARGAIN

by

VICTORIA PADE

Corporate raider Adam Benson vowed to bring
down the man he blamed for his family's ruin.
And what better way to start than by marrying
his enemy's daughter? But he hadn't planned
on falling for his own prisoner....

**MONTANA MAVERICKS:
WED IN WHITEHORN** continues with
BIG SKY LAWMAN by **Marilyn Pappano**,
available in October from Silhouette Books.

Available at your favorite retail outlet.

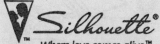

Silhouette®

Where love comes alive™

Visit Silhouette at www.eHarlequin.com　　　PSMM4